CHAI TIME *at C* [barcode: MW00572238]

'*Chai Time at Cinnamon Gardens* is a lyrical, stirring, accomplished exploration of the trauma we carry, the secrets we keep, the histories we harbour, and the family we find. Chandran's characters are so vividly drawn you can sense them sitting across the table long after you've closed the covers. Deftly traversing time, culture and continent to weave a tale of both home and unbelonging, this is truly a novel not to be missed.'—Maxine Beneba Clarke, author of *Foreign Soil* and *The Hate Race*

'Chandran is an excellent storyteller.'—*The Weekend Australian*

'This is an engaging story that feels both urgent and necessary. It is also a terrific read.'—*The Daily Telegraph*

'this story both burns with anger and sings with optimism, sprinkled through with moments of levity and humour'—*The Canberra Times*

'Wise and dignified.'—*The Australian Women's Weekly*

'An engrossing, urgent, warm, wise and utterly, utterly beautiful novel.'—Emily Maguire, author of *An Isolated Incident* and *Love Objects*

'a powerful, compassionate novel about friendship, family, community-building, and the racism faced by members of diasporic communities in this country'—*The AU Review*

'might at first appear to be a straightforward feel-good tale, but quickly reveals itself to be firmly grounded in the light and shade of real life'—*The West Australian*

CHAI TIME
at
CINNAMON GARDENS

SHANKARI CHANDRAN

ultimo
press

Originally published in 2022 by Ultimo Press,
an imprint of Hardie Grant Publishing.
This edition published in 2022.

Ultimo Press
Gadigal Country
7, 45 Jones Street
Ultimo, NSW 2007
ultimopress.com.au

Ultimo Press (London)
5th & 6th Floors
52–54 Southwark Street
London SE1 1UN

A catalogue record for this
book is available from the
National Library of Australia

Chai Time at Cinnamon Gardens
ISBN 978 1 76115 140 8 (paperback)

Cover design and illustration Jessica Cruickshank/The Jacky Winter Group
Map illustration Jessica Cruickshank/The Jacky Winter Group
Text design Simon Paterson, Bookhouse
Typesetting Bookhouse, Sydney | Baskerville MT Pro
Copyeditor Ali Lavau
Proofreader Rebecca Hamilton

10 9 8 7 6 5 4

Printed in Australia by Griffin Press, an Accredited ISO AS/NZS 14001
Environmental Management System printer.

The paper this book is printed on is certified against the
Forest Stewardship Council® Standards. Griffin Press holds
chain of custody certification SCS-COC-001185. FSC®
promotes environmentally responsible, socially beneficial
and economically viable management of the world's forests.

Ultimo Press acknowledges the Traditional Owners of the Country on which we work,
the Wurundjeri People of the Kulin Nation and the Gadigal People of the Eora Nation,
and recognises their continuing connection to the land, waters and culture.
We pay our respects to their Elders past and present.

This project is supported by the
NSW Government through Create NSW.

For Ellora, Kailash, Hari, and Siddharth

PROLOGUE

The Cinnamon Gardens Nursing Home sleeps deeply on this summer night. The heat trapped in its brick walls radiates outwards, through the skin of its painted facade. It forms a gentle nimbus around the building. Arabian jasmine climbs the wooden trellises staked in the garden beds. They are bold travellers, dark vines carrying white stars up the two-storey walls and around the windows of the residence. The plant grows obediently in the quiet suburb of Westgrove, Sydney, but its tropical ancestors are a wilder breed, a vine that grows rampant in the villages of Sri Lanka, a home more familiar to many of the residents. They remember this fragrance from their childhood, and it creeps into their sleep, turning nightmares of war into dreams of their parents, long gone but still loved.

To the passer-by, the grand old Federation building has been restored to its colonial corpus. It looms over a circular driveway, wide enough for ambulances to speed in and for hearses to crawl out. The driveway curls around a small garden of giant agaves. In the moonlight, the succulents look like granite statues; spiky oversized sentinels that hide a sandstone plinth in the centre.

The plinth is empty; no statue sits astride it. Without a purpose, it has been forgotten by almost everyone.

The southerly swells around the nursing home. The residents are used to a more feverish summer that rots the wooden bones and crumbles the clay muscle of their homes. But they welcome the southerly and breathe more easily when it slips through the mortar of Cinnamon Gardens and lifts the blanket of heat from their ageing bodies.

The wind, now reduced to a breeze, explores the nursing home as it has many nights before. While the outside of the building has been restored, the inside has been completely transformed. A few vestiges of its history remain—high ceilings with ornate bas-relief carvings here and elegant architraves there. But the inside of the building is functional, repurposed to hold and house a community of elderly men and women.

The southerly passes the office and the industrial kitchen on the ground floor of the old building. In a few hours, the cooks will begin frying onions, curry leaves and green chillies for the breakfast omelette, served with idiyappam, sothi and sambal. Omelette on a bed of steamed rice noodles, topped with milk gravy and a side of freshly grated coconut tossed in chopped chilli. It's something to wake up for.

Ascending the wooden staircase to the second floor, eight residents, the longest serving, sleep and dream of the books they want to write, the battles they haven't finished, the lovers they didn't marry and the children they couldn't protect. Each resident has their own room along a corridor that leads to a large shrine room. Its altar is heavy with the gods of the Hindu pantheon, the main faith of the nursing home. But there are other statues too, representing both the Hindus' hedging of divine bets, and the religions of the rest of the community.

The nursing home's previous owner built a shiny, red-brick monolith behind the old Federation one. Its four floors and ample girth cast a shadow across the elegant grounds. This wing is home to the other fifty residents of Cinnamon Gardens. The two buildings are connected by a covered ramp on the ground floor: a tunnel with a gentle gradient for the wheelchairs and trolley beds. Maya, the nursing home's current owner, and the resident of Room 1 in the old building, named this new wing Sivam, in honour of the god of destruction. Shanthi Segaram in Room 6 asked Maya if she thought she was being funny.

A wide garden stretches around these buildings. Over the four decades that Maya has run the nursing home, it has been terraformed from a neglected wilderness to orchards and large beds of vegetables that feed the residents. The crops are more comfortable in the red, hard earth of Jaffna in northern Sri Lanka and the verdant flatlands of the Vanni jungle to its south, but Maya and her family have ploughed and tilled and nurtured. They have coaxed and cajoled the earth of Westgrove to yield manioc, vallaarai, murungakkai and kariveppila.

At the very bottom of the garden, beyond the vegetables and ayurvedic herbs and almost hidden by a row of black jamun trees, stands a house. With only two bedrooms, a generous bookshelf and a kitchen that's more of a kitchenette, the house is small in stature, but the memories it holds are immense. It is rightly called the caretaker's cottage. The different people who have lived there over the last four decades have accepted that responsibility and burden with courage.

MAYA

Maya shuffled towards the front desk. The new linoleum of the nursing home floor bubbled and curled in places, the heat expanding under its synthetic skin. The lino was only six months old, a change required by new aged care regulations. The old blue gum boards underneath it would outlive the new Minister for Health.

The teenager at the desk studied her mobile phone with surgical intensity, her thumb skating across its screen, both aimless and purposeful.

Maya parked her walker against the desk, her swollen fingers still wrapped tightly around its cushioned frame. She could move from her bed to her bathroom without it, but the walker was essential for long-distance travel.

'It's just arrived, Aunty,' the girl said, picking up a package. She turned it over but didn't hand it over. '"Mrs Maya Ali",' she read the name on the label and shook it. 'What is it?'

'Carnatic music tapes, lots of them. My cousin in America sent it,' Maya answered, not too quickly. 'Recordings of MS Subbulakshmi's last concert in Colombo. Your grandmother will remember her.

5

My cassette player still works.' Maya tapped the small tape recorder clipped to the frame of her walker. She took the recorder with her everywhere.

'Oh, is that all.' The girl gave her the package and went back to her phone.

Maya's daily mail checks had started to raise suspicion but not enough to compete with the allure of other people's gourmet dinners, exotic holidays and impossibly talented children. Maya was relieved her deep-fried eggplant curry never had to stand up to the scrutiny of millions of Tamils on Instagram, just that of the constantly dissatisfied Mrs Sivaguru, a former resident of Room 15, God damn her soul to perpetual reincarnation.

Maya had worn her caftan especially. Its batik folds were capacious, allowing her to hide an entire packet of Kingston biscuits. Old Mr Padmanathan's grandchildren brought them for him, but ever since Mrs Padmanathan died, he was sleeping his life away. He would never miss them. Plus, he was diabetic, like most Sri Lankans over the age of fifty-five from their generation. It was thoughtless of the family, really. She placed the package in her caftan pocket, next to the biscuits, and adjusted her incontinence underwear. One midnight treat next to the other. She shuffled back to her room.

Ruben was already there, changing her sheets.

He winced as he straightened his back, pulling the sheets off awkwardly. The bruises on his face were healing. The colours were hardly visible against his dark skin but the swelling couldn't be hidden. The damage was fresh, not like the wounds he carried from before she knew him. Both were unexplained.

'Leave it, mahan,' she said, the heat rising in her face. 'You don't need to do that. I was going to let it dry. I don't mind.'

'Doesn't matter, Aunty,' he answered in Tamil. 'I don't mind either.' His wide smile triggered the dimple on his left cheek and his skin shone faintly with sweat. His daily shift started at 6 am, but on Fridays he worked the first half of the day in the garden.

He had been hired as a cleaner, shortly after Zakhir had disappeared, but over the last ten years Ruben had demonstrated a collection of skills as innumerable as they were random. He knew how to grow things because, as he explained, his grandfather had been a manioc farmer near Kilinochchi. He knew how to translate things because his father had made him study languages. He knew how to clean things because his mother had raised him properly. Most intriguing to Maya, he knew how to hide things.

She stood at the doorway of her private room on the top floor. It was a luxury in a place like this, where there were usually two residents to a room, sometimes three. She was different. Shanthi Segaram called her the Maharani of Cinnamon Gardens, behind her back but loudly. Maya was the co-owner and then, after Zakhir died and her daughter Anjali took over, she was the owner's mother. Legally, she was still the owner.

Ruben flipped the heavy mattress over; the muscles of his arms flexed and released from the strain. Something under the bed caught her eye but before she could bend forward to look at it, he dropped the mattress in place and it was gone.

His shirt lifted at his waist, revealing a tattoo of torn skin that hadn't healed properly despite the many years that must have passed since it had been scored into his body. Maya only ever glimpsed the tips of the pattern, the place where the design had come to an end—or was it the place where the design began? She would never know. The fingertips of the scar beckoned her, daring her to ask the questions: how did it happen; when did it happen; who did this to you? And the question that plagued her the most: does it still hurt?

As if sensing her scrutiny, Ruben pulled his shirt down and deftly tucked the clean sheets around the mattress, his hospital corners tight and geometric. The freshness of Sunlight soap powder blended with the cloying but familiar sweetness of her Ponds talcum powder. She always left it out for him, right next to her eau de cologne. He had once said the smell reminded him of his mother. It reminded every Sri Lankan of their mother. She still used it for the same reason.

'It's not appropriate for a woman of your age to stare at me like that,' he said, smiling.

He helped her to her writing desk and threaded her wasted arms through her husband's oversized cardigan—her writing cardigan now. The desk was the only piece of furniture she'd insisted on bringing with her to the nursing home. Zakhir had bought it for her on their honeymoon, forty-three years ago. He had carved their wedding date, *3rd December, 1977*, on the inside of its drawer.

Ruben lowered her gently into the chair and arranged the folds of her caftan. She held on to his shoulders longer than she needed to. He heard but ignored the rustling in her pocket.

'I'm only eighty. It's inappropriate for me to admire my gentleman caller?' she asked.

Last week's movie club had been the Bollywood remake of *A Streetcar Named Desire*, starring Abhishek Bachchan, the son of the great and far superior Amitabh. It seemed unlikely to Maya that Kajol would want to dance in the streets of a Mumbai slum after her brother-in-law had essentially raped her. But who was she to critique the fusion of mid-century American literature with modern Indian cinema? Plus, in India, #metoo would need more time and more than Reese Witherspoon to catch on.

Ruben laughed. Again, the dimple danced. He arranged the pillows on her bed and retrieved the emergency button from under the mattress, placing it where she could reach it.

'Inappropriate and salacious. A predatorial grandmother of Sri Lankan ancestry will make headlines, demonstrating why we shouldn't let refugees into Australia.'

'Because we're all sexual predators and terrorists?'

'Exactly,' he replied.

He rolled her dirty sheets into a bundle. There was soil under his fingernails from this morning's labour. A dark half-moon encased the ridged pink of his nails. In Jaffna, the half-moon would have been a rich red.

'Which one are you?' she asked. She pushed strands of grey hair behind her ears and straightened her thinning plait.

He paused and looked at her directly. She held her breath. Such sad eyes, even when he laughed at her jokes or made small talk with the staff. The muscles of his face shifted the right way, his body made all the right movements, but his eyes remained the same. He had learned to mimic the behaviour of others, to respond with the language that was expected of him. You only noticed his eyes if you were looking.

If you were looking and longing to be seen.

She knew him well now. He had worked for her for ten years, and had been changing her sheets for nine. In the last twelve months, the sheet changing was done with increasing frequency and discretion. He didn't pity or patronise her. He didn't use that sickening tone the other staff used. They all called her Aunty. They all called every resident Aunty or Uncle, as was their tradition. The title was respectful but sometimes the tone was not, revealing the judgement that the young had for the old.

It was the same tone her daughter, Anji, used when talking to her recalcitrant seven-year-old.

'Darling, it's time for you to put your shoes on otherwise you'll be late for school.'

'Darling, it's time for you to take your blood pressure tablets, otherwise you know what will happen in the middle of the night.'

False patience and forced lightness.

'Well?' She raised an eyebrow. She had lightly shaded the wispy hair with her kohl pencil. Nothing excessive, like that painted racoon Shanthi Segaram down the corridor.

'Neither. I'm an Australian citizen. Just like you.' He smiled again and tucked the sheets under his arm. He didn't seem to notice the odour, or if he did, he never shuddered the way some of the staff did.

'Don't let the matron catch you with the contraband.' He gestured to her left hand, resting on the bulge in her caftan pocket. 'And always dispose of the evidence. It's the best way to commit a crime,' he said as he shut the door.

Her heart pounded.

She smiled at the photograph of Zakhir seated in the middle of her small shrine, and adjusted the necklace of japa mala beads around his neck, her fingers lingering on his wide smile. The twins, Anji and Siddharth, smiled like him; a beautiful, painful reminder. The photo was taken in 1978, a few years before they migrated. The day he got his second PhD in ancient Tamil architecture. As if one was even useful. She had made Zakhir stand outside the Jaffna Public Library. The heat melted the Brylcreem and collapsed his thick puff of hair that was very fashionable back then. She remembered resting the camera on her pregnant belly while he tried to revive the pompadour.

She took the package from her caftan and placed it on her writing table. It contained the proofs of the twelfth Clementine Kelly novel, sent by the publisher for her to review before it went to print. She was ending with a cliffhanger, Clementine potentially dead. She was sorry to do this to her heroine and her readership, but it was time. They had come a long way together, but even the best partnerships had to end.

Cinnamon Gardens, 1981

'Come, come.' Cedric ushered Maya and Zakhir down the path to the nursing home. He almost skipped towards the front door in his Savile Row three-piece suit. Maya stumbled behind him, dabbing the sweat from her neck with her cotton sari pallu.

Three-year-old Anjali and Siddharth ran ahead towards the building. On the flight from Colombo to Singapore to Sydney, the dense clouds of cigarette smoke had kept them awake the whole way.

But their fatigue was forgotten as they surveyed their new kingdom. Zakhir turned back for the suitcases in the van.

'Leave it, we'll do it later. I want you to see the place first,' Cedric said proudly. 'It's not much right now, but it will be.' He pointed to the swollen and sagging floorboards of the verandahs that circled the building, the plaster stucco that flaked away like leprotic skin, revealing crumbling red brick underneath. 'Once the last of them die, we will fix it up and sell it off.' He opened the front door with the key and his shoulder.

'Welcome to Cinnamon Gardens,' he said with a florid bow that suited the elegant manor home the building *used* to be, not the dilapidated nursing home it was now.

Cedric Furholmen was descended from three generations of plantation owners. He had grown up next door to Zakhir's family in Cinnamon Gardens, Colombo. It was after this fashionable suburb of moneyed families, aristocratic exiles and alcoholic diplomats that he had named his business venture in Sydney. He and Zakhir were like brothers. Their mothers had played bridge together for decades, leaving their children and their husbands in the care of their ayahs.

Cedric could have moved to Woollahra with all the other Sri Lankan burghers who had migrated to Australia in the 1950s, deemed worthy of entry by virtue of their European ancestry, colonial affectations and milky complexions. But Cedric was nursing a prematurely failing liver and the eternal shame of his parents. Hiding in Westgrove's western suburbia suited him. He had been sent down from Oxford, stripped of his robes and dignity. During his undergraduate years, Cedric had a taste for pretty English girls, with their translucent skin and the confidence that can only be born of class. Although he was the top of the social food chain in Ceylon, he was still a colonial underclass in Oxford; white, but not white enough. A darkie to those who knew his accent was British but his blood was not; exotic and appealing to the bored ladies who were looking to rebel one last time before they married the rowing captains they were destined for. One such heiress actually broke his heart. Cedric drank the rest of his Commonwealth Scholarship, had a cocktail named after him at Magdalen College (the 'Cedric Special') and was exiled from Oxford. He was refused entry into the family home in Cinnamon Gardens and found himself on a journey of redemption in Westgrove.

He was reinventing himself as an entrepreneur, and his first venture was the rundown nursing home with a diminishing clientele. As the old residents died, new ones were not being recruited. The bones of the building were strong and the original features of a once-proud family home still gleamed with ageing beauty. Behind the small Federation mansion, the previous owners had built a modern monstrosity to house another thirty residents, giving the whole nursing home capacity for thirty-eight pensioners.

Cedric was able to afford Cinnamon Gardens because, as a business, it wasn't working. The nursing home was on notice from the Department of Health and due for another inspection in six months—an inspection Cedric intended to fail. He would then accept his sanction from the government, apologetically dump the remaining residents at the local hospital in Westmead, and begin renovating the home back to its former glory.

Maya walked the corridors of the nursing home, lightly touching the walls, scabs of paint sticking to her fingertips. The building had absorbed the memories of decades of residents who had lived the last years of their lives here. The stories lifted out of the pores of the walls. They were released into the air and inhaled into her body and then her blood.

She looked at Zakhir. He had climbed halfway up the sweeping staircase and stopped at the landing before the stairs circled around to the top floor. He did that a lot; he began a task and then stopped, as though the thought behind the act had been abruptly confiscated from his mind. He was confused by it but also compliant, waiting until the intention returned or, as was more often the case, until Maya touched him gently and reminded him of what to do next.

Standing in the early morning light at a tall sash window, he was still beautiful. A noticeable presence in any room, with his tall frame and skin the colour of milk toffee. When trauma receded and he returned to her, he was the intelligent, kind and often irreverent man she married.

Dust motes danced around him like a halo of quizzical fairies.

'Don't close the home,' she said to Cedric. 'We can do something with it.'

'There's no money in it,' Cedric protested.

'There doesn't have to be money in all our endeavours.'

'You would say that,' he replied. 'You're a failing author.'

'True, but we can build something here. Zakhir can do it.'

'He's a temple architect, not a magician. Or a geriatrician. Even a mortician would be more useful. And with whose money?' Cedric asked, his eyes on Zakhir, frozen in the sunlight.

'With your money for now, and then with our money. We'll work it out.'

Cedric shook his head but his eyes gleamed. He liked a futile challenge, as his previous love interests had demonstrated. And he loved Zakhir.

And so Maya, Zakhir and the twins moved into the caretaker's cottage, fifty metres from the nursing home at the bottom of the property's wild garden. They had to cut a wider path through the shoulder-high weeds when Maya's three trunks of books finally arrived by sea, months later. The name of the cottage suited her. She was a caretaker now.

Cinnamon Gardens, 1982

Cedric and Zakhir unfurled the roll of thick paper across the dining room table. Maya weighted the corners down with the heaviest books on baking. Between the three of them, they had borrowed eighteen books on home improvement. Although she'd treated them with suspicion initially, Mrs Vandermark, the cardigan-clad librarian at the Westgrove Public Library, had since extended their borrowing privileges. She even ordered in specialist trade manuals for the amateur renovators and Australian cookbooks for Maya. Australian cooking seemed to be just a variation of English cooking, which seemed to be just a variation of one piece of meat accompanied by three vegetables, but no coriander, cumin, turmeric, fried onions, chilli, garlic or mustard seeds. It was confusingly simple. And very bland.

The nursing home dining table became their work table. It was covered in colour charts, tile samples and lists. Zakhir was a pedantic draughtsman who insisted on producing 2-D and 3-D scale drawings of the nursing home. Cedric prohibited the creation of scale models in balsawood.

'According to Dave at Mitre 10, we need to strip the walls back to their base layer of paint, bleach them at least twice to kill the mould and then repaint. The wallpaper in the common rooms is a violation of three new health codes, so that has to go.' Zakhir opened a book at the marked page. He searched his shirt and then trouser pockets for a pencil, eventually locating it wedged behind his ear.

'The wallpaper has to go because it makes those rooms look like a brothel in Madras,' Cedric responded. 'Not that I've seen one, but I've heard they have embroidered wallpaper in fleur-de-lis prints.'

Zakhir laughed. He was doing that a lot lately. Maya laughed too, more with relief than mirth. Zakhir hadn't laughed so freely since Appa died.

Zakhir flicked through the pages of the reference book. 'If we mix turmeric with the paint, it will slow future mould growth too. Maya has chosen Arabian jasmine white for the colour. It has undertones of pink that will become duskier with the turmeric.'

'No more institutional white,' Maya said.

14

'This place *is* an institution,' Cedric pointed out, studying the colour chart.

'This place is a *home*. I read an article that said colours can change a person's mood. *Reader's Digest*—they get that here too,' she said, more to Zakhir than Cedric. 'White is clean but it's also cold. We want warmth; a sense of welcome.'

'Have you been sniffing the paint samples? People come here to die, Maya. We want a sense of people paying upfront before they do that,' Cedric argued.

'They come here to live with dignity and community.'

'They might die faster if we don't sort out the mould,' Zakhir noted, his head inside another encyclopedia-sized book, this one devoted entirely to bacteria and aptly titled *Home Bacteria: Kill it before it kills you.*

'According to this book, we're going to have to excavate the sub-floor to create proper ventilation and stop spore proliferation. I did that once in Anuradhapura,' he said, referring to his former job in the ancient capital of Ceylon. 'Sydney has a very high clay content which retains water, promotes spore reproduction and, in the event of a tectonic shift, will most likely cave in on itself. There's new sub-floor fan technology evolving in Singapore but we can buy that in phase two.'

'Phase two? We can't afford phase one! Is it possible he's reading too much?' Cedric asked Maya.

'There's no such thing,' Maya replied. 'I have a plan.' The nursing home would restore her husband as much as he would restore it. '*We* have a plan.'

Zakhir looked up from his book and smiled.

∼⌒

Mr Petsas, aged eighty-eight, in Room 7, was a welder. He had come to Sydney from Psarianos, a small village in southern Greece, in 1910 at the age of seventeen. He had met his wife, Soula, a northerner with hair the colour of sunflowers, at a Hellenic club dance. She was light in his arms and laughed with him instead of at him. She didn't mind that he was riddled with scars from the sparks and the shards of half-molten metal that flew like miniature comets and burrowed deep into his body.

For decades, he worked on the bridges of Sydney, canisters of liquid fire strapped to his back, an umbilical line from a harness tethering him to a platform suspended a hundred metres above the earth. The world was easier to love from a distance, he said, leaning into Maya's new tape recorder.

When younger men and machines replaced him, he spent the rest of his life as a mechanic working for other younger men, fixing the cars of richer men.

Maya often noticed that when she visited Mr Petsas, something in his room had improved. Once, it was the window jamb, previously sealed shut by a sloppy painter. She found it now opening and closing, its inner wheels cleaned and oiled. A mosquito net had been inserted too. Another time, the curtain tracking around Mr Petsas's bed, which had slipped its cracked brackets, was refitted with new brackets and new plastering.

Someone with skills and commitment to aesthetics was fixing things.

'It's my youngest son, Ahilleas,' Mr Petsas explained proudly, when she told him he had the most operational and attractive room in the nursing home. 'He can fix anything. He has a whole crew, mostly my nephews. They even do mansions on the North Shore for posh white people. Make sure you write that down in your notes.'

Maya smiled appreciatively. Ahilleas was clearly successful and exactly what she needed.

'If I may ask, Mr Petsas, why do you live here and not with one of your sons?'

Mr Petsas smiled, his sun-weathered skin cracked and crenellated like the pictures of the Nullarbor she had been studying.

'Your families are like ours, yes?' he asked.

'Yes, I think so. I don't know, because you're the first Greek person I've met, but given the quantity of dolmades and moussaka your daughters-in-law bring you when they visit, I think we may have things in common.'

He laughed. 'Their spanakopita is improving. Not like my wife's, but not bad.' He paused and looked towards the window, leaning back into his bed. 'I gave the house to my eldest son, Costas. There's plenty of space for me there, but without Soula it feels empty and unjust. Life feels empty and unjust. Does that make sense?'

It made perfect sense. Since Appa's death, Zakhir had occupied their marriage intermittently. Sometimes he was there and sometimes he was not. Sometimes it felt empty and unjust, although he was still living, unlike Mr Petsas's wife. Since moving to Australia and starting the nursing home project, Zakhir had occupied their marriage more often and more joyfully.

'How's business?' Mr Petsas asked.

She shrugged. 'You can see for yourself.'

In the months since she and Zakhir had moved in, two residents had died, four had left and three more had given notice under their residency agreements. Four staff had left too.

Cedric didn't say anything; he didn't need to.

Families had noticed the new management.

'Don't worry about it,' Mr Petsas reassured her. 'They were like that when the Greeks first moved here, and now look at us: we own Melbourne. They'll come back.'

The truth was they wouldn't come back; they would die somewhere else. But she couldn't do anything about that for now.

Maya hired Ahilleas Petsas and his crew of cousins to move everyone into the west wing of the big nursing home (now renamed Sivam) at the back, and they began work on the old house at the front of the property. Over the next few months, the Petsas family stripped and bleached walls, excavated and created new ventilation, re-rendered and painted everything Arabian jasmine white with a touch of turmeric. At lunchtime, Maya fed them kolokythokeftedes, using a recipe from a library book. Zakhir became an apprentice tradesman and learned everything the Petsas family would teach him. They were impressed with their new assistant and tutored him generously. He had spent years restoring temples and was an intuitive, patient nurturer of a building's potential.

Ahilleas heard that Primrose Preparatory School in Mosman was renovating and he negotiated with them to strip and bring their laminate back to the nursing home. Zakhir covered every floor in Sivam in synthetic parquetry, while the young men of Primrose Prep were treated to the new hardwood parquetry their future-leaders-of-Australia feet deserved.

Maya removed the plastic shower curtains that separated the beds and enlisted Mrs Borkowska in Room 6, who was once a seamstress, to sew new curtains for each of the shared rooms, even the empty ones. Maya chose a palette of pastel blues and greens, as she had read these colours were soothing for babies and the elderly.

The sun-bleached and time-faded prints of impressionist paintings were removed. Maya convinced the art teacher at Westgrove High School to lend her art by Year 11 and 12 students as a revolving exhibition. She invited the young artists into the nursing home to see their work and to use the residents as subjects. Mrs Borkowska's offer to pose nude was politely declined.

The night before the Department of Health's inspection, Maya, Zakhir and Cedric moved the last resident into one of the newly renovated rooms. Maya took the team of low-level public servants and their clipboards on a tour. She showed them what had been achieved in one half of the nursing home and what could be achieved in the other half, if they had more time. The department gave them a stay of execution.

Cedric reluctantly took her aside. 'I respect what you've done here, Maya. It's beautiful and warm, and it *is* more like a home than a nursing home. But I can't afford to keep pouring money into renovations. The place needs to cover its costs at the very least, and if we're going to keep it open, which I'm still not convinced we should do, we need to grow our client base.'

'They're residents, not clients.'

'*That* is part of your problem; they *are* clients. When they die, they need to be replaced; I've got sixteen empty beds.'

'We need more time, Cedric, but we can do this. We can transform these buildings into a home where people will be valued. We'll build a community of the elderly, not just a place to hide them until they die.' She held his arm as she spoke, shaking it to control the tremor in her body. She wasn't just talking about the building, and Cedric knew it.

He nodded, tears in his eyes. 'You'll ruin or restore us all, Maya.'

Zakhir emptied the cabinets in the office and together they went through clinical files that revealed nothing except what medication each patient was on. Half the records were for dead patients and the other half were incomplete. Many records hadn't been updated since the residents had arrived.

'These files don't tell me who they are,' Maya said, adjusting the folds of her sari so she could sit on the office floor among the papers.

Zakhir interviewed each patient and set up a new file, updating their health status and current drug protocols.

But Maya wanted to know more. On the pretext of learning about their family medical history, she interviewed the residents, tape recorder in hand. She found out who loved them and who they loved back; who looked after them, who visited and how often. Who they longed to be visited by and why they weren't. She found out their religions, their traditions and foods. She created a filing cabinet of stories—about the years that had passed and their dreams for what lay ahead, because even though they were old, they still had hopes for themselves and those they loved.

Zakhir converted a large walk-in wardrobe into a prayer room, complete with a second-hand copy of the Quran he'd found in the local St Vincent de Paul and his own prayer mat.

Maya converted the linen cupboard next to it into a small Hindu shrine. She hadn't brought enough deities from Ceylon to properly furnish it, but the local Hare Krishna Society in Paddington was happy to contribute the rest of the Hindu pantheon on the proviso that they were allowed to conduct a cleansing ritual for the nursing home.

The local priest from St Mary's was invited to meet the Catholics and fewer Christians, and conduct a weekly service for those too old to be wheeled to the church two streets away. He also offered to administer the last rites for a small fee.

Zakhir opened the drawers in the office with trepidation. They were stuffed full of receipts, unpaid bills and notice letters. He had been trained by his father to run the family business and, although he had rejected it in favour of 'digging holes in the ground' and 'restoring obsolete heathen temples', he was still sufficiently fluent in the accounting system required to run a 100-million-rupee business. The double entry bookkeeping required to run a nursing home was significantly less complicated.

Maya studied the patient profiles she had created. She memorised the medical histories. It was important to know which patients were diabetic, which ones had high blood pressure and heart disease. Which ones were morbidly obese and which ones were anaemic or undernourished. Which ones were from which countries and liked what food.

She gave the nursing home's menu to an old friend of her father's, Mrs Ranganathan, who gave it to her youngest daughter-in-law Vidya, who made the best kathirikai kulambu in Keerimalai before the war, when people had enough time and oil to deep-fry eggplants properly. She replaced the fleeing kitchen staff with Vidya and two other Tamil women who had no catering experience but, like Maya, knew how to cook for their families.

Vidya spoke to Dr Sanchayan, the cardiothoracic surgeon from Colombo General who now worked as a GP at the Westgrove Medical Centre, and together they designed a new menu for the nursing home. Dr Sanchayan reviewed the patient files. Vidya and Maya reviewed the recipe sections of *Women's Weekly* back issues. They created a menu that was rotating and evolving. Clinically acceptable and culturally adaptive, as Maya liked to call it.

She tested recipes and went to the Westgrove Public Library to borrow more cookbooks. She learned that Jewish people liked to eat honey cake on Rosh Hashanah, that Polish people ate babka on Easter Sunday and that Greek families celebrated Easter a week later than other Christians and ate tsoureki. There were no Tamils in the home, and there might never be, because the Tamils wanted to die in Ceylon or in the homes of their daughters, as was their birthright. But she cooked Tamil food anyway and introduced it to the residents.

Weetbix (breakfast), devon sandwiches (lunch) and meat/three veg (dinner) were replaced with delicacies such as string hoppers, Jaffna omelette and sothi (breakfast), antipasti and orecchiette ai funghi (lunch), rugelach or Sri Lankan butter cake (afternoon tea), pierogi or rice, parippu and an iraicci curry (dinner) followed by kithul pani and curd (dessert). Turmeric was added to everything because it was an antiseptic, an anti-inflammatory and, according to the *New England Journal of Medicine* she borrowed from Mrs Vandermark, a cholinesterase inhibitor. She would fight dementia one pierogi at a time.

The kitchen in the nursing home was Maya's masterpiece. She begged Cedric to renovate it but he refused, saying it would be like giving a new kidney to a dying man; a wasted transplant.

She insisted that he at least install a new oven.

'A European oven, are you mad?' Cedric asked, punching the keys of the calculator as if, by hitting it, he could compel it to reveal a different numerical outcome.

'I need it for my butter cake. And one of those steel benchtops like you see in restaurants. It's more hygienic and it makes rolling rotis easier.'

'Rotis? *Rotis*? Mrs Smith-Jones isn't craving rotis, Maya,' Cedric shouted. 'She wants her chocolate-flavoured laxative and a hot-water bottle. And frankly, that's all we can afford to give her. God, I need a drink.'

'Mrs Smith-Jones, and you, need to aim higher.'

Eventually, Maya and Zakhir turned their attention to the caretaker's cottage that had become their home.

An enthusiastic shop assistant tried to sell them a showerhead guaranteed to provide a tropical rainforest experience. As she talked them through the apparently impressive range of shower strengths, Zakhir leaned over and whispered, 'Do Australians know that the rainforest experience in tropical countries involves mosquitoes the size of bats and dengue fever?'

Maya shushed him. The showers of her childhood were conducted at the village well, partially clothed. Every second day, she and her cousin-sisters would huddle together, sitting on their haunches. Her father's sister, her chinnamma, would haul the briny water up in a bucket and tip it over them, the salt stinging their eyes and knotting their curly hair. The children looked forward to the monsoon and the sweet rainwater it brought, first in generous and then dangerous abundance.

They couldn't afford a tropical rainforest showerhead but Maya wanted one. Maybe she just longed for tropical showers.

They slowly started breathing life into the rest of the cottage, often using second-hand or fifth-hand fittings from Ahilleas Petsas, who admired Zakhir's eye for structural innovation and Maya's spanakopita, which was better than his wife's but not as good as his mother's.

One year, they peeled back the skin of the dark carpet. Its coarse and stained fibres released droplets of oil from her deep-fried eggplant curry, sending them stale and spinning into the air. The exploration revealed hard wooden floors, wide boards the colour of amber.

The twins returned from school to find their mother lying on her stomach, inhaling the floor.

'Come, come,' she said, beckoning for them to join her. She wasn't inhaling so much as listening. 'Trees still speak, even after they've died.'

The children were used to these moments and, not realising there was anything unusual about a parent who communed with floorboards, they lay down on their stomachs and listened too.

'This house is one hundred years old, but these trees could be hundreds, maybe thousands of years more. They saw the first brown people come here and then the first white people.'

Maya traced the path made by an insect that had bored its way through the hard flesh of a living, breathing tree.

'And now us,' Anji, the youngest by a few minutes Siddharth never let her forget, whispered. She was the most like Maya, the most willing to close her eyes and see the universe beneath the world.

'What do you think they're saying?'

'That the memories of trees will not be included in your exams so you should get up and do your tutoring homework.' Zakhir's disapproval was affectionate but final. The children scattered, grabbing their schoolbags on the way to their shared room.

With the guidance of the Petsas cousins, Maya and Zakhir sanded, stained and nurtured the boards back to life. When the last coat of varnish went on, Maya stood at the doorway and prayed to the mighty trees beneath her feet.

The memories of her family were now sealed in the fibre of their floorboards.

RUBEN

Sydney

Ruben stepped off the train and onto the platform. The all-stations from Mount Druitt to Westgrove took an hour, but late at night, he always got a seat. He used the time to read, and at Aunty Maya's recommendation, he was trying Latin American magic realism. She read translations but he was remembering a disused skill, drawing vocabulary and verbs from dormant grey matter, matching them to the words on the page. *Pretérito imperfecto* defied him. He couldn't see its logic or feel its rhythm, even when he first studied languages at Jaffna University. Now, his forty-year-old brain rebelled against the conjugation of verbs more vehemently than before, and he was beginning to hate Vargas Llosa for his famed lyricism. *Pretencioso pendejas*, he muttered.

Ruben put the book in his backpack, next to the English homework he had set for his tutoring students, and looked around. The platform was empty except for the winged cockroaches. They scuttled away and launched themselves into the ribbon of fluorescent light that flickered down from the lamppost.

His body still hurt from last time. He braced himself as he left the false security of the train station's CCTV cameras.

For the last few weeks, the gang had been waiting for him. It wasn't a routine but it wasn't random. They had observed his schedule and they followed him down Rochester Street until he neared the section of the road that passed the empty playground. It was surrounded by apartment blocks, dark towers of sleeping tenants.

'Hey, boong,' they called.

He had googled that one. Ethnically incorrect, but this wasn't the time for pedantry.

'Boong! We're talking to you,' said a recognisable voice.

'He's not a boong,' said another. 'He's a Paki.'

Not even close. Over 2500 kilometres from Pakistan to Sri Lanka, a completely different religion, and many cultures and languages between them.

'Hey, Paki!'

'Osama, we're talking to you.'

The footsteps grew faster and louder. He didn't turn around but he could feel them. Three men; boys, really. They were close enough for him to smell the deodorant of one. It was Lynx Africa. Old Uncle Gana in Room 5 used it too. They were close enough to touch him.

His body jerked back as he was swung around by the straps of his backpack to face two of them. They wore hoodies but, in the moonlight, he could make out their features. There was something about their easy banter and the way they didn't need to finish sentences that he recognised. It was the familiarity of brothers. Ruben liked to do a lot of things with his brothers when they were alive, but not this.

Lynx Man, the third one, always held him. Perhaps he was the strongest. Perhaps he didn't want to look at his victim's face. Ruben cried out as Lynx drove a knee into his back. His legs buckled and he fell to the ground.

'Hold him up, hold him up.'

25

Lynx obliged and Short Brother pummelled Ruben's stomach with his fists. The sharp jabs found their mark beneath his rib cage, forcing the air out of his lungs in small bursts, faster than he could draw it back in.

'How many times have we told you? Go back to where you fucking came from.' The brother took his hoodie off and pulled his t-shirt away from his sweaty body. Ganging up on fellow citizens was hard work.

Ruben slumped. He willed his legs to stand but the pain in his back radiated to his feet, like a metal wire inserted through his spine, threading its way down his nerves to the soft rubber surface of the playground. Lynx let go of him and ripped the backpack from his body.

'What's this, Osama?'

Tall Brother flicked through the pages of the novel.

'Big words for a Paki,' he said, hurling it at Ruben's head.

Ruben looked at the book, inhaling the musty smell of its second-hand pages. He conjugated slowly in his mind.

Estoy doliendo. I am hurting.

Estás doliendo. You are hurting.

He paused and corrected himself.

Meh *estás doliendo.* You are hurting *me.*

He rolled back onto his knees, palms on the ground, supporting his body on all fours. He reached for the book but a boot landed on his right hand, pinning his fingers to the ground. A second boot stepped on the book, breaking its spine, grinding it into the dirt.

He had been beaten by these boys before. He had been given his beating and he had accepted it. He didn't know what was different about tonight; why he fought back this time.

Over a decade ago, the Third Battalion of the Sri Lankan Army had taught him well. He knew what to do.

With his free hand, Ruben grabbed the boot and stood up, tipping Lynx onto the ground. He flexed his right hand. It hurt to tighten but nothing was broken. The two brothers didn't move, surprise paralysing them for a dangerous moment too long.

Ruben drove his foot into Lynx's head and then picked him up by the hair. He cried out but was too dazed by the blow to fight back. The others stepped towards him but Ruben shook his head, his arm wrapped tightly around Lynx's neck, holding the man's back close to his chest with one arm.

With his free hand, he took Lynx's left hand in his.

'I'm not a Paki,' he said, slapping Lynx's face with his own hand. 'I'm Sri Lankan Tamil and I'm Australian.'

He slapped Lynx again. It wasn't enough pain.

'Are you?' he asked.

'What?' Short Brother asked.

'Are you Australian?' Ruben held Lynx's fingers gently but firmly in his own.

'Of course we are,' said Tall Brother. 'What kind of a question is that?'

'A fair one,' Ruben answered, adjusting his fingers to wrap them around one of Lynx's. 'We take a citizenship test to prove our worthiness. Do *you* know how the Australian nation was founded?'

'What?'

Ruben repeated the question slowly and clearly. 'Was it negotiation? Referendum? Or both? Think carefully before you answer.'

The brothers looked at each other, Short Brother prompting the other to answer.

'Um . . . referendum?'

Ruben shook his head. 'The correct answer is referendum *and* negotiation, but the citizenship test conveniently overlooks the founding genocide. Either way, you're wrong.'

Ruben tightened his grip on Lynx's finger and snapped it back. Lynx screamed and shuddered against him but Ruben was ready. He held him hard against his body, the way he'd seen men do to Anil, his youngest brother.

'Question two. An easy one. What is Australia's official religion?'

'I know that.' Tall Brother raised his hand like a child answering a question in class. 'It's a Christian country. Not—' He stopped himself.

'Not Muslim like those Pakis,' Ruben finished for him.

Lynx slipped a little in his arm, their sweat mingling together. *Lynx* was an everyday antiperspirant. Torture, it seemed, was not an everyday occurrence in Australia.

'Is that your final answer?' Ruben's voice trembled. He adjusted Lynx and tightened his grip around him. The man started to shake.

'Yes, that's my final fucking answer. We're all Christian. Australia is a Christian country.'

Ruben shook his head. 'Australia is officially secular.'

Derived from the Latin word *saeculum*, meaning 'worldly', he remembered from Jaffna University.

He twisted Lynx's finger back; the sound of the pop followed by the scream made him want to vomit. He dropped the man, grabbed his backpack and the book and ran towards the nursing home.

He heard footsteps sprinting behind him and a strange sound in his ears, like an animal whimpering. The sound was coming from him. He was crying as he ran, his face wet and cold, his breathing ragged. His heart thrashed painfully inside his chest. The gates of the nursing home were in sight, the windows black and empty. One light hung over the front door of Cinnamon Gardens.

He was almost there when the force hit him from behind, like the waves of the ocean he swam in as a child. One wave after another hurled him forward, his hands outstretched to break his fall as he hit the gravel driveway, palms first then chin, tasting blood in his mouth as a tooth pierced the soft lining of his lip.

'Hold him, hold him, wait for Ned.' One of the brothers dragged him to his knees, his arms twisted hard behind his back.

Lynx—Ned—had finally caught up with them, holding his hand tenderly against his chest. The knuckles had started to swell already. Tomorrow the hand would be the size of a small balloon. Hopefully a big balloon. Tomorrow, Ruben would wake up in Westmead Hospital's emergency department, if he was lucky.

'Fuck, are you in trouble, Paki.'

Vanni jungle, north-eastern Sri Lanka, 2009

'Fuck, are you in trouble, Osama.' The Sri Lankan soldier tightened the straps around the old man's legs and stood back. Arms and legs were secure, although one of each was already broken so the man was going nowhere. And even if he could move, there was nowhere to go. The village had cleared out days before the Third Battalion arrived. Only a few aid workers remained, caring for the wounded who couldn't leave.

The wounded who would now die a little faster than before.

And the aid workers too.

And the old man, who didn't quite fit.

'He's not a Saudi,' Ruben corrected him. 'Osama was a Saudi.'

'He prays like a you-know-what.'

'He prays like a *Muslim* because he is a Muslim. Not a Saudi.'

'Same same,' the soldier replied.

Not really.

Sydney, present day

'Fuck, are you in trouble, Paki. You're gonna pay for this.' Ned lifted his hand then, wincing, cradled it to his chest once more.

Ruben looked up. The dim light of the nursing home door was behind him. The brothers holding him threw long shadows, a blackened rainbow that arched around Ned but left his face illuminated. Over the last few weeks, Ruben had become familiar with their voices, their silhouettes, their gaits and treads. He even knew who was hitting him by style and strength. But he had never looked one of them clear in the face as he did now. Ned was younger than he expected; fine featured, almost feminine. His skin looked pale in the light, but it was hard to tell. He could have paled with the pain. People often did.

'Hold him up,' Ned instructed.

Ruben struggled against the brothers and lowered his body, receiving the first kick in his gut instead of its intended target. A boot in the crotch hurt like hell. He doubled over, feeling the air and contents of his stomach rush out of him.

'Christ, he's spewing.' The brothers dropped him and jumped back.

Ruben rolled onto his side, eyes still on Ned. The young man lifted his good hand, his fist clenched and aimed at Ruben's head.

'Stop!' a voice screamed behind him. 'Stop! I've called the police. They're on their way.'

The woman stepped out of the nursing home and ran towards them.

The brothers bolted and didn't look back. Ned stood, frozen, his fist still clenched but lowered in hesitation—or was it fear?

The woman crouched down next to Ruben, one arm protectively around his shoulders.

He shrugged her off. 'I'm fine, Nikki,' he said.

'You should go,' Nikki said to Ned. 'If I see you here again, I'll report you.'

'You wouldn't.'

'I would. This is a nursing home. He works here.' As if his place of employment entitled him to protection and proper treatment.

'Can you stand?' she asked him.

'In a minute,' he said, wiping the vomit from his swollen mouth.

Nikki's eyes widened when she saw his face properly. She turned back to Ned. 'You're an arsehole,' she said. 'What's wrong with you? Get off the property, before the police get here.'

She placed one arm gently under Ruben's chest and helped him stand. He leaned against her for a moment and then steadied himself. He could feel her slight body trembling beside him, her words all bravado.

'How can you touch them?' Ned said.

'Get out.' There was an edge to her voice Ruben hadn't heard before. 'Get out!'

She dragged Ruben back towards the front door of the nursing home, her eyes still on the man. Once inside, she slammed the door shut and twisted the deadlock.

'The police aren't coming, are they,' he said. It wasn't a question. He slumped against the door and let himself fall to the floor. Pain slipped through the receding wall of adrenaline. She was standing with her palms pressed against the door, as though keeping the enemy at bay with her body.

'No,' she replied softly. She didn't say it but they both thought it. *What would be the point?* The first three times she'd called the police they arrived thirty minutes later, asked perfunctory questions and a few provocative ones ('Tell me, mate, who threw the first punch, you or them?') and promised to investigate. She hadn't heard from them since.

'Let me help you back to your place,' she said, reaching for him again.

'I'm fine,' he lied. Something settled in his chest, heavy and disappointing. He pulled himself back up but grimaced and stooped, his hand across his belly.

'Room three is still empty,' she said, as if he hadn't spoken, and led him to the elevator.

The original nursing home only had rooms on the top floor, reserved for the eight most important residents. One of them—the old librarian, Mrs Vandermark—had died recently and her room hadn't been reallocated yet.

Nikki helped him onto the bed then, shutting the door, instructed him to take off his shirt.

Every movement hurt. He wouldn't be able to work tomorrow.

Nikki wet a towel in the sink and wiped his face, cleaning the blood and vomit gently. She took her stethoscope from her coat pocket and held its cool disc to his chest. She moved it from one side to the other, from his chest to his back and then his chest again. The light pressure soothed him. He imagined the beat of his heart travelling up its cord and into her mind, a message contained in its rhythm. Golden strands of hair escaped the loose bun at the nape of her neck. He wanted to pull at it, feel its softness on his face. During the day she swept her hair into a tight ponytail that moved playfully of its own accord as she walked. It contrasted with the austerity of her demeanour and the economy of her clothing.

'There's nothing wrong with my heart.' He pulled away.

'I'm listening for a punctured lung.' She ran her hands over his chest and abdomen, testing him for pain, feeling for breaks. 'Don't try to be brave; I need to know if it hurts.'

'It hurts,' he replied.

'On a scale of one to ten, talk me through it.'

How did one measure pain? he wondered.

Pain that dwelled briefly in bruised muscle and fat. Nurofen and Tiger Balm would heal it.

Pain that was inflicted regularly and deliberately. Death would end it.

'It's all about a five,' he answered. 'I've experienced worse.'

He was being flippant, trying to move the conversation on, but she looked at the scars on his body and nodded. She placed a hand on the scar that started at his sternum and scrawled its way down to his hip and beyond, as though someone had taken a scalpel and graffitied their name on his body, scratched it out and tried again and again, using his skin as their canvas. She traced its path from the place where it started to the place where it had not ended soon enough. That pain was more than a ten.

He placed a hand over hers, stopping her as she reached for his zip. He kept her hand there, her fingers hooked into the top of his trousers, her wedding ring catching on his hair, a pinprick in his belly, if not his conscience.

She tilted her head and looked at him, as if uncertain of the next step in the dance.

He slipped his hand behind her back and brought her closer to him, so he could rest his head on her shoulder. He felt the ridge of her collarbone. She had lost too much weight over the last year. He inhaled the familiar scent of her perfume, something gently floral that interlocked with the astringent smell of the nursing home's disinfectant.

He closed his eyes and let his breath deepen and slow. He desperately needed to sleep. He saw the younger one in his mind. The features of his dimly lit face shimmered into focus and then fractured again, rage distorting them. He tried to recall that moment when Ned had spoken. 'How can you touch them?' he had said. She had challenged him and protected Ruben. He wanted to say more to her but he needed to sleep. Everything would be clearer in the morning. Everything would be better. He couldn't make it to his cottage at the bottom of the garden.

He pulled back and looked at her. She kissed him lightly, tentative and gentle, finding a path around the pain. He tried to kiss her back but the pain forced him to stop.

'Nothing seems to be broken,' she said. Part doctor, part something else.

'Nothing that can't be fixed, I suppose,' he replied. He swayed and leaned against her again.

She rolled him back onto the bed, pulled off his shoes and covered him with the blanket.

He closed his eyes, heard her leave the room. The blanket was soft and smelled like sandalwood; the laundry detergent Maya insisted on shipping over from Cargills in Colombo. It was heavy too; an anxiety blanket. She had ordered them especially for some of the residents.

He heard Nikki return and felt the ice of an alcoholic swab and a sharp prick in his arm.

'I borrowed Mrs Segaram's corticosteroid. It will help with the muscle inflammation and stiffness you can expect tomorrow.' She pulled the needle out of his arm and wiped the droplet of blood away with the swab. 'The injection works faster than the tablets. I've given you a dose of Endone as well. My personal stash, not the nursing home's; they'd notice that. You can thank me later.' She pushed his hair back and kissed his forehead. 'I'm sorry I didn't call the police. I should have.'

He reached for her hand and held on to it. 'I'm glad you didn't,' he whispered. He tried to anchor himself to Nikki, the sound of her voice, the feel of her hand in his, but sleep pulled him away.

Alaveddy, northern Sri Lanka, 1995

Ruben's blood dripped from his nose onto his torn school uniform and the dirt floor of his family home. Red blood absorbed into the red earth of his village. He sat crumpled in the corner of the room, his breath ragged. The nails fastened to the tip of the policeman's whip had gouged deep cuts into his small body. The man had used a sharp flicking motion, but sometimes the nails caught and the man would drag the whip through Ruben's skin to free it. Covered in blood, tears and sweat, his skin was on fire, flaps of it dangling from his body.

The police were there to interrogate his older brother. Sanjay Anna had been helping the Tigers for months. He was over-ordering supplies at Jaffna Hospital and sending them to the Tigers somehow. One of the administrators at the hospital had reported an issue with the stocktake.

'We don't want to hurt you,' the policeman said. 'We know the Tigers are persuasive. We know they brainwash you and threaten you. What kind of people's movement is that?' He spoke in English, adjusting the whip in his hands, making Ruben cower. 'So, I'll ask you again. How do you make the deliveries? Give me names and times. Tell me how they do it. How do they get past our checkpoints? Who else is involved?'

Sanjay Anna shook his head.

'Anna,' Ruben whispered. He flinched again when the policeman looked at him. 'Anna, please tell them what they want to know.' He willed his older brother to speak. He willed it in Tamil, the language of his parents, he willed it in Sinhalese, the language of his nightmares, and he willed it in all the other languages he was teaching himself during hours spent hiding in the school library.

'Still no?' the policeman said. 'Maybe now.' He nodded at one of the other men in the room.

Ruben stared in horror as the man ripped his young sister, Nimi, from his mother's arms and dragged her into their parents' bedroom at the back of the house.

His mother opened her mouth and a deep sound escaped from her body like an endless serpent. It crawled along the walls and rafters of their home, coiling around him, squeezing the air out of his body.

Sanjay Anna thrashed in the arms of a police officer. He begged the policemen to stop, promising to tell them everything. He broke away and tried to follow their sister. The police officer bludgeoned him on the back of the head with his gun and then held him down with a knee on his neck. Ruben could see his brother's bruised face, blood and tears streaming down his cheeks. His eyes looked distant and glazed. He had never seen his brother cry. Not when their father died of dengue or when his friends left to fight with the Tigers and nothing remained of them but a hero's portrait for the families to keep in their shrine rooms.

One of the police officers lifted Anil, Ruben's younger brother, by his shirt, his legs kicking in the air. The man held the boy close to his chest with one arm and gripped Anil's wrist tightly in his other hand.

'Ready?' the officer asked.

Sanjay Anna opened his mouth but his voice wouldn't come out, his eyes unfocused and red, as if his brain was struggling to fathom what was happening to his family.

'Not talking?'

The policeman shook his head as if he regretted what he was going to do next. Then, still holding Anil tight against him, he snapped one of the child's fingers out of its socket.

Anil screamed, his legs flailing.

The police officer held him effortlessly, and Ruben realised why Anil had been chosen and not him. His brother was so much smaller.

The policeman took another tiny finger in his hand and separated it from the rest.

'Please,' Amma begged. 'Please stop.'

The other policeman returned, dragging Nimi with him. He kicked her towards them. Amma pulled the girl's trembling body into her arms. Nimi's dress was torn and bloodied; her skin smelled like the sweat of the policeman in front of him.

Ruben crawled towards them. Amma opened her arms and Ruben buried his face in her sari. The smell of her Ponds talcum powder wrapped itself around him. She held her hand up to the policeman and Anil. She was looking at them but pleading with her eldest son.

'Tell them,' she begged in Tamil.

'The first Monday of the month,' Sanjay Anna replied. He put both his hands up. 'The first Monday of every month. They come to the hospital, north exit, where the garbage is taken. They wait on the other side of the big bins. I wheel the supplies out in a waste trolley and leave it for them there.'

'Who comes? The same person every time?' The policeman tightened his grip on Anil's finger. The boy bit his tongue in pain. Blood dribbled from the side of his mouth.

'Yes, the same person every time. Mr Sampath, the geography teacher from Chundikuli Boys High.' Anna closed his eyes.

Ruben tightened his hold on his sister. Mr Sampath had taught Anna. He had lost three sons when their bullock cart went over a landmine. They were returning from a wedding.

'How does he transport the supplies?'

'He brings the school van and takes everything, I don't know where. I don't ask questions. Sometimes he gives me a list of things they need. Sometimes I just steal basic supplies. Antibiotics, painkillers, anaesthetic drugs, dressings. Lots of dressings. The school van has a compartment under the last row of seats. He hides the supplies in there; that's how he gets past the checkpoints.'

'Good. Thank you. That's very helpful.' The policeman dropped Anil onto the floor and the boy crawled into Amma's arms, holding his hand to his chest.

The policeman walked over to Sanjay Anna, the gun in his hand.

'You understand why it has to be this way,' he said.

Ruben didn't understand.

'Please, not the others—they're only young,' his brother said, shifting to his knees, his eyes lifted to meet the barrel poised in front of him. He glanced over to Ruben. 'Take care of them, thambi.' He looked back at the policeman. 'I beg you, not the children.'

The policeman nodded. 'As you wish.'

ANJALI

Sydney

Anji watched as Nathan deftly rolled the last balls of dough into rotis.

When they renovated their kitchen last year he had specifically asked for a roti station. 'No other home in Westgrove will have one.'

'That's because no self-respecting Tamil mother makes her own rotis anymore,' Anji had replied. 'We buy them premade by a machine and frozen.'

'I'm not a Tamil mother,' he responded.

'True.'

Nathan was white and an excellent maker of Sri Lankan carbs. He got his roti station. It was more like a stainless-steel teppanyaki grill that could cook eight rotis at a time. It was next to their gas stove, so once the rotis were cooked he dropped them onto an open flame, where they inflated into balloons of bread. He tossed one with a pair of tongs, charred its rim and frisbeed it onto a plate. The children loved the game and, tonight, their guests loved the theatre.

Anji loved coming home from work and being served very hot rotis by her still-warm husband. Nathan caught her checking him out and flexed gratuitously as he singed the edges of the last roti, small geysers of steam escaping from holes in its surface. She reached up and brushed the atta flour from his brown hair, careful not to get it on her kurti.

'Honestly, you two.' Mel shook her head and heaped more eggplant curry onto her plate. 'Fifteen years of marriage and three children. Have the decency to resent each other more.'

'We do resent each other often,' Nathan replied, rolling the sleeves of his shirt down. 'I can sense my forties are going to be all about escalating resentment. But I pour that anger into my perfectly rolled rotis and monthly therapy sessions.' He laughed and sat next to Mel. She laughed along hesitantly, as if unsure whether he was joking about the therapy.

Mel and her husband Dave had moved to Westgrove a few years ago, but their son Jacob had only recently started playing chess with Anji's son Kailash and Nikki's son, Oscar. Year 4 competitions in far-flung public schools had extended into combined family dinners on a Friday night.

'Seriously, how do you know about making Indian bread?' Mel asked, wiping the tamarind gravy from her plate with the steaming bread.

'My mother taught him,' Anji replied, smiling at the memory of Nathan's early failed attempts.

'I wasn't allowed to marry Anji until I could make roti and three Sri Lankan Tamil curries,' Nathan added. 'Amma's rules.'

'Amma?'

'Yes, my mother-in-law,' he replied. He called Maya *Amma* but had always referred to Anji's father Zakhir as Uncle. Uncle and Amma. It was imbalanced but accurate.

'Is she the one who lives in your nursing home, Anji?' Dave asked, between mouthfuls.

Anji pointed apologetically at her mouth, which was full of food. Amma always said she ate too fast, but growing up, if she didn't eat fast, Siddharth would take her rotis.

Nathan answered for her. 'Actually, she lives in *her* nursing home. She owns Cinnamon Gardens. She developed it with Anji's dad and a friend of theirs, Uncle Cedric, who passed away a few years ago.'

Uncle Cedric had died without children, leaving his sixty per cent stake in the nursing home to Maya. He had descendants in Colombo, distant great-great-nieces and nephews, but they were as indifferent to him in death and probate as they were in life.

'After dinner, Mel, I'll make you his favourite cocktail,' Anji offered. 'A shot of gin, a shot of tonic and a lightly roasted star anise. He called it the Cedric Special.'

'Sounds strong,' said Dave. 'So how long have you been running the place, Anji?'

Mel threw him a warning glance and his face reddened, confused.

'Sorry, hon.' She smiled apologetically at Anji and shook her head at her husband.

'It's no problem, Mel, honestly,' Anji assured her. 'I used to work there as a geriatric psychiatrist, but about ten years ago . . .' She coughed to clear the familiar tightening of her throat. The psychiatrist in her made her repeat segments of the story as often as she could. Talking about it without reliving it. That was the key. 'About ten years ago, my father left us. He and my mother ran the place together with Uncle Cedric for almost three decades. After Appa . . . in 2009, my mother handed the management over to my twin brother and me, but Siddharth lives in London. So, it's just me. Well, no—that's not true.'

She paused and looked at Nathan. He may have been slightly fearful of her father, but he had loved him too. Nathan counselled Anji, Maya and Sid whether they wanted the support or not.

'Nikki's there, our talented geriatrician.' She looked at Nikki, who lifted her gaze and smiled. They had each other too, for work and grief. Her friend's body relaxed a little, but not much. Nikki gave the illusion of inhabiting social groups while really only observing them from the margins.

Nikki's husband, Gareth, sat opposite Anji at the dinner table. Nikki and Gareth were also on the margins of each other, circling their marriage from its periphery. He was much broader but shorter than Nathan, which, according to her husband, made him an excellent midfield in the Westgrove FC's under-forty-fives, third-division team. Fast and not afraid to put his shoulder into a tackle, apparently.

'I grew up in the house at the bottom of Cinnamon Gardens,' Anji continued. 'It was years before I realised that other kids didn't have a nursing home in their front yard. I hung out there, did my homework at the cards table, and I helped out on weekends and holidays. It was as much my home as the family home. A lot of the staff have been there for years and Amma still tells me what to do. She can't help herself.' She laughed.

Last week, her mother had given her hairpins because Aunty Shanthi in Room 6 had said Anji's long, curly hair made her look like a rakshasi rather than a doctor. Shape-shifting goblin was a bit harsh, even for Aunty Shanthi, but she took the hairpins.

'So, it's not just me at all,' she said, trying not to touch her hair.

'Your mother sounds like such an interesting person,' Mel said. 'It would have been unusual for an Indian woman, or any woman of her generation, to run a business, wouldn't it?'

'Yes. Interesting and unusual are both good words for her,' Nathan replied. They both ignored the *Indian*. 'She was always well ahead of her time. Still is, I'd say.'

'Is she happy being a . . . ?' Mel floundered in search of the most appropriate noun.

'*Resident*,' Anji supplied, smiling. 'We prefer not to call them inmates.'

'Yes, resident. Was it hard for her to go from being the owner to a resident?'

Anji paused to let a stream of children run past the dinner table to the garden outside. Her younger two boys, Hari and Kethes, at seven years old, were the naughtiest in any group. Though named after the temples Haridwar and Ketheeswaram, they were anything but peaceful or contemplative.

'No, I don't think so. It's how she's maintained control over her life. She made that decision for herself, about a year after Appa died. Just packed up her things and took the best room in Cinnamon Gardens. She said she felt her duty to the nursing home had ended.'

What Maya meant was that her duty to Zakhir had ended with his disappearance and presumed death. Her mother had finally chosen herself over her family, and Anji respected that.

'Do you miss being a psychiatrist?' Dave asked.

Anji relaxed. She had expected Dave to ask about her father.

'Not at all, I love the nursing home. Like I said, it's home.' She shrugged. 'And I'm still using my clinical skills in this madhouse.' She smiled at Nathan, who picked up on the cue, as he always did.

'Are we ready for dessert? I bought gulab jamuns from the spice store in Homebush. No self-respecting Tamil mother would make those herself.'

The crowd laughed at the bad joke as they were meant to. Nathan stood up and signalled for Gareth and Dave to help with the plates.

'I'm so sorry, Anji,' Mel repeated. 'He's hopeless sometimes—just can't read a room.'

'Honestly, there's nothing to be sorry about. It was years ago. It's a reasonable question. People talk about work. And I know I need to keep practising talking about my father. It's healthy, even if it's hard. Speaking of jobs, Nikki, how's Gareth going? The council's been getting great coverage in the *Westgrove Chronicle*. I see acting Councillor Gareth Barton opened the new Bharatanatyam studio last week.'

Nikki startled, and a mottled red tinge crept up her pale neck. 'The new dance school?' It seemed to take her a moment to focus on the question. That happened a lot; she was present without being present. Anji was used to it; her father had been like that too.

'Yes,' Anji prompted her. 'Gareth was a natural, cutting the ribbon at Aunty Subhadra's new dance school. They were very proud to have him there. I still can't convince the boys to take up dance. Not hip-hop and definitely not Bharatanatyam.'

Nikki smiled gratefully and picked up the thread of the conversation. 'The job's going quite well. It's just a temporary position, until the council works out what to do after the scandal,' she said. 'But he's really keen to prove himself. You know, show them he can lead, not just write comms. He's very focused on the job so he misses a lot of things at home—' She stopped suddenly, her face flushed again. She glanced towards the kitchen. 'He misses out,' she corrected herself. 'On a lot of things.'

Things had been hard at home for a long time for Nikki and Gareth. Anji was ready to change the subject if she needed to.

'But overall,' Nikki continued, focusing on a more comfortable narrative, 'he loves working at the council. The community has really taken to him. He's not quite Nathan, so for now the aunties of Westgrove Shire are asking him to cut ribbons and crack coconuts outside their new businesses, but not roll rotis.' She said it humorously, but Gareth's inability to make Tamil food was not his key failing.

Mel dropped her voice conspiratorially. '*No one* is Nathan. Did you have to train him or did you pick him up at the store this way?'

Anji smiled, her eyes still on Nikki's face. 'I bought him online actually. He came fully house-trained.'

Mel laughed. 'Seriously, where did you two meet?'

'We were at medical school together,' Anji replied. 'He's the oldest of four boys and his mother had no patience for fair-weather feminism, as she called it.'

'Fair-weather feminism?' Mel asked.

'Yes, the kind espoused by men who insist their wives work because we're all feminists, but then are incapable of engaging in domestic work, because they're men. They only value unpaid work when they do it.'

'God, I wish his mother had raised my husband,' Mel lamented.

Gareth returned with two bowls of gulab jamuns, the fried dumplings shifting precariously in the thick sugar syrup.

'Are we talking about everybody's favourite back-up husband?' he asked, a little too jovially. 'The successful child psychiatrist who gave it all up for this.' Drops of syrup splashed onto his shirt cuff. 'A real hero.'

'Hero?' Anji laughed. 'If I was at home doing all of this'—Anji gestured at the dinner table, filling quickly with a diabetic disaster— 'while he ran the family business, I wouldn't get more than a "thank you so much for a lovely evening".'

Nathan brought the last bowls of dessert to the table with Dave. 'Sounds tense in here, people. Have some cardamom-infused deep-fried donuts—they make everything better.'

They all laughed.

'Make what better?' Dave asked.

'The fact that if I gave up my career for Nathan to pursue his, it wouldn't be noticed because it's expected,' Anji replied, reaching for a bowl.

'Whereas right now, I'm enjoying the adoration of the wives of Westgrove Public School,' Nathan said, breaking his gulab jamuns into small pieces. 'I do the same domestic duties as them but my stock is worth more than theirs simply because I'm a fucking unicorn in the playground.'

Anji laughed. He *was* a fucking unicorn.

'Well, I think it's the most important job in the world, being a mother. Or being a stay-at-home parent, I mean,' Dave said.

'Jesus, Dave.' Mel shook her head.

'What? What did I say?'

'Leave him alone, Mel. He's fine.' Anji took a scoop of the Maggie Beer Murray River Salted blah-di-blah ice cream. Nathan had gone all out tonight.

'It *is* the most important job,' Dave said defensively. 'Raising children and creating a home—what could be *more* important? I think every man—or person—would agree with that.'

'To be honest, mate, I think every man *says* that shit so he doesn't have to *do* that shit,' Nathan responded.

Nikki laughed out loud and then tried to snort the sound back into her body. It was too late. Gareth wouldn't look at her, his eyes still on Nathan.

'You're such a feminist icon, Nathan,' Gareth said.

'No Gareth, applying feminist theory is the only way my gorgeous wife will still have sex with me.' Nathan reached for the tub of ice cream.

Anji laughed at the word *gorgeous*. Nathan exaggerated like a Tamil. After a hard week at the nursing home, showered and awake was the best they could both hope for.

'That's where I'm going wrong,' Mel replied. 'I should hold out until I see personal growth. Or at least a few more adjectives like that.'

'Thanks for that, mate.' Dave shook his head. 'I wasn't bullshitting when I said mothering—I mean parenting—is the most important job. I didn't mean to offend you.' He blushed again, more deeply this time.

'You've got no chance, Dave,' Gareth replied. 'No matter what you say, you're going to offend someone: the working mum, the part-timers, the stay-at-home mum, the stay-at-home dad. Best not to say anything, and I was in political communications for years.'

'You're fine, Dave,' Nathan reassured him. 'I'm not offended. And at the risk of speaking for Anji when I'm not entitled to, I don't think she's offended either.'

Anji shook her head. 'I'm not offended at all. I agree: it's a shit job *and* the most important one. Someone has to do it, or you both have to do enough of it, to get it done. Whatever works and whatever's fair. Right now—and I *am* going to speak for you, unicorn husband of mine—we're mostly fair. But sometimes we're not. Then we resent each other and we fight about it, like everyone else.'

Anji had spent her childhood observing her parents' marriage, and she had promised herself she would never let things go unsaid. Ever. Even if the saying was too painful. Nor would she stay married, if the staying was too painful.

'On those days, I go into the kitchen and take it out on the rotis,' Nathan replied, mixing the small pieces of his gulab jamun with the ice cream. He could be such a vellaikaaran sometimes. No one except white people ate gulab jamuns like that.

'Or I do, but mine aren't as good as his.' Anji turned to Gareth. 'I was saying while you were in the kitchen that we love all your community activities. You're getting great local coverage. When does your re-election campaign start?'

The table exhaled collectively with the subject change.

'Too soon.' Gareth took the lifeline she'd thrown him. 'It's been a great three months and I think we're past the Incident That Shall Not Be Named.' He was referring to a scandal that had led to the Mayor's sudden resignation and a council purge. 'I've worked hard to rebuild public trust, so I'm hopeful the next few months will go smoothly.' He placed his hand on Nikki's back.

Anji saw Nikki tense. Anji had known her a long time; it'd been more than three decades since they met at kindy netball. Nikki was the first friend she had made at primary school and one of the few who were privy to the torment of the last decade. She tried every day to be that kind of friend to Nikki; to hold her while Nikki gave herself to the full scale of the loss. The irreversibly gone.

But Nikki had other coping mechanisms: work, exercise and, more recently, family grief counselling with Nathan at Oscar's school. Perhaps Ruben was a mechanism too, for both Nikki and Ruben.

Nikki nodded slightly at Gareth's touch. The muscles of her beautiful face arranged themselves carefully into neutral; her blue eyes focused on the ice cream.

'It's great to be able to contribute to the community you live in,' Mel said.

'It is,' Gareth replied. 'I know the neighbourhood and I drafted so much of Attwood's policy speeches that often I'm just reciting an old script with new adjectives.'

'For now,' Nathan said. 'Give it time and you might find yourself throwing out the old script and starting over for the Democratic Alliance Party. I think the electorate wanted more from former mayor Attwood. More dessert, people?' He went to the kitchen and returned with a second serving.

'And former mayor Attwood wanted too big a piece from the corporate pie,' Anji noted, testing Gareth.

Gareth smiled and nodded. 'He did indeed.' He tilted his bowl and collected the last drops of the sugar syrup in his spoon. 'I suppose you're right, Nathan. Attwood was a lifetime politician, a born-and-bred Westgrove boy, but the neighbourhood's changing now.'

'The neighbourhood has been changing, moving forward for decades,' Nathan said, placing the gulab jamuns in the centre of the table. 'But the country's regressing and the party has to decide whether it's going to follow, or lead us away from that.'

'What will you do, Councillor Barton?' Anji assumed her best investigative journalist voice. 'Will you lead us away or lead us astray?'

'I haven't had time to develop a new platform yet.' Gareth laughed. 'But, Anji, you're as beautiful today as you were the day I met you, so I'd be happy to lead you astray.'

'Oi, settle down, Councillor.' Nathan skipped Gareth's outstretched bowl and served Dave an extra dumpling. 'Westgrove couldn't cope with any more scandals.'

Gareth raised his hands in surrender and then folded them together in prayer, and everyone laughed. Nathan gave him the last gulab jamun.

'Could be the start of bigger things for you,' Dave suggested. 'Today Westgrove, tomorrow Canberra?'

'So true.' Anji nodded. 'Gareth, you're a photogenic guy. Somehow, you manage to say reformed rugby player meets under-tens cricket coach meets scholarship winner.'

She didn't mention that his recent family tragedy also gave him an emotional depth that he lacked in reality. She wanted to invite him to visit the nursing home as part of his Meet the People strategy, but it was too soon for that, after everything that had happened there. She had visited the council a few times as part of his Look, I have Sri Lankan Friends strategy.

'Ambitious local boy returns to his roots,' Nathan added. 'You're a compelling package.'

'Enough.' Gareth laughed. 'I feel like you're both hitting on me.'

'Mate, you'd never get that lucky,' Nathan said. 'But seriously, every politician starts somewhere. Why not Westgrove? It's the natural place for you to build a career. You grew up here and you've got a strong base of support. You can test your ideas, refine your platform and make a few mistakes in relative obscurity.'

'You must have thought about it,' Anji said. Gareth had been politically inclined even at university, although back then, he was running student political campaigns behind the scenes rather than fronting them; a true believer from a young age.

'Thought about what?'

'About being more than just a local councillor.'

'Give him a break, Anji,' Nikki said. 'He's only an *acting* councillor, and Westgrove is more than enough for now.'

Gareth's predecessor, Ben Attwood, was a party conservative who appealed to the 'ethnics' because they thought he would help them keep their hard-earned first-generation wealth. He appealed

48

to the swing-voting whites because he was white, on an otherwise unpronounceable ballot sheet. He even appealed to the 'radical' liberals because his child was gender diverse and Attwood had proudly walked them down the aisle, although critics suspected this was part of a strategy by the then communications manager, Gareth, to broaden his appeal.

A development scandal had stripped the local council of its head as well as its entire upper echelon, tainted by association, if not complicity. Gareth was on indefinite personal leave at the time and had escaped the cull. When the party approached him with a temporary reassignment he accepted the faulty baton that was passed to him. As acting councillor, he had three months before the next election to prove his competence, declare a few coherent policies for his ward and avoid a scandal.

'What does the council have to say about the attack?' Anji asked. 'The police haven't been much help; could be time to re-educate them about what constitutes racism in post-race Australia.'

When Gareth looked at her blankly, she looked over at Nikki.

'Sorry, we haven't had much chance to talk lately.' Nikki shrugged, her face firmly neutral. 'It's been so hectic with Oscar and work. You know how it is.'

'Of course,' Anji lied. The last incident had been more than slogans on the fence. Ruben had been attacked and hurt on his way back home from his tutoring job in Mount Druitt. Despite her interrogation, he hadn't revealed much, except when she had asked if he had been attacked before. 'I need to know, so I can help keep you safe,' she'd said.

He had laughed at that. Not unkindly. Just with surprise and amusement. 'That's my responsibility, not yours,' he replied.

'We're in this together, Ruben.' She reached for old words then. 'Ondraaher kudumbam mathiri.' Together, like family.

'Om,' he answered. Yes. But he refused to say more.

'I know you had some graffiti recently. Are you saying there's been something more than that?' Gareth asked, looking at his wife.

'The graffiti was just the start,' Anji replied. 'We thought it was random but now we know it's more organised. Gangs—at least, we think it's gangs. We can't tell because the security cameras keep getting broken. It's more than one person. Damaging the fences, spray-painting words.'

'Imaginative things, like, *Go back to where you came from*,' Nathan said. 'And, *Ban the burqa*, which is particularly confusing since no one in the nursing home wears a burqa—but, whatever, small detail.'

'I didn't realise it was getting worse.'

'Last week, one of our employees, Ruben, was attacked. It's not the first time, either,' Anji said. 'The police have been treating it as just random, unfortunate incidents. Regrettable as opposed to criminal. Kids being kids—although unlike most of the kids I know. Nothing to worry about, apparently. It'll pass.'

'You don't think so?' Gareth asked. He sounded genuinely concerned, his eyes still on Nikki, who didn't look up from her empty dessert bowl. She had allowed her hair to fall forward, hiding her expression.

Anji shrugged. 'In my family's experience, these things never pass.'

'This is not Sri Lanka, Anji. We have laws here, rules that protect people. I'm sorry, I didn't mean . . .'

'That's okay, Gareth. I know what you mean and you're right. There *are* laws here. There are laws in Sri Lanka, too.'

Anji checked her phone for messages. No calls from the nursing home. Uncle Saha in Room 2 was tucked away and sleeping safe for the night. The old man's midnight jailbreaks were becoming more frequent. He had found a way to exit the building without tripping the perimeter alarm, and in the last month Anji had had to send Ruben out looking for him three times. Somehow Ruben always knew where to find him.

She put her phone in her back pocket, finished loading the dishwasher and started it. She ran the tap, filling the pan with hot water. Oil and eggplant remnants floated to the top. Nathan drained his glass of wine then came to stand behind her and rinsed his glass. He turned off the tap and she looked at his reflection in the window above the sink.

'They all think you're the husband of the century,' she murmured as he moved her hair to the side and kissed her neck. She turned to face him, standing on her toes to reach his face.

'The bar's pretty low with that crowd,' he pointed out.

'Dave is a nice guy,' she said.

'He is. He may be in the doghouse tonight. You were very diplomatic when Mel tried to show you her yoga.'

She laughed. 'She's lovely but the yoga's not for me. Nikki was more distant than usual.'

'I don't want to talk about her or them tonight.' He pushed against her body gently, his fingers threading through her curls. He really did make her feel gorgeous.

'You smell like roasted cumin,' she said.

'I'm wearing it just for you,' he replied, tickling her face with his beard. 'It's called Eau de Ceylon.'

NIKKI

Sydney

Nikki half carried, half dragged Oscar into the house. Her son was reassuringly solid; he had a density that created its own gravity and tethered him to the earth. And tethered her to him. Gareth tried to take him from her but she shook her head. She hoisted the sleeping boy onto her chest and placed Oscar's arms and legs around her body.

'Hold on to Mummy,' he whispered and bent his head towards her.

She moved away.

She carried Oscar up the stairs and placed him in his bed, lingering a moment to smell the top of his sweaty head and run a finger along the crooked line of his eyebrow, the small scar where a cricket ball had clipped him last season. Loving was in the detail. Missing was in the detail too. Florence's ears curled tightly and were pointed at the top, making her look like a baby elf.

She tiptoed from her son's bedroom, leaving the door ajar, and hesitated at the top of the stairs. She could get ready quickly and slip into bed, claiming the fatigue of a long week. Instead, she braced herself and returned to the kitchen, unsure what to do if Gareth reached out to her again. He'd had a few drinks at Anji's.

He was at the fridge looking for the open wine bottle.

She went to the sink, pulled her hair back into a tight ponytail and began emptying the drying rack.

'Did you have a good night?' Gareth asked. 'You seemed pretty quiet.'

'Just tired. There's a lot going on at work. People aren't getting any younger.' She shrugged her shoulders.

'Hard to get a word in when Nathan goes on his feminist rant. At least he admits he only does it to get Anji to sleep with him.' He laughed.

Nikki looked down. Anji and Nathan had sex because they still loved each other. Still liked each other even.

'What?' he asked when she didn't say anything.

'Nothing,' she replied, keeping her face turned away, absorbed in removing food stains from the hob.

'You don't think he's serious, do you?' he asked. He poured himself a glass of red and tilted the bottle towards her but she shook her head. He added more to his large glass. Droplets spilled onto the stone benchtop. They would stain if he didn't wipe them fast enough. She waited for him to do it.

'Serious about what?'

'About being a stay-at-home dad.'

'He's not a stay-at-home dad,' Nikki replied. 'He works at the school part-time.'

'Yeah, counselling upwardly mobile middle-class kids whose immigrant parents send them to the educational equivalent of a sweatshop for fifteen hours of coaching a week. He'll be handing out antidepressants like Ovalteenies when he should just be telling them to get out in the playground.'

Gareth hadn't noticed the wine. It settled into the shiny surface.

Nikki had begged Nathan for antidepressants. He eventually allowed them, but with regular dosage review and only as an accompaniment to regular talk therapy with Oscar. She told Oscar the tablets were a vitamin and she gave them to him in the car on the way to school.

'It's an important job; anxiety and depression affect a lot of kids,' Nikki said. And a lot of men and women, she thought.

'Yes, but he makes parenthood sound like fucking sainthood.' Gareth drained his glass and refilled it. 'We all do it, he's not special, just because he can make a naan.'

'Roti,' she corrected him.

'Sure.'

'I don't think that's what he was saying.' She squeezed the drying cloth and hung it on the oven door handle. 'He was just making the point that people talk about motherhood as though it's some sacred duty, but they don't really value it or see how hard it is—especially when women do it, rather than men.'

When women do it.

They pay attention to everything.

'Yes, I remember,' Gareth said. 'He's been reading too many angry feminists on Insta. And he's got too much time between pretending to be a doctor at the school, pretending to be the perfect man and making the perfect naa—roti.'

'He's not the perfect man.'

'I *know*. What kind of man quits a successful career to stay at home?'

'A confident one,' she replied. She regretted it immediately. It must have been the wine. Either the wine she'd consumed at dinner, or the three drops of wine sitting on the benchtop she'd just cleaned.

'A *confident* one?' Gareth repeated, the edge in his voice familiar and cold.

'I just mean he's confident enough to leave something he enjoyed to try something different. The family needed him to do that, so he did. His self-worth isn't defined by his job or his lack of a job . . .'

She needed to stop talking. This conversation would reappear in weeks or months, her words given a new colour and sharpness because they had simmered in his mind.

'Maybe he's in the fortunate position that his self-worth can be improved by her net worth.'

'Yes,' she replied, wiping the droplets of wine near his wrist. There was a purple shadow on the surface. She would need to Jif that. She dropped her shoulders and focused on making her voice sound steady and sincere. 'You're right. It's different for them. He's in a completely different position.'

She didn't say to what.

Gareth moved closer to her. He placed his hand on the small of her back. She forced herself to breathe more deeply, concentrating hard on not flinching.

'I don't want to fight.' He rested his head on hers. 'Come up to bed. I can't make Indian food but I have other husbandly talents.'

She could smell the wine on his breath, in her hair. She kissed him quickly on the cheek. He stiffened.

'I'd love to, darling, but I've got an early start. You know how it is . . .'

'Yes, patients not getting any younger,' he repeated.

Neither were they. But one of them wasn't getting any older either. She pulled away and reached for the Jif, massaging the grainy cream into the benchtop with her fingers. She didn't look up until he had left the kitchen, taking the stairs to their bedroom. When she heard the sounds of his night-time routine, she left the kitchen and followed him up, but turned left at the landing, towards the children's rooms. She checked on Oscar, who was fast asleep, then kept walking towards the bedroom whose door was always closed.

Before she opened it, she allowed herself a few moments. She wasn't supposed to do this. During Oscar's counselling debriefs, Nathan had told her not to, but she did it anyway. What the hell did he know? With her hands and head resting on the door, she allowed herself to hear the deep and steady breaths of a living child. She allowed herself to imagine that she would open the door and the moonlight would cast a gentle blanket on Florence. Her dark brown hair was always matted during the night. She imagined touching its softness, bending down to inhale the shampoo she had used since Florence was a baby, locking her fingers into its untamed mass, feeling the warmth of her daughter's head underneath her fingertips.

She opened the door. The room had been left as it was the last time Florence had slept there. The preschool photo still on her bedside table. The dirty clothes still in a small basket by the beanbag. A dance leotard, jeggings with a sequined butterfly on the pocket, a t-shirt drenched in sweat. Time had dried it. That was her final smell. Sweat, covering her skin like a sheath.

The sheets hadn't been washed either. Sometimes, when she was alone in the house, Nikki slipped under the doona, put her head on the pillow. She inhaled deeply and willed her mind to re-create the silkiness of her hair, the curve of her head, the sensation of stray hairs tickling her nose, the sound of her breath, rising and falling, inhaling and exhaling with the certainty and steady thrum of endless life.

No one used this room now. She had thought she was the only person who ever entered it, but recently she'd noticed that books had been moved, and the Shopkins miniature shopping trolley and cash register had been picked up and replaced, but not where Florence had left them.

It was most likely Oscar. Gareth respected Nikki's request that nothing be touched or changed. But he had insisted the door be kept shut; like a tomb.

And every night, after he fell asleep, Nikki came to the bedroom door and opened it. The moment of imagining and pretending always ended. The bed was always empty.

~♋

Nikki liked to finish her morning rounds of the nursing home in Maya's room. She kissed her hello and wrapped the cuff of the blood pressure machine around Maya's arm, careful not to pinch her soft flesh.

'Too tight, Aunty Maya?' she asked.

'No, mahal.' Maya patted her hand.

Nikki squeezed the pump: three quick compressions to inflate the cuff and then two longer ones. She released the air slowly, watching the mercury drop down the scale magnified behind the glass. She adjusted the stethoscope in her ears and repeated the process to be sure.

'One hundred and ten over sixty,' she said, satisfied. 'That's excellent. How's the pain?'

Maya shrugged. 'It's a six. If I keep a heat pack on it and steal an extra Mobic from the Drug Cupboard every now and then, I can get it down to a four.'

'If you need an extra Mobic, you just have to ask. Drug theft isn't necessary.'

'Technically it's not theft—I own this place.'

'You do. Just ask me, Aunty. I'll prescribe it.'

'Thank you, mahal. It's a slippery slope, that one.'

'Yes. Anything that numbs the pain is a slope,' she replied. A slope to be feared and longed for. 'You're all good. Blood pressure is fine. Swelling, pain and mobility issues is what we would expect with such rapid-onset arthritis in the hip. But since you've refused the surgery and insist on stealing drugs, there's not much more I can do for you today.'

'How are *you*?' Maya asked.

'I'm fine,' Nikki lied. She tried again. 'I'm okay.' It was her turn to shrug. Maya had known her since she was a little girl in a

57

Westgrove Public School uniform and ribboned pigtails. Nikki had always been a terrible liar.

'I understand.'

Maya did understand a little. Her children were still alive but her husband was lost to her. She carried that pain everywhere. Her hip was a welcome distraction.

'And your father?' Maya asked. 'I visit him sometimes.'

Nikki smiled. 'I know you visit him every day. Thank you, Aunty. He has good days and bad.'

Like them all. Her father, Ray, lived down the corridor in the old building with Maya. Sometimes he forgot to leave his room, so Maya would drop in on her way to prayers or the games room and take him with her. Nikki tried hard not to think about one of Ray's bad days: the day Florence died. The day he couldn't remember anymore.

As she packed up the blood pressure machine, she asked, 'What does "enne manichi kolungo" mean?'

Maya frowned. 'Say it again.'

'Sorry, my pronunciation is terrible.' Nikki cleared her throat self-consciously and repeated the words. 'Enne manichi kolungo. Mr Balendran in Room 24 says it sometimes.' Another lie. Ruben whispered these words in his sleep.

Maya smiled sadly. Her eyes were large in the deepening hollows of her face. 'Forgive me,' she said. 'It means "forgive me".'

Nikki nodded. 'Do you have time to talk today, Aunty?'

'Always, mahal.'

MAYA

Cinnamon Gardens

Every day, Maya visited the large shrine room at the end of the corridor for her morning and evening prayers. On Saturday mornings at ten o'clock, she attended the weekly poosai, conducted by Mrs Shanthi Segaram from Room 6.

Shanthi Segaram had definitely let her status as de facto high priestess go to her head, which was inevitable. Even when they worked together at the Jaffna Public Library, Shanthi always thought she was better than everyone else, just because her husband was the son of Proctor Segaram.

The Westgrove Hindu temple three streets away was once a scout hall, but Tamils didn't 'do camping' unless they were internally displaced by war, so the local scouts platoon moved further east, freeing up prime real estate, zoned for community benefit. Civil engineer Vijay Sundaralingam set up a fundraising committee, and within a few years of the scouts vacating the building, it was reincarnated as a Ganesha temple. Vijay Sundaralingam's father, Potato Sundaralingam, was not only the Jaffna peninsula's most successful potato farmer, he was also widely but secretly reputed to be the main producer of the local vodka. Everyone ignored the fact that the Ganesha temple was partially funded by illicit alcohol money because the intergenerational transfer of wealth was highly applauded, regardless of how that wealth was generated.

The priest from the Westgrove Hindu temple came to the nursing home one Saturday a month to conduct a poosai and abhishekam for the deities. When he first started, he had inflicted the full range of Sanskrit mantras on the residents and ritually bathed the divine statues in milk, then sandalwood paste, then honey, then jasmine-infused water. Zakhir politely advised him that the congregation were afflicted with varying degrees of continence and consciousness, and brevity would not be mistaken for a lack of piety.

Maya entered the shrine room to find it was already teeming with residents dressed in their tenth-best saris or their first-best caftans and cardigans. Even Ray had worn a collared shirt for prayers, flanked by Nikki and Ruben.

The teachers had taken the back row and were preparing lessons while waiting for the prayers to begin. On weekends, the nursing home was full of children visiting their grandparents and also coming to receive tutoring from chemistry masters, biology masters and maths masters who had dominated Sri Lanka's education system decades ago. Even in their old age, they still had formidable recall of organic chemistry, anti-differentiation and trigonometric functions. Maya called the back row the Jaffna Teachers' Union, and they were as respected now as they were back then.

Saha Anna was in his usual spot, seated at a small table in the corner of the room by the largest window. The morning sun streamed through it, illuminating his work. Every day, Saha Anna worked in the shrine room with his heavy box of tools. The deities he carved from sandalwood were given as Deepavali gifts to residents and their families. Ganesha, the remover of obstacles, and Lakshmi, the goddess of wealth, were by far the most popular. Saha Anna used the bronze, brass and iron statues of the shrine as his muses, but he also drew on his decades-long study of temple art. His memories of all the forms of the divine were still as strong as the memories of his family, now dead for almost forty years.

Sometimes, by special request only, he created the Amman thali, using a small collection of cannisters, one containing compressed liquid gas for melting, and one containing compressed liquid nitrogen for freezing. The twenty-two-carat gold pendant was moulded and carved into the Mother Goddess, to adorn the wedding chain of a bride. He would use his diamond-tipped chisel for this task, which could only be done on auspicious days. And he would only do it for refugee families who could not afford to pay for a jeweller in Colombo to create the pendant, bless it and courier it back to Westgrove.

Saha Anna lifted his microscope headset to acknowledge Maya's presence and then he returned to his carving.

Mrs Ragupathy and her younger sister, Devaki, had come early too and taken the prime spot near the priest. They were third-generation classical Carnatic singers and never missed an opportunity to remind everyone that they had sung in Sri Venkateshwara Hall in Chennai, performing at the Thyagaraja Festival, the most prestigious Carnatic music festival in Asia.

The altar in the shrine room was predominately a showcase for Hindu deities. It reflected the main religion of the nursing home, but like any Hindu shrine, it held statues of the Buddha, Jesus Christ and his poor mother Mary. Siddharth, Maya's son in London, had also sourced a more racially accurate Jesus statue for her, and after some resistance from the Christians and Catholics, of all ethnicities, Brown Jesus (as he became known) had finally been accepted into the fold. There were also pictures of Sai Baba, the afro-haired avatar in India, and surah Al-Fatiha from the Quran. Maya looked at the shrine and felt the familiar rush of irritation.

Every evening, she arranged the deities in a particular hierarchal order. Every morning, she found them rearranged. As well as being in charge of the weekly poosai, that bossy boots Shanthi Segaram had appointed herself the keeper of the gods. A showdown of Hindu mythological proportions was inevitable.

Ganesha still sat in priority position at the front. Obviously, the night-time deity disarranger had some respect. Nataraja, the cosmic dancer, was three feet tall and two feet wide. Made of solid bronze, he was impossible to move and he stood at the back, presiding over the rest of them.

Saraswathi, the goddess of learning, had once again been demoted. Every night, Maya promoted Saraswathi to the front, as co-leader of the divine team, to give Maya the words and wisdom to create stories. She had organised the rest of the deities behind Saraswathi and Ganesha, so she could focus on her key praying priorities. Every morning, when she came to the shrine room, she found that Saraswathi had been moved back and Shiva, the destroyer and the head of the Hindu trinity of male gods, was promoted in front of her. He was flanked by Vishnu, the protector, and a small iron statue of Brahma, the creator. Shanthi Segaram was determined to preserve the patriarchal hierarchy that placed the Hindu male gods above the female gods. Strictly speaking, Brahma shouldn't even be there, because legend had it he'd been stripped of his right to be worshipped after offending Shiva.

Maya began restoring the divine order.

'Help me.' She motioned to Nikki and her father. 'Quickly.'

She couldn't reach the heavy Saraswathi statue. The goddess sat cross-legged, with her celestial instrument, the veena, across her lap. Maya had to reach over a row of gods and thrust her chest inappropriately into the Buddha's blissfully enlightened face. Nikki looked confused, but Ray sprang into action. He had been commandeered for this task before and knew exactly what to do. The man's mind might be fading but he was still physically stronger than Maya, and he had chosen her side in this religious war.

Shanthi Segaram shuffled into the shrine room.

'You!' she declared. 'Again! Why do you do this?'

'Why do *you* do this?' Maya had learned from watching question time in parliament that returning a question with a question surprised the opponent and gave her time to rally a defence. In this case, she needed time for Ray to move the statues around.

'We need Shiva more than Saraswathi, you know that. You're playing with fire, Maya,' Shanthi insisted. She wrested the bronze statue of Shiva from Ray's hands with surprising strength and clutched the god, also inappropriately, to her sagging breast.

Shanthi had a point. Shiva's deep meditation sustained and destroyed the universe. Maya had contributed two children and five grandchildren to the world of men and she wanted them to live long and happy lives. If anyone could cause or stop a global apocalypse, it was Shiva.

'It's sacrilegious,' Shanthi continued. 'No one puts Saraswathi at the front. You're destroying the proper order of things. You'll invite retribution. *This* is what happens when you marry a Muslim and run your own business instead of running your own family. You forget our ways. You think you're the boss around here.'

'I am well-versed in our ways, thank you, Shanthi. According to scripture, the male and female energies of the divine are equal, they are two halves of one whole. Shiva is as masculine as he is feminine.'

'Are you saying Shiva is a woman? Shame on you. This is disgraceful.' Shanthi's sari slipped a little, placing only her sari blouse between her body and Shiva's.

'No, this is ridiculous. All of these deities represent stories that help us understand our own divinity. The deities are supposed to be meaningless in the end.' Maya shook her head, trying to avoid eye contact with Shanthi's heaving chest.

The use of the word *meaningless* was ill-advised. Shanthi lifted Shiva, her emaciated arms shaking with rage and the supernatural effort. The statue slipped from her grasp in slow motion, and the meditating form of the god of destruction fell face first towards the ground. Twenty-five elderly Hindus dropped their canes, let go of their frames and wheelchairs to cover their mouths in horror.

'Aiyo, aiyo!' they whispered collectively through their fingers. 'Kadavule!'

'Holy shit,' said Ray as he lunged forward, his crooked fingers reaching for the bronze cobra draped around Shiva's neck. Catching the god by the snake, he swivelled him back upright and fell forward onto the altar with him. The table shuddered and listed to one side, the statues all beginning a slow slide towards his body.

'Jesus, Dad!' Nikki shouted.

Suddenly Ruben was at his side, supporting the table with one hand, Ray with the other, and kicking the table leg back out to its rightful position.

'Told you this was better than *The Bold and the Beautiful*,' he said to Nikki.

'Thank you so much, Ray. Are you all right?' Maya asked, her hand on Ray's back. She took it away abruptly.

'All good, love. Happy to help.' He gave her a wink.

Nikki suppressed a smile and Ruben coughed. Maya recognised a familiarity in the conspiracy of their humour but she didn't have time to ponder it. There were giggles from the rows of wheelchairs behind them.

'I'm reporting you to the Saiva Siddhanta Society for heresy,' Shanthi shouted. 'You're disrespectful and shameful. I'm going to demand an investigation.'

'Yes, you do that. I'm sure my daughter will take you very seriously. You're completely mad.'

'I'm mad? *I'm* mad?' Her voice escalated to shrill. 'Your husband was mad!'

Before Maya could respond, Ruben guided her away from the table and placed her walking frame between the women.

'Hush, Aunty,' Ruben whispered under his breath. 'She's angrier than usual today; please don't start something.'

'But she's been telling everybody I'm a Muslim disguised in a Hindu's clothing.'

'I can hear you, Maya,' Shanthi called. 'It's true: you're a traitor to your religion.'

'Now, now, Aunty,' Ruben placated Shanthi. 'People from all religions and backgrounds are welcome here at Cinnamon Gardens.'

'But we are mostly Hindus. Do you think people will still send their people to Cinnamon Gardens if they know you're converting them to Islam? People come here because they feel comfortable and safe.'

'No one is converting anyone, Shanthi Segaram,' Maya retorted. It was definitely time for Shanthi's medication.

'You think you're special just because you're educated,' Shanthi said, firing up her victimisation complex of Bollywood proportions. 'You think you're better than us because now you're rich.'

Maya tried to interrupt, but the old woman kept going.

'I knew you when you were a poor spinster living with your mad father, before you married your mad husband. I knew you when you were in university, and you were as arrogant then as you are today. You always got what you wanted. You didn't respect me then and you don't respect me now.'

'You're all special at Cinnamon Gardens,' Anji said from the door of the shrine room. She must have been summoned to end the dispute. 'Come, Aunty, let me take you to your seat. As soon as the poosai is over, we're having a screening of *Sankarabharanam*.'

The crowd quietened down immediately at the mention of the classic Indian film. Anji moved Shanthi to a seat at the front row and nodded to the priest, Mrs Ragupathy and Devaki to begin the singing.

'Just like in Chennai, Aunty,' Anji said.

Mrs Ragupathy smiled at her radiantly. Anji was good at her job. So good that Maya knew what was coming next.

'Amma, let me take you to your room.'

'I don't want to go to my room.'

'Let me take you anyway, please.'

Maya relented. The argument had exhausted her.

Anji escorted her back to her room down the corridor. Once they were safely inside, with the door shut, she said to her mother, 'You and Appa wanted to create a space here that reminded your people of home.'

'*Our* people,' Maya corrected her. Anjali did that a lot.

'Our people,' Anji repeated. 'And our people don't like change, Amma.'

'It's one of their many failings,' Maya replied.

'*Our* failings actually,' Anji said with a smile. She took Zakhir's cardigan from the chair and helped Maya put it on, arranging her plait down her back and smoothing the lines of her caftan.

'Fine,' Maya replied.

'Please don't rock the temple, Amma. Aunty Shanthi is difficult, and for some reason you make her angry.' She put her hands up in a mollifying gesture. 'I'm not saying it's your fault. I'm just saying we need to keep her happy. Let's respect the patriarchal distortion of Hinduism, don't tell her we pay Zakat and we'll keep the peace, at least until she dies.'

Maya stood in front of her personal shrine. It was a small table, laden with the deities she had brought from the caretaker's cottage, including a small statue of Saraswathi her father gave her when she was a child.

'She said nasty things about my appa and Zakhir.'

'I know; she's a nasty person,' Anji replied. 'But something has made her that way. When we were children, and people called us names at school, you told us to be defiant instead of defensive.'

'Nice use of alliteration.' Maya smiled.

'Yes, you were always good with words. You also told us that people were rarely born nasty, they were usually raised that way. Let her be, Amma. Aunty Shanthi will die before you if she keeps stealing milk toffee from the kitchen. After that, I'll let you teach Gender for Geriatrics in the games room. You can start with Hinduism and work your way through to contemporary Christianity.'

Anji gave her mother the small pot of holy ash from her shrine and bent her head, her hands folded together in prayer.

Maya placed a smudge of ash on her daughter's forehead.

'I won't live long enough, but again, nice use of alliteration, mahal.' She kissed her daughter and straightened Saraswathi, moving her just slightly in front of Shiva.

GARETH

Sydney

Gareth looked at his phone. The Monday morning round table was supposed to start at 9.30 but it was already 9.55. Mike Davidson's secretary had texted to say the MP would be a little late, due to a prior commitment. It was a brief, unapologetic message. Even the admin staff of their state member considered themselves higher up the food chain than the local councillor of an increasingly vulnerable local government area.

Gareth straightened his meeting papers. They were ordered by agenda items. He searched his suit jacket for the extra highlighter. Orange meant *Action Immediately*, but he needed green for *Action Later*. If he left this meeting with the papers annotated entirely in fluorescent orange, it would annoy him. People laughed, but when he was a speechwriter he'd written word-perfect speeches, policy statements and last-minute press releases because he had systems in place that worked under pressure. The colour-coded highlighter system was one of them.

Davidson strode in. He was a big man, a former union player for the western suburbs private school they had both attended, decades apart. Gareth remembered seeing Mike's name on the faded wooden boards that adorned their assembly hall. These rolls of honour listed the legends in their small universe. A few of them, like Davidson, would become masters of a much larger universe, accepting this birthright as casually as they did their first investment property in Summer Hill.

With his broad chest and tall frame, Davidson carried his thickening around the waist confidently, as though it was intended. All part of the man's plan, Gareth noted enviously.

Davidson had been playing early morning golf with other state MPs who represented their western region. He was still in his beige trousers and navy-blue polo shirt. He wore the collar turned up.

'It's to protect my neck against the sun, Gareth,' Davidson had once told him. 'The girls in PR say I shouldn't do it, that it's alienating to the rising middle class. Makes me look like I have the two-door, S-Class weekender they yearn for but will never achieve.'

Davidson did have the two-door, S-Class weekender. He heard the advice and ignored it. His collars remained resolutely upright.

He sat down at the head of the large meeting room table, his face flushed with the morning's exertions.

'Tell me,' he commanded, looking around the table, 'how are we travelling?'

Travelling? What did that word even mean in this sentence?

Gareth sat on Davidson's right. Opposite him was the MP's twenty-seven-year-old daughter, Bella. She was immaculately constructed. Her hair was expensively blonde, cut into a short, executive bob. Her barely there and yet definitely there make-up gave her face the pleasing sense of being finished. Her skin was consistently tanned to a hue that in most lights looked impossibly healthy but in the over-lit boardroom looked like it was approaching *Action Immediately.*

Richard Lewis sat on Davidson's left, his fingers resting on the keyboard of his laptop. He was an accountant with three decades of local government experience. He had served Mayor Attwood well and the mayor before him. Ben Attwood's brief descent into white-collar crime had eluded his scrutiny, only because the scene of the crime, the golf course, had been a place Richard Lewis rarely frequented.

The scandal had made the accountant even more vigilant and he would only accept Bella onto their staff if her salary was paid personally by Davidson as a fully declared, non-tax-deductible expense from his personal earnings and not from the council budget. Davidson refused and, in the end, Bella was employed by the state party and seconded to the local office. Parental love knew no shame, thought Gareth. He revised his position; he had plenty of shame.

'I see the local papers are still running the Attwood story,' Davidson said, throwing the *Westgrove Chronicle* on the table, its pages open on the headline: GOLF-GATE: SECRETS TRADED AT THE 18TH HOLE. CADDY FINALLY TELLS ALL. NEW REVELATIONS.

At his weekly golf game, then Mayor Attwood had passed inside information to his old school friend, the CEO of Robertson Constructions Pty Ltd, who was awarded the tender to refurbish the town hall.

When Golf-gate hit, Gareth had been on bereavement leave, ring-fenced from the scandal by a personal tragedy that made him a good candidate for the unexpected vacancy. He was able to temporarily ascend to the throne of his local ward without an election. Davidson visited the council offices every fortnight, on the pretext of visiting his daughter, but Gareth couldn't shake the feeling the party didn't trust him, and Davidson was there as supervisor, micromanager and spy until democracy could be restored and the people of Westgrove appointed a complete and scandal-free council.

Gareth shrugged, ignoring the newspaper. 'There's nothing new in there.'

'There doesn't have to be,' Davidson replied. 'You know that. What's on today's agenda—aside from our failure to move the elec-torate past this bullshit?'

He was right. *Any* words were damaging words on this. Any words kept the story and the party in a spotlight it didn't want. It was time for a strong policy statement or a new school refurbishment. But not Oscar's school, nothing improper. Maybe even just a small bushfire at Captain Cooks Reserve would help.

The door opened and they were joined by Pete Woodbury, or Woody, as he was called. He was their liaison with the state and federal police and 'other agencies'. No one, including Gareth, knew which other agencies, but no one had the nerve to ask Woody. According to party rumour, he was former special ops, and there was something about him that made all of them want to salute him and then delete their search histories. Woody only joined them a few times a year, when requested by Davidson or instructed by the other agencies. Today, he was here on Davidson's instruction.

Bella, who liked to chair these briefings, usually began by providing a confusingly unnecessary and unnecessarily confusing overview of everyone else's agenda items. She used the personal pronoun 'I' more than anyone he had ever met, giving the audience the impression that she was singlehandedly running every program she described. Once her introduction was done, she flashed a dazzling smile, and it was clear from her body language that she expected gratitude and possibly applause for her contribution. Then she turned the floor over to Gareth and Richard to provide the substantive briefing to her father. To mask his irritation, Gareth imagined her blowing up balloons, contorting them into complex animals, perhaps even endangered species, and handing them out to everyone at the meeting. It helped him smile appreciatively at the right moments.

Woody spoke before Gareth could open his mouth. 'I'm sorry I'm late and I'm sorry to interrupt your usual run sheet, but I have to get back to the city. Would you mind if I cut in?'

No one minded but everyone braced themselves. Woody's stakes seemed higher than theirs.

'We've had more reports from head office about gangs here. There was an attack on the Indian grocery store on Rochester Street on Wednesday night, and then on Thursday night residents living close to the Kapunda playground called about an attack. Three men beating a fourth man. The victim got away and they chased him, but we don't know what happened. We called Westmead Hospital and the twenty-four-hour clinic on Herbert Street, but no one seems to have been admitted.'

Davidson interjected, 'There's no way of knowing if these attacks are committed by the same people, Woody. So far, we're looking at random acts of violence.'

'I don't think so, with all due respect, sir.' Woody had this way of saying 'with all due respect' that indicated he had no respect for you but dared you to suggest otherwise. Gareth had asked him once why he always referred to each of them by their title and never their first names as they had invited him to do.

'I don't serve the man,' was his reply.

'You serve the office?' Gareth had asked.

'I serve the country and the office serves the country.' Until it doesn't, Gareth had thought at the time.

'These acts of violence are escalating.' He nodded to Richard, who tapped on his laptop and brought up a file, projecting a map of western Sydney with coloured dots on the screen at the front of the room. The red dots were clustered around their suburb and spread like an angry rash westwards. Gareth couldn't decipher the scale so he wasn't sure how far the red dots were spreading. He squinted to read the suburb names.

'Hatfield. It stops at Hatfield,' Woody told him. Hatfield was only twelve kilometres away and still within the boundary of their council area.

'How do you know it doesn't start at Hatfield?' Davidson asked. He leaned back in his chair, elbows on the armrests, hands resting on his lap, cupped as if he were about to catch a cricket ball. Gareth was sure that, under the table, his legs were outstretched and crossed at the ankles. A casual taking of other people's space.

Woody picked up Richard's remote control and clicked at the screen. With each click the red dots grew in number but not in distance. It was a localised infection, with the greatest, reddest cluster in Westgrove.

With each image, he intoned the dates. Over four months, the attacks had increased in frequency. They had also increased in intensity.

'That still doesn't tell me where the perpetrators are from. It only tells me where they're attacking.' Davidson still hadn't moved. Gareth had seen this before. When Davidson disagreed vehemently but did not want to show an emotional investment in a proposal, his brain instructed his body and his voice to show relaxed disinterest.

Woody didn't care. He had seen combat. Conversational conflict simply got in the way of the strategy he would implement with or without local government support. He answered to the country not the party.

'Our analysts have also cut the data looking at the specific time and location of the attacks. Many occurred on the same night, first in Westgrove and then extending further west later in the night, following the train line. With this kind of violence, typically we see the group peak early and then wane in interest and energy as the night progresses.'

Gareth wondered what other kinds of violence there were. Woody seemed to read his mind.

'This is in contrast with mob violence, where the mob grows in size, bloodlust and confidence. The killings start here, and escalate quickly to here.' He moved his hand from his chest to above his head.

Gareth swallowed hard.

'Don't ask where "here" is. It varies, but it's never good. In this case, the assailants were initially targeting Indian stores, Indian restaurants and Indian businesses. My concern is that the violence is escalating from property damage to attacks on people. This transition, once made, does not de-escalate without state intervention.'

Woody said the words *state intervention* so matter-of-factly, but Gareth needed a few seconds to imagine what that might involve.

Davidson hadn't picked it up at all, instead asking, 'What's an Indian business? An IT store?'

'I should say South Asian businesses. Businesses where the signage indicates the owners are of South Asian origin, such as local GP surgeries.'

'Could be drug addicts,' Davidson suggested.

'No drugs were taken. Local accountants and dentists were hit; again, no money or drugs taken. When the attacks involve individuals, the victims are always people of identifiably South Asian origin.'

'Are we using PC language with the ethnics now too, Woody? When did the political correctness police get to you?' Bella laughed. *'People who identify as South Asian,'* she quoted and smiled widely at him.

Misquoted. He didn't smile back.

'South Asia is comprised of seven countries, over one billion people, five major religions, over twenty-five languages and more than two thousand ethnic groups.' Woody recited the data from his cerebral regional report. He had mastered an intonation and cadence that could only be categorised as professionally neutral, but everyone in the room heard the judgement. It sat in the air between them, dust motes laden with disdain. No one, not even Davidson, dared call it out or stop Woody's security assessment.

'I said the victims are always people of *identifiably* South Asian origin because they are brown but not Indigenous. The average white assailant incorrectly identifies them as *Indian.*'

Gareth was quite certain that if Woody was instructed to execute the one Sri Lankan at a multi-ethnic, multi-racial South Asian wedding at the Westgrove Bowling Club, the ex-soldier could identify and kill him before the Bhangra band started. People had such varied skill sets. Gareth shook his head. It was moments like these he used to laugh about with Nikki. He felt the pain of that loss in his chest, below his heart, above his gut.

'Right, okay. Thank you, Woody. This is your wheelhouse and we respect that,' Davidson said, cutting off his daughter before she could frame an offended response. 'Let's do a deep dive into some of the information you've got. You've noted the assailants are white. Do you have CCTV footage?'

Woody shook his head. This had been the problem with his last two briefings on the attacks. But the US had invaded Iraq on much less evidence and significantly less plausible inferences than Woody's.

'There's no footage of their faces because they're aware of the cameras and they're only attacking after dark. However, we've interviewed numerous local residents and all of them confirm that the assailants were white.'

'If the attacks all took place at night,' Davidson countered, 'how could they tell?'

'Given the targets of the vandalism—'

'South Asians are just as vandalous as white people, Woody,' Davidson interrupted him. 'They are just as violent and just as capable of these kinds of attacks. You've only got to watch BBC Asia to see how violent Asia is.'

Gareth doubted Davidson watched BBC Asia. Or the BBC.

'I just think if we start saying "white gangs are attacking brown people", we're causing unnecessary alarm and unfairly racialising these one-off incidents,' Davidson persisted. 'We need solid evidence before we start suggesting that Westgrove has a race problem.'

'Westgrove does have a race problem, Mr Davidson. Some of its constituents are racist. We can deduce this from the fact that the targets of their attacks are consistently people of particular racial origins.'

'Accusing Australians of racism does not play well in the polls, Woody. We're looking for headwinds to bring the community together, not tailwinds.'

Davidson had just described possible racial violence as a tailwind. That was new.

'There's more at stake here than just a few Indian video stores,' he continued.

'You're right, sir. The attacks are escalating in frequency and violence. There *is* more at stake here.'

'What are you suggesting, Woody? A public safety announcement? There's no footage of their faces, so we'd be asking every South Asian in the suburb to be wary of every Australian in the suburb. That's simply not practical. We need a more "whole of community" approach.'

Gareth sighed. He had worked in politics for long enough to know what Davidson was doing. This was an election year. The party needed to prove they had been given a clear mandate by the community, and they had distanced themselves from Attwood. While Woody saw a problem brewing in Westgrove, Davidson saw an opportunity, but Gareth didn't yet know what the local member would do with it.

'What do you suggest we do, Woody?' Gareth asked, wanting to pre-empt Davidson.

'I suggest you do make a public safety announcement. Ask people to stay off the streets at night until the authorities have tracked down and arrested key suspects. Invest in better local surveillance. These guys aren't brain surgeons. They've quickly formed patterns with the times and places they attack. Proper covert surveillance will get us identities. And think about your communications strategy.' He turned to Gareth. 'You want key messages on community, cultural unity, respect and acceptance. Our forensic psychologists tell us those are the words you need to repeat. Strong leadership can shape what happens next just as much as strong law enforcement.'

'Understood, Woody, I'll prepare something,' Gareth said. They needed a short, simple loop, like George W, post 9/11. There was nothing magical about it; he just kept repeating the same reassuringly patriotic and patronisingly simplistic messages. Gareth wrote the words *community, cultural unity, respect* and *acceptance* down, and underlined *community*.

'If you identify and arrest these guys, doesn't that take care of the problem?' Richard asked.

'Not necessarily. It depends on how deep the problem runs. If it *is* just a few racist idiots beating on a few South Asians, then all we need to do is arrest the lone wolf or the lead wolf.'

'You're not suggesting there's a deeper problem here, are you, Woody?' Davidson said. 'This is educated suburbia. We're the rising middle class. Our residents have finally started skiing in Japan. This is not Cronulla or Redfern, for God's sake.'

'Redfern residents are skiing in Whistler and Verbier, sir. The world is changing and rarely for the better. My job is to anticipate situations and stop them before they become a problem. Councillor Barton, I'll send you the scripts our guys recommend. You can tailor that to suit your actual speaking style and language.'

'Thank you, Woody, that would be helpful.' Gareth wondered if 'recommend' was code for 'insist'.

'Yes, thank you, Woody, we'll take all of that on board and craft a communications strategy around it.' Bella flashed her signature smile. 'Let's see if we can shift the dial on this.'

Gareth saw a muscle twitch in Woody's jaw. The soldier gathered his papers and nodded tightly. It was his signature goodbye.

Davidson turned to his daughter after the door shut behind Woody. 'That was surprising,' he said. 'I didn't pick Woody for an alarmist. There's no way we're making a public announcement. He doesn't appreciate the political consequences of telling Australians they're racist. We pride ourselves on tolerance and respect in this country.'

'They're all Australian,' Gareth said.

'What?' Davidson turned towards him, confused, as though he had forgotten Gareth was there.

'They are all Australian, Mike,' Gareth said. 'You keep referring to the South Asian Australians as South Asians and the white Australians as Australians. They are *all* Australian.'

Richard Lewis looked at the imaginary Excel spreadsheet on his laptop with renewed interest. Bella Davidson seemed to pale under her fake tan.

Davidson's eyes narrowed as he weighed his options. 'You are absolutely right, Gareth. I'm sorry. I was just trying to distinguish between the different groups in our rich multicultural society.' He smiled and turned back to his daughter. 'No public announcement, but I'll talk to RMS and New South Wales Police about the additional surveillance. I'm sure I can persuade them to put some budget behind it. Don't you worry, Richard. I'll find the money for you. Leave it with me.'

He smiled magnanimously at Richard then shifted his gaze to Gareth. 'I'll see you this afternoon for our four pm? I'm in the city for meetings, so if you could meet me there, that would be great.'

The city was a two-hour round trip in traffic.

Davidson didn't wait for a reply. He stood up, checked his phone and closed Gareth's council meeting.

∼ↄ

Afterwards, Gareth called Nikki and left a message on her voicemail.

'Hi, darling, it's me. Just wondering if you were free for a quick coffee? We could meet at the usual place.' He tried not to make every sentence sound like a plea. Cafe Blue Lotus hadn't been their usual place for over a year.

He looked at his phone. No call, no message. She might not pick up her messages if she was with patients. He started to text her, abandoned it and then tried to text her again.

Quick coffee at Blue M? I'm free any time. BD said shift the dial again.

He waited. Thirty minutes later, she replied:

Back 2 back patients. Sorry. Thnx anyway. C u at home.

MAYA

Cinnamon Gardens

Maya put a new tape into the recorder and labelled the case. She smiled at the photograph of Zakhir on her shrine table and dabbed holy ash on his forehead, her fingers lingering on his wide smile. She wrapped his cardigan around her body, pulling it close. Recording her own story was Ruben's idea. She had initially felt self-conscious, but she had found a way to do it, for her children and grandchildren. She looked at the photo of Zakhir and imagined him in the room with her in Cinnamon Gardens. She spoke directly to him.

Cinnamon Gardens, 1984

Maya had written hundreds of thousands of words. With Zakhir's help, she extracted and edited the best ones into a novel. He sat with her night after night, urging her not to throw the words away but to find ways to make them better.

Finally, she submitted the novel to every agent and publisher she could find in the heavy Sydney phone directory. She and Zakhir spent hours in the nursing home's office, photocopying the

80

typed manuscript and putting it in envelopes. Together, they took the envelopes to the post office and posted the manuscript into the wind, wishing it a fruitful journey.

Nine envelopes were posted and over the next six months she received eight envelopes back with polite letters of rejection. One had not even bothered to reply. The letters were all variations of the first one.

Dear Mrs Ali,
Thank you so much for your submission dated 12 August 1984.
We enjoyed reading your work. It was very exotic. But while
it is well written and engaging, no one will read it and no one
will buy it. Unfortunately, we are unable to make you an offer
of publication.

Zakhir made her call each publisher and ask for feedback.

'Feedback will help you improve,' he said.

Feedback crushed her. It was always the same.

'There's no readership for your kind of work here; it's too ethnic. Perhaps seek a publisher in India . . . Oh, that's right, sorry—you're from Sri Lanka. Excellent tea, excellent cricketers. Who knew they were so violent?'

'Sri Lankans know,' Maya replied. 'And I want the world to know; that's why I wrote this story.'

'That's lovely, dear. Perhaps look for a publisher in Sri Lanka. Thank you so much for calling, very brave of you, shows commitment. Keep trying.'

'No readership?' Zakhir retorted. His pompadour shook with anger. 'If Woolf and Austen are published in Sri Lanka, why couldn't *you* be published *here*? No readership,' he repeated. 'What is wrong with their readers? We all have eyes.'

And we all have hearts, she thought. Woolf broke her heart. Maya wasn't brilliant like her, but she could break hearts too.

'What do they mean, I'm not right for their brand?' she asked Zakhir, Cedric and any resident who would listen. What was so *esoteric* about her work? Or had the publisher said *ethnic*? What was ethnic about a story set in Ceylon?

'Ethnic? There are over fifty million Tamil speakers in the world. Sri Lanka's population is the same as Australia's. Who are they calling ethnic? White people are ethnic,' Zakhir said, taking the phone out of her shaking hands.

It was the last phone call which told her that her literary career was over before it had begun. Clara Rose, a former commissioning editor now turned literary agent, called her back, raising her spirits.

'It's a beautifully written story. Perhaps you could change their names, make them more pronounceable. More um . . .'

'More white?' Maya asked. 'Perhaps you'd like more white people in the book? Would you like me to give your readers more white people because they struggle to enter other people's worlds?'

'There's no need to get defensive, Mrs Ali. It's just not very Australian.'

Not very Australian. She couldn't think of anything more Australian. The story was about the loss of one identity and the creation of another.

'There isn't a lot of space in the Australian market for migrant literature,' the agent continued.

'Mrs Rose,' Maya began.

'Miss Rose,' the agent corrected her.

'Miss Rose, *National Geographic* tells me that everything written by a non-Aboriginal writer could be considered migrant literature.'

'It's just not *English* enough.'

'Not English enough? It's set in a post-independence nation. It's about colonialism and its consequences. It's about genocide, about dispossession and migration. It's practically "Advance Australia Fair".'

She didn't call another publisher.

'I want you to take my work,' she said tearfully to Zakhir. 'Take it all and put it on the barbecue. That would be a fitting death to my brief literary career.'

'I know sustaining tension is important in a novel but don't be so dramatic,' Zakhir replied, adding more charcoal and then inserting fire starters in strategic places. He had recently bought himself a barbecue at her request, despite his complaint that cooking on an open fire was for impoverished villagers.

'Not in Australia,' she had replied.

'This entire place is one big culturally impoverished village. You have to speak to them in their language, Maya.'

'My novel *is* in English,' Maya replied, confused.

'I don't mean *English*. I mean in their language, through their eyes. They only see *their* stories as valid. Give them that. Give them their stories but write them better. You've studied English literature; you know how it works.'

He provoked the charcoal embers with the tongs.

'I need more kindling.'

She gave him the rejection letters for the barbecue, but not the novel.

Maya put her failed manuscript down and picked up the Australian canon; gripping novels about the hardships of early European settler life, stories about men doing battle with unforgiving landscapes and unjust penal systems. They often involved horses, but not many women or Indigenous people. She studied harder than she'd ever studied before, reading the literature and observing the language, taking notes on the idioms and idiosyncrasies of Australian English.

She read the recommendations of Mrs Vandermark at Westgrove Public Library, books written by people called Michael and Sarah about life in modern Australia. Hard-boiled detectives, damaged childhoods and beguiling cities where more souls were lost than found.

She also studied the bestseller lists, which told her what books were bought by other people called Michael and Sarah. For the first time in her life, she thought about the readership rather than just the writing.

She planned a completely different novel.

Her second failed manuscript, written by Sarah Byrnes, was called *A Pocketful of Gumnuts*. It was a children's story about a gutsy koala called Barry who leaves the bush and heads for Sydney's Kings Cross in search of his missing son, Redmond, armed with nothing but his wits and a pocketful of gumnuts. It was once again rejected, but the agent, Clara Rose, sent a letter asking to meet with her. She felt Sarah's writing style had promise.

Maya wrote back, declining the meeting.

Sarah Byrnes was a recluse, recovering from a mysterious personal tragedy, and she did not meet with people. However, she agreed to engage in conversation by letter, her preferred form of communication.

Clara explained, by return letter, that Sarah's voice was strong and had an authenticity of place and purpose. She felt that Barry's story was too derivative of Blinky Bill and took the koala to darker places than were appropriate for a children's novel. She noted that Sarah had an edge that she should apply to literary fiction or perhaps even romance.

Maya placed *A Pocketful of Gumnuts* on the barbecue.

'Are you sure you want to do that?' Zakhir asked, tongs poised to rescue Barry.

'Yes, it was terrible,' she replied. 'No more marsupial misadventures.'

'Thank God. It *was* terrible. What's next?'

Maya considered the things she'd learned about Australia from reading its literature. The dreams and delusions contained in the stories of her new home. The presence of some people and the absence of others. The contradictions. She remembered a lesson from her father; the memory hurt and helped her: *If you read the literature of a country, child, you will understand it; you will fall in love with it.*

'Maya?' Zakhir prompted.

'I want to write a story about a complex heroine. She lives in a hard world and learns to accept both it and herself.'

'Sounds like a bestseller,' Zakhir replied, pushing Barry deeper into the barbecue.

Thus began the Clementine Kelly series of Australian crime-with-a-bit-of-romance-and-increasingly-more-sex novels. Maya sent the first three chapters to Clara, who pitched them to local publishers. Several came back with offers. Maya accepted one and used the advance to upgrade the nursing home kitchen, to Cedric's amusement.

'It's your money,' he said, straightening the waistcoat of the three-piece suit he refused to relinquish. 'If this is what you want to do with it, do it.'

'It's our money, and I'm investing it in our nursing home,' she replied.

Clementine Kelly was an instant hit with the Country Women's Association, whose members could not stop talking about how well Sarah Byrnes had captured the Australian spirit in her vivid, evocative writing. The chair of the CWA was quoted as saying, 'Her rendition of the brutal landscape that tames and is tamed by Clementine's wild spirit has awakened the frontier woman in all of us. She makes us want to stop baking and start tearing the shirt off the nearest, cleanest shearer.'

Clementine was a flawed heroine in an era of conventional and commercially viable protagonists. She navigated the legacy of a complicated childhood that hung like an albatross around her neck in every relationship. Tragedy and misfortune seemed to follow her as she escaped her dysfunctional family, only to find herself trapped in a loveless marriage to an abusive sugarcane farmer.

The Women's Weekly ran a feature:

Who is Sarah Byrnes and what personal tragedies keep her hidden behind the veil of secrecy?

Sarah writes from a place of such deep pain. Her portrait of a colonial woman transcends time, and speaks to the challenges of the modern woman, while remaining deeply rooted in the ancient soil of 1800s Australia. Her readers ache with her . . .

Based on the success of the first book, the UK rights were sold and then the US rights. Publishers and readers wanted more. Maya wrote another book, and when Queenwood Entertainment approached her agent to option the film rights, Clara Rose insisted on a face-to-face meeting with her most lucrative client.

Maya and Zakhir sat next to each other at a small table in the games room. The bingo cards were being cleared away by staff, and the Tuesday afternoon bridge class would start soon. Mrs Napoli was warming up her vocal cords in front of the whiteboard, where points were tallied by Mrs Shanahan, her bridge partner of many years at the nursing home, and now her co-instructor.

Mr Napoli was a poor bridge player but he had other talents. He sat opposite Maya, wearing his church clothes, his hair specially oiled for the mock interview.

'Agents are slippery characters. They'll make you feel as though they're doing you a favour but they're not. You are her meal ticket. *You* are doing *her* a favour,' Mr Napoli coached, his crooked forefinger punctuating his words. He had been the director of an amateur theatre company back home in Greve, Italy, as well as a bank manager. He had the perfect combination of artistic and commercial insight.

'Trust me, I know the type. Don't agree to anything at the meeting. Look disappointed with everything she offers you. Tell her you need to talk to your lawyer. No, your husband—she'll believe that.'

Anjali ran into the games room, screaming. Siddharth was close behind her, his hands full of homemade boomerangs. He took up a defensive position behind Mr Napoli's wheelchair and the seven year olds began hurling the boomerangs at each other. On impact, the weapons disintegrated into the paddlepop sticks they were made from.

'Siddharth!' Zakhir shouted. 'We're working. Both of you go outside and help the nurses with the exercise class.'

During school holidays, Siddharth and Anjali helped with classes, throwing soft beach balls and adjusting the elderly into their modified Sun salutes. The residents also participated in Siddharth's complicated battle scenarios against Anjali, becoming enthusiastic and sedentary castle walls, bunkers and lookouts.

Maya was terrified about the meeting with her agent. She briefly contemplated sending her good friend and fellow school mum, Bek South, in her place.

'You need to do this yourself. Publishers are offering you advances for two more books. You can't keep negotiating by letter,' Cedric said, sipping his latest cocktail invention.

Maya agreed to meet Clara at Cafe Blue Lotus, the small curry house on Bourke Road. She had seen a picture of Clara Rose in a publishing magazine so she knew who she was looking for. Also, there would be no other white people in the curry house, which was reminiscent of roadside stops in Sri Lanka.

When she arrived, Clara was already waiting, peering at the menu in confusion.

Maya sat next to her and Clara looked up, startled. The glasses perched on her nose slipped off, saved by the chain around her neck. Her permed brown hair surrounded her head in a wild halo. It contrasted with the thick straight fringe that cut across her forehead, like a line that underscored a very important point. Her nose turned up like a mini ski jump, sharp and just as pale.

'I'm sorry,' Clara said, 'but you can't sit here; I'm waiting for someone.'

'You're waiting for me, Clara.' Maya extended her hand for Clara to shake. 'I'm Sarah Byrnes. Well, I'm Maya Ali, but I didn't think you'd read my work if I told you that.'

Maya ordered the mildest food on the menu for the agent and they talked while customers eyed Clara with interest and then amusement as she struggled with the sambal and had to wash the coconut chilli medley down with an emergency lassi.

'What do you want to do?' Clara asked, shaking her head at the heat and in disbelief that this was her client.

'I want to write. I want to raise my children and I want to help my husband build a nursing home. If I'm being honest, I want to do it in that order, too. But you and I both know there is no place in the Australian market for me, even if everyone loved my first two novels. I have at least one more adventure for Clementine Kelly. I'm going to break her heart but not her spirit. My readers will weep for her and grieve for her and they will want more of her.'

She exhaled. She had practised this speech with Zakhir and Mr Napoli for weeks. She knew it by heart. Her memory and her resolve did not fail her.

'What are you proposing?' Clara asked, exactly as Zakhir had predicted she would.

'She's a businesswoman,' he said. 'She will know what that third book is worth before you've even written it. Don't sell yourself short. Think tall, Maya. You are a woman of great intellectual and literary stature.'

She had kissed him then, so relieved that he was having a good day, one of those days when he believed in himself and in her.

'I'm proposing that Sarah Byrnes write another Clementine Kelly book, and perhaps another and another,' Maya replied. 'It's my words and my character they want; the mystique of the author behind her only adds to Clementine's appeal. Let's keep it that way.

You're my agent. Represent me with the public. I can do written interviews but nothing face to face. Nothing on the phone, either; my accent is far too convent-educated-in-a-former colony. They'll know immediately that I'm not one of you even though I've written a book about you that you can't put down.'

'We wouldn't want to deny the CWA their heroine of the hour,' Clara conceded.

'I think we both know Clementine Kelly is here for more than just an hour,' Maya countered.

She pushed the first chapter of the third Clementine Kelly novel across the table. The young waitress hovered over Clara's shoulder with a plate of egg hoppers. 'Uncle Sinathamby asked you to try this, latest on the menu. The thaachis have just arrived from Jaffna. He said to tell you he can get more for the nursing home.'

Maya nodded at Uncle Sinathamby, who was watching from the counter as he stacked fish patties that had been freshly deep-fried. He winked at her. Maya winked back and admired the egg hopper. Its concave body rose up towards crisp but not crumbly edges in an algorithmic sweep that followed the curve of Uncle's new pans. In the centre, an egg had been cracked and partially cooked, the albumen shining in the fluorescent light above, giving the egg yolk in the middle a glow, a small sun setting against the pancake's moon. She wanted to dip her fingers in and break the yolk, watch it bleed into the pancake. But she kept her hands clasped, controlling the tremor that started in her stomach, spread to her shoulders and surged down into her fingers.

'Keep your hands together and breathe deeply but not obviously. I find that helps me when I'm in trouble,' Zakhir said. He held his hands together too often.

Maya sat silently as Clara read the chapter and then looked up, eyes wide with surprise and something else: hunger.

'It's good,' Clara said.

'It's excellent. Can you sell it?' Maya asked, repeating Mr Napoli's script.

Clara was the third-most-senior agent in Australia's premier literary agency. There weren't many literary agencies in Australia, but this was the one that counted. *Booksellers Monthly* had suggested that Clara had been third-most-senior for too many years.

'Yes.' Clara nodded, her fringe unmoving. 'I can sell it, but we like to sell the author as well as the book.' The agent scrutinised her without judgement, just an honest appraisal of a commercial prospect.

'I know. That's why I sent you the first two in the mail, not in person. You sold those books without a feature in *Women's Weekly*; without the photo of me baking in the kitchen with a labrador and blond children at my feet.'

'Yes, but I'm not sure I can do it again.'

'I'm sure you can.' Maya remained on course, despite the sweat sliding down her body. Zakhir and Mr Napoli had coached her well.

'Do you have blond children?' Clara asked.

Maya laughed. 'No, do you?'

It was Clara's turn to laugh. 'No, thank God. How many more books can you write?' She raised an eyebrow that disappeared into the inscrutable wall of hair above it.

'As many as you can sell. You'll get tired before me,' Maya lied.

She had mapped out two more manuscripts, including the one Clara was holding now. But how many more adventures could Clementine have in country New South Wales before the community around her noticed that every adventure started with a dead farmer and wondered if she could be causing the mysteries as well as solving them? In Sri Lanka, Clementine would be less heroine and more harbinger of doom, chased from her home by superstitious villagers.

Also, running Cinnamon Gardens was demanding. She would wake at four o'clock every morning to begin the day's cooking with Vidya. This was inevitably followed by calls to plumbers to fix the heating system, typing up invoices and speaking to the anxious families of residents. The days were full and fast. Cedric and Zakhir helped her, but Zakhir's bad spells were erratic and unpredictable.

'Let's make a deal,' Maya suggested. 'Represent me, speak for me, and hide me. I'll keep sending the Clementine Kelly novels to you and no one else.'

Clara wiped the remnants of egg yolk from her manicured fingernails. A thin sheen of sweat had formed on her upper lip. She drained the last of her lassi.

'Deal.'

Maya reached over the debris of egg hoppers and sambal, and shook her agent's sticky hand.

Maya would go on to write another ten Clementine Kelly books, each one a bestseller. They were all published under the name Sarah Byrnes, without readers ever knowing who she was.

Eschewing the conventions of the time and genre, by book four, Clementine had rescued herself from her abusive husband and bought herself a cattle ranch in far-west New South Wales. She ran the ranch with her best friend Viv Maurer, a Barkandji woman whose family adopted Clementine into their own. Clementine rejected the shackles of societal expectations by taking lovers as and when she felt like it. She had a riding crop and she wasn't afraid to use it. She was a frontier feminist and an unashamed masturbator. The CWA loved her for it.

NIKKI

Sydney

Nikki shifted in the chair, peeling her legs away from the hard plastic. The backs of her thighs felt damp. She looked around at the posters in the small room; inspirational slogans and soothing acronyms surrounded her. Was this what her life had come to—weekly meetings with her son's school counsellor? Was this what it depended on—R U OK alerts on her iPhone and a small window smothered with a **H**old **O**n **P**ain **E**nds poster? HOPE. She winced. Pain ended for some, for others it endured. She wondered if that acronym had been tested with suicide experts and determined to be comforting rather than suggestive. Perhaps she was unduly focused on the Pain Ends part. She longed for an End to her Pain.

Nathan entered the room, weaving through the colourful mine-field of small toys strewn across the carpet. Each toy had been placed as a distraction, a tension breaker, a conversation starter, or something for a child to focus on while they avoided eye contact with Nathan but navigated their own internal minefield towards his voice. He had a reassuring voice when he was in clinical mode. Deep and more soothing than any of the posters that loomed over them.

'Thanks for coming in, Nikki,' he said. The edges of his trousers lifted, revealing Snoopy socks. Oscar wouldn't tell them how his sessions with Nathan were going, but every week he reported what socks Dr Cheney wore.

'Oscar is doing well, all things considered.' All things considered. Net positive, not net disastrous. On balance, he's okay. R U OK, Oscar? Yes and no, but a little more *yes* than *no*. For now. Please, God, forever.

Nikki didn't say anything. Usually Gareth asked the questions, extracting as much as he could from Nathan's debriefs, always pushing him for more, always trying to prove how engaged he was with the process. How sorry he was for all the debriefs he had missed. How sorry he was that they needed to debrief at all.

'Is Gareth joining us?' Nathan asked, checking his watch.

Nikki shook her head. 'An important meeting with his boss, couldn't move it. Sorry.'

All of Gareth's meetings were important. So important.

'No problem; I just didn't want to start without him. At our last session, Oscar talked about her for the first time,' Nathan continued.

For the first time since she died, he meant. They had all stopped talking about her. They learned very quickly to navigate their own minefield, where even her name would cause the earth to explode into hot shrapnel. Actual memories—Remember when she made all of us macaroni portraits for Christmas? Remember when she broke my stunt scooter and didn't tell me until I tried to ride it?—were even worse than her name. The blast radius of those words could shear off an entire limb; blow up an entire marriage.

'That's good, right?' Nikki asked.

The grief literature Nathan made her read said that removing Florence from their home and conversations would only make the grief worse. She had laughed at that. Nothing could make the grief worse. Attempting to excise her, Nathan explained, slows the development of the survival skills you need. There is no healing. There

93

is loss and there is acceptance of the loss. There is learning to live with the loss.

'What you learn now will affect how you all cope, live and love others for the rest of your lives,' Nathan had said kindly. Sometimes when he talked, Nikki didn't listen to the words so much as follow the cadence of his voice. It cut through the grief that kept pulling her back into a blinding mist of rage and regret.

'Yes,' Nathan said. 'Talking about her is good. It means he's accepting that she's gone and testing out what that feels like for him. He's reorientating his world—not to fill the void but to carry the void with him. Like trying to work out the best way to carry an awkward and heavy bag, he's setting it against his body and then adjusting it so it's easier to carry.'

Nikki smiled. If Florence was a bag, what kind of bag would she be? Something Italian like her name and Gareth's side of the family. Something elegant and unassuming, perhaps with a quirky lining and hidden pockets. Something small and soft to touch; when you wore it, you never wanted to take it off. Her eyes stung with tears.

'Not every memory and thought about her will make you cry,' Nathan said softly.

'They do. Every one of them. Every time. I can't function if I let myself think about her. I can't be a mother to Oscar. I can't be a doctor. I can't think about her, but I can't stop thinking about her,' she said, pulling at her neck as if there was a hand around her throat and she had to prise away its fingers so the words could claw their way out. She knew that talking and the right pharmacological cocktail were the only things that enabled her to Be OK. The literature said clinical responses to suicidal ideation involve talk therapy, medication, proper support networks and constant vigilance.

'You didn't say, *I can't be a wife*,' Nathan noted.

'What?' She feigned puzzlement.

'You listed your roles, those that give you meaning and purpose, and you didn't mention *wife*.'

'It was a mistake,' she lied. 'Do you like your job? Does it give you meaning and purpose?'

'That's not relevant. How are you both?' Nathan asked. 'The other night, you seemed more tense than usual.'

The 'usual' bar was so low for them, and still falling.

'We're okay.' There was that word again. What the fuck did 'okay' mean, anyway? 'We're coping. Things have been easier since he went back to work. I don't think him being at home was helpful—for either of us. The new job's only part-time but it's a good distraction, I suppose.'

Gareth grieving at home while she returned to work had quickly turned from understandable to enraging for her.

'Distraction is an important tool,' Nathan said.

'I thought we were supposed to acknowledge our grief and all of our other shitty emotions,' Nikki replied. 'Face them head on. Look anger in the face and say, *I see you. You are not helping me, therefore I am not taking you with me today.*'

'You've been listening to the podcast.'

Nathan had recommended a podcast which she listened to for thirty seconds. 'Yes, the psychologist is very enlightened.' He sounded like he'd never lost a child.

Nathan shrugged at that, a smile tugging at the corner of his mouth. 'Distraction is an important tool. Denial is a damaging crutch. There's a difference, and you're smart enough to know where you sit on that spectrum on any given day, at any given moment. Use the tool but not the crutch.'

She nodded and looked at the posters again. The Lifeline poster was faded, more an imprint now than an image. A child talking into a phone, the dialling kind that no longer existed. Obsolete. A leftover from previous counsellors at Westgrove Public School.

She felt her morning coffee start to rise in her gut.

'Water,' she whispered, swallowing rapidly.

'Yep, hang on.' Nathan grabbed her a child-sized bottle from a box of supplies.

He watched her as she downed the water and loosened the collar of her blouse.

'Nikki, you've been coming here for months, with Gareth but also without him. I can counsel you as a family, but I can't counsel you individually. You're Anji's best friend and I know Gareth. It creates complexities in my interactions with him that aren't fair on either of you.'

She felt her anger flare at that. She didn't care about what was fair for Gareth. Nor did she want the grief counselling recommended by everyone from her GP to her mother to the school canteen lady.

Ten months after Florence's death, her friends had stopped sending her frozen lasagnes but the shared articles on Facebook continued. Articles titled 'Living with Loss' and 'Grief's Journey'.

Grief's fucking Journey.

They recommended support groups, church groups and meditation retreats. One of them had given her a salt lamp the size of a toaster, which she accepted but only so she could refuse the sage-burning cleansing ritual. She didn't want the house cleansed. She had finally agreed to have their weekly cleaner back, but Lily and her army of Chinese women were not allowed into Flo's room. The stray hairs, the epithelial fragments, the sweat-impregnated sheets, the bitten nails embedded in the cracks between the floorboards; these were the last cellular remains of her daughter.

'I won't go to anyone else, Nathan. I know I need help and you have to be it for now. Screw Gareth. Oscar needs me, so, as his counsellor, you'll need to counsel me too.'

Nathan sat back in his chair, shifting his leg and revealing the Snoopy socks again.

'Do you like your job?' she repeated. Years ago, before Anji took over the nursing home from her parents, Nathan had run his own private practice, ministering to the increasingly anxious children of the west. He also worked at Westmead Hospital's acute psychiatric unit. Nikki was determined that Oscar would not end up there. *She* might, but not Oscar.

'You could have been much more,' she prompted.

'Thanks,' Nathan said, and the corner of his mouth twitched again. '*I* need counselling after time with you.'

'I'm sorry. I just look at you and admire your . . . ease. I guess the changes must be worth it.'

Nathan laughed. 'I've lost tax-deductible holidays to Xanax conferences in Switzerland, but look around you and behold all I've gained in return.'

It was her turn to laugh. 'You never answered my question.'

'That's because I'm meant to ask the questions. I do enjoy this job, Nikki. I think I'm doing good work here and I'm making a difference.'

'At least you'll always have a job,' she said. Nathan would never have to worry about that. He would never fear losing his job so much that he paid more attention to his job than his family.

'I suppose so; anxiety is a growing problem for children,' Nathan said without sarcasm. 'Nikki, I'm not valuable because I'm employed. And I'm not valuable because others value me. I'm valuable because I value myself.'

'That's easy for you to say,' she replied, concentrating hard on the poster behind Nathan's head. 'You've kept three children alive. And you know Gareth resents you because somehow you make baking masculine.' She tried to smile.

Nathan's eyes darkened. 'Our three children are alive through dumb luck more than anything else. But one of our parents is dead and it forced a new value system on us. It forced a new world on us. You know that. You saw what it did to Anji and her mother. Families are an ecosystem. We have to adapt for the ecosystem to survive.'

'Thrive,' she corrected him. 'You're thriving.'

Anji and Nathan had all the things she wanted for herself. All the things she could have had. All the things she'd once had for a moment. When she allowed herself to look back on her life with Gareth, she could sometimes admit that they'd started to lose those things even before Florence.

'You make it sound so easy,' Nikki said.

The poster was a cartoon child in a Dick Tracy trench coat and fedora, armed with a magnifying glass. The Emotions Detective was asking her to investigate and identify her feelings. Nikki had tried to, but the answer to that question was not appropriate for a primary school counselling room.

GARETH

Sydney

Gareth's meeting was pushed back from 4 pm to 5 pm, a strange time slot, but he had always loved the State Library. He tried not to be early and ended up walking past the building, down to the bottom of Martin Place and back up again via Phillip Street to kill time.

He didn't come into the city much anymore, aside from party meetings. He used to bring the kids in for shows at the Opera House, but Oscar wasn't interested these days. Maybe Gareth wasn't interested either. In their cultured youth, Nikki always bought season passes to the Sydney Theatre Company. No, it was Belvoir Street. She thought their plays were more provocative.

He completed a second circuit of the CBD and entered the palm-fringed gates of the library feeling calmer. The afternoon sun caught the pink in the sandstone, giving the building a rose warm nimbus. He was ready for his meeting.

When he arrived at the library cafe, Davidson was already there, chatting to a waitress.

'Gareth!' Davidson greeted him as though they hadn't seen each other that morning. 'What will you have? Coffee? A pastry?

The Portuguese tarts here are amazing; I've just had one and am contemplating a second.' He leaned back and placed his hands on his belly.

'Just coffee, please.' Gareth looked at the waitress apologetically.

'He'll have a piccolo, Siobhan,' Davidson clarified. Then, to Gareth, 'Take a seat.' He motioned to the chair opposite him.

'I'm sorry, Mike, am I late?' Gareth checked his phone. It was 5.01 pm.

'Not at all; I just love the coffee and sweets here. I'm glad you could make it. I thought it would be nicer to talk here, rather than the office. We're taking over the fourth floor as well, but the renovations, the noise . . . You know how it is.'

'The team must be growing, if you need more office space? You've already got the second and third floors.' Gareth smiled at the waitress as she placed the small coffee in front of him. The crema on top was shaped like a fern. Expansion of the Democratic Alliance Party was good for them and good for him. It was good for Australia, he reminded himself. He was in leadership now, not just comms.

'That's what I wanted to talk to you about, Gareth.' Davidson took a sip of his coffee and assembled his features into a reluctant and sympathetic expression. 'Over the last six months we've been polling our electorates, getting a better picture of where our safe seats are and who our safe candidates are.' He swirled his coffee cup and drained it. 'We're using a new team of data analysts from the US. They're expensive but good. They assess the data in a lot of ways, giving us insight into what's not working for us at the moment, and what could work for us in the *future*. They've done phone and online surveys as well as convening a number of focus groups.'

Davidson was an accomplished script reader.

'The data is telling us that in Westgrove, people *like* you and they feel for you and your recent tragedy, but they just wouldn't *vote* for you.'

'They like me but wouldn't vote for me?'

'That's correct, Gareth.' Davidson looked at his plate and pushed the flaky remains of his pastry across his plate for no reason. Was it discomfort or boredom? Gareth saw him glance at the phone sitting by his plate. It was boredom. Indifference even.

'Did they say why?' Gareth's voice sounded strange in his ears. Strained. A little pleading; a little desperate to be liked. He sounded like that sometimes with Nikki. 'If there are reasons, we can address them.'

Thank God he'd stopped himself before he could say, *I can change.* He rallied his professional rhetoric. 'Politics is a constant process of reinvention. Let's talk about what I need to do.'

He could deep-fry curry puffs at the harvest day celebration. He could show up at the temple. Nikki would join him if Anji was there. She might even agree to wear a sari and a henna tattoo. He could wear one of those ridiculous white sarongs he'd seen Nathan in. He could smear holy ash on his forehead and namaste with the best of them.

'I'm not sure there's anything you *can* do,' Davidson replied. His eyes met Gareth's certain of how this meeting would unfold. It wasn't a discussion. 'This electorate is changing, just like the rest of Australia.'

He was right. Westgrove was white until, one day, it wasn't. Civil war broke out in Sri Lanka and a handful of migrants became the deluge of refugees that those racists in the Southern Cross Party talked about. Educated and earnest, they were changing his neighbourhood, and him doing Ashtanga yoga once a month wasn't enough to impress them anymore.

'It is changing,' Gareth agreed. 'If you're looking for stronger ethnic credentials, my great-grandfather was born Gaetano Bastiani. He changed his name when he moved here.' It wasn't a rejection of the immigrant's ancestry; his forefather just wanted to create a future unencumbered by his past.

'Yes, we know that. The historic name change tested as insincere and opportunistic.'

'All politicians are insincere and opportunistic, Mike.'

He hadn't always thought that; there was a time when he believed that politicians actually stood for something.

Davidson shrugged. 'You're looking like a career politician with no real core values, someone who can accurately assess what will win votes and then portray it—a chameleon,' he said, articulating the very definition of the career politician.

'You're a career politician,' Gareth replied.

'Yes,' Davidson said. 'But I don't look like one.'

'What does the rest of the party say?'

'The last campaigns you were on, you were Attwood's director of comms and Sewell's chief of staff . . .'

'I won those campaigns. I'm being penalised for being successful?'

'Like I said, you're being penalised for not really standing for anything. Attwood and Sewell are from two ends of the spectrum.' Davidson said this as though it explained everything.

'Two ends of the spectrum of the same party—my party,' Gareth argued. 'The one I've belonged to since university. The party chooses which candidate to run based on which way it thinks the wind is blowing. I just did what I was told. I supported the candidate you told me to support.'

'And we're grateful for your loyalty.'

'But?' Gareth said.

'But we're a centrist party and that's always played well with upwardly mobile migrant communities. They want us left enough to allow their extended families to migrate, but they want us right enough that they can hold on to the wealth they're rapidly accumulating for their future generations.'

Davidson paused when he saw Gareth wince. 'I'm sorry, mate. Jesus.'

102

Davidson had never called him *mate* before. It was a word he'd only heard the MP use on the campaign trail when forcing friendships and winning votes.

'It's completely fine. It's me, not you,' Gareth replied. He swallowed hard, wrapping his hands around his warm piccolo glass to stem the tremor he could feel creeping down from his shoulders. At least Davidson would think it was because of Florence, rather than the conversation he would have to have with Nikki tonight. Rather than the feeling of failure this job had allowed him to shelve briefly but not entirely forget.

Florence's closed door was a daily reminder.

Nikki's face, too. The way she recoiled when he came near her. She thought he didn't see it, but he saw it all. He'd learned to pay attention the hard way.

'I feel the same way, mate. This decision is about the electorate. It's them, not you.'

Gareth was starting to feel light-headed. He tried to breathe deeply through his nose without Davidson realising. He placed his feet wider apart under the table, and imagined them anchored to the ground. He needed to get out of there, fast.

'What . . . what's next? What do you want me to do?'

'That's the spirit, mate. I knew you'd be professional about it.'

Gareth thought if he heard the word *mate* come from Davidson's mouth one more time he might dive across the table and strangle him with his Paul Smith tie. And when did the word *professional* become code for 'submitting quietly to shitty behaviour by one's employer'?

'The data is telling us it's time for a change. We need a candidate to differentiate us from the ones we've previously run in this electorate. We need someone completely different from you and Attwood. Someone who can appeal to the new Australians and connect to the new Australia they're building, whether we like it or not. Someone who can engage with the Sri Lankans, Koreans, Chinese and Indians in this electorate without seeming too closely aligned to any one of those groups. The voters are getting younger too. It's not just the second-generation immigrant; it's the students and new money from China and India.'

Excellent, Gareth thought. Voter antipathy towards him was transnational and transgenerational.

Davidson had someone in mind. Gareth realised he'd had someone in mind for a long time. Perhaps even before the overpaid data analysts had told him it was time for a leadership change. Gareth was a placeholder.

'Sure, I can understand that.'

'That's what I told the party secretary. I told them you'd do what was best for the party. You'd see it wasn't personal.'

It was a little personal. The electorate liked him but wouldn't vote for him. Who would they vote for? A Sri Lankan neurosurgeon in a photogenically biracial marriage to a Korean accountant. Kings Curry Powder meets kimchi. A couple more like Nathan and Anji, damn them and their handmade naans. They were taking over his world.

'So?' Gareth prompted. 'Who's my replacement?'

'We haven't decided that yet,' Davidson replied.

'Sure you have.'

'What?' Davidson seemed startled by the tone in Gareth's voice.

So was Gareth for that matter. He felt the tremor in his arms subside. He leaned back in his chair, exhaled and crossed his legs under the table. His political career was over. As a failed candidate, he might struggle to get a job in the party, even in comms. He was unemployed, possibly unemployable and, worse, Florence was dead. He didn't have much more to lose.

'You've already decided on my replacement. At least do me the courtesy of telling me who it is.'

In his mind, he scrolled through the high-profile Sri Lankan doctors in the party. It would have to be a doctor, someone the whole community trusted and respected. Someone who sent his kids to the local selective primary school, followed by the local private high school. Someone who played for the Westgrove Cricket Club with his sons and whose wife taught Bible Study at the local Korean church, where she also did pro bono accounting for refugees. Something like that. Gareth could do pro bono. He made a mental note to ask Bella Davidson to find him some pro bono work; maybe serving curry at the local soup kitchen run by the Ramakrishna Mission at the back of the Hindu temple.

It was Davidson's turn to cough nervously. 'The polling tells us you're too vanilla . . .'

'I can imagine,' Gareth replied, his mind still searching for his successor.

'We need to be agile in the face of this data. After a lot of consultation and blue-sky focus groups at the national level, we've decided to go with—'

'Bella,' Gareth interrupted, the name rising from his subconscious and storming out of his mouth before his usually fail-proof filter could stop it.

'Excuse me?' Davidson said.

'Bella. You've decided to nominate your daughter.'

What was it Nikki used to say? The only thing worse than white male privilege was white female privilege. It had the entitlement of male privilege, a heavy dose of fake empathy for the disadvantaged, and complete blindness to the intersectional nature of its own advantage.

Bella fucking Davidson.

'Yes, that's right. She's an economic pragmatist with excellent human rights credentials.'

Eight years ago, Bella Davidson had done a three-month unpaid internship at the Southern Poverty Law Center in Alabama, during which she bunked at the Four Seasons. She would dine out on her 'human rights' qualifications for the rest of her career, part-RBG, part-Gwyneth Paltrow, and now, it seemed, part-ethnic.

'She'll have broader appeal with the ethnics,' Davidson said.

'She's whiter than me.' Her skin colour was a fake tan, for God's sake.

'She's a woman, and we think she has the moral courage to stop the corporate speak and really shift the dial on the issues that matter to people.'

Gareth imagined Bella making balloon animals, each one labelled with terms such as 'affordable housing', 'energy prices' and 'job security'. He took a pin to each balloon in his mind.

'This race thing could ramp up. If we come out and call Australia racist, the party will lose at the state level. As I said this morning, Australians don't like being called racist. But if we don't pacify the ethnics in Westgrove and reassure them we're taking their concerns seriously, we'll lose the shire and others like it.'

'Of course.' Gareth tried to nod but found there was a piercing pain developing behind his right eye that commanded him to sit absolutely still. 'I've been with you a long time, Mike. I assume that you're asking me to retire from office, but you'll redeploy me in the party. I'm happy to go back to comms.'

Gareth made some rapid calculations in his head, trying to recall his mortgage plan. In the last few years, Nikki had returned to work on a full-time basis, dividing her time between the nursing home and a private clinic in Hatfield. She was the primary earner now, but they still needed his income.

'We're rethinking our identity,' Davidson started.

'I've helped shape that identity.'

Gareth had been in comms roles that took him close to the nucleus of power but never into it, until now. Comms was an easy job if you knew how to read the demographic data. All he had to do was create looping narratives with buzzwords. The ethnics responded to *education* and *jobs*. The whites responded to *border security* and *resource boom*. Everyone responded to *affordable housing*.

Now the data was telling the party that the voters did not respond to him.

Now the nucleus was breaking all covalent bonds.

'I know, Gareth.' Davidson stood up; the meeting was over. 'Like I said, we're rethinking our identity. Let me get back to you.'

∽つ

Gareth checked his phone. No messages from Nikki. Two missed calls from the office and one from Anji. He called her back.

'Gareth.' Anji's voice often held a smile. She was a lot like her mother that way. Gareth remembered Maya serving them chickpea curry and rice while they studied for their uni exams in the nursing home games room.

'I've got a missed call from you. Everything okay?'

'Yes, everything's fine. I'm sorry—I didn't mean to worry you.' She paused, as if choosing her next words carefully. 'I've been meaning to ask you, Gareth—and please say no if it's too soon or if it's not appropriate.' She paused again and then hurried through the last part. 'But I'd really love for you to come down to the nursing home; see the damage the vandals have done for yourself. I'm worried about where this is going, and it would be great to have your support when we're talking to the police.'

'Of course, that's what I'm here for, Anji. I'm your friend *and* your local councillor. I'll talk to the office and find a time as soon as possible.'

He finished the call just as the waitress brought him the bill. He looked at the itemised list, most of it Davidson's.

'I'll have three Portuguese tarts to go.' He opened his wallet, his fingers moving past his personal credit card to the council card. 'Make it six.'

∽つ

Gareth placed the tarts on the kitchen bench and pulled out a Tupperware container of leftover lasagne from the fridge. Nikki's handwritten note on the bench told him that Oscar was sleeping over at Mel and Dave's place and she was working late.

'Catching up on paperwork,' she said.

Second night this week.

He checked his phone. Both Nikki and Oscar were where they were supposed to be. He checked Nikki's roster, pinned to the fridge with a Leaning Tower of Pisa magnet. The list indicated that her shift finished at 4 pm. The head of the leaning tower pointed to another magnet at the top corner of the fridge; Oscar and Florence, their last photo taken together. Side by side. Her hair in an uncharacteristically neat ponytail, a few dark curls escaping the hairband and shiny purple ribbon. The sibling photo Oscar hated doing.

He picked up his phone and called Nikki again. It went straight to voicemail. Eight o'clock. He checked the roster again, as if that would bring her back to him.

Nikki, the blameless grief-stricken mother. It's harder for the mother, his own mother had told him. Mothers have a different relationship with their children, a deeper, more physical connection. It's biological.

He kept his eyes resolutely away from the photo.

He binned the tarts and left the lasagne on the bench, untouched.

NIKKI

Sydney

Nikki followed Anji and Mel into Cafe Blue Lotus. Anji had reluctantly agreed to attend the trial yoga class with Nikki and Mel, but she flatly refused to pay $16.50 for a 'Bliss Booster' at the Bondi studio's cafe. Nikki agreed that mango lassis were better than kale puree, so they had returned across town for lassis and lunch at her favourite cafe in Westgrove.

'You're right,' Mel said, licking the yoghurt from her lips. 'This is delicious. What do you recommend for lunch?' She turned the menu over, squinting at the names and badly printed photographic aids.

'Ask Nikki,' Anji replied, checking her phone. 'She's the regular.'

'Of course.' Mel laughed. 'You have Nathan. I'd still have sex with my husband if he cooked for me like that. I'd have sex with *your* husband if he cooked for me like—' Mel stopped abruptly, her face reddening.

Nikki burst out laughing and Anji clearly wanted to, but choked on her mango lassi instead.

'Nothing to be embarrassed about here, Mel,' Nikki replied, hitting Anji on the back and passing her a silver tumbler of water. 'You just saw me wee myself a little during the Crow.'

Anji nodded. 'That's a hard one.' She wiped the yoghurt from her chin. 'Anything that involves opening my legs and relaxing my pelvic floor is a disaster. As for the sex, not often. Food or no food, I'm pretty knackered most of the time. What I really want is a cup of tea and Netflix. My mother gave me a device for Mother's Day one year.'

'Your mother?' said Mel. 'Maya?'

'Yep. It was horrifying and helpful. I use that or I think about Chris Hemsworth to get in the mood. Sometimes Elsa. One or the other but never both at the same time. I'm not greedy.'

'I'm more of a Liam girl, myself,' Mel offered. 'How about you, Nikki?'

It was her turn to blush, the image of Ruben in her mind, naked in his bedroom, a sheet over his scarred body. His dark skin against her white skin, unscarred on the outside. He was so clear to her, she was terrified she had said his name out loud instead of a Hemsworth. She looked at Anji to check it was the fear talking and not her mouth.

'Nikki's definitely a Chris,' Anji replied, pushing the menu towards her. 'Surfer Chris, though, rather than Superhero Chris; you've always had a thing for surfers.'

Nikki nodded, smiling at Anji gratefully.

'That so?' Mel said. 'Does Gareth surf?'

'He does. He used to be really good when we were at uni,' Nikki replied. 'He'd go holidaying with friends in surfing hotspots, that kind of thing.'

She loved being with him back then. She would read on the beach, a small sun tent protecting her pale skin. Watching him ride the waves, her breath would catch when he went under. He always resurfaced, battered but exhilarated, his eyes scanning the beach for her. Across warm sand and churning water, they'd find each other.

She didn't look for him anymore.

'He doesn't have a lot of time for it these days. Now he just teaches the kids—' She caught herself too late. She wondered when she would stop that. When would she move from the plural to the singular? 'He teaches Oscar in the summer. He loves it.'

Mel cocked her head to one side, her eyes wider than usual. The sympathetic pose that people always adopted with the bereaved. Nikki's friend Jay, a psych at Westgrove Medical Centre, called it the *grief eyes*, which were similar but different from the *cancer eyes* people used when you told them you had cancer.

Before Mel could make soothing noises, Nikki waved her hand to get the attention of Vanita, the waitress.

'I recommend we do the mini masala dosai lunch special. Keep it simple and not too spicy. Is that okay?' she asked.

'Perfect,' Anji said.

'That's with potato inside, right?' Mel said, her hand reaching for her yoga abs. She really did have the most incredible body: a walking advertisement for giving up commercial law and retraining as a yoga instructor.

'It is, and you could do with some, Mel,' Nikki told her. 'Please don't make the rest of us feel guilty. Life's hard enough without curried carbs.'

Mel couldn't argue with that. 'How do you know the menu so well?'

'I come here a lot. After drop-off, I often grab a vadai and masala tea for breakfast. The staff know me. I think they'd judge me for not feeding myself at home, if they weren't so delighted by my constant business.'

Breakfast here, and lunch and dinner at the nursing home often— leftovers from Maya's generous industrial kitchen. Cafe Blue Lotus used to be *their* place; the place she and Gareth would take the kids to after sport or dance class, for a quick mutton roll and fish patty en route to another sport or dance class. The place for an easy Sunday night dinner, eating hoppers while Florence watched Bollywood dancing on the cafe's TV.

She couldn't remember the last time they had gone out together, with Oscar or even alone. It was before Florence's death, maybe not even because of her death. It was too hard to address the normal marital resentments of the past without exploring the exceptional one that was ever present. She couldn't separate the blue wire from the red wire without touching the live wire that ran through the core of their existence.

'I'd eat here every day too if I could, but my yoga career would be over before it started if I did that,' Mel said.

Nikki smiled as Anji reached for her phone again, getting ready to make up a meeting or patient emergency she urgently needed to attend to. Nikki gently nudged her under the table.

'Speaking of yoga, Anji . . .' Mel said.

No one was speaking about yoga. They were speaking about comfort carbs, tossed in coriander, cumin and turmeric. Vanita approached them, bearing three steaming plates of mini dosais, which she placed in front of them. Her brother, Venki, was behind her. He bore increasingly complicated facial hair and a cup of masala tea, just for Nikki.

'Thank you, Venki,' she said, wrapping her fingers around the hot cup.

'You're special,' Anji teased.

'I am.'

Mel didn't break stride. 'I know the nursing home runs yoga classes for the residents, but I was wondering if I could show you what I've been learning. Perhaps I could run a trial lesson with the old—elderly?'

'Maybe you should *attend* a trial lesson at the nursing home,' Nikki suggested, blowing into her tea. The cooler liquid on top had formed a caramel-coloured skin, flecked with minute fragments of undissolved cardamom.

'What?' Mel and Anji said in unison.

'You should attend a lesson at the nursing home,' Nikki repeated. 'Then you'll see how good they are. Aunty Yagnik, the resident who runs them, trained in India. She's amazing and makes it accessible for everyone. Even I attend, although you'd think I'd have better bladder control, after all that meditative clenching she makes me do.'

Anji started to laugh and couldn't stop.

Mel smiled, confused. 'I don't get it.'

'Sorry,' Anji replied, wiping her face. 'I'm very susceptible to wee jokes. It's really childish, something Nikki has been preying on since we were in netball together.'

'It's true. Very childish, but we *have* known each other since we were children. I'm serious about the classes, though, Mel,' Nikki continued. 'If Anji and Aunty are okay with it, you should do a class or at least observe one. It's really helped me, the chanting and mindfulness training, plus the yoga.'

Not as good as medication. But better than prayer.

Nikki had refused to speak to God from the time Gareth had brought Florence home from Cinnamon Gardens, her body lifeless in the back of his car. She had screamed for God or somebody to help them then. Pulling Florence from the back seat, shouting at Gareth to call the ambulance. She remembered the fierce animal inside her chest that rose up from her gut, threatening to drive her mad with fear. She remembered taking a deep breath, the one that Aunty Yagnik had taught her in yoga class, and then a few more until the animal was under control and she could position her child carefully on the grass outside their home. She opened Florence's mouth and scooped out the remnants of something blue and familiar. She rolled her back, tilted her head and began the rhythm of compressions to breaths, her mouth over the girl's. A kiss. A long and frantic kiss. Her child's only chance of survival. Her sweet child. Her beautiful Florence.

Anji saw the tears in her eyes and clapped her hands.

'You're a genius,' Anji said loudly. 'Mel, you'll love Aunty Yagnik. She also does a Vedic philosophy class once a week, explaining the asanas. I'd love for you to attend.'

'That's very generous of you, Anji, thank you,' Mel said. 'It's just that the Energetic Mindfulness Centre takes a much more holistic approach to body, mind and soul. We're on a journey.'

'A journey?' Anji repeated.

Nikki felt better already, but she was out of lifelines for Anji.

'Yes, a journey, and I feel like I've come so far in such a short time. I really want to share it with people.'

Sharing is caring, Florence used to say.

Nikki laughed a little. The sound surprised her. 'Sorry, I was thinking about something Florence used to say.'

Anji turned sharply at the name. Nikki nodded. Nathan was right. She *could* think about her and say her name out loud without crying.

'That sounds so interesting,' Anji stalled, unsure of how to extricate herself.

'Is it therapeutically approved by the Department of Health for use in aged care facilities?' Nikki asked.

'Therapeutically approved? I don't know,' Mel faltered.

'Yes, therapeutic approval,' Anji said, catching on. 'It's required by the department before we introduce any new . . . therapy. You're right, Nikki; I don't know why I hadn't thought of that. Let me look into it for you, Mel. But thank you for offering. Let's get some masala tea to go.'

'Sure.' Mel stood up to leave.

Anji reached across the table and took Nikki's hand. 'Florence,' she whispered.

'Florence,' Nikki whispered back.

~

Nikki smiled as warmth spread down her back, from her neck to the base of her spine. It followed the path of Ruben's kisses, a relaxed, almost lazy exploration of her body. It was different from their first few months together. Those initial furtive encounters after Florence's death were an aberration for her. An urgent alternative reality that helped her escape the confusing one she was condemned to live in, without her daughter. Months later, they had formed a more comfortable, less urgent pattern; a relationship of sorts. She had never been unfaithful to Gareth before. Fidelity was an assumed quality of her nature and her life. But after Flo, many of life's assumptions were no longer valid.

Ruben had been a gentle presence at the nursing home, reserved but still noticeable for the deep sadness that inhabited the cells of his body. She loved to touch that body now, naked and shining with the sweat of sex and the early summer humidity. She imagined the sadness in the cells of her body mingling with the sadness in his, and somehow this was sadness not doubled but sadness supported. They understood and helped each other. They distracted and comforted each other.

'I need to go to work. Early shift,' he said, his voice muffled under the sheets. His head surfaced, hair wild and upright. She laced her fingers in his black curls and locked one leg around his body gently. His ribs were still tender from the attack. Her fingers traced a path across his lower abdomen, following the map of scars. Lighter skin, tracks shining and stretched, weaving through the hair on this belly.

'You need to stay here and finish what you started.' She held his earlobe in her mouth. She could feel the tiny hairs on the rim of his ear, the tight curl of it between her lips.

Loving was in the detail. Missing was in the detail too.

She pushed the thoughts of Florence away.

'You also need to be at work soon.' He kissed her one last time and then pulled away. 'Your father will be waiting for you.'

Her father had moved into Cinnamon Gardens a year ago, after his dementia worsened. She wondered what would have happened if they had chosen another nursing home. Or if he had another disease. Or if she had kept him at home.

'Uncle Ranganathan isn't eating his meals since Aunty Vidya died,' Ruben said. 'He won't admit it. If he drops more than ten per cent of his check-in weight, then he has to be case-managed. It'll be easier for him and you if you catch it before it hits the ten per cent.'

Nikki shook her head, grateful for something else to think about. 'What are you doing here, Ruben, carrying old people in and out of showers, fixing toilets and changing beds? You speak six languages; you could work anywhere you want.'

'I speak ten languages,' he said.

'Seriously? That's amazing,'

He shrugged. 'Most of those languages are from South Asia, but I have some choice phrases in Mandarin too.'

'Like what?'

'I can say, "Thank you, China, for your soft loans and heavy artillery. Please take our homeland by the testicles."'

'You're funny,' she said without laughing.

'I am. And I'm serious.'

'I know you are. I'm serious too.' She sat up and pushed her hair away from her face, assembling it into a loose bun. 'You know that no one at the nursing home believes you were a farmer in Sri Lanka, no matter how hard you try to hide your education.'

'Sri Lanka is a highly educated postcolonial nation. Our farmers are no fools. Neither are Australia's, for that matter. I'm offended by your urban elitism.'

'You always do this: random digressions so you don't have to tell me the truth. What are you doing at the nursing home, Ruben?' she repeated. 'Surely you wanted to do more with your life—more than helping old people and tutoring Tamil.'

'I tutor English too, don't forget.'

'What?' she said. He was infuriating at times.

'I tutor Tamil children in Tamil in Sydney's mid-west, and I tutor Tamil children in *English* in Sydney's *far* west. I'm employed from Mount Druitt to Westgrove. I even tutor the occasional Tamil child of gay parents in Paddington.'

She shook her head. 'I could help you get interviews; I could—'

'I'm happy here. You don't need to fix this.'

'I wasn't trying to.'

'You were, and I'm grateful you care. But as I said, I'm happy; happier.'

'Happier,' she repeated. 'I'm happier too.' She felt the guilt in her chest like a minor myocardial infarction. She put her hand to her heart and felt its rhythm, fast but persistent.

She stood up and went to him, the sheet wrapped around her body. The swelling around his eye had subsided. You would only notice the puffiness around his brow if you looked as closely as she did. Perhaps only if you stood as close to him as she did.

'You look good,' she said, placing her fingertips near but not on the healing skin above his eye.

He caught her hand and put it to his lips, kissing the tips of her fingers and then the palm of her hand.

'You look great,' he replied, pulling her towards him.

ANJALI

Cinnamon Gardens

Anji had ignored Mel's text for a couple of days but eventually relented, agreeing to a meeting at Cinnamon Gardens to talk about Mel's new career.

Anji asked Mel to come at 10 am so she could attend the yoga class that was held every day in the exercise room. It was an inspired idea by Nikki, a pre-emptive strike to deal with the ongoing pitch for business. Mel had half-asked twice already and Anji was running out of indirect ways to say no or to pretend to talk to the Department of Health about therapeutic approval of Mel's 'holistic approach to body, mind and soul'.

Mel arrived in her yoga wear, with a diaphanous linen blouse thrown casually over it, the way one throws $350 from Seed over $400 from Lorna Jane. Nathan said Anji was a reverse snob—which, he clarified, was a thing, unlike reverse racism.

'Thank you so much for including me,' Mel said, her hands pressed together and her head bowed. 'Namaste. I feel so honoured to be a part of this.'

Anji instinctively put her hands together too and returned the Namaste with the Tamil Vanakkam.

'You're welcome,' she said. 'Thank you for being open to it.' She mirrored Mel's sincerity, because it came from a good place.

The nursing home's classes were led by old Aunty Indumathi Yagnik, from Room 12. She was seventy-two with the muscle tone, mental acuity and flexibility of a forty-five-year-old. She had trained in Coimbatore and had qualifications in Saiva Siddhanta, Vedic neuroscience and Ayurvedic healing from Madras University. Her sessions at Cinnamon Gardens were a masterclass, a peaceful but challenging space to learn, contemplate, evolve, and pass wind. The classes were always oversubscribed.

'What did you think of Aunty Yagnik's class?' Anji asked at the end of the gruelling hour, hopeful Mel would take the hint.

'Oh, it was wonderful,' Mel gushed. 'Just wonderful. The teacher is obviously very good.'

'Obviously.'

'But,' Mel said, rallying her pitch once more, 'I'd still love to talk to you about teaching yoga here as well. I've just finished my training and I'm looking for people who might benefit from the ancient wisdom I've learned.'

Anji kept her smile in place. She deserved a gold star for this.

Mel definitely thought she did too.

'Yes, well . . .' Anji floundered as she tried to frame a positive-but-negative response for the third time.

'I know you're still waiting to hear from the Department of Health. It's just that at the Energetic Mindfulness Centre,' Mel continued, 'we have a patented sensory system that we use, and I was hoping I could do a demonstration for your residents.'

Mel reached into her oversized tote bag.

Anji pressed her lips together. She prayed Mel wouldn't bring out a Himalayan salt lamp and singing bowl. Not that she had anything against either.

Mel handed her a brochure, which Anji received with relief. It was covered in people holding synchronised standing bows and cobras, the zenned-out smiling faces of the whitest people she'd ever seen. Not that she had anything against that either.

'Thank you so much,' Anji said, scanning the list of courses. Her father would have given the aspiring yoga teacher a lecture on selective cultural appropriation. But he didn't have friends like Mel, and Anji loved her friends, the magical range of them.

'Let me read this and get back to you.'

She gave Mel a hug and guided her out the front door before the other woman could Namaste her again.

Anjali sat on the bench outside the cottage. It was handmade by one of the Petsas sons, using wood they had reclaimed when part of the roof collapsed back in 1987. Her father used to sit on this bench after work. From the cottage's small verandah, Zakhir could look back up the garden at the nursing home.

As a child she would sit with him. If he was aware of her, he would put her on his lap and tell her stories about his life in Ceylon. Tales of long summers spent with cousins, hiding, running and fighting in a family home that she later suspected he had borrowed from an Enid Blyton book. Tales of school days supervised by fearsome reverends wielding fast canes with deadly accuracy.

There were many nights when she just sat with him in silence. He didn't acknowledge her presence. His face and eyes were turned to the nursing home, but his mind had turned inwards, towards a time and place she was denied entry.

She watched Ruben approach from the nursing home. 'You can go in, you know,' he said. 'It's your home. You've still got the key.'

'It's your home. Amma gave it to you.'

'She didn't give it to me; she said I could stay here for as long as I wanted,' Ruben replied.

'Why?' she asked him. Why had her mother given their home to him? Her skin prickled, the confusion settling on it like cold sweat. He wasn't family, but he wasn't other people. Her whole family had grown to love him over the years he had been with them. *She* had grown to love him and depend on his presence in their lives.

'Why not?' he asked.

'That's what Amma says when I ask her. Is Uncle Saha okay?' Uncle Saha was becoming more determined to escape the nursing home. He treated it like a game; a dangerous one, if he fell on the street. Or fell climbing out a window; they still didn't know how he did it.

Ruben nodded. 'He's fine.'

'How do you always know where he is?'

'I pay attention to his stories,' Ruben said.

'Like Amma,' she replied.

'Because of Amma,' he said.

He opened the door of the cottage and she followed him in. She could tell by his movements he was still in pain. He did that thing the elderly did; they moved slowly and deliberately, aware of the parameters of their pain, the boundary where it began, always navigating away from it.

'If you need the cottage, you could always evict me.' Ruben smiled and then grimaced, raising his hand to the cut on his lip.

'I'm too afraid of my mother,' she said.

'No, you're not. You were afraid of your father, but not her.'

'How do you know that?' Anji asked, startled. 'You never met him.'

'Your mother talks about him a lot.'

'Has she told you how they met?'

He shook his head.

'It's a good one. I'll let her give you the details, but a Hindu girl and a Muslim boy fell in love and dared to act on it. My father was excommunicated and exiled by his parents.'

Zakhir had once told her that the cuts from their curses had bled for many years. She didn't understand what he meant, but she nodded and placed her small hand in his, checking his shirt for bloodstains throughout her childhood. In her adulthood she realised he hadn't meant it literally, although she also realised that she had never seen him without his shirt.

Ruben had scars too, old keloid on his arms, the fine print of its braille message undecipherable to her. 'Shrapnel,' was all he said when she asked once.

'I like what you've done with the place,' she said, looking around the cottage.

He laughed and winced again.

The cottage was the same, but simpler, the contents of family life stripped back to the basics. No photos or anything that told her who he was now or who he was back in Sri Lanka. The floor-to-ceiling bookshelves that Zakhir had made for Maya were still crammed with her books. Several shelves contained the entire Clementine Kelly series, in the different translations that Ruben could no doubt read.

The dining table was covered in papers, notes with handwriting that she recognised. There was a laptop open and a cassette player by its side.

'You're still writing for her?' Anji asked.

He nodded again, tidying up the papers; hiding them, perhaps. 'Her hands and hip are getting worse but her mind is still writing.'

'She needs to write,' Anji replied, sitting down at the table. It was solid and covered in scratches, children's scribbles and turmeric stains: the patina of life.

'It comforts her; she blames herself,' Anji said slowly. She rubbed at a mark on the table she knew wouldn't come off. 'She thinks she could have stopped Appa from going back to Sri Lanka. She thinks she wasn't enough for him, wasn't strong enough to keep him here with us.'

'She thinks that about herself?' Ruben asked, sitting down next to her but not looking at her. 'Or *you* think that about yourself?'

Anji exhaled deeply. 'Maybe we both do. Uncle Gana has petitioned the new Information Commissioner in Sri Lanka and its Office of Missing Persons. New processes, as part of Sri Lanka's commitment to reconciliation.'

She said this without bitterness but also without hope. Uncle Gana, in Room 5, was a veteran of Sri Lanka's legal failures, but he cared for Maya and knew Zakhir from their university days. He wrote letters, sent emails and filled out forms for Maya, requesting then demanding then begging for someone to find her husband's body.

'Does it trouble you?' Ruben asked. 'Not knowing what happened to him?'

She shook her head. 'We're sure he's dead, even Amma. He went back to the north and he disappeared with all the others. Seventy thousand people died in those last months of the war and he was one of them.'

She swallowed hard and made herself sit in that feeling. That truth.

Her father was one more Tamil buried deep in the earth, waiting to be excavated like the temples he used to find and restore. Except that Zakhir Ali would never be restored, even if one day he was found.

Ruben stood up abruptly and walked to the window. Anji wiped the tears from her face and studied the bookshelf she had perused millions of times before. An eclectic collection that ranged from literary fiction to Danielle Steele to academic works on South Asian temple history, archaeology and architecture.

They never discussed the impact Clementine had had on the nursing home. Maya was adamant about retaining her anonymity and she breached it only when she had to. For some reason, it hadn't surprised Anji that her mother had confided in Ruben about the books.

'We lived here our whole lives,' she said to no one. Ruben already knew that. 'It took a long time for the nursing home to make any money. It was only when things in Sri Lanka got worse, and the

Tamils here brought their parents and grandparents over, that we suddenly had a much larger clientele.'

'Your parents sound like war profiteers,' he said.

Anji smiled. She could understand Nikki's attraction to him, and given everything that had happened to her, she could understand the adultery.

'Profiteers, that's them. When they finally had a decent income, they could have bought a bigger place, but neither of them wanted to. They liked being next to the nursing home.'

From the kitchen window of the cottage she could see the kitchen window of the nursing home. When her father stood there, he would have watched her mother, up before dawn chopping onions, frying them with green chillies and curry leaves from the tree he had planted in the front garden, beating eggs mixed with coriander and cumin to make the sixty-four-egg omelette that was served every morning with puttu.

'Her friends used to tease her for staying here. Sometimes she let them blame Appa and his eccentric academic ways. But the truth was they both loved the place.'

Her parents were more than close to the nursing home, or next to it; they were inside it. Appa was the nursing home's brain and Amma, Maya, was its heart.

'They were happy here.'

Anjali had been happy here too. She looked around. The kitchen windows had swollen in the humidity and the jamb had fused to the frame, making it impossible to open them. When her mother fried fish or eggplant, she had to open the front door to get enough ventilation, the smell of burning oil curling out towards the nursing home.

'Do you ever want to go back?' she asked.

He shrugged. 'I'm safe here.'

'Really? Look at you, Ruben. I know you don't want to talk about it, but I have to tell the police. If you're not interested in

124

protecting yourself, then think about the other staff. You won't be the only one targeted.'

'It wasn't targeted. It was—'

'A random act of violence; yes, you said. And the police said. The problem is, I don't believe either of you. I can understand why they'd prefer to think of it that way. So much easier, isn't it? Australia's not racist, don't be ridiculous. But you—you know what can happen.' It was the closest she had come to acknowledging his background. The closest she could come to asking him about his past.

'This place is nothing like Sri Lanka, Anjali.' It was the first time he had used her first name and they both looked at each other, surprised. His face darkened. 'Dr Ali,' he corrected himself. 'This is nothing.' He motioned to the bruises on his arms. 'Nothing at all. No police. If you call them, I won't talk.'

'When the police ask questions, you have to answer them,' she said. 'You have to do what they tell you.'

'In some countries, but not in this one,' he replied.

RUBEN

By Week 3 of the new academic year, Ruben's students were used to the eccentricities of their young professor. He had a reputation at Jaffna University for unusual teaching methods, but his students were prepared to trust him.

He finished writing the Sinhala script and walked to the back of the classroom. The fan juddered above him, its fits and starts keeping pace with the ebb and flow of their intermittent electricity supply. The army kept removing parts of the university's generators for their own in the camp on the outskirts of the city.

'Distance,' he told his students. 'Gives you an important perspective, often a better one. Always be prepared to give yourself distance.'

Leaning against the back wall, he surveyed the expanse of the alphabet.

All languages had an internal logic, in script, grammar, and composition. If you could see the logic and sit in it, rather than fight it, a language would reveal itself to you willingly.

He could admire the beauty of Sinhalese when he stood back from it. Its curved and spiralled letters formed a network of white

126

shells across the black ocean of the chalkboard. The language was beautiful to look at. Perhaps beautiful to listen to and speak, too, but he had never heard it uttered in love.

'For homework this week, I want you to memorise the sixty letters you see in front of you.'

He raised a hand to quell the students' protestations.

'You have absorbed the two hundred and forty-six letters of the Tamil alphabet without even realising it. The pathways in your brain have been primed for Sinhalese. You've spent a few weeks being immersed in the sounds you need to make, but now you must learn the building blocks of language. By the time you leave here, you'll be fluent. You won't speak it like a Tamil who has learned Sinhalese. You will speak it like the Sinhalese.'

'But, sir, what if we don't want to speak it like the Sinhalese?' a student, Murugan, asked. 'We're Tamils. Our literature, poetry and songs are revered. The Tamil language has an ancient tradition—'

'—that will not survive in the new world, if we do not adapt,' Ruben told him. 'You can spend your time contemplating the Tamil language's glorious past. You can take your chances, get on a fishing boat and try to make it to Tamil Nadu, where you will be in fine company in refugee camps and prisons in India.

'Or you can adapt. Sinhalese is the language that's spoken once you leave the north. Beyond Vavuniya, this is the mother tongue of the people around you. In some parts of Sri Lanka, it is spoken exclusively and people do not have English as a common tongue. You do not have the means to find a common understanding if you do not have a common language.

'From what I can tell, most of you were born after 1983 and, like me, you know about Black July only from the memories of survivors. I was three years old, living safely here in Jaffna.'

Another student, Vijayan, put his hand up. 'My parents used to live in Colombo. They only just survived. My uncle and his wife were killed.'

Other students murmured their own experiences. Everyone had lost loved ones in July 1983. That pogrom, twenty-five years ago, had been the catalyst for the civil war.

'I am sorry to hear that, Vijayan. In Black July, Sinhalese mobs roamed the streets of Colombo. They stopped people in the streets and they shook a bucket at them. They said in Sinhalese, "What is this?" If the person replied, *Valli*, in Tamil, the mob covered them in petrol and set fire to them. If the person replied, *Bhaldiya*, in Sinhalese, the mob moved on.'

Ruben paused to give his students time to reflect on the story they all knew.

'At various times in our history, the inability of the Tamil people to speak Sinhalese has resulted in their deaths,' he said. 'Your parents have sent you to Jaffna University, to this course, because they know that the language I teach you here may save your life.'

There was a knock at the door. Ruben closed the Mandarin dictionary and looked up. 'Come in,' he said, expecting to see a line of anxious students at his door. He focused hard on maintaining his smile when the door opened to reveal a man in army fatigues. He stood up and extended his hand.

'Please sit down,' the soldier said. He looked around at Ruben's small office and his desk, strewn with books, papers and stained coffee cups. He motioned to the maps of the world behind Ruben's desk. 'Do you teach geography too?' he asked in Sinhalese.

'No, but as part of my course, I track the historical and geographical spread of languages. It helps students to understand the evolution of grammar.'

It also helped them to understand the history of conquest and colonialism that propelled some languages into supremacy and beat others into submission. It helped them to remember the origins of their own language and its importance as the resilient genome of culture, if not race.

He didn't tell the soldier that.

'I am Brigadier Chandima Fernando. I'm the head of the Third Battalion that's stationed here on the peninsula. We're currently based at Kankesanthurai in the north and Elephant Pass in the south.'

Ruben knew exactly where they were stationed. The Sri Lankan Army's occupation of Jaffna had been quick and effective, pushing the Tamil Tigers south into the Vanni region, where they were regrouping in the jungle.

The president, Mahinda Rajapaksa, was equipped with newly purchased Chinese artillery. He and his brother Gotabaya, the Minister for Defence, were committed to ending the war, once and for all.

'I heard you were expanding the army base at Kankesanthurai,' Ruben said, keeping his voice and face neutral.

'Yes, it's an important vantage point to stop supplies coming in from India,' the brigadier replied.

And to stop refugees from fleeing to India or taking a boat to Mannar on the west coast of Sri Lanka, outside the war zone. Even better, a boat to Indonesia. But for that, they had to get to one of the port towns further south.

Ruben had been saving money to buy his mother and younger siblings a seat on anything, to any place out of here. He'd take what he could get.

'Your Sinhala is excellent,' the man said.

'Thank you. I work hard at it.'

'You're an accomplished linguist and interpreter; all the foreign aid agencies and diplomatic missions speak very highly of you. You've mastered a lot of languages for someone so young.'

Ruben shrugged. 'As I said, I work hard at it. There's not a lot to do here.'

'There's not a lot to earn here, either.' The brigadier looked around Ruben's office again. 'Jaffna University doesn't pay as well as the universities in the south. You've never thought of moving to Colombo, or abroad even? Canada, perhaps; they could use your skills. You have French?'

Ruben's mouth went dry. The brigadier knew he had French, Mandarin, Sinhalese, Hindi, and a number of other languages. He would have known that Ruben had applied for permission to leave Jaffna and pass through the Vanni into the south, but that his applications had been denied. His brother's involvement with the Tigers made them suspects to the army. The only safe passage would be illegal passage, and that was expensive. Ruben needed more time.

When he didn't answer, the brigadier continued. 'There's no need to be afraid of me. I'm not here to hurt your family or threaten you. I'm asking for your help.'

'My help?'

'Yes. The Third Battalion will be here for the foreseeable future. We'll create a permanent base at Kankesanthurai. You know that. It's inevitable. Now that we have Jaffna, we won't let it go. And it's only a matter of time before we win this war. Not a lot of time, either; it's almost over. My soldiers will be stationed here on tours of duty lasting three to six months, depending on their personal circumstances. Jaffna will become their home.'

Their home in his homeland. He was starting to understand.

'I need you to teach my soldiers Tamil. Classes five times a week. Intensive classes for the senior soldiers. And interpretation services for both the soldiers and the police.'

'Many of us speak English in Jaffna; you don't need Tamil.' His mind raced through plausible reasons to decline. Refusing the brigadier was dangerous, but accepting his offer would make him complicit. Police stations had been proliferating all over the north for years. Now the army would expand its hold on Jaffna. The soldiers

130

would bring their families or even create new ones, and the basis for a separate homeland would be eroded over time.

'Yes, but most of my soldiers don't speak English. They're from the south. Not knowing what people around them are saying frightens them. When people are frightened, they do stupid things.'

Ruben nodded.

'Language is a bridge to understanding,' the brigadier said. 'If the Tamil people see us trying to speak to them in their own language, they might see that some of us are trying to build a bridge, not destroy one.'

Ruben looked down at the Chinese dictionary on his desk. 'I need to think about it. I have a heavy teaching load this semester.'

'Yes, your classes are very popular. I've read your CV. You have a master's degree in Mandarin from the Lekikuang Institute. You could get a job as an interpreter for the Chinese embassy in Colombo or down at the new port in Hambantota earning ten times your teacher's salary.'

'More, actually,' Ruben replied. 'They've approached me already. It's something for me to think about in the future.'

The Chinese government was building its own city around the new military port it was developing in Hambantota, at Sri Lanka's southern tip. The string of pearls was tightening its chokehold and Hambantota, with its view across the Indian Ocean, was a critical part of China's strategy. The Chinese government had offered to compensate him well for his interpretation services. Again, the Chinese workers who were building the port were bringing their families with them. Apparently the street names of Hambantota were already signposted in Mandarin rather than Sinhalese.

The poetic justice would be satisfying if it wasn't so frightening. Once the Chinese were settled in Hambantota, they would look to Trincomalee in the north-east. And it was Chinese weapons the Sri Lankan Army was storing at their bases in Jaffna. Chinese weapons being deployed in the imminent final offensive against the Tamils.

'We can pay you well,' the brigadier said. 'Perhaps not as well as the Chinese, but far more than the university.'

'There is more to life than money.'

'Not when you're poor. I know you're poor and that you pay your family's rent and your brother and sister's tuition fees. You'll be saving for the future too.'

What kind of future would they have in Jaffna? In Sri Lanka? The brigadier knew he was saving to get them out of the country.

'Ruben, you have no reason to help the army and no reason to believe me,' the brigadier said. 'We're all Sri Lankan, and language has been used by both sides to divide us for too long. The mistrust between our communities has gone on for too long.' He smiled at Ruben encouragingly. 'We're not trying to trick you into betraying your people. We're trying to help them understand the new reality. You can do that for them. You can do that with us.'

There was truth to what he said. The Tigers had fought hard for a different reality, two separate people in two separate states. It was a dream, one for which they had all paid a heavy price.

'I know I'm asking you to work with the enemy.'

'Your words,' Ruben said. He would lose friends, maybe even family over this.

The brigadier nodded. 'Yes, but you're not very good at hiding your thoughts. I'm trying to tell you we are *not* the enemy, at least not here. You said there was more to life than money. I can offer you more than money.' He paused, waiting for Ruben to catch up.

Ruben held his breath.

'I can offer your family what every family wants: safe passage.'

GARETH

Cinnamon Gardens

'Councillor Barton.' Anji put her hand out with a little irony and a lot of affection. Gareth laughed and pulled her into an embrace. He wasn't much taller than her, and the stray curls of her hair brushed against his face. They stood outside the front gates of the nursing home. It was just as he remembered it. Except different. He was different too.

There was a cool breeze in the morning air, lifting the jacaranda flowers from their branches, a lilac cloud that descended in purple rain. Florence's favourite colour. She was speaking to him through each Florence-coloured flower, each Florence-coloured haze in the early morning or early evening sky. A message from her to him.

'You don't have to do this. I tried to call you last night to cancel.' Anji placed a hand on his arm. He couldn't remember the last time Nikki had touched him there. A piece of his skin that had not connected with skin for such a long time.

'I got your messages.' He smiled back at her reassuringly. 'Let's do this. I can't avoid the nursing home forever. I want to see what's happening. It's obviously upsetting and, as your councillor, I need to address it.'

Anji walked him around the nursing home's perimeter. He had known this building for almost two decades and it had become more beautiful with age. Anji put her profits back into the facilities, both the old house at the front and the newer one at the back. The two-storey Federation facade of Cinnamon Gardens had been restored, its brickwork repointed, the stucco redone and painted in a gentle hue of eucalypt. The trellis around its verandahs and gabled roof had been restored too. Charcoal and shining, the wrought iron fringed the old building assertively. Maya had apparently read an article about colours, drawing on recommendations by some expert in Spain who was the colourist for juvenile detention centres and mental institutions. According to the Spanish, colour mattered.

The building sat on a corner block and when he walked around to the other side, he saw what she was talking about. The wall had been spray-painted, large words scrawled in black and red, shouting at him from above:

> GO BACK TO WHERE U CAME FROM
> BLACK BITCH,
> FUCK. OFF

The erratic use of punctuation distracted him.

The lampposts and security cameras around the wall had been decapitated.

'You see what I mean?'

He did. The words were ugly but not surprising.

'I'm sorry, Anji. There's no place for this here or anywhere.'

'I agree, it's disgusting. We've filed a police report and we'll paint over it this afternoon. I was waiting to show you first. Photos don't really do it justice.'

'Do you mind?' He held his phone out.

'No, go ahead. It's the third time this month. If you look at the wall closely you'll see the variations on a theme underneath this

134

layer. And it's not just the vandalism. As I said at dinner, one of our employees, Ruben, was attacked again last week. I'm worried it's going to escalate.'

He nodded, took a few photos and then turned to her.

'Would you like to come inside? Mr South should be almost done with physio.' Anji still referred to Nikki's father as though she was a child. It was a respect thing, she explained.

'It'll be lunchtime soon. I'm sure he'd love some company.'

Gareth turned back and pretended to look at the wall. He tried to remember the breathing exercises Nathan had taught Oscar.

'Let me check in with the office; I'm a bit back-to-back at the moment,' he prevaricated. 'And I'd like to talk to one of my colleagues about what's going on here. See if we can't motivate the police to do better.'

'Of course. Thank you for coming, Gareth. I know it must be hard—'

'It's okay,' he broke in. 'It's okay. It was time.' He leaned over and kissed her goodbye. 'I might see you in there.' He tilted his head towards the nursing home.

'Room four, in the old building—top floor,' she reminded him.

He hadn't forgotten.

$\sim$

He walked the hallway, familiar in its colours and smells. Urine cleansed by disinfectant; small atoms of it that permeated the plastic bed covers and burrowed deep into the adjustable beds. A smell, a memory that lay sleeping with the bed's occupant. On top of that, another fragrance. Lunch. He recognised the spices that had wafted out of Anji's—Nathan's—kitchen.

He took the long way around to his father-in-law's room. He wanted to stretch his legs, he told himself. Legs that were slowing in pace even as his heart rate picked up. He pulled his shirt away from his armpits. He had known it would be like this. Of course it would be like this. He had avoided the place for ten months. Pull the bandaid off nice and fast, he told himself. Just keep walking. He nodded at the residents in their rooms, smiled tightly and raised a hand. Eye contact but no physical contact. The thought of their thin, papery skin made him shudder. Decay. People blessed and burdened with longevity. They should all be put out of their misery.

He passed a nurse in the Cinnamon Gardens uniform: black cargo pants and a simple cotton blouse. An Indian top in sea blue, with a lightly embroidered collar. All the women wore the same top, Indians in Indian clothes. The male nurses had them too, but the collar was different, less ornate and more shirt-like. He remembered when Anji had brought the new uniform in.

'Amma says sea blue is soothing,' she updated them. 'The uniforms are bespoke designed for the nursing home, so they have a pocket on the front for a pen and notepad. The trousers have extra pockets for stethoscopes, spare gloves and so on—although each corridor has supplies, obviously.'

'Obviously,' Gareth and Nathan had replied simultaneously, neither sharing Anji's fascination with nursing home efficiency or Maya's with feng shui. No, not feng shui. 'Vasthu, the Hindu equivalent,' Anji had explained, while Gareth hoped she would stop talking so they could discuss the by-election in Redfield. 'The science of positioning your home to maximise positive energy flows.'

As Gareth stood in the corridor that led to his father-in-law's room, he wondered if there were enough positive energy flows to pick him up and carry his leaden body the rest of the way. He felt the saliva in his mouth disappear. He needed water but didn't want to use the fountain in the corridor.

And then he heard it. Laughter. A woman's happiness. Not restrained by resentment. Not fettered by grief. Not undermined by regret. It started low, the way he remembered it, in the back of her throat. Or maybe it came from the base of her belly, where all the beautiful things in their lives began. A vibration of energy and music that picked up speed and sound as it rushed forth from her body and into the open air, received by a surprised and grateful world.

He stood at the door and watched, all of them unaware of his presence. They were a closed and comfortable circle.

Nikki laughed at something a male nurse was saying to her and Ray. Her father was clapping his hands at the punchline of the story. She laughed again and then said something to the nurse. Her voice had none of the quiet but palpable rage that surged through every word she said to Gareth, and every word she hadn't said since Florence.

He coughed, and Nikki and the nurse turned. The man looked familiar. It was Ruben, Gareth realised; the employee Anji had mentioned earlier. He recognised him now.

'Ruben.' Gareth put his hand out. 'Good to see you again.'

'Mr Barton.'

'Gareth is fine, please. I'm glad to see you're still here. I remember you're a favourite with the residents.'

Ruben laughed, his teeth bright against his dark skin. Nikki kept her eyes firmly on her father. He could feel her exhale and will herself to look at him, her husband.

'I'm not sure about that.' Ruben smiled again and turned back to Ray. He bent down and Ray put his arms around Ruben's neck and shoulders. Ruben picked up the old man easily and placed him in his chair, sliding the table next to him. Ray reached out for Ruben, squeezed his arm and let go.

'Is he okay?' Gareth asked Nikki.

'Hurt myself breaking up a fight in the prayer room,' Ray said, pulling the table closer. 'This place is rougher than it looks, Gareth.' He winked at Ruben. 'What time's lunch?'

'It'll be here soon, Uncle,' the nurse assured him.

'What am I having?' the old man asked.

'Your favourite: chicken curry, a boiled egg and idli. Don't tell anyone about the idli; everyone else is getting puttu, but Aunty Latha likes to spoil you.'

Gareth felt an ugly sensation in his gut. There was a time when Gareth was a good son to Ray; when they had shared jokes and shared treats. When they'd rolled their eyes together at Nikki and had one too many beers at Oscar's cricket games.

Ruben nodded at Nikki and then Gareth and left them together, alone and quiet, as though the laughter had belonged to him and not her. Maybe it had. It no longer belonged to Gareth.

'It's good to see you here,' Nikki said finally. 'You okay?'

He shrugged and tried to smile, but the gesture felt false. The social conventions that propelled him through the door and had sustained him—barely—through the encounter with Ruben were in freefall now.

There was a photo of him and Nikki with the kids on Ray's bedside table. It had been taken last Christmas, at their house. They didn't have many photos of all of them together.

'It's beautiful, isn't it? I . . .' Nikki swallowed hard.

It was beautiful.

'I look at it every day.'

It was the most she had said to him in months. He wanted to say he understood, that he felt the same. That the photo made him feel whole and broken at the same time.

But the sound of her laughter was still echoing in his brain. The laughter she offered to someone else, and the grief she offered to him.

A nurse came in with a tray of food.

'Good afternoon, Uncle Ray—I have your lunch for you.' The woman placed the tray in front of Ray and fastened a bib around his neck, looking towards Nikki for instructions.

'I'll feed him, thank you, Manju.'

'Thank you, Dr Nikki.' The nurse left the room, calling out to someone in the corridor in a musical language he had heard before.

'What happens when he wants a sandwich?' Gareth asked.

'What?'

'What happens when he wants a sandwich?' Gareth repeated. 'Or just something other than a curry?'

'He doesn't want a sandwich,' Nikki replied, confused.

'But what if he *did*? What if he didn't want chicken and idli.'

'The fermented lentil cakes are really high in protein and fibre. He needs both. The chicken curry is cooked in bone broth with a combination of spices that neuroscientists and immunologists at Johns Hopkins have studied.'

'Why would they do that?'

'Because the combination enhances immunity and neurological acuity.'

Whatever it was, it really did smell good. 'You know what I mean.'

'No, I don't, Gareth.'

Gareth wasn't sure he knew what he meant either. He hadn't come in here to fight. He hadn't really wanted to come in here at all, but he knew it was time to face this demon. He was steeling himself to see Ray and feel the full force of all his regrets, reframed as unfair anger and resentment towards the old man. Instead, he saw Nikki in this place that claimed so much of her life, and inadvertently theirs, and he felt something he couldn't name. Something that confused and shamed him.

She was beautiful when she laughed. Beautiful even in the depths of her grief or when her face was contorted in blame and anger. Beautiful the day he first met her. Beauty that was intended for him and no other.

'Gareth?' she said. 'What's going on here?'

'Nothing. Sorry, Nik, I'm just . . . it's just my first time back here. I'm not myself. You can understand that . . .'

He picked up the Old Spice cologne on Ray's bedside table and showed it to Nikki.

'I haven't seen this for a while.'

Nikki smiled tentatively. 'Anji imports it from Cargills, a department store in Sri Lanka. Apparently, the version sold there is slightly different from the one you get at Chemist Warehouse. Aunty Maya's instructions on nursing home management are specific, if not always economically rational.'

Gareth inhaled the cologne's cedar muskiness, which inevitably conjured an image of a ship on its way to the colonies. He placed the bottle back on the table, thinking about what to say next.

'How's work?' Nikki asked, filling the silence.

'It's great. Time to shake things up. Good projects in the pipeline. Really good, thank you,' he lied. 'You look well, Ray.'

'Thank you, son.' Ray smiled at him. 'It's good to see you. How are the children?'

Gareth flinched. Children.

He saw the old man's spiky eyebrows furrow, a grey grevillea sitting above his blue eyes. Blue eyes like Nikki. Blue eyes like Florence.

'They're good, Ray. They're good.' He exhaled and tried to imagine his heart pumping blood, imagined slowing it down to a gentle river. A wine-dark river that he could urge into calm submission. He closed his eyes.

Nikki had mentioned that Ray didn't always remember what had happened; his dementia had worsened since the accident, intensified by the trauma. Gareth envied him the loss of memory and the pain that attended those memories.

If you can't recall the pain, then you can't recall the joy. You can't remember the love you gave and the love you received. You can't remember the smell of her skin or the laughter in her voice.

Laughter. He felt something cold and hard congeal in his chest.

He opened his eyes.

'Ask them to come see their old grandpa, will you? I'll take them on a tour of my new place.'

'Sure, this weekend.'

'After surfing? They love surfing with you.'

'Yes, after surfing,' Gareth repeated. 'It's good to see you too, Ray.' He nodded at Nikki and the old man and left.

~⦿

'Gareth.' He heard Anji's voice behind him, stilling his hand on the nursing home's front door. The sanitiser dispensers stood like sentinels on either side, at two heights: one for adults who were able-bodied and one for adults in wheelchairs. Or for children. He turned to face her.

'How did it go?' Anji asked. She looked just like her mother from this angle.

'All good. I saw Ray. He looks well.' Anji would know that he hadn't seen Ray since the funeral.

'Let me walk you out.' She brushed past him and pressed the door-release button. Sunlight streamed into the foyer, the smell of frangipani with it. Maya's favourite flower. It was strange the things he remembered from decades of knowing these people, this place.

They walked together in silence to his car on the street.

'The place looks the same. It's a great thing you're doing here, Anji. A business and a community service.' He had seen the posters for the mix of cultural celebrations, the rosters for Fun-Fizio, games and karaoke lunches, the inter-floor bridge competitions and wheelchair tug of war. It was a fun place to live and die, for those whose time had come.

'You okay?' she asked, her hand on his arm, her eyes searching his face. Her mother must have been a beautiful woman in her youth. He leaned towards her, not sure why. She instinctively stepped back, creating distance.

Hot shame rushed through him, for the second or perhaps it was the third time that morning.

'Gareth, are you okay?' she asked again. 'I know this must be hard for you. You're so brave, so good to come. I know it's confusing.'

She was managing him; her clinical training kicking in. Nathan said her diagnostic and de-escalation skills were excellent. They hadn't helped her with her father, though, he thought. Cruel but true.

'I'm fine, thank you, Anji. Nothing to worry about. Small steps; it takes time. You know that better than me. I need to keep doing this, for Oscar and for Nikki.'

'And for yourself,' she answered. 'Don't forget about yourself. You are entitled to your grief.'

He felt the tightness spreading down into his chest.

I am entitled to my grief, he repeated inside his head. *I am entitled. To my grief. My grief. Grief.*

What about my rage?

He exhaled.

'Business seems to be doing well.' He looked back at the nursing home towering over them. 'Nikki mentioned that you'll be investigated in the next round of the Royal Commission.'

The Royal Commission into Aged Care Quality and Safety was nothing to be concerned about, according to Nikki. At least, not for places like Cinnamon Gardens, which were run properly in full compliance with federal regulations and global best practice. Nikki really did drink the nursing home Kool Aid.

'Yep, next month. It's a postcode lottery and our number came up. Nothing to worry about.'

'Nothing to worry about,' he echoed. 'You've expanded? There seem to be more beds, or more staff.'

She nodded. 'Both. We expanded the footprint of the newer building by twenty per cent; there was a lot of land behind it. We were doing that renovation the last time you were here. More rooms, more beds, more staff. People aren't getting any younger.' She smiled. Nursing home humour.

'Too true,' he replied. 'The staff seem happy. Nice uniforms. I like the sea blue. It *is* soothing.'

She laughed, clearly remembering the conversation about it. 'Thank you, I'm glad you agree.'

'The staff all seem to speak the same language. Are they all from Sri Lanka?'

'No, they're from a mix of places originally. They're all Australian now.'

'Of course, I wasn't—'

'I know, sorry. Asserting national identity is a bad habit of mine. They're Sri Lankan, Indian and Nepali mostly. They speak Tamil, Hindi and Nepali between themselves, although the Hindi and Nepali speakers are picking up Tamil faster than the other way around.'

'Not picking up English?'

'They're all from former colonies, Gareth,' Anji said. She was smiling, but her tone was controlled and careful. 'Their English is better than yours.' There it was, a flash of the temper that Nathan found so attractive. Gareth thought it could get tiring after a while.

'Australia is a former colony,' he countered, although he wasn't sure what he was trying to say.

'But a white one, so it's never had to try very hard.'

Not as white as it used to be, according to the Australian Human Rights Commission's last report on multiculturalism. That ex-commissioner, Tim Something-or-other, had a lot to say about it. Suddenly Australian politicians had to learn words like 'multiculturalism' and acronyms such as CaLD. He'd learned them, but it hadn't done him any good.

Fuck Bella Davidson and her darker-than-vanilla fake tan, her faker-than-her-tan wokeness and her greater marketability to the Westgrove electorate.

Fuck the party, too.

'Right.' He knew he should stop before this conversation spiralled out of control like his conversation with Nikki. 'You're right, Anji. Quite right. Thank you for having me here. Let me talk to the office—and the police—about the vandalism. See what we can do.'

He leaned down and kissed her quickly. His lips on the softness of her cheek. He longed to feel his skin against skin.

Then he was in the car, not looking at her watching him leave.

~ා

Gareth walked into the office. Bella was leaning against Richard's table, her legs crossed, her pink skirt riding up her legs, revealing more of her thighs than Richard seemed comfortable with. Poor man, Gareth thought. Bella was wasting her efforts; she'd be better off trying to dazzle him with an exposition on statistical modelling.

As Bella leaned into him, Richard leaned away. He was on the verge of tipping off his chair when they both noticed him. He could tell from the look on their faces that they both knew about his change of circumstances. Davidson was such a dick. Made sense he would tell his daughter and heir apparent. But Richard?

Bella stood up abruptly. 'Gareth, you're here.'

'Good observation, Bella.'

What did she expect? That he would quietly clean out his desk overnight and save them the discomfort of making eye contact and small talk? He had a three-month notice period, and unless the party wanted to pay him out, he was entitled to be there. It was his office until his contract said it wasn't.

'I just thought . . .'

'There's a lot of work to be done before the end of my tenure. I'm sure a public servant like yourself would understand that.'

'Yes, yes, of course.'

Richard stood up and straightened his shirt and tie. 'Let me know how I can help.' He offered Gareth his hand.

Gareth shook it. 'Thank you, Richard.' He moved off towards his office, his defiant stride broken by a half-formed, quickly consolidating thought.

'Bella, you're a human rights expert, aren't you?'

Three fucking months in a human rights organisation, probably just photocopying memos for the real lawyers, and she was an expert. Great credentials for an electorate too stupid to know any better.

'Well, yes, I've done some work in human rights.'

'Your father mentioned you're an expert. Do me a favour and prepare a research brief. Doesn't have to be as detailed as you're used to. I want to know what laws prohibit racism in Australia. Is it still the—?' He stopped. Let her work it out; she was the expert. 'Give me the full range of legislation, state and federal. I want to know what constitutes racism. Is there a test for it or a standard that has to be met? And what recourse do I have when I see it taking place? Can you do that? Thanks, mate.' He winked at her the way Davidson winked at him.

'When would you like it by?' Bella asked.

'Close of business would be grand.'

He went into his office. Three months left, unless Davidson managed him out. He shut the door behind him.

He spent the afternoon reading his employment contract. He called his union rep and sought advice which reassured him. Local government afforded him surprisingly strong employment rights, apparently. He emailed his employment contract and his last three appraisals to his rep and copied it to his personal email address. He also created a file note of the conversation with Davidson at the State Library yesterday. He left out the part about buying Portuguese tarts on the council credit card.

There was a tentative knock on the door.

'Come in,' Gareth called out from behind his desk.

Bella entered, her face flushed with the exertions of actual legal research and perhaps confusion over why he was still there. And why he was giving her instructions. Navigating confusion and uncertainty were important skills for a local councillor: he was training her; helping her. He would serve this office until the end of the eighty-ninth day of his notice period.

'I think I have what you asked for,' Bella said, handing him the research memo. It was certainly brief. 'The relevant legislation is the *Racial Discrimination Act 1975*. Race discrimination is a federal offence and it can be committed by anyone; an individual, or governments and organisations. There's no direct state equivalent legislation, but the New South Wales *Anti-Discrimination Act 1977* overlaps with it somewhat.'

'Somewhat,' Gareth repeated. Good legal language, that. He bet *somewhat* didn't fly at the Southern Poverty Law Center.

He scanned the memo, and stopped at the extract of the act, reading it closely.

Racial Discrimination Act 1975 (Cth)

Offensive behaviour because of race, colour or national or ethnic origin

(1) It is unlawful for a person to do an act, otherwise than in private, if:

    (a) the act is reasonably likely, in all the circumstances, to offend, insult, humiliate or intimidate another person or a group of people; and

    (b) the act is done because of the race, colour or national or ethnic origin of the other person or of some or all of the people in the group.

'There's also this really helpful guideline from the AHRC—that's the Australian Human Rights Commission,' Bella offered, clearly delighted by her ability to explain acronyms already referenced in the legislation she had downloaded.

'Which says?'

'Sorry?' Her sparkling eyes were confused.

'What do the guidelines tell us, Bella?' he asked. 'Surely you did more than print pages off the internet at that human rights organisation?'

Her face reddened as she scanned the guidelines, tried to understand them, and threw key words at him. Her balloon animals were deflating rapidly, flaccid pieces of coloured rubber descending from the sky.

'The RDA tries to strike the balance between freedom of speech and freedom from racial vilification,' she began.

'Yes, anyone who's watched *Q and A* knows that. I want to know what the process for making a complaint is,' Gareth said happily, leaning back in his chair, eyes on Bella as she frantically scanned the document in her hands.

'Um . . . let me see . . . Oh yes, if you—'

'Never mind, I can work it out myself.' He looked down at the memo in his hands and then back up again. 'That's everything, thanks, Bella. Leave the guidelines on the table.'

He looked back down again, the sudden sense of power making him dizzy. It was true: power did go to the head.

~⁀

Gareth loosened his tie as he poured a glass of red and then another. He set them on the kitchen counter to breathe and turned his hand to dinner, taking the sweating containers of Sri Lankan food from their plastic bag. If she wouldn't go to Blue Lotus, then he would bring Blue Lotus to her. He pulled out two plates and waited. He flicked through TV channels, stopping at the local news. He looked for the nursing home story but couldn't find it. Local news wasn't as local as a local nursing home graffitied by local racists.

He heard the front door open. His heart pounded the way it used to, only louder and more urgent in his chest.

Nikki walked in, tired and surprised to see him and dinner laid out.

'You're home early,' she said. 'Where's Oscar?'

He masked his disappointment and ploughed forward. 'He's sleeping over at Anji's house tonight. He's been asking for a sleepover.'

'On a school night?'

'He's in primary school.' Gareth shrugged. 'I've got dinner. I know it's not quite up to Nathan's standards, but I got all your favourite dishes from Blue Lotus.'

Remember? he wanted to say. Remember when we used to go there every Sunday night? Remember when the kids loved to watch the TV bolted to the corner of the ceiling, the fan underneath it slowly stirring the smell of spices and sweat throughout the small cantina? Remember how Florence would copy the Bollywood dancers, their hips thrusting and their arms turning the light bulb or milking the cow or something. Florence, with her tiny hips and big attitude, would dance and laugh and laugh and dance.

Why had they stopped going? He couldn't understand it. They had stopped before she died, not because she died. But the Blue Lotus, like so many other traditions and trappings of family life that had disappeared, was swept into the post-Florence morass of grief, a convenient blanket excuse that covered a multitude of forgotten or forgone interactions that had bound them together as a family, with or without their little girl.

He would try harder now. He would push through their pain and ignore her anger and suggest date nights, movie nights, curry nights. Anything that might inch them closer together from the opposite sides of the empty continent of the marriage they now inhabited.

'Smells great,' she replied, her back to him as she washed her hands in the sink with pre-surgical precision. 'You should have told me you were going to Blue Lotus; I already ate.'

'You ate?'

'At the nursing home. I like to eat there sometimes, if there's leftovers in the kitchen. It's easier for me just to cook for Oscar and you. One less person—you know how it is.'

Did she eat alone? he wondered.

'I hadn't realised,' was all he said.

Had it been that long since they had sat down together, the three of them? Coming and going from the family home, passing but not intersecting. Not touching. He burned with shame at the memory of Anji today. Would she have said anything to Nikki?

'It's good food. Delicious actually, despite your cheap shots at it this morning.'

There it was.

'I wasn't taking cheap shots. I just think it's a legitimate question to ask about the options residents are given at Cinnamon Gardens. I get that Anji is proud of her heritage; it's wonderful and, *yes*, the food *is* delicious. It's just that—'

'It's what, Gareth? What exactly is it?' She turned to face him. Her voice was quiet—she was always quiet—but the anger coursed through the strained cordons in her neck. Her delicate neck, a steep gradient from her jawline down to the gently raised muscle of her shoulder, a small mole on her left side, the hard nub of bone where her collar met the top of her arm. Territory that he was once entitled to travel.

'It doesn't matter. I'm sorry, Nikki,' he said. This wasn't the way he had planned this evening. This wasn't the plan. 'I know you're angry at me, and I'm sorry.'

He handed her a glass of wine and gently touched his glass to hers. 'It's just . . . it was hard for me to be there. Harder than I expected, and I was expecting the worst.' He leaned into her, the way he had with Anji that morning, pushing the intruding thought away.

'Let's skip dinner, if you've already eaten. I bet I can think of something to do tonight that you *didn't* do at the nursing home.'

Her eyes narrowed, just a little.

Something pulled in his mind, an unformed thought at the edges. Easy laughter and a circle of intimacy that didn't include him.

He tried to ignore it.

He took another sip, smaller this time, and placed his glass and hers on the counter.

Before she could move away, he pulled her towards him, her body stiff. He kissed her lips gently at first and then harder, prising them apart with his tongue, insistent on entering the softness inside.

'Kiss me back,' he urged her. 'You used to love kissing.' It was her thing. He could make her weak, he could make her wet, when he kissed her. He held her head in place with one hand, and with his other hand he touched her, moving down from her neck, the fine bones of her throat, to the curve of her breast. He pushed hard against the thin fabric of her blouse, fingers over warm flesh, thumb on the joint between her ribs. The erratic pulse at her neck mutated, rhythm becoming form, a mass trapped in her chest, beating at the walls of her rib cage.

She pulled her arms up against her heart, palms on his chest, pushing him back. He pushed forward. He knew he should stop, but he didn't want to. He missed her. He wanted her. He was incomplete without her body, her love and her acceptance. She had withheld all of it and now he wanted it. He deserved it.

She pulled away from him, her head still locked in place by his hand, her body angled awkwardly. He pushed her back against the counter so she couldn't move, she couldn't refuse. Her hands were balled into fists now, hitting him. She was making a sound, but it wasn't the sound he wanted. She gasped for air, her breath fast and short, in through her nose and out into his mouth. Her air was his air. He inhaled her into him.

He pushed his body against her, bent his knees and then raised his body into hers, again and again, waiting to hear her moan like she used to. Clothing divided and separated them still. She tried to pull her head back, breaking the seal in their lips, sucking in air and spitting words back out. Her mouth bruised and angry. No. She was scared.

'Stop, Gareth, stop!' She turned and twisted her face away, her fists pummelling him harder and faster.

'Please,' he said. Why did he have to beg? Why did she always make him beg?

He tried to kiss her again.

Why couldn't she see how they still fit together? A piece of them was missing but they still fit.

'Please,' he repeated, hating the tone in his voice. The tone he used with her, the tone he used with Davidson. It wasn't him.

'Nikki,' he said, releasing his hold on her a little. 'I—'

Before he could finish the sentence, she hit him hard across the face.

He stumbled back a step and she slipped away from him, holding her hand to her chest, rubbing her palm.

His face stung. He closed his eyes so he wouldn't have to see her disgust and then made himself look at her. He deserved it all.

'I'm sorry,' he whispered. *For so many things*, he wanted to say. He reached out to her, but she shook her head.

'No, Gareth,' she replied, wiping the tears from her face. Her voice hard, her blue eyes now clear and distant. 'Enough.'

She picked up her handbag from the counter and walked out.

MAYA

Cinnamon Gardens

Maya knocked on Mr Sahadevan's door. Ruben stood close behind her, carrying supplies from Bunnings in his hands and a child's backpack slung over his shoulder.

'Go in,' Ruben said. 'Sometimes he can't hear you. The TV,' he explained.

Mr Sahadevan, or Saha Anna as Maya called him, was wealthy enough to pay for his own room on the top floor of Cinnamon Gardens, unencumbered by the Sun TV preferences of other residents, who all watched the Tamil soap operas. Saha Anna watched two channels on the Indian digital package. He followed cricket continuously, including English county cricket, where the Sri Lankan development squad often trained during the off season. He also watched the Hinduism Now channel, which live-streamed religious ceremonies from India's greatest temples. When asked about his dual obsessions, he replied simply, 'I worship both gods,' giving him a reputation for being deeply devout.

Maya knew better. In Colombo, Saha had been a well-known gemologist. He worked at Piyadasa, the prestigious chain of jewellers, and he liked to watch the temple channel because the deities were made of gold and covered in obscene amounts of jewellery.

'What are you making today?' Maya asked him, watching the old man sand down a small block of wood.

Ruben placed the supplies at Saha's feet. The old man patted him on the back, confident Ruben had procured everything he needed for his work.

'It's a little Shiva for Mrs Segaram to take to the hospital next week. She's worried about her cataract operation. This will fit in her handbag.'

'Shanthi Segaram.' Maya tried not to scoff. 'She's not a very nice person.'

'She's not a very happy person,' he replied, putting the wood down. 'There's a difference.'

She nodded reluctantly, ignoring Ruben's smile.

'Are you comfortable, Anna?' she asked Saha, who felt like an older brother to her. She pulled Zakhir's cardigan tight around her body. Saha was one of her husband's oldest friends from back home and he understood what her loss felt like; his loss was greater.

Saha locked his hands together in his lap, the tremor barely restrained, a fierce energy in his fingertips, scratching to get out. Some mornings he woke up screaming and the nurses knew that he was no longer with them. In the night, his mind had travelled back to the moment, the reason, he had left Sri Lanka.

The first time Saha Anna told her the story, his voice and body shook, even though many years had passed. Maya recognised the signs of trauma; she had lived with them her entire married life.

She sat with him every Friday morning, after the last televised temple poosai in India had ended and before the next cricket game began, somewhere in the world. Every week, she let him tell his story. He gave it to her and she took it from him. She carried a small piece of that burden so that he carried a little less. When his son came to see him, every Friday night, he could see that the old man was lighter, but he never knew why.

Saha's story took place in 1983, two years after Maya and Zakhir left Sri Lanka. Colombo was burning with anger and fire—a fire that had been four decades in the making. Black July, they called it.

Colombo, Sri Lanka, 1983

A crowd of men came to the jewellery store in Colombo 7. Saha and the other Tamil employees sat on the floor of Mrs Piyadasa's office, above the front door. They huddled together and listened to the mob swelling below.

The men had an electoral roll and a list of employees who were identified as Tamil. It was only the first day of the burning, and people were yet to realise what would happen over the coming week.

The security guard lowered the iron grille over the shopfront, a simple lattice that was designed to keep out petty thieves at night. It was no match for the crowd that gathered outside the store, holding flaming torches and machetes. The knives, intended for cleaving bananas from their trees, now glistened with sticky blood.

The guard stood his ground, a baton in his hands.

The men swelled in the darkness, their number and faces concealed by the shadows. The ones at the front surged towards the grille and wrapped their hands around its bars, shaking it, testing its strength.

The leader of the mob stepped forward and challenged the guard.

'We're here for the Tamils.' He read from a crumpled sheet of paper. He named them all.

'We know they work for Mrs Piyadasa. I can't believe she trusts them. They are liars and thieves. They'll steal your fancy jewellery from you, just like they've stolen this country from us. Hand them over and we'll go quickly.' He shook the list in the guard's face.

Saha felt sick. One of their fellow employees, someone who worked with them, ate with them, laughed with them; someone here had told them there were Tamils in the building.

Someone led this mob to them.

The Tamil employees moved closer together, some clasping hands with each other. They could smell the smoke from the bodies, the buildings, the school buses and cars. They could smell the burning tyres, toxic fumes seeping through the cracks in the windows.

Saha had called his home over and over again, desperately dialling the number, each time praying that someone would pick up. Each time realising that, if someone picked up, they were still in danger because they lived in Wellawatte, in Colombo 6, where all the Tamils lived.

He called everyone he knew, every number he could remember. They all did. No one answered. They sat on the floor, holding each other, listening to the shouts from the street below. Listening to their names being called. Saha heard his name clearly. He cowered against the wall. The men below rattled the grille again, their anger and impatience growing.

Mrs Piyadasa placed her hand on his. It was the first time she had ever touched him. So out of place; her refined hand on his knotted one.

She was wearing something he had designed and made for her seventieth birthday, a wide gold bracelet with burnished filigree that curled around her wrist like a jasmine vine. He had set it with clusters of small diamonds, cut and placed in the formation of the delicate flowers she loved. In the daylight, they shone white. But at dusk, when the jasmine released its perfume, the diamonds picked up the blood red of the falling sun, and glowed with the same gentle pink as the flower they honoured.

Every woman in Colombo 7 wanted that bracelet after they saw it, but he refused to make more.

'Send them out,' the man in the street demanded. 'Send them out or we will burn everything.'

Mrs Piyadasa adjusted the bracelet on her wrist and released his hand. She walked down the stairs towards the front door. He knew she was going to hand them over. She had jewellery in the store worth tens of thousands of lakhs. She could not allow them to breach the grille.

The Tamils huddled together, crying and praying. Saha peered through the plastic blinds, holding his breath and waiting for the end to come.

Mrs Piyadasa walked into the centre of the mob, her head high and her contempt for them worn as artfully as any piece of jewellery her great-grandfather had designed.

The crowd shrank back a little, unsure of how to respond to both her status and her audacity.

'We've come for the Tamils,' the leader repeated. 'Hand them over and we'll leave you in peace.'

'*You* will leave *me* in peace?' she said. 'Get off my property now, and I will leave you in peace.'

Anger rippled through the crowd. Saha held his breath, certain they would kill his boss first and then them.

Mrs Piyadasa spoke again before the leader could issue an order. 'I am the jeweller to the kings and queens of the world. Not *a* jeweller. *The* jeweller. Queen Elizabeth visited me when she came here in 1956. She bought Ceylon stones cut and crafted by *my* staff. Their hands are worth more than the jewels themselves because, without them, rubies and sapphires are merely pretty-coloured stones. And without these pretty-coloured stones, the presidents of Ceylon would have nothing to present to the leaders of foreign countries.'

The crowd stepped back further, as if intimidated by this small, imperious woman who was not afraid of them. The leader lifted the hem of his sarong and wiped the sweat from his face with it.

'Unless you want to explain yourselves to President Jayewardene himself, you had better leave. Do remember that I make *all* of his wife's jewellery.'

Mrs Piyadasa returned to the office, a faint sheen on her upper lip, her pencilled eyebrows smudged a little, the kohl bleeding down towards her eyes giving the impression that two caterpillars had fallen onto her forehead.

She looked at Saha, her master gem cutter since he was sixteen, a talent identified by her father more than thirty years ago, at one of their mines in Kandy. She placed her hand on his again.

'Keep calling your home. Tomorrow morning, my driver and I will take you there. We'll find your family.'

The next day, Mrs Piyadasa kept her promise. Before sunrise, they drove through Colombo's smouldering streets until they reached the charred remains of Harmers Avenue. The mobs had used the electoral roll to find the Tamil homes.

Saha got out of the car and stood before the burned and blackened cinders of what had been his home. A simple but cherished existence.

'Stay with the car,' the driver said. 'I'll look.'

The young man had a heavy stick in the boot of his car. He had done this before. He picked his way through the debris, sending ash into the air wherever he stepped. He looked like he was walking on clouds.

The ash caught in Saha's throat.

He heard the driver cry out.

Saha stepped forward, towards what had been the front door, now just half a frame leading to the embers of the house. Mrs Piyadasa grasped his arm to restrain him.

'Stay back,' the driver shouted in Sinhalese.

Saha pulled away from Mrs Piyadasa and ran towards the driver's voice.

He found him in the kitchen. Saha's wife and two of the children were there, collapsed in the corner, her arms wrapped around them. Their heads separated from their bodies. Their bodies burned and fused together like the metals he worked with, one inseparable from the other. A new and hideous alloy. His third child, a son called Gunam, was in Galle, in the south of the island, playing cricket in a school competition. The other boys were supposed to go as well but they had chicken pox and stayed home with his wife. He wished he had stayed with them too.

Cinnamon Gardens, *present day*

Maya and Ruben sat quietly in Saha Anna's room, Maya waiting for the right moment to speak, to draw him back from his daily memories.

'Are you comfortable, Saha Anna?' she asked him again, gently.

'I am, thank you.' He looked at the calendar pinned to the wall next to his work table. It was Thursday not Friday. 'You're a day early.'

'I'm here on official business.'

He laughed, revealing a wide gap. 'Bring me my glass, thambi.' He motioned to Ruben, who retrieved the glass from the bedside table and handed it to him.

Saha fished out his dentures and shook them off before popping them in his mouth. 'They're new. Do you like them?'

'I do. They're bigger and whiter than the old ones,' Maya observed.

'My granddaughter,' he said proudly. 'I get them for free. American style, she says. What is your official business? In all the years I've lived here, you've never asked me to value your jewellery. You don't seem like a suspicious person.'

It was Maya's turn to laugh. Although Saha's eyes and hands were failing, the residents of the home still brought their jewellery to him for appraisal and reassurance that they had not been cheated by their miserly in-laws. Saha would verify whether the stones were as real and superior as their mothers-in-law had once asserted.

'My mother-in-law never gave me any jewellery. She told me not to marry her son.'

'She's not a very good listener, is she?' Ruben said to Saha Anna, lifting the backpack on his lap and setting it down. It hit Saha's work table with a thud.

Maya pulled out a key from her sari blouse and unlocked the bag. It had belonged to one of her grandchildren, its plastic facade cracked with misuse, only segments of a robot face remaining.

'I want you to sell all of this,' she said. 'It's not mine; my father sold my mother's small dowry when he lost his pension. This belonged to Cedric's family and he didn't have much use for it either. No wife to lavish with jewels, no daughter to inherit.'

'You don't want them?' Saha Anna asked.

'I have no use for them.'

Maya's friends came to weddings and festivals, their bodies dripping in layers of gold and Ceylon gemstones. She wore her traditional wedding chain, the thali kodi, that Zakhir had commissioned from Saha when they were all much younger. She also wore the single gold bangle her grandmother gave her. Her friends teased her but she didn't mind. Cedric's gift sat unused and hidden in her sock drawer.

Saha nodded his approval. 'We send boys into bottomless shafts. Over the decades they return from the dark as hard, wiry men, but only a shadow of the people they might have been. There is a deep tragedy in the life and beauty we suck from them to feed our desire for stone. We destroy their potential in order to realise the potential diamond in the compressed coal.'

'This, from Colombo's finest gem cutter.'

'I would know. May I?' Saha Anna asked. He reached inside the backpack and arranged the pieces in front of him, his eyebrows raised in surprise.

'These are beautiful. Have you kept anything for your children?'

She smiled and nodded. 'I've given Anji the engagement ring you made me and a couple of Cedric's pieces. My naughty grandsons have even told me which ones they want, after I die. Can you imagine that? Will you speak to your grandson, Saha Anna?' Once a year, Saha's grandson, who worked for a renowned jeweller in Dubai, came back to Australia to visit his family. 'Would he do this as a favour to you?'

'He'll do this as a favour to you,' Saha replied. 'He pays all his suppliers a fair value because that's what I taught him. It isn't just the skill of gem cutting that I passed down. However, he will pay you full value. Many of these designs are antique. These pieces are held in families for generations and never sold. Are you sure you want to do this?'

'I'm sure,' she replied.

'Then I'm sure he can find Emirati wives who like to dress like South Asian royalty underneath their burqas.'

Saha Anna set his loupe to his eye and squinted, the muscles of his cheek holding the lens in place. He picked up a ring and turned it in the light.

'Most gem cutters think that cutting a stone is a physical act. They are taught when to use the turntable of the lap machine and when to sand by hand. They learn when a stone requires the gentle coaxing of a man and not a metal plate to bring the stone to its full brilliance.'

'That sounds like a physical act,' Ruben said.

'It's not. It's a mathematical one. It's about the physics in the angles and the refraction of light. It's about chemistry, the strength of the bonds between the elements that comprise a gemstone and how hard you can test those bonds before it shatters in your hands.'

Saha turned the ring over in his hands, letting the diamond catch the light.

'It's science and parenting.'

'You *parent* the stone?' Ruben asked.

'Yes. The average stone cutter identifies the stone's weaknesses and works within the parameters of those fissures to produce something that can be set in gold. A good stone cutter reads the stone and senses the exact limit of the fissures, sets his blade to the fissure and not a millimetre before it. He does this so that the weaknesses of the stone do not undermine its strengths.'

'And you?'

'The beauty of a stone is not in its strengths but in the uniqueness of its failings.'

'You are a master gem cutter,' Maya said.

'I am,' he said, without pride. Saha Anna valued what others feared. He found the flaw and he cut facets, highlighted occlusions, not to reflect the light but to harness the light, not to sit in gold but to ride gold like it was a celestial palanquin.

'My family can sell these for you. It won't take long, with quality like this. Do you want cash or an electronic payment?'

He was looking around for the TV remote. Ruben turned the cricket on and gave the remote to the old man.

'Cash,' Maya replied.

She had access to money. Theoretically, she still owned the nursing home accounts. She didn't need cash, but Maya liked the informal economy of the nursing home. A lot of the residents paid for things with cash. Nothing illegal, just items their well-meaning children might not allow them to have. At her request, Ruben recently bought Womanizers for half of the residents. Using her cash but his card on the internet, the transactions were untraceable to her or Mrs Ragupathy or the others who were now blissfully indebted to her.

'This is how we do things in Sri Lanka,' Maya had argued when Anjali sought to prohibit the cash transactions occurring under her nose. Anjali could be such a wet blanket. That was probably one of her mother-in-law's genes in her.

'Amma, in Sri Lanka, ninety per cent of the wealth is in the hands of three per cent of the country, and ninety per cent of that three per cent don't pay any tax,' Anji replied, laughing when Maya showed her the backpack months later, the jewellery replaced by rolls of cash. 'I'm not trying to set up a little Sri Lanka here in the nursing home.'

'But, mahal,' Maya replied, squeezing her daughter's face, 'that's exactly what your father and I tried to do.'

NIKKI

Cinnamon Gardens

Nikki knocked on the cottage door. It was late, and when Ruben opened up, she hesitated, lingering in the darkness. He drew her into the warmth of the cottage and then saw the bruising on her mouth and arms.

'I'll kill him,' he said.

Nikki shook her head. 'Can I stay here tonight?'

'You can stay here forever,' he said, taking her into his arms and holding her gently. She let herself believe him.

~◡

The next day, she walked up to the nursing home and, passing her father's room, entered Maya's. She shut the door behind her, locking it from the inside. Maya was the only resident who had a lock. Ruben had fitted it for her but Anji insisted that the office keep a key, in case of emergency. The older woman was finishing her prayers at the small shrine in her room.

'You're early,' Maya said, putting out the oil lamp with her fingers. The flame hissed, leaving a wisp of smoke that curled towards the photograph of Zakhir. She wiped her fingers and then anointed her husband with holy ash. 'No rounds this morning?'

'Anji will do them for me today,' Nikki replied.

'Chollungo, mahal,' Maya said. Nikki knew this meant: Tell me, daughter.

So she did. She set up Maya's tape recorder and spoke into the microphone, slowly and clearly. She recorded every act she could remember; every emotion.

She started with the night before and told Maya of her pain, of the fear and the rage that had propelled her hand to his face, severing his hold on her body. Then she told Maya the rest of the story, because it began with friendship and then passion and then love, and that should be recorded too.

She thought she'd be scared of how this story ended. But sitting in Maya's room, looking at the photos of Zakhir, the writing table with its papers and the hard drive that stored Maya's words, she felt calm.

And then she did something she had never done before but had seen Anji do many times before. She kneeled down and touched Maya's feet. She took her blessings from this old woman, her best friend's mother. She asked for Maya's strength. Maya, who had loved people and lost people too. Maya, who lived life courageously and recorded life honestly.

Maya raised her up and placed a little holy ash on her forehead.

'Neengal enda mahal mathiri,' she said.

Nikki understood the important word in that statement. *Mahal.*

Maya took Nikki's face in her withered hands and kissed her the way all Tamil mothers kissed their children, inhaling her. The Sri Lankan kiss, they called it. It always made her laugh, and Nikki laughed then, even though she'd thought she'd never laugh again.

~⌒

Ruben parked Anji's big Volvo outside Nikki's house. The location app on her phone had told her that Gareth was still at the council chambers. She gave her phone to Maya with instructions to call Ruben if Gareth moved. Uncle Gana in Room 5 had printed a list for her from the internet, so they were fast and methodical.

Clothes for her, clothes for Oscar.

The hard drive with the photos of the children.

The two passports and birth certificates.

The diary with the passwords to all the bank accounts.

The last tax return and super details.

On Uncle Gana's advice, she had already called the bank and their lawyer, accountant, and broker. Uncle Gana said women almost always walked away with less money and often had no idea how much was at stake to begin with. She had to think about Oscar.

She took her mother's jewellery from the safe at the back of the shoe cupboard and placed her engagement and wedding rings there in return.

Finally, she went to Florence's room. She stood at the closed door and allowed herself the moment of imagining and pretending.

She sank to the floor and pressed her ear to the wood. She could hear Florence playing with her Shopkins, chatting away, laughter cascading from her child's sweet mouth, through the door and into her aching heart. Little feet padded from the bed towards her.

Ruben touched her back, lifted her gently and held her.

'We have to go. Aunty Maya said he's heading to the nursing home. I've put everything in the car.'

She nodded.

The moment of imagining and pretending always ended. She opened the door. The bedroom was empty.

MAYA

Jaffna, 1977

The Jaffna Public Library was Maya's favourite place in the world, with its dark floorboards and white stuccoed walls that were covered in books. She corralled the children from Alaveddy Primary School through the halls of the library, waving a newspaper at them to be quiet.

She caught the headline in English.

TAMILS VOTE TO SECEDE FROM SRI LANKA. POST ELECTION BLOOD-SHED. 300 DEAD. A SEPARATE STATE — AT WHAT COST?

She folded the newspaper the other way before the children saw the photographs on the front page.

Maya had spent her childhood playing in the library's corridors while her father restored maps and coded and catalogued archives in his spare time. Now, in her adulthood—at thirty-nine she was, as Shanthi Segaram liked to point out, in her spinsterhood—she found herself still living among the library's towering shelves of books and historical records.

Her father had helped curate the archaeology section of the library, treating it as an extension of his department at Jaffna

University. The library offered him more space for the books and hundreds of maps that meticulously recorded the geographical scope of the ancient Tamil civilisation; a scope vastly different to the diminishing territory of the Tamil people in Sri Lanka.

Maya taught Tamil literature and language to people from across the northern province. Like scholars from around the world, Tamil people came to the library for its famed collection of ancient manuscripts that detailed the longevity and richness of the Tamil culture.

More recently, she had agreed to teach English as part of an outreach program funded by the British Council, something she'd had to justify to her father.

'Appa, the program ensures that poverty is not a barrier to literacy,' she argued.

Her father had snorted. 'The program ensures that *illiteracy* is not a barrier to economic colonisation. It's been thirty years since India and Sri Lanka's independence from those marauding imperialists. The British Council is funding English literacy in the colonies so it can plunder our workforce to enrich its economy. Why don't you study that? Study how much of the Commonwealth is in fact *common* wealth. Let me tell you, mahal, exceptionally high English literacy does not make a successful democracy. It just means we can read about our own demise in more than one language.'

Her father's comments only strengthened her resolve. English was the back-up plan of every Tamil she knew: an escape route from the rising violence between the police and unarmed Tamil protesters. Increasingly, the violence was between the Sri Lankan Army and armed, angry Tamil youth calling themselves the Liberation Tigers of Tamil Eelam.

Despite Appa's disapproval, Maya taught the English classes. Her father's pension had been revoked after the scandal with Jaffna University and she was on a teacher's salary. It was just enough for them to live on, but she wanted to take him to India to see the

Kailash temple at the Ellora Caves. It was supposed to be exquisite. The British Council supplement was too good to turn down.

Maya didn't feel traitorous. She was happy to teach in any language and happy to take droves of children through the corridors of the library. She showed them the parchment maps of Tamil empires, the scrolls of a second-century Tamil census, the textbooks on Ayurvedic medicine and pre-Pythagorean Tamil geometry.

'Public libraries are a beautiful, important place,' she whispered to the children, reminding them to lower their voices too. 'When I was your age, my father told me that if you read the literature of a country, you will understand it; you will fall in love with it.'

The children giggled at the words *fall in love*.

She gathered them around her, shaking her head at their laughter. 'You are never alone in a library. You can never be lonely in a library. You have thousands of friends here.'

She motioned to the books on the nearest shelf, which was somewhat incongruously filled with Irish literature. Although the Jaffna Public Library was a celebration of Tamil culture, a subversive librarian had started to stock Western literature, but only if it was of an equally subversive nature. And so the library contained Irish writers, because they had waged war against the British through their literature as well as through their militants. Maya recognised the subliminal rebellion, the appropriation of language in retaliation for the appropriation of land, and she respected it.

'Children,' she whispered, pulling them closer. 'If you listen, you will hear the voices of generations of people who have tried to understand and record the human condition. These are their efforts to honour human strengths and weaknesses. Our achievements and our failures are all recorded here so that we can better understand ourselves, so we can better achieve our potential. Words are a gift. Books are a gift.'

She took a breath and surveyed her diminutive audience. The children, of course, had no desire to receive these gifts and were hoping to visit the Keerimalai temple pond where a recently rescued family of orphaned baby turtles had been installed. She wasn't expecting applause from them and she received none. However, someone behind her did applaud.

She turned, intending to berate the owner of the ironically delivered accolade, to find a handsome man smiling at her without a trace of irony. His eyes were gentle and clever, his smile broad and confident. He was the kind of man who assumed the recipient of his smile would smile back. She bit her lip in defiance of the rising impulse. What kind of a man applauded a single woman with a group of children? More importantly, what kind of woman would smile in response?

The children were all paying attention now, the rascals. They were watching her intently, and they knew her well enough to detect that she was uncomfortable.

'I would thank you, sir, to leave us alone.' She set her shoulders back to make herself seem taller and more powerful. Then, worried that she was pushing her breasts out, she hunched a little. The entire sequence made her look like she was exercising.

'I don't mean any harm,' he replied, not chastened and not moving away.

'Perhaps not, but still, I would—'

'Thank me to leave you alone. You're terribly polite.'

And this time, she did detect the irony and felt the heat of embarrassment rise up her sari blouse into her neck and cheeks.

That would have been the end of it, except that little Akshay fell to the floor, his body stiff for a moment and then convulsing, his head hitting the ground over and over again. The children scattered and screamed.

'Take them,' the man ordered, motioning to the children. He looked at his watch, and Maya wondered incredulously if there was somewhere else he needed to be right now. He kneeled next to the child and held Akshay's head, stopping it from thrashing. He whispered words of comfort, gentle and at odds with the firmness of his grasp on the boy. Maya could see the sweat on his back soak the crisp white shirt.

When the seizure subsided, Akshay was exhausted and confused. He saw the children staring at him and started to cry.

The man put his arms around him and held him against his chest, wiping his tears and hair. 'It's okay to cry. It's frightening, but you're all right now. Did you know Charles Dickens used to have seizures?' He looked up at Maya as he asked the question. 'It's a mark of brilliance. If you treat it properly, it's not a burden. It's just part of your life, like any other part.'

Akshay nodded and wiped his eyes and nose on the man's shirt.

The man threw his head back, closed his eyes and laughed. It was a carefree laugh. The laugh of someone who found something funny and didn't care if others did or not.

Maya found it funny too and laughed with him.

'My name is Zakhir. Dr Zakhir Ali.'

'You're a doctor, thank God,' Maya said.

'A doctor of archaeology, specialising in Pandya Empire architecture and temple restoration, nothing useful. I threw that in there to impress you. I'm doing some research on the competing histories of Sri Lanka, as told through archaeological discoveries and suppression.'

Had Maya been paying more attention to what Dr Zakhir Ali was saying, and not how he was saying it, she might have realised that he would know her father. Instead, she was increasingly absorbed by the movement of his mouth.

Maya wasn't a frivolous woman, easily seduced or interested in charm. But Dr Zakhir Ali was right. Dickens, one of her favourite authors, was an epileptic and it had never stopped him from achieving greatness. He had instead used it in his work, giving two of his characters the disease, as was the God-Author's prerogative.

And so she replied, 'Do you read Dickens?'

'Or do I simply memorise the medical statistics of famous authors to try to impress young English teachers in the public library?'

'I wasn't impressed,' she replied falsely. She wasn't young either.

'I wasn't trying,' he replied, and she believed him. 'He should go to Jaffna Hospital for a full check-up. It might happen again. Will you speak to his parents about it?'

She nodded. 'Are you sure you're not a doctor?' She was fishing for information.

He laughed. 'I'm sure. But I come here to research and I'm easily distracted by any reading material that does not pertain to Tamil architecture in pre-Buddhist Sri Lanka. I now know a lot about seizures and knock-knock jokes.'

She looked at him, confused.

'*Reader's Digest,*' he said, shrugging his shoulders.

He helped Akshay up and steadied him on his feet. 'You need to rest, thambi; the excursion and journey through literature is over. You have a bus?' he asked.

Zakhir walked with them to the bus and ruffled Akshay's hair before ushering him up the steps to the vehicle. He stood with Maya at the door. The children pressed themselves against the windows, watching, listening and giggling.

'I read Dickens,' Zakhir said. 'He's funny and clever. He notices everything and spares no one.'

'True. Do you study here often?' Maya asked boldly.

'Every Thursday and Friday. I've seen you many times before, but you're so lost in your books you never see me. I'm studying the work of a disgraced archaeologist whose academic work and primary resources are stored here.'

Her heart began to race. 'Which archaeologist?' she asked.

'Dr KN Sriskandarajah,' he replied. 'He's the head archaeological archivist of the library and something of an unsung hero in academic circles. A doomed rebel and a wrongly accused rogue. He famously argued that the Tamils of Sri Lanka arrived on the island first. There are records here at the Jaffna Library and archaeological sites in Jaffna that prove it—sites that have been deliberately destroyed by the government at the insistence of the Buddhist clergy. Dr Sriskandarajah's work has been suppressed and silenced.'

'Possession of land is nine-tenths of the law,' Maya quoted her father. 'Possession of history is nine-tenths of the future.'

'Yes! He says that. Have you read his work?' Zakhir asked.

'Some of it.' It wasn't a lie. She hadn't read all of her father's work.

'I'm always at the Irish Writers section,' he offered.

Her pulse quickened. 'Why there?'

'Because they're all doomed rebels and wrongly accused rogues.'

'Like you?'

He laughed at that. 'No, but I understand that women find them more attractive.' He looked up at the children in the bus. 'I hope I'll see you in the library again. Words *are* a gift. You have lots of them. You should put them down on paper. I would read them.'

With that, he left, a departure that annoyed and confused her.

Maya did return to the Irish Writers section of the Jaffna Public Library every Friday. The first time, she was embarrassed by her own audacity and hopefulness, but rewarded by his presence and his relieved smile. He moved his books over and made space for her. She sat next to him in silence and studied, until finally he spoke.

'You teach here?'

'I do. I also teach English at Alaveddy Primary School and I'm studying English literature.'

'That sounds very useful,' he remarked.

She looked at him closely, searching for sarcasm. He was an archaeologist who specialised in ancient Tamil architecture; what could be more useless?

'It is,' she said. 'I want to be a writer. I've only published short stories so far, but I'm working on my first novel.' She didn't know why she'd told him that. She waited for his response.

He opened his mouth and then closed it.

'Yes?' she said.

'I just wonder why you would study English literature when you could study Tamil literature? Study Kamban and Tiruvalluvar. Study Avvaiyar and Manikkavasagar. If you must, study the north Indians. Study the Bengalis; they're always going on about how clever they are with language. Study the Malayalis; they're always pretending to be Bengali. And they all secretly wish they were Tamil.'

Maya burst out laughing. 'You sound just like my father. You'd like him.'

She caught herself. Had she just suggested she wanted him to meet her father? What was wrong with her? When had she become so forward? Zakhir was studying her father's work and regularly petitioning him to be his post-doctoral supervisor, which her father continued to refuse. She hadn't told Zakhir she was his hero's daughter.

'I already have a degree in Tamil literature and language,' she said.

'You do? How old are you?'

She felt the heat rise in her neck and up to her hairline.

'I'm sorry, I didn't mean to be rude. I'm forty-one years old, Maya, and my parents have told me that my unmarried condition is killing them. Unfortunately for me, not fast enough.'

She laughed. 'I'm thirty-nine. I don't expect to marry. I only have my father and he needs me. I have my father, my books and my writing. Marriage would get in the way of that.'

'How very Virginia Woolf of you. Remember, she died sad and alone.'

'You know it was more complicated than that for Virginia. I want people to read my work. That's why I'm studying English literature.

No one outside of Tamil Nadu and the northern province of Ceylon reads Tiruvalluvar.'

'True. So, you have important stories to tell and the world needs to hear them.'

'You're mocking me.'

'Only a little; you seem like you can take it.'

Their weekly study sessions extended into shared cups of tea. On Fridays, her father took a mobile library to the villages in the Vanni region, so she was able to join Zakhir without his knowledge. Every Friday, they waited for the warden to do his rounds and checked that nosy parker Shanthi Segaram had finished shelving books in their part of the library.

Maya and Shanthi had done their undergraduate degrees together at Jaffna University, but Shanthi's husband Thillai was the son of Proctor Segaram, and Shanthi didn't need to work or study after marriage. Shanthi volunteered at the library, often giving the impression that the venerable institution was lucky to have her, not the other way around. If anyone was going to betray Maya to her father, it would be Shanthi Segaram.

Once they were certain they were safe, Zakhir brought out a thermos and poured two cups of sweet, milky tea, the steam carrying the fragrance of ground cardamom to the back of her throat and making her cough.

Hot tea and wonderful conversation. Over several months, she learned that he was from a Bohra Muslim family who had bifurcated into the Merchants Branch and the Lawyers Branch. The lawyers thought they were more respectable than the merchants. The merchants knew they were richer than the ungrateful, social-climbing lawyers who were standing on the shoulders of generations of spice traders and latex tappers.

'My father likes to talk as though he toiled in the southern lowlands; as though it was his strength that carved and gouged the flesh of the rubber trees until they bled latex, his body that was broken by the weight of all those vats the labourers carried, his sweat that drenched the factory floors, his lungs that inhaled the fumes the enslaved men suffocated on decades before their time.'

'I take it he wasn't a labourer then?' Maya asked.

'Him? No, our forefathers became labour owners more generations back than we can count. We are the buyers of men and manpower. The sellers of the fruits of *their* labour—rubber, coconuts and spices have enriched us.'

'Still, they've worked hard and done well,' said Maya. 'You should be proud.'

'I am proud. No'—he paused—'I'm grateful. They've educated me and, despite trying hard to make me into another spice baron, they have supported me as I follow my dreams.'

'You dreamed of studying obscure temple architecture?' she asked. 'The Pandya Empire ended sometime in the 1300s, following numerous sultanate invasions. No one has needed it since.'

'Perhaps,' he said with a smile, pouring her a second cup of tea. 'I dreamed of building places that brought people together. I dreamed of creating communities and families through stone, wood and cement. I love the Pandya temples because they are simple but audacious testaments to our reverence for mankind.'

'Don't you mean God?'

'No, I mean mankind. Pandya temples are designed for families to pray, study, eat, bathe, and even sleep in their precincts. They are a place of worship and refuge, but also a place of living.'

He blushed. He might have been a rebel, unwilling to follow in his father's footsteps, Maya thought, but he was definitely not a rogue.

'How do you know so much about the Pandyas, anyway?' he asked.

'My father,' Maya said tentatively. 'He likes to read and learn and teach. He studied them, so I studied them. There are remains of the Pandya kings here in the north.'

Appa would love Zakhir. Zakhir already respected her father, the archaeologist. He would love her father, the man.

'Your father sounds very inter—' Zakhir stopped mid-sentence. 'Maya?'

'Yes?' she said, waiting.

'*Maya*? As in *Mayanilayam*?' He was referring to her father's greatest archaeological find, which he had named after her. 'You're his daughter?'

'I am.'

'Why didn't you tell me? Aiyo kadavule!'

'I didn't want to tell you before I knew if you . . .'

'I do. Of course I do. Maya . . .' Zakhir laughed. 'Your father is going to hate me.'

'No, I promise he won't. Just keep talking to him about the Pandya Empire. You'll be fine.'

'Easily done. There are remains of the Pandya kings on the rest of the island too, but the Buddhist monks don't like to talk about that, do they?'

'No, they don't,' Maya answered. Her father had wanted to talk about that and he had been punished for it. 'I went on excavations with him as a child. He's quietly proud of that hidden history. I think he'd like you.'

This time, she *was* inviting him to meet her father. He nodded and she blushed too.

~)

Appa swallowed the last of the tea, which Maya had brewed the way her father liked it.

'You've been generous with the condensed milk,' he noted, placing the empty cup on the table between them. 'What's wrong?' He unfurled the old handkerchief that contained his betel leaves, areca nuts and the rusted cutter that he used to slice them.

'You'll get tetanus from that,' she said, watching him place a small, hard nut in its jaws and slice off wafer-thin shavings.

'You'll get a frontal lobe haemorrhage from storing too much information.'

'That's neurologically impossible.'

'You're a student of language not medicine.'

She explained that she and Zakhir intended to marry.

Her father snorted, causing betel pulp to shoot out of his nose like a blood clot. 'You'll do no such thing!' Despite his resistance to English literature, Appa had been schooled in the English canon like the rest of the country and he couldn't help but sound more like Mr Bennet than Dr Sriskandarajah.

'Shanthi Segaram was delighted to inform me that she'd seen you carrying on with this Dr Ali. The look on her face. I would have fired her there and then, if Proctor Segaram wasn't a patron of the library.'

'That Shanthi Segaram is a rat. She's been waiting to get me into trouble. She hates me, Appa.'

'She doesn't hate you, mahal. She's envious of you. And that doesn't change the fact that you're not marrying him. He's been stalking me, you know: sending me letters, studying my work and asking me to supervise his. He's working on a book expanding my theory of pre-Buddhist proto-Dravidian migration. Dr Mailvaganam says he's always digging around in our archives. Polite fellow. Clever, too.'

'Then you approve.'

'I completely *disapprove*. If you marry him, then I shall be obligated to help him with his fool's errand of a thesis. He's been writing to me for months, asking for my guidance on his work, ordering microfilm from India, using the library's contacts, *my* contacts, to access records, and all the while he has been secretly romancing my daughter. He's a thief and a liar.'

'He's an academic, Appa, not a Kaurava. He's a lot like you, in fact: an erudite Pandava, if you will.'

'Your mythological references, while endearing, are not helpful. All of the Pandavas were erudite, mahal, even the dummies. That's the advantage of a princely upbringing. If he's at all like me, then you should run. The world does not need another academic with an esoteric and unemployable expertise.'

'You'll love him.'

'His family will hate you. They will hate *us*.'

'We're all Tamil.'

'We're Hindu Tamil. They will never accept you. Even if they do allow him to marry you, do you want a life of purdah? I thought you were a feminist.'

'They're not like that. They're Bohra Muslim. They're very modern.'

'Of course they are. Those Bohras think they're better than the rest of their community. Too proud, too rich, too beautiful to have the decency to cover up like the rest of them.'

'Your criticisms are selective and contradictory, Appa. Tamil Hindus are as bigoted as Tamil Muslims, maybe more so. I don't even know how to respond.'

'Respond by saving yourself a lifetime of judgement and get rid of this fellow immediately. If you must get married, Maya, I'll find you a quiet tenured professor from Madras University. Move to India before this country goes to war with itself. It won't matter what kind of Tamil you are then, as long as you're a dead one.'

~⁀

Zakhir stood at the Sriskandarajahs' small dining table. It was covered in maps of archaeological sites, pinned down by stacks of old textbooks and second-hand copies of *National Geographic*.

Maya's father flicked through the handwritten draft of Zakhir's thesis then placed it on the table. 'Sit.' He motioned to the chair opposite him.

Zakhir exhaled and took a seat.

'You too, Juliet.' Appa nodded at Maya.

'I've read all of your work about Mayanilayam, Dr Sriskandarajah, connecting the site in Jaffna to the Sangam and pre-Sangam period temples in South India.' Zakhir was more uncomfortable than when he proposed to Maya. 'I've studied your theories about proto-Dravidian architecture that tie the sites together, and the Tamil-Brahmi script you found carved beneath the Buddhist stupas.'

He took a breath and Maya prayed he would keep talking. Temple archaeology was the way to seduce her father into permitting their marriage.

'Mayanilayam was carved and created first. I want to build on your theory that the early Hindu Tamils of India migrated south to Sri Lanka, before Prince Vijaya and the Sinhalese kings; before Buddhism.'

'I am familiar with my work and its potential for expansion,' Appa said.

'Then you know that the Jaffna Public Library holds all of the archives that cross-reference and confirm your findings. It has all of the primary sources as well as your secondary analysis.'

'Mine and Dr Mailvaganam's. Yes.'

'Dr Mailvaganam has been helping me secretly,' Zakhir said.

'He told me. And there's a reason for his secrecy. If you publish your thesis, you'll have to leave Sri Lanka for the same reason.'

'My thesis builds on your work.'

'I know. I've read it. The language is a little laboured, but Maya could help you with that; she's an excellent writer.'

'Appa!' Maya scolded. 'I asked you to meet my fiancé, not critique his thesis.'

179

'I'm trying to help him. If you're going to marry him, then I don't want to see him excommunicated by the academic community. He needs to be able to get a job and support you.'

'I've supported myself very well, thank you very much. I don't need his money.'

'Good, because his parents will disown him and no university in Sri Lanka will employ him. No one will allow you to publish your findings, Zakhir, let alone teach them.'

Zakhir looked down, his face flushed.

'But you already know that. Why spend so much time and effort on a fool's errand?' Appa asked.

'You are the curator of one of the largest collections of Tamil archaeological archives in the world. You have explored South India and the length and breadth of this small country, looking for and preserving sites that demonstrate who we are and how long we have been here. Why?' Zakhir asked, though Maya was aware he already knew the reason.

'Because national identity, territorial sovereignty and self-determination are grounded in history. Who was here first won't determine who will be here last, but it will help us to understand who has the right to be here at all.'

'Exactly,' Zakhir replied. 'Possession of land is nine-tenths of the law. Possession of history is nine-tenths of the future.'

'Tell me what your parents said about this marriage,' Appa ordered. 'Did they curse my poor Maya as a temptress? Did they try to persuade you to give her up?'

'They did. The imam from the Jami Ul-Alfar Mosque was summoned. He told me that Allah was disappointed in me because I am a faithless son.' Zakhir looked Appa in the eye as he spoke.

'I should have tried that, but Maya would never listen to the brahmin at Nallur temple. She's also a faithless daughter with no respect for authority.'

'She respects you.'

'She does. And I respect her. What else did they say?'

'They reminded me of the slaughter in India during partition. The flare-ups anytime a cow is run over or a Pakistani military vehicle accidentally strays over the border.'

'How dramatic; partition was thirty years ago.'

'That's exactly what I said. I may have added that the carnage was mostly the fault of the British, and Muhammad Ali Jinnah was as bad as Nehru and the rest of them. Then I reminded them that military vehicles on either side of the Indo–Pakistan border rarely stray *accidentally*.'

When she saw Appa suppress a smile, Maya knew he would agree to the marriage.

Her father took Maya's hands in his and touched the engagement ring on her finger. 'You designed this yourself?' he asked.

'I copied a design you copied from the Saraswathi statue at Mayanilayam,' Zakhir replied. 'I had a friend in Colombo make it. Mr Saha works for Mrs Piyadasa and he occasionally accompanies me on my restoration projects. Mrs Piyadasa wants him to learn the ancient designs.'

'It's a faithful reproduction of a piece the world may never see,' Appa whispered.

'It's an homage,' Zakhir said. 'To Maya and to you.'

Maya was both terrified and relieved when Zakhir's mother, Shazia Ali, finally arrived at the Sriskandarajahs' door, dressed in a tailored skirt suit she later learned was Chanel, bought in Paris that year by Mrs Ali personally, not through a relative. It was from the 1977 Spring Collection, which apparently meant something.

Mrs Ali did not cross the threshold into Maya's small house. She stood at the doorway and her eyes drifted inside. Maya flushed red as the woman's gaze took in the Sriskandarajahs' modest furniture, recycled from other family members, the towers of books, scrolls of maps and dusty relics that her father had salvaged from his travels. She lifted her chin defiantly. They were who they were.

Mrs Ali asked only one question: 'Will you leave him?'

Maya had anticipated the moment and she understood that she must stand her ground. She would not be bullied into sacrificing what she wanted.

'I will not. But if he leaves me, I will let him go.'

Mrs Ali raised her hand, fine-boned and armed with heavy rings. Maya braced herself in anticipation. That engagement ring was going to hurt. She closed her eyes but the blow never came.

Her father was at her side.

'Your son's heart knows the way. Let him run in that direction.'

'Rumi was an idiot. You think it is his *heart*—'

'Don't belittle yourself as a mother or your son as a man.'

'Or me as a human,' Maya said, her face ablaze at the woman's implication.

Her father nodded. 'It's time for us to accept that this marriage will happen with or without our blessings. Your son wasn't my first pick either, don't forget that. He's an archaeological architect, for God's sake, and not even a useful one like that Geoffrey Bawa. Unless you're telling me he's going to give up the study of temple architecture and sell renovated old houses to gin-soaked expatriates for a small fortune instead?' He paused. 'No, I didn't think so. But life is a balance of holding on and letting go. I am letting her go so I can hold onto her and our future grandchildren.'

At the mention of the word *grandchildren*, a strangled cry escaped Mrs Ali's lips. She shook her head and backed away, then turned and strode towards her car. Her driver was having a smoke, leaning on the glossy Bentley. He dropped the cigarette abruptly.

'When did you start reading Rumi, let alone quoting him?' Maya asked. Her father was a learned man but he favoured the Tamil poets, not the Sufi ones.

'Since I discovered my grandchildren might be praying in Arabic as well as Tamil. She's right about one thing. Rumi was an idiot. That kind of optimism can only come from drugs.'

Maya laughed and held her father tight.

'Don't mistake me, mahal. I'm worried. Your life will be hard. *You* will never be without family. But *he* will be lost. He will be the branch of the tree cut from the body. It will wither and die. All of us, we are connected, a part of the whole that gave us nourishment. We cannot survive without the whole.'

'You're starting to talk like Rumi. I will be his whole. I will be his tree and his family. I will nourish him; me and the family we create together.'

'Perhaps. I hope so. We were not meant to live like this. We have been joined to our families, our people, and our homeland for a reason.'

Zakhir's father, Farhan Ali, disinherited him. He declared that he had not laboured for decades in mosquito-infested plantations and toxic factories just to see a Hindu girl defraud the family of their hard-earned legacy. He threw Zakhir out of the family home and forbade their extended family from taking him in. He called the university and insisted that the dean of architecture withdraw Zakhir's funding. The dean, a personal friend who had benefited from the Bohra community's generous donations, had no choice but to comply.

Farhan assured his rebellious son that all these privileges would be returned to him if he would agree to give up the impoverished, gold-digging heathen who had seduced him at the Jaffna Public Library.

Zakhir moved in with his uncle Mozammel, who was too rich and too old to care about the scandal. Uncle Mozammel performed the rites at Zakhir and Maya's small wedding at Nallur temple in Jaffna.

'Thirty minutes and four people attending, that's how a wedding should be,' the old man declared. 'None of this six hundred people subjected to a ten-hour pretentious extravaganza business. Who has time for that?'

'I agree,' Appa said, wiping the tears from his eyes.

Maya and Zakhir fell at the feet of the two old men to receive their blessings.

'Your family, your community and your ancestors are here in spirit.' Uncle Mozammel helped the couple up. 'We wish you a long and happy life together, filled with health, happiness and an abundance of children. Inshallah.'

'Inshallah,' Appa repeated. He kissed his daughter and his new son, and then, overcome, he kissed the old uncle too.

Jaffna, northern Sri Lanka, 1978

Maya paced the length and breadth of her father's small living room. She adjusted her sari around her growing belly, loosening the pleats at her waist. At her last appointment with Dr St George, he had palpated her abdomen several times, as though searching for a lost item at the beach. He hurried from the room and called for another doctor, who did the same. After a whispered conferral, they announced apologetically that Maya was probably expecting twins.

'Probably?' Appa repeated. 'Probably twins? Or an eight-limbed foetus?'

Even the memory of this conversation couldn't make her laugh, as she waited for her father and Zakhir to return from Zakhir's latest job interview in Colombo. They were three hours late and Maya could feel it in her heart; something was wrong.

Appa had been right about Zakhir's work. Jaffna University wouldn't employ him or even publish his book. At first, Zakhir thought it was his father's influence. He appealed to the university board of publications and then finally the dean, who explained that the subject material was too controversial. He said had they known the exact nature of his research, they would never have agreed to fund it.

Zakhir was devastated but neither Appa nor Maya were surprised, given that Zakhir's work was based on Appa's work, which had already been silenced. With Appa's help, Zakhir published the book himself, using a small publisher in Colombo who operated out of his garage and was widely rumoured to subsidise his publishing business by secretly printing flyers and manifestos for the communists.

Appa edited the work and agreed to be its co-author, giving it the academic credibility of the head archaeological archivist of the Jaffna Public Library. Her father had been sanctioned for his complicity, suspended and then fired.

In the ten months since his book was published, Zakhir had job interviews with universities, technical colleges and now with private schools in Colombo. Each of them had said the same thing. His findings about the contested histories of Sri Lanka attracted unwanted attention. If he recanted his book, they would consider hiring him. Zakhir refused.

Maya stood on the verandah of the house, staring at the gate. She had walked from the house to the gate to the train station three times already. She had sent Uncle Mozammel to the station to check a further two times. Zakhir and Appa were supposed to be returning on the overnight Yal Devi from Colombo. If they missed that, they could have caught the six o'clock or the seven o'clock. If they were going to be late, they always called. They hadn't called.

She rang everyone they knew in Colombo, including the school, St Anthony's College, where Zakhir had gone for the interview. Appa had spent his final two years of school at St Anthony's, on a scholarship, and Zakhir's interview with the headmaster was a favour to the former student. The headmaster informed her that neither of them had shown up for the interview.

Panic threaded through her muscle and bone, like a cold electric current, making her shake. She held on to the children inside her body, fearful she might loosen them from their peaceful walk through water.

The next morning, she and Uncle Mozammel called everyone they knew in Colombo again, including Zakhir's parents. Appa and Zakhir had been seen getting on the train in Jaffna, but no one had seen them arrive in Colombo. Zakhir's parents started making calls too—to judges and police commissioners. By the end of the second day, Maya packed a small suitcase.

'No, mahal,' Uncle Mozammel said quietly.

Maya checked the contents of her handbag. She had money, the address of Zakhir's family in Colombo, her identification papers and a photograph of them both, taken at their wedding. She had a phone number for her father's friend's son, Mr Gana, a human rights lawyer in Colombo, who had promised to help.

Uncle Mozammel shook his head. 'No, mahal,' he repeated. 'You're staying here. You're a brave and clever girl, but you're not going to Colombo. Your father chose to live here in the safety of Jaffna for a reason. I am going and Proctor Segaram will come with me. The rest of my family—Zakhir's family—will meet us in Colombo, and together we will find them. Stay by the phone. I'll call you. Nahn sathiyama cholluren,' he promised.

Reluctantly, Maya agreed to stay behind.

Four days later, Proctor Segaram's blue Morris Minor saloon arrived at the front of their house. The proctor and Uncle Mozammel had found the missing men and were bringing Zakhir home. Appa's body would not be released.

Apothecary Kathiravel was in her bedroom, his black bag open to reveal painkillers and antibiotics. The bed had been made with clean sheets, and bowls of warm water stood beside it, dressings ready. The old apothecary had been briefed. No hospitals, no records, the police superintendent had insisted.

Proctor Segaram's driver carried Zakhir inside. Maya stood frozen on the verandah, her hands covering the eyes of her unborn children as she forced herself to look at what remained of their father. Gravity seemed stronger than her body, pulling her down to the earth, but Uncle Mozammel was at her side, supporting her.

'Come, child, he needs you now.'

The apothecary cut Zakhir's clothes away from his body. In places the cotton had become fused with the open flesh, and when it was peeled back layers of skin came with it, causing Zakhir to cry out. The whites of his eyes gleamed in pain, and he lashed out with his arms and legs, kicking and pushing them away.

The apothecary pulled Maya back to the doorway. 'The babies. He mustn't kick the babies. We'll take care of this,' he said calmly, like a man who had seen this before. Maya had not seen anything like it. Zakhir's body was covered in lacerations, some deep, some shallow. Some short, some long. From his navel to his penis, his skin was burned—the small, blackened holes were the size of a cigarette, she realised later. She had first wondered *what* had done this. She later wondered *who*.

Her husband's beautiful body, every inch of which she had touched with her fingers and lips, had turned deep shades of purple and orange, colours she had never seen on a body before. She would never be able to watch a sunset without remembering this land-scape of pain, the shifting colours, the swelling and ballooning of flesh, stretched within skin, that shone and cracked at the effort of containing the whole that had been broken into a million parts.

In the quieter moments of her later life, she wondered what her father's body had looked like at the end, and shuddered at the pain he must have felt. The fear.

The apothecary worked quickly and efficiently, despite his age. He washed and dried Zakhir's body and surveyed the damage, making notes in a tattered exercise book. He mixed a combination of drugs from three vials into one injection, and administered it. Zakhir's breathing slowed, his chest finally settling into a steady rhythm. His eyes closed.

The old man threaded ten needles and placed them on the tray next to the sterilised scalpels and scissors.

'Put those gloves on and thread a few more,' he instructed Uncle Mozammel.

Maya watched as the apothecary sewed her husband back together. Some of the wounds were so deep that he sewed the flesh back layer upon layer.

'I'm taking him to Jaffna Hospital for an X-ray,' he said when he was done. 'There are breaks everywhere, and I need to check for internal bleeding. This is beyond my diagnostic skills. There are doctors who will help us. They will be discreet.'

Proctor Segaram shook his head. 'I have no doubt they will, Apothecary Kathiravel, but the superintendent was clear in his instructions. No hospitals. If we take him to the hospital, someone will report this to the Jaffna Police Station, who will refer it to the Central Colombo Police Station. And they will refer it to the people who did this to him.'

'Who did this to him?' Maya whispered, holding on to the doorway for strength. 'Who would do this to them?'

Where is my father? she wanted to scream over and over again. *Bring me back my Appa*, she had cried every day and every night since the proctor had called her from Colombo. Uncle Mozammel had been too broken to speak.

'It doesn't matter; it's done now,' Proctor Segaram answered.

'It doesn't matter?' Maya repeated, confused. 'What do you mean, *it doesn't matter?*'

'I mean the people who did this to him can do it again and again until he doesn't come back to you.'

Proctor Segaram looked at the blood on his hands—her husband's blood.

'He's here now, but there are so many who are not, more than just your father—and you have more to lose. Don't forget that. I'm sorry, Maya, but that's the truth.'

~つ

Zakhir had been held for four days by the Criminal Investigation Department in Colombo. After the fifth hour of interrogation, he had agreed to give them what they wanted. He would have given them anything to stop the pain, and the fear that the pain would go on and on and on. The policemen brought him back to his cell and laid his body next to the lifeless body of his father-in-law.

He agreed to retract his book on Mayanilayam and contested histories. He signed, with broken fingers held in a shaking hand, a letter declaring that he was mistaken in his findings, and that both his work and his father-in-law's had deliberately drawn a false link between temples in India and the temples in Sri Lanka in order to progress their careers. He unequivocally apologised in his letter, on behalf of both of them, for misleading the academic community. He renounced his previous academic accolades. His eyes were swollen shut when the letter was placed in front of him, so he couldn't read it. Nor could he find the place he needed to sign. Blood and sweat dripped onto the letter and he had a muddled recollection that he had been asked to sign a few times, with policemen holding his body upright and directing his hand to the right places.

He agreed to destroy all copies of his book, and all copies of his father-in-law's work were withdrawn from universities across the country. Only the Jaffna Public Library refused the dictum from the Department for Education and maintained a full set of the academic works of Dr Sriskandarajah, including his final contribution to the history of Sri Lanka, the book he had co-authored with his son-in-law.

When Zakhir returned to Maya, he never told her what happened to him. It was only decades later that he told the last friend he made in the world how the police interrogated and tortured him for five hours, and then, even though he gave them what they wanted, they had held him for a further four days and tortured him some more.

For months, Zakhir barely spoke. He followed Maya's instructions and helped around the house when he was asked. He ate when reminded and he bathed when implored. When the twins finally arrived, it was Shanthi Segaram's much nicer younger sister, Prashanthi, who held Maya's hand in the delivery room. Zakhir was outside in the corridor, Uncle Mozammel holding his body as he trembled with her every agonised scream.

The babies gave Zakhir purpose and a routine. Maya returned to work as soon as she could, and Zakhir stayed at home to look after them. His career was over, but he approached the twins like a delicate archaeological project that required thoughtful planning, specialised tools, restoration timetables and appropriate allocation of labour. Books on archaeology were replaced by books on babies.

Maya put away Appa's papers, something she had never been allowed to do before. The dining table underneath was a dark, teak desert, its skin marred by the ink stains that had seeped into the wood from maps that had not been moved for years. It was now both study table and nappy-changing table.

Between Zakhir and Uncle Mozammel, the babies thrived. Zakhir struggled to leave the house without support, but Uncle Mozammel, along with his driver and housekeeper, fetched whatever he needed. Maya hurried home from her job at the Jaffna Public Library and the Mannipay Girls School three times a day to feed them, but her body eventually succumbed to exhaustion and Zakhir weaned the babies off breast milk and onto brown rice kanji several months earlier than she wanted. Zakhir was still a shadow of the laughing, teasing, loving man he used to be, but the children's call was strong and most days he heard them.

Jaffna, 1981

Maya tasted the smoke before she saw it. She heard the fire before she felt it. The roar of Agni, the god of fire, raised against his will and unleashed on the Jaffna Public Library. He raged against his own nature to devour everything in his path. Once started, he was unstoppable, a god with no control over his own power. His river flamed through every floor and corridor, its gluttony aroused but not sated by the sacred texts of the ancient Jaffna kingdom, the Vedic scrolls etched into ola leaves, the yellowed pages of newspapers from the British, the diaries of the first Portuguese traders who came in search of cinnamon, the Dutch who followed the Portuguese, the songs that venerated the Tamil kings who conquered from the northern lands, who made war and peace with the people of Ceylon.

Maya and Zakhir stood on the side of the road watching as the building was eaten from the inside. The people of Jaffna stood with them and cried. The security forces stood in front of the inferno, armed with torches and impunity. The police stood apart from them all and did nothing.

And suddenly, Zakhir was running away from her and into the fire. She screamed and tried to follow him, but people, strangers, were holding her back. He disappeared into the fog of black smoke billowing from its windows and then from its fractured body, splitting open.

She begged the strangers to let her go. She begged them to follow him. She screamed his name and begged him to come back, even though she knew he couldn't hear her above Agni's cry. She screamed at him in anger for leaving her and sank to her knees, remembering her children and why she had to stay, why she had to live. She stared in disbelief as the building she loved gorged on the man she loved.

And then she saw him. Stumbling out of the mouth of the god of fire, rejected by him and returned to her. He was covered in black sweat, his chest heaving with sobs, eyes streaming with tears. He collapsed, too close to the building, and its rain of hot bricks and burning books fell from the sky around him. Men ran forward and dragged him towards her by the shoulders. In his arms, he clutched something tightly to his chest. She turned him over and pried it loose. It was their book: *Reclaiming the Past, Claiming the Future*—the book he had written with her father.

Maya watched over her children as they slept in their bed together, limbs entwined, each breathing in the other's air. Her hands lingered on Siddharth. He was smaller and seemed more fragile than Anjali. She felt the gentle rise and fall of her son's chest. He looked just like Appa when he slept. Her eyes stung with tears.

She couldn't get the smell of smoke out of her home. She had thrown away the clothes Zakhir wore that day; they were singed and torn in some places, and covered in blood in others. He had managed to save more than the book; stuffed into a satchel slung across his body were the maps Appa had drawn based on his work all over the island. She wanted to throw away the satchel along with his clothes, but Zakhir wouldn't let her. He folded the maps neatly and placed them back in the bag along with the book.

The Tamil newspapers told them that no one would be brought to justice for the burning. They would all remember and grieve for the night of 1 June 1981. The houses of Jaffna were infused with the smell of the library's destruction. Maya washed the sheets and frayed rugs, she wiped the inside and outside walls of the small home she had shared with her father since birth. She swept and scrubbed until her body ached almost as much as her heart. Uncle Mozammel visited them daily, his elderly servant Letchumi often accompanying him, pulling a small trolley of food behind her.

He sat down at the dining table with her and pushed an envelope towards her. She needed the money but the shame of it was hard to bear. Her teaching jobs were only just enough for them to live on and the children's needs were changing, increasing.

'Uncle, please. I can't keep taking money from you.'

'I'm not giving you money to live, mahal.'

At the old man's use of the word 'daughter', Maya's eyes filled with tears.

'I'm giving you money to leave.'

It was his turn to cry. Silent tears that found the small canyons and crevices of his ageing skin and made their way slowly to the edge of his jaw. She watched them fall to the table, sit in the dust and then sink into the wood. A small portion of this man captured by the table. Were Appa's tears preserved in this table too?

'Mahal,' Uncle Mozammel repeated.

She lifted her eyes reluctantly.

'It's time. Ceylon will only get worse for the Tamils. Pack up your family and go somewhere—anywhere. You must get out before it's too late.'

'I can't leave. This is my home. This is . . . *was* Appa's home.' She looked around the room, cluttered with the relics of a life spent digging up and deciphering the stories of the past. A life spent recording the stories of their forefathers. A life sacrificed, and another life barely hanging on. Zakhir had good days but he had bad days too.

'Few civilisations are truly dead, mahal,' Appa used to say. 'They have evolved and adapted. They have been killed to the point of extinction but not beyond. They have been absorbed into others, but something of their bloodline and their culture remains in all the future generations. Nothing is ever completely lost.'

Appa was wrong.

'Where would we go?' she asked the old man.

～⁀

Uncle Mozammel bought her father's house from her for an outrageously inflated price. 'When I die, I'll leave it to the twins in my will,' he said as he signed the contract. His lawyer, Mr Abdullah, shook his head in disbelief when called on to witness it. Uncle Mozammel took all of her father's books, except one.

'When they rebuild the library, I'll give them everything,' he promised. Maya could not imagine the library standing over Jaffna again.

Maya kept the book Zakhir had risked his life to save from the fire. She wrapped the satchel in her wedding sari and placed it in her suitcase.

'Will Zakhir bubba like Australia?' Letchumi asked, wiping her tears on the edge of her sari then tucking it back in place. She folded the baby clothes neatly and handed a pile to Maya. 'What is it like?' she asked, reaching for more clothes.

Maya's two cousin-brothers had moved to Perth, on the other side of Australia from Sydney. They helped her apply for a student visa so she could finish her studies in English literature. It seemed that all former colonies were enamoured with the British canon.

'According to Ashan and Nishan, Australia is "very hot and very white".' Their only other alternative was to go to Britain, which Kishan, the third cousin-brother in the set, had described as 'very cold and very white'.

Letchumi shuddered in horror.

Maya applied for a scholarship at the Australian Catholic University in Strathfield, in Sydney's west. It was the only course she could do by correspondence and it accepted most of her current degrees as credit.

Maya and Zakhir started to read about Sydney. Zakhir was a little more like his old self. Motivated and engaged, he researched the strange animals that lived in Australia, like the wild dogs called dingoes, which they should avoid. He showed the twins books with pictures of the sweet but aggressive tree-dwellers called koalas.

He called his cousins in Colombo, the few rebels who were still talking to him after he married Maya, and had them trawl the collection of the Colombo Public Library for him. They found journals written by a Christian minister, Henry Winterbottom, who had settled in the island paradise of Serendib, eventually known as Ceylon and now known as Sri Lanka. The unfortunately named Reverend Winterbottom had spent a gruelling time in Australia, failing to convince the diminishing populations of Aborigines of the value of Christianity. His litany of complaints ranged from the torturous weather to the predatorial snakes to the rugged terrain for which he had not brought the appropriate footwear. However, he reserved his most scathing diary entries for the 'recalcitrant and savage' natives. On arrival at one settlement he grudgingly accepted their hospitality and marvelled at their capacity to cultivate land which, to his British eye, was a desert wasteland.

'He's very pompous, isn't he? Look at these drawings.' Maya leafed through the book Zakhir's cousins had sent him. 'He has no problem breaking bread with them when he's lost and starving, but when they insist on keeping their own religion, he turns quite nasty. What on earth was he thinking?' Maya asked.

'The same thing every coloniser is thinking,' Zakhir replied. 'That he's entitled to dominate, using military technology, religion, and disease, simply because he is who he is. His sense of moral superiority renders him morally depraved, capable of far greater savagery than the savages he presumes to conquer, convert, and steal from.'

Maya leaned over and kissed Zakhir. It was wonderful to hear so many words come out of his mouth.

'They're beautiful, aren't they?' she said, flicking past the diary extracts to the photographs. The Aborigines were as dark-skinned as her father. In one colour portrait, an older woman had large, deep-set eyes and a wide nose. Her thick black curly hair fell to her shoulders. This woman could have been any of Maya's cousins.

When she suggested this to Zakhir, he looked over at the photograph.

'She is beautiful,' he agreed. 'She looks like you.'

Maya put her arms around Zakhir and placed her face in the warm space underneath his jaw. He had shaved for the first time in weeks, and his skin was smooth and a little raw. She inhaled the smell of Sunlight soap from Cargills. He wrapped his arms around her and held her tightly.

She was frightened. The furthest she'd ever been from home was an archaeological dig with Appa in Kathirgamam, in the south of the island. In a week, she would be getting on a plane with Zakhir and the children. Zakhir's childhood friend Cedric had invited them to move in with him. At least they had somewhere to stay when they arrived. Cedric was a bachelor and, by all accounts, a dilettante, but his failing nursing home had spare rooms that he had offered them for free.

'We won't impose on you for long,' Maya had promised when they spoke on the phone.

'It's no imposition, Maya. Zakhir is like a brother to me.' Cedric had paused. She could sense that he wanted to say more, wanted to ask more, but didn't know how.

Her throat tightened. 'Thank you,' she whispered.

'No need for that,' Cedric replied. She could hear the tears in his voice. 'Stay as long as you want. I'm lonely here, and I'm afraid I don't know what I'm doing with a nursing home. It seemed like a good idea at the time. I was going to renovate it to sell, but these old people are taking forever to die. Sorry, that was stupid of me.'

Maya laughed at that. Laughed until she cried.

She often thought of her father's words in the last weeks before they left their home. Families were branches of a tree. Each branch needed the tree but the tree needed soil. The soil of Sri Lanka, which her father and husband had excavated to find the truth, had hardened against them. She didn't want to leave, but she knew she couldn't stay.

NIKKI

Cinnamon Gardens

Nikki sat in the security room, her heart racing. She watched Gareth enter the building, spray sanitiser on his hands and smile at the receptionist. The young woman acknowledged him with a nod but didn't stop flirting with the orderly. Another lady walked in behind him, a Sri Lankan and a regular. The receptionist and the orderly put more distance between themselves, the receptionist assuming a more professional expression, smiling and greeting the lady with a demure, 'Hello, Aunty, how are you?'

She watched Gareth call her again. She had retrieved her phone from Aunty Maya and switched it to silent. He was checking his phone but it couldn't ascertain her location in the nursing home. Her blue dot and his were physically in the same place, but she was out of his reach. She was safe, she reminded herself. She was safe, but Ruben had warned her that her brain would remember the trauma and make her body react in surprising ways.

'Your brain and body are just trying to protect you, Nikki,' Ruben had said. 'But remember, you're here and you're safe.'

Nikki exhaled, invoking his words, repeating them to herself.

Gareth called again.

She picked up this time.

'Nikki. Hi, it's me,' he said.

There was a pause.

'Gareth,' she replied. 'Wait for me in the games room. I'll meet you there.'

'How did you know I was here?' he asked, turning around to see if she was nearby.

'I'm in the security room. We're getting new cameras for the outside walls and gates. Uncle Saha, one of the residents, keeps finding a way out, despite all the security.'

He looked around and saw the camera in the front corridor. He looked into the lens and, for a moment, she thought he could see her.

Her body went cold and she started shaking.

No. She was safe, she repeated. She was safe in the nursing home. She could see him but he couldn't see her. Not unless she wanted him to.

'Of course. Thank you, Nikki. I'll be in the games room.'

She exhaled. She switched to another TV screen and watched Gareth enter the games room and take a seat at an empty table by the door. A group of residents were seated in a circle in their wheelchairs and chairs, blankets across their laps. Also present were a nurse and Farmer Rob, who was taking small rabbits and guinea pigs around the group and offering the residents a chance to interact with them. The residents were laughing with delight, many taking a turn at hugging the docile creatures to their chests.

Nikki left the security room and went to the games room.

'Pet therapy,' she said.

Startled, Gareth turned around.

'Farmer Rob comes once a month from Dural,' she continued. 'It does wonders for the residents emotionally, while lifting the animals strengthens their upper bodies and fine motor skills.'

'Right.'

There were children in the room too, playing with the animals. Although a home for the elderly, Cinnamon Gardens was often full of young people visiting their grandparents and great-grandparents. It was a place where extended families were constantly running into each other.

She turned and walked from the room. Gareth followed her through the old nursing home and down the covered walkway to the newer nursing home behind it.

She left the building and walked to Ruben's cottage at the bottom of the garden. She motioned to the bench on its verandah but neither of them sat down. They stood at either end of the verandah, staring into the garden without facing each other. It was easier this way.

'Nikki,' he whispered.

He wasn't entitled to say her name like that anymore.

'Nikki,' he tried again. 'I'm so sorry. I—I had no right.'

She didn't say anything. She was poised for flight if he moved the wrong way, but she felt her shoulders shift a little, a fragment of ease in the tight coil of her body.

'I'm sorry. Please tell me what I can do to make it better. Please . . .' Tears shone in his eyes, but the shame on his face didn't touch her. Nothing about him could touch her anymore.

'Please,' he said.

'Please what?' she asked.

'Tell me, talk to me, please. What can I do?' he repeated.

'Nothing at all. There's nothing you can do, Gareth. We're fine.'

'We are?' He took a step towards her.

She took a step back; her body shuddered without her permission.

'Yes. We're okay.'

Okay. Such a nothing word. They weren't nothing but they weren't something good.

'We're okay, finally,' she exhaled on the word *finally*, as though she had been holding her breath. Holding her breath for the hours since he had hurt her. For the ten months since Florence had died. Finally, she exhaled and could inhale again.

She welcomed the clean and cleansing air. She inhaled deeply.

'We're okay, because we're over. We've been over for months, maybe since she died, maybe even before that. It doesn't matter now. After last night, there's no going back for me. For us. There *is* no us.'

She paused to catch her breath. Another clean and cleansing breath. She felt her body expand and her heart rate slow. She turned her face towards the sun and let it warm her body. Surya, the sun god. Her tremor dissolved in the light.

'We should sort out the details as soon as possible, but I have patients now. I'll email you later.'

Nikki stepped off the verandah and walked up the path towards the nursing home. She didn't look back.

GARETH

Cinnamon Gardens

Sort out the details. What were the details of their life together? Love, marriage, one child and another child.

That was before he had tried to—he couldn't even say the words—his wife. He wished he could go back to that moment yesterday when he had only been a dick outside the nursing home instead of . . . He shook his head.

He wished he could go back to that moment when he took Florence to the nursing home to visit Ray. If he could just change that one moment, it would change all the others that followed.

He remembered the look in Nikki's eyes that night. And last night. She shuddered and then drew herself inwards. He had never seen that cold resolve in her before. Her profile still, the features of her face set hard and unrelenting. She was right to look at him that way. He was repugnant.

The details. What were the *other* details of their life together? Love, marriage, one child and another child. A drifting, a death, a sinking.

The panic in Gareth's chest turned to a sharp pain. He couldn't pull air into his lungs. He stumbled forward and reached for the bench, just missing its arm, falling to his knees next to it and then toppling forward onto his stomach. He rested his face on the wooden floor, placed his palm on its knotted surface, worn and splintered by the passage of time. Even the verandah of this cottage was given the privilege of ageing.

He lifted himself back onto his hands and knees, his head dropped between his shoulders. Between the gaps in the floorboards, he caught a glimpse of a grey face staring back at him. Eyes open but lifeless. Face haughty but unmoving.

He jerked away in shock at the sight of the dead body, and then looked again, afraid of what he would find. A familiar face, stoic and unimpressed with Gareth's unspooling, returned his gaze. Searching for more gaps in the floorboards, Gareth paced up and down the verandah, finally recognising what he was seeing but not understanding why he was seeing it.

He stepped off the verandah, lay down on his stomach and used his elbows to propel himself towards the man trapped there. He reached the body, bronzed and hardened by captivity. He raised himself over the man, coming nose to nose with a face he had seen so many times that he had stopped noticing him.

Later, Gareth would look back and try to identify what it was about the statue of Captain James Cook that so incensed him. Once he realised he wasn't looking into the eyes of a dead body, hidden among the weeds and overgrown grass, his fear subsided. The incongruity of the great explorer lying prone, his body discoloured by lichen blooms and oxidisation moving like a rash across his clothing, should have made him laugh. He should have thought, How strange.

Instead, he didn't think. He couldn't think.

'Gareth, what are you doing down there?' Anji was squatting by the steps, shining her phone torch at him. 'There are spiders—come out.'

Gareth commando-crawled out, as ungracefully as he'd crawled in, and emerged covered in grass, dirt, bindis, and the faint tendrils of imagined spiderwebs he kept trying to swat away.

'What's that statue doing down there?' he asked, brushing down his clothes and adjusting them.

'The statue?' she replied, confused, looking back at the verandah. 'Oh, that.' She kneeled down again and flashed her phone torch into the darkness. 'There you are,' she said to the statue, as though it were a lost child she'd been looking for.

She stood back up again. 'I'd totally forgotten about that. How did you find him?'

'I . . . I dropped my keys. Why do you have a statue of Cook . . .'

'Stashed under the verandah of our family home?' She shrugged. 'There was nowhere else to put him.'

Gareth instinctively smiled back at her. There was something about Anji and her mother too: the humour was always gently teasing, but not harsh. You wanted to be teased by them; it made you feel as though you mattered. You were loved enough to be the subject of a loving joke. A joke between friends. Nikki obviously hadn't told her about last night yet.

'Are you coming back to the nursing home?' she asked.

'Yes—actually, no. I should head back to work. I just popped in to see Nikki. I'll let myself out, thanks, Anji. See you later.' He walked away quickly, his heart still pounding.

Gareth sat at his desk, relieved that Richard and Bella were out for lunch. Remembering their hushed tones and pitying expressions from the morning, he clenched his hands into fists over his laptop and then relaxed them as he stared at his monitor. He typed *Cinnamon Gardens* into Google and found a map of a suburb of Colombo, many references to a book of the same name by Shyam Selvadurai and tourist information about Cinnamon Gardens, the suburb.

He typed in the additional search term *nursing home*, and found the website of the Cinnamon Gardens Aged Care Home. Nikki had mentioned that one of Anji's second cousins was in IT (of course), and she had designed an impressive site, complete with sun-drenched photos of happy old people who looked as though they had found a second lease on life since moving in with other happy old people.

Gareth flicked through the website.

No, he did not wish to apply for a room. He wished Nikki had never applied for a room there. He kept going back and forth, finding no clue as to the existence and destruction of the statue. He closed the website and tried a new approach, searching the address itself.

This revealed far more.

The building was once the municipal office of the Parramatta Council. It had been a seat of power, hence its grand architecture and grounds. The previous nursing home owners had built the second building at the back and Anji's family had restored the heritage house and added another wing to the newer building as well as a small visitors car park.

He searched for images, pulling up a series of black-and-white photos, and finally found what he was looking for: an old photo of the nursing home in the heyday of its government glory, before a wall was built around it. The statue stood at the front, resting on a sandstone plinth. It was imposing, despite the grainy tone of the photograph. He pinned that image and looked for others.

After scrolling through more old photos, he found a close-up of the statue. It was taken from the ground, looking up at Cook's face, so that the man towered above them all, his eyes staring into the vast and sweeping continent ahead of him. Gareth tried to zoom in on the plaque beneath the statue but its words were blurred.

～つ

Gareth's hands shook as he tried to fit the key into the front door lock. He had spent the afternoon researching the history of the building that was now Cinnamon Gardens. Most of the photographs of the nursing home were relatively recent. Some revealed the empty plinth that he now remembered in the front garden but had never scrutinised before.

His house was dark and empty. On the kitchen bench, Nikki had left another note.

Oscar and I are sleeping at Anji's. Please don't come there. I need space.

Gareth drove straight over, hesitating before he knocked on the door. Inside, he could hear the opening music from the ABC's 6 pm news and then footsteps coming down the corridor towards him, Anji's silhouette pausing before she opened the door.

She didn't know before, but she knew now, the judgement barely masked by tightly controlled neutrality.

'Gareth.'

'Anji.'

'I can't let you in, Gareth.' She shook her head. 'You know I can't. She doesn't want you here. Oscar is doing his homework upstairs with the kids. He doesn't know what's going on.'

'Neither do I,' he replied. 'I made a terrible, terrible mistake. I know that. I wasn't thinking. I just . . . I just lost control. If I could take it back, I would.' He could feel the tears streaming down his face. He wasn't just talking about last night and she knew it.

'Take it back?' Anji said softly. 'Take it back?' An edge sharpening and rising in her voice. 'There's no—' She stopped herself, her mind seeming to sort through possible responses as she tried to frame a reply.

'She said you can talk to her at the nursing home tomorrow. She's there all day.'

'Is she—how long is she staying here? Is she coming back?' The questions clung to the inside of his throat, as if once spoken, and once answered, there was no going back.

Anji shook her head. 'You need to talk to her when she invites you to talk to her,' she said. 'Goodbye, Gareth. Take care, and please don't come to the house again.'

She shut the door and he stood there for much longer than he should have.

～◯

Gareth was waiting at the nursing home door when Nikki arrived the next morning. She tensed when she saw him and then steeled herself.

'Gareth, I can't talk. Uncle Saha has disappeared again and I need to do Anji's rounds. She has to find him before he hurts himself.'

She tried to push past him but he moved into her path, careful not to touch her this time.

'Nikki,' he began.

He had thought through every word and rehearsed his speech over and over last night until he could recite every aspect of his carefully crafted apology.

'Nikki, I'm a monster. What I did was unforgivable. I need help, real therapy, like you've suggested from the start. Since Florence.'

At the mention of their daughter's name, Nikki looked up sharply. Something shifted in her eyes. He recalculated. He wasn't trying to blame his behaviour on Florence's death. There was no excuse for it. But since her death, he had not been the same. *They* had not been the same.

He tried again. 'Nikki . . .'

'Don't,' she whispered. 'Don't bring Florence into this.' She stopped and took a deep breath. 'I'm moving out of our home, Gareth. Anji's letting me stay with her until I work out what I'm going to do. On the weeks I have Oscar, he'll be there with me too.'

'The weeks you have Oscar?' he repeated.

'Yes. For now, if you're agreeable, let's do week on, week off. When he's with you, I'll get out of Anji's way and stay at the nursing home. There's an empty room here I can use until I work out something more permanent.'

'More permanent.'

There were never any empty rooms at Cinnamon Gardens, not for long anyway. The waiting list was extensive. It was a running unfunny joke that Anji and Nikki looked after the residents so well they didn't die often enough.

'Yes, more permanent.' She too had prepared for this meeting.

She walked past him and swiped her card to enter the building before opening hours. He sat on the front step and loosened his tie and shirt collar. The empty plinth stood in front of him. It was surrounded by giant agaves, the leathery leaves of the succulents pointing up to the sky and obscuring a clear view of the sandstone.

He walked through the agaves and circled the plinth. The monument had been removed and the top of the plinth had a small mosaic in the centre instead, all traces of its original purpose erased.

'Gareth? Is everything okay?' It was Anji, standing in the nursing home driveway. Behind her, he saw Ruben walking with an elderly man at his elbow. The missing Uncle Saha had been located.

'Hi, just checking out the plinth. I guess the statue used to stand here.'

Anji nodded hesitantly. 'Cook's ears must be burning. He hasn't been talked about this much since . . . well, since Appa took him down.'

'Appa? Your father?' Gareth asked, recognising the Tamil word. Anji had rarely talked about him since his death.

She looked at Gareth uncertainly, as if unsure of how to respond to him, then fell back on politeness.

'Yes, Appa took him down a few years after we moved in. Uncle Saha here helped him.' She nodded at the old man, who smiled and nodded.

'I was responsible for the reconstruction work afterwards,' he said. 'The plinth took a beating and those Greek boys destroyed the garden. We were lucky no one lost an eye that day.'

'Right,' Gareth said, confused. 'When was this?'

'I think I was about six or seven,' Anji replied. 'I remember Appa took us to see *Back to the Future* afterwards, so that was, what, 1985?'

'Why did he do that?'

'Because it was a great movie.'

'I mean—'

'I know, I know, sorry. I just . . . this is . . . I don't know what this is.' She wasn't talking about the missing statue. 'I asked him about it later. He said Captain Cook was a symbol of colonisation and he wouldn't celebrate it. He had lots more to say but that was the crux of it.'

She whispered instructions to Ruben in Tamil and kissed Uncle Saha on the cheek, scolding him at the same time.

Ruben walked the old man slowly back to the nursing home. There was something about Ruben's face that told him he knew what Gareth had done too. He remembered the sound of easy laughter and the circle that didn't include him. Unformed thoughts coalesced briefly into sharp clarity and then dissolved again.

'I never thought of your dad as an activist, Anji.'

'Me neither. He wasn't an activist so much as very principled about certain things, and this was one of them.'

When he didn't say anything, she continued. 'Listen Gareth, about you and Nikki . . .'

'You don't need to say anything. I know you're her best friend and she needs you right now. Thank you for looking after her.' Gareth had rehearsed his response to Anji already. He wouldn't gain anything by alienating her, even though he wanted to beg her to plead his case with Nikki. Or scream at her for giving Nikki an easy way out.

'Okay, sure,' Anji said. 'Well, I've got to get going—meetings. Take care of yourself, Gareth.'

She reached forward automatically to touch him and then stepped back awkwardly, as if remembering that his presence was unclean. She left him alone, staring at the empty plinth.

~つ

His hands lingered on the laptop, reading the online complaints form again. Gareth whispered the questions out loud, afraid someone might hear him in his empty house and judge him for what he was contemplating doing. The questions on the Australian Human Rights Commission website were straightforward and easy to understand. Designed for people with significantly less education than him, the needy demographic much more likely to make such an application.

'Who is the complaint about?' he repeated to himself.

He filled in the nursing home's details, typing in Anji's name as the respondent.

'What is your relationship to this respondent?'

His heart pounded. If he did this, he would have no relationship with Anji and Nathan going forward. He typed in: 'A family member is a resident at the nursing home.'

'When did the alleged event(s) happen?'

He typed in today's date.

'What happened?'

Gareth reread the brief prepared by Bella, checking the definition of offensive behaviour again.

The nursing home also met the definition of a public place. Anji's 'offending act' was not made in private and it didn't fall within the exceptions listed in the legislation. He took a deep breath and began to type.

ANJALI

Cinnamon Gardens

The Australian Human Rights Commission had called to tell her about Gareth's complaint, so Anji was expecting the email when it landed in her inbox, but not the exact content of it. The Commission's complaints manager had advised her to cease all communication and contact with the complainant, as he was now known, and to be civil if she saw him at the nursing home or elsewhere.

She had always tried to be civil to Gareth, even when Nikki couldn't look at him after Florence's death. Even when he came across as 'a bit of a prick', as Nathan would say after their dinners together, Gareth having been invited for Nikki and Oscar's sake.

She read Gareth's complaint several times and then forwarded it to Nathan and her lawyer, Uncle Gana in Room 5. She had briefed both already, based on the call from the AHRC. Uncle Gana—or Advocate Ganapathipillai as he was known to his former clients—talked her through the Racial Discrimination Act. He had been a junior barrister—more of a clerk, according to his wife, Aunty Rudra—at the chambers of the famed SS Sivagnanaratnam, the barrister, King's Counsel and politician who had opposed the

210

Sinhala Only Act in Sri Lanka's Supreme Court in 1956. It was the most racist legislation ever approved by the country's failed Westminster system.

Aunty Rudra used to remind her poor husband that she could have married a Sivagnanaratnam if she wanted to. No one reminded her that SS Sivagnanaratnam's son, Giri Sivagnanaratnam, had later been executed in his car at close range, allegedly on the orders of the president of Sri Lanka, Chandrika Kumaratunga, whose own father, former prime minister SWRD Bandaranaike, had been responsible for the Sinhala Only Act.

Coming from a high-profile family of activists came at a cost in Sri Lanka, and Uncle Gana was delighted to spend his life preparing the briefs that other advocates argued in the compromised courts of their homeland. Their son, Kogulan, was a successful maxillofacial orthodontist in Toronto and would, God willing, live much longer than any of the Sivagnanaratnams.

Uncle Gana's legal opinion was that while Anji's explanation of the reason for the removal of the Captain Cook statue from the nursing home might have been regarded as offensive to Australians who considered themselves to be descendants of European settlers, her comments—in fact, her father's comments and actions—were not made *because of* the race, colour or national or ethnic origin of Gareth or of some or all of the people in the group that he considered himself a part of. The act was not done or directed to Gareth or his race; and it was not done because of Gareth's race.

Uncle Gana noted that conciliation was designed to avoid the parties ending up in the Federal Court, which Gareth could appeal to if they failed to agree to a resolution and/or the president of the AHRC rejected his complaint.

Anji felt a rush of fear at the words *Federal Court*, but Uncle Gana assured her that according to the AHRC's extremely helpful website, very few matters progressed from the Commission to the Federal

Court, given their limited prospects of success and the expense of making an appeal.

This all required the complainant to be rational, which Anji wasn't so sure about.

She looked at the last section of the complaint form, which asked: 'How do you think this complaint could be resolved?'

Gareth had suggested that the statue be returned to its 'rightful' place.

Not a chance, Anji thought to herself. Not a fucking chance.

Uncle Gana instructed her to draft her response to the complaint. He would review her work tomorrow after yoga and bridge.

And so Anji sat at her computer in her office and cast her mind back thirty-five years . . .

Cinnamon Gardens, 1985

A maritime compass in one hand and a telescope in the other; these were the tools that would take Captain Cook to lands he would claim for the Crown. When they first moved into Cinnamon Gardens, Siddharth would hoist Anji onto the plinth and then she would drag him up with her. Barefoot, they would hold on to the man's legs, each desperate not to be the one with their face pressed against his bronze buttocks.

They would then empty their pockets of food from the previous night's dinner they didn't want to eat, hiding it in the contours of his regal uniform. Thus, magpies and Indian mynas were drawn to poo all over the great man, until Uncle Cedric realised what they were doing and shooed them away with an affectionate, 'Chee chee, defiling the captain, no respect for authority, just like your mother.'

Every day, Anji walked past the captain, saluting him on the way to school and on the way home. She did the same when she passed him at other times, too, such as when Appa was 'suffering from a medical illness', as Amma put it (as though there were non-medical illnesses that people could suffer from). On these occasions, Anji and Siddharth were given a job to do. They went to their parents' room and rolled around on their father's body until he stirred awake. Then she and Siddharth each took one of their father's hands and dragged him outside for a short afternoon walk. There was always something Amma needed from the newly opened Sri Lankan store at the bottom of their street: Brylcreem, Horlicks, arthritic stalks of lady's fingers—the random list went on. The shopkeeper, Uncle Varatharajan—who later retired to Cinnamon Gardens—gave them Bulto candies, imported from Sri Lanka, and tried to engage Zakhir in conversation.

On these walks, Appa was mostly silent. Anji prayed they didn't run into her school friends. They would see that her archaeologist and historian father was less like Indiana Jones and more like the Indian zombies who had drunk Kali Ma's poison in the second film—which, incidentally, was set in Sri Lanka and not India and featured many cultural stereotypes and inaccuracies according to Amma, who wouldn't let her watch it again after the first time.

Aunty Selvadurai in Room 10, on the other hand, didn't care about racial stereotyping, whatever that was, and she had a VCR in her room which she let Anji watch *Indiana Jones* on, if she stole cigarettes for her from Nurse Devi's locker.

Anji was ashamed at the embarrassment she felt over her father. Siddharth didn't care what Appa was like or what people thought of him. Anji cared about all of it. She didn't like the kind looks Uncle Varatharajan gave him or the funny looks from the nurses when Appa would run up from their cottage in his pyjamas, his banyan stained with sweat and his hair fanned out like a palm tree. He frantically searched the corridors of the nursing home, looking for Amma and the children. Amma would reassure him that everyone was safe then gently lead him back to bed, slipping a crushed tablet into the warm turmeric milk she prepared for him.

But on one walk, when they entered the nursing home grounds and Anji and Siddharth saluted the captain, as they often did, her father froze.

'What are you doing?' he asked, softly. He looked startled by the sound of his own voice, strange even to his ears.

The children were startled too.

'What did you do just then?' he asked again, flicking his head towards the bronze statue. Cook's brown skin glistened in the afternoon sun, chocolate deepening into black, with random bursts of green. 'Oxidisation,' Chemistry Master Puvana in Room 9 called it.

'We're saluting the captain,' the twins replied, speaking in unison as they often did.

'Saluting the captain?' Appa repeated slowly, practising the sounds as he spoke, each syllable emerging stronger than the one before it. 'Why?'

The children looked at each other, confused. Everyone knew *why*.

'Because he's the captain,' Anji replied.

Appa looked at her, his eyes clear and shining. She met his gaze. His dark pupils were flecked green. Amma said this was the Moor in him; her father was descended from Arab traders. Biology Master Chelvanayakam came to visit Chemistry Master Puvana at the nursing home once. He said her Moorish father was genetically predisposed to mental weakness and mercenary tendencies. Amma told the biology teacher not to visit ever again.

Anji waited, holding her breath.

'The captain?' Appa repeated. 'Not of this ship,' he said, and smiled.

~⌒

The next day, Anji and Siddharth sat on the front steps of Cinnamon Gardens, eating freshly fried murukku, snapping coils of it off and grinding it into a pulp in their mouths. Appa was in the front garden, sizing up Captain Cook.

214

Uncle Cedric walked out holding two buckets with their bottoms cut out and split open. The old chemistry master walked behind him with the help of a nurse, holding a large tin in both hands. The nurse held a second tin. Each was branded with the words Mitre 10 and an ominously large skull and cross.

Chemistry Master Puvana instructed Uncle Cedric to wrap the adapted buckets around Captain Cook's feet, like cuffs, and to seal the bottom of the buckets with the tape.

'We're going to be deported,' Uncle Cedric complained, 'I know it. First Oxford and now Australia. The shame is going to kill me.'

'The intense exothermic heat, molten bronze or falling statue is more likely to kill you,' Appa said.

Old Mr Petsas's four sons had been summoned along with six of their cousins, all of whom had the stocky physiques of men who laboured hard their whole lives. They tied safety ropes and harnesses around the body of Captain Cook, and connected these to the muscular boughs of the eucalypt that towered over the garden.

'The tree will catch him when he falls,' one son explained confidently.

Uncle Cedric took a step back.

They wrapped a second harness around the captain, attached to a small wheel that was also thrown over a bough of the tree.

'This one's a winch,' another Petsas son said. 'When the statue falls, the first harness will catch him, and the second harness will help us lower him to the ground in a controlled manner.'

Uncle Saha was called. He brought his own tools. Amma said he was a famous jeweller in Sri Lanka.

'Will he be hiding gems in the plinth?' Anji asked Siddharth, imagining an *Indiana Jones* scenario taking place in their own front yard. Finally, she was living the archaeologist's dream.

'Don't be stupid,' Siddharth hissed back.

Amma came to sit between them with a cup of tea and a packet of sparklers. 'She's not stupid. He *is* going to put gems in the plinth.'

They both turned to her, eyes wide.

Amma laughed and explained. 'Uncle Saha will create a navarathinam for our family at the front of our home. He will place nine gems on the top of the plinth, each representing one of the nine celestial gods in our mythology.'

'Like Paata's ring?' Siddharth asked, opening the sparklers and pulling one out.

Amma nodded, her face pained at the mention of her father. Their grandfather had died before they were born, and they only knew him from the stories that Amma would sometimes tell, with tears in her eyes. Appa never talked about him at all.

'Exactly—like Paata's ring.' Their mother wore the ring on a chain around her neck, next to her heavy gold wedding chain. 'Uncle Saha has chosen the gems for us. A Ceylon ruby in the centre to represent the sun, and a Ceylon sapphire to represent Saturn, and then Australian gems for all the other planets.'

'Why only two stones from Cey—Sri Lanka?' Siddharth asked.

'I want the two most powerful planets to be represented by stones from our old home. Saturn has to be appeased for all of us, especially your father.'

Amma looked at Appa, who was standing in the centre of the chaos, calling out words like *tension*, *torque*, *yield strength* and *megapascals*. He was waving his arms around, mimicking the potential flight path of the statue and issuing instructions, his voice clear and full of energy.

'It's working already,' Amma said, smiling at Appa.

'Already?' the children whispered, Anji thinking about the magical gems that were about to be entombed in the plinth.

'What if someone steals them?' she asked. Archaeological sites were always being raided, hence the need for booby traps.

'No one will steal them because no one will know. Uncle Saha will do it quietly.'

The children nodded, not doubting the gem-concealing skills of Uncle Saha.

'Okay,' Appa shouted. 'Everyone ready?'

The four Petsas sons nodded, each holding a support rope in gloved hands, their legs braced. Their cousins all took sections of the rope, similarly gloved.

They watched as Mr Petsas put on thick but fitted gloves and a helmet with a drop-down visor that made him look like a storm trooper. He fired up his propane gas torch.

Appa shook his head. 'Chemistry Master Puvana says we won't need it.'

Mr Petsas nodded at the chemistry master holding the two large tins.

'Just in case your science doesn't work,' Mr Petsas said.

'Everything is science and science always works,' Chemistry Master Puvana replied.

Mr Petsas scoffed in return.

Appa grinned at Amma, and Anji saw her mother blush.

Under the supervision of the chemistry master, Appa poured the contents of the tins into the plastic cuffs around the statue's feet until the powder reached the top of the bucket. He stirred the combination together with a wooden chopstick until he seemed satisfied he had the combination he wanted.

'Anji?' Appa held out his hand.

She ran forward with the packet of sparklers and presented them ceremoniously. He nodded and she ran back to the verandah.

Appa pulled out a box of matches from his pocket. 'Behold, chemistry. Iron oxide and aluminium powders, mixed together. Ignited with this sparkler'—he raised the sparkler like a magician's wand—'it will create a thermite reaction, reaching a temperature of almost nine hundred and fifty degrees Celsius, and then burn out quickly, but not before melting the feet of this man.'

He turned and shoved several sparklers into the chemicals, lit them and ran to the verandah, where he stood in front of the children as if to shield them.

The bright sparks traced a path down the thin wire to the deadly combination in the buckets. Anji held her breath. For a moment, nothing happened and she exhaled, disappointed. And then she saw the light glow from within the buckets. Seconds later, Captain Cook's feet were sparking in every direction, each one of them a star of white light shooting out. And then, beneath the light, Anji saw red molten metal ooze like lava down the plinth and towards the earth. The statue began to sink into the liquefying feet and then swayed forward.

The men on the ropes were not distracted by the fireworks display. Seasoned welders and builders, they'd seen liquid metal before, although admittedly not bleeding from the feet of Australia's founding explorer.

Just as Appa had said, Captain Cook swayed and then toppled forward, cracking off from what was left of his feet. The ten men on the ropes all leaned back into the cables, their legs wide and feet firmly planted. If even one of them slipped, the statue could swing fatally the wrong way. The mighty gum whose torso and limbs were bearing much of the weight seemed to groan and then rally, holding its place, anchored to the earth by deep roots that were older and stronger than Cook.

Appa clapped his hands and jumped off the verandah.

Mr Petsas turned off his propane torch and shouted instructions to his sons and nephews in Greek, guiding the gradual transfer of weight from stone plinth to tree and man. Together, their skin sweating, their muscles and tendons raised and stretched, sucking in air through gritted teeth, the ten men lowered Cook towards the ground. Appa rushed forward with the massive dolly and, inch by inch, they placed him horizontally on its metal base.

Two of the Petsas sons used their ropes to strap Cook to the dolly, a prisoner bound and ready for transport.

Old Mr Petsas beamed at his family with pride, then looked at Appa. 'Where do you want him?'

∼ↄ

For the next week, Anji and Siddharth were famous at school for having a dead body under their house. CJ Cook was a criminal who was never convicted for his unspecified but heinous crimes. Anji alluded to murder and theft of profound proportions. She offered eyewitness testimony in the playground: CJ Cook came to a fiery end and his body disposed of.

'You never can be too sure,' she told her best friend Nikki, who told her mother Bek, who called Maya to find out whether Maya was a nursing home operator by day and a vigilante by night.

'That's my husband, Zakhir,' Amma replied. 'Sri Lankan justice is swift and waits for no court.'

Bek laughed. 'What really happened?'

Amma explained that a resident with dementia had been scaring the children with suburban ghost stories.

Anji's playground fame turned to shame when Nikki's mother told Georgie Jones's mother. Georgie Jones was golden-haired and captain of the under-eights netball team. She called out Anji on the netball courts one Friday afternoon. Georgie teased Anji so much she weed herself in front of the other girls, a seemingly endless amount of warm urine pooling in her sandshoes and spilling onto the asphalt. Nikki marched right up to Georgie Jones and kicked her in the shins. All three girls got into trouble.

'Why didn't you just tell her it was a statue, not a real person?' Appa asked Amma, holding Anji as she sobbed.

'Because Captain James Cook is a national hero and people are protective of their national heroes,' Amma replied. 'Don't cry, mahal,' she said to Anji. 'The dead body is our little secret, just like the gems. Uncle Saha is back—why don't you and Siddharth help him?'

Anji ran outside to the plinth. Uncle Saha and Siddharth were already standing there: Uncle Saha with his hands on his hips, studying it; Siddharth next to him, copying him.

Mr Petsas's sons had cleaned up the plinth, freezing the molten copper with liquid nitrogen and then gently chipping it away, leaving the sandstone column standing in the centre of the small garden, which itself stood in the centre of the regal circular driveway.

With a chisel and hammer, Uncle Saha scraped back a layer of sandstone the size of Anji's palm. He opened up several tins and began mixing the substances together.

'It's a polymer-based resin used in Hindu temples,' he explained, stirring the substance harder as it thickened and darkened quickly.

'Are you ready?' he asked Siddharth, who was holding the gems in his hands. Her brother gave half to Anji carefully. 'The resin will dry in a few minutes. That's why we have to work quickly.'

Siddharth nodded and Uncle Saha spread the mixture in the indentation. Without a word, he took the gems from their outstretched palms in an order that only he knew, and placed them in a design that only he understood. Eight stones orbited the Ceylon ruby in the middle.

The design was small, like a flower blessed with petals of different colours. In the afternoon sun, the ruby glowed, casting a pink haze around the other stones.

'The beauty of a stone is not in its strengths but in the uniqueness of its failings.'

'You are a master gem cutter,' Anji said, repeating her mother's words.

'I am,' he said, without pride.

～

Over the years, the agaves around the plinth grew tall and wide, obscuring the plinth until it was largely forgotten. Every Saturday morning, Anji's mother threw a mixture of palm sugar and roasted black sesame seeds into the garden bed, an offering to Saturn and the crows who were His celestial vehicle.

Her mother's efforts to pacify Saturn met with mixed success. Sometimes Saturn listened and their father was himself: affectionate, loving and curious about the world around them. Sometimes Saturn was cruel or indifferent, and their father would wake them up in the middle of the night with his screams, begging someone to stop hurting him, promising he would 'take it back'.

Siddharth would get into Anji's bed and they would lie there, listening as Amma spoke to their father in a soft, soothing voice, until his screams turned to sobs and eventually to whimpers and whispered apologies. Anji and Siddharth stopped trying to work out what 'take it back' meant. As they got older, they each lay in their own bed; the trajectory of their father's trauma was familiar now and less frightening.

Anji and Siddharth discovered another way to reach their father; something far more powerful than the capricious Saturn.

It started with a question about CJ Cook, shortly after their father had removed the statue. The defiant act of engineering and high school chemistry had lifted his spirits, and the children were emboldened to ask him the obvious question—*Why?*—at dinner one night.

'Appa, why don't you like Captain Cook?' Anji asked.

Amma stood over Appa, serving him parippu. His appetite had returned since he felled the mighty explorer and she was on a mission to rebuild his body, if she couldn't quite fix his mind. Her hand froze, a ladleful of creamy lentil curry suspended in mid-air.

'I don't like him because he was a conqueror and a coloniser,' Appa said. 'History reveres him as a bold and courageous explorer of new worlds. He was, in fact, a plunderer of old worlds. When he came here, he told a new story about this country. His story erased the past and rewrote the future. The battle for territorial legitimacy is fought on many grounds. It begins with the battle of competing and contested histories. Cook was a liar and a thief; he has no place at the front of our home or in this nation's pantheon of heroes.'

'What about under our verandah?' Siddharth asked, brave now that Anji had asked the first and hardest question.

'That's just perfect. I've always wanted a dead body buried under my house.' He looked at Anji and winked.

Emboldened, Anji asked Appa for more. 'What does terra . . . territory leg . . .' She scowled at Siddharth's smirk.

'Territorial legitimacy,' Appa repeated slowly. 'Don't smirk at people seeking knowledge, Siddharth. It doesn't hide or help your own ignorance.'

'Sorry, Appa,' Siddharth answered.

Appa coughed.

'Sorry, Anji,' Siddharth muttered.

'Territorial legitimacy is a nation or people's right to be where they are. Their right to own and defend their land and operate to the exclusion of other states. Territorial legitimacy goes hand in hand with notions of territorial sovereignty and integrity.'

Anji and Siddharth stared at him blankly.

'Aiyo, Zakhir.' Amma shook her head, emptying the last of the lentils onto Appa's plate. 'They're seven years old. They're barely able to do their homework by bedtime, let alone understand the finer points of statehood.' She waved the ladle at him, her tone reproving but her eyes alive with laughter that matched their father's.

Anji would remember that moment for the rest of her life. So would Siddharth. It was a key to their father's inner life. Something that could unlock and release him from the monsters in his head. When the nights were very bad, Amma would emerge from their room, exhausted from nursing him. Appa would take the tablets that helped him calm down but also settled like a blanket on his mind.

Anji and Siddharth would come home from school to find him still in bed. This would go on for days until he emerged from his room and the family continued as though the previous week was an aberration to be ignored, rather than a problem to be addressed.

Until Anji and Siddharth discovered what they called Cook's Thurappu, or Cook's Key. Whenever Appa got sick, they would go to his room and talk to him.

'Tell us more about self-determination, Appa,' they would say. 'Tell us more about competing and contested histories.'

They went to the Westgrove Public Library and asked Mrs Vandermark, the librarian, for books about Sri Lanka (there were none) and for books that explained Australia's history before Captain Cook (there were none). They braved Mrs Vandermark's quivering moustache and asked her to order books on these topics from another library. They left the books lying around Appa's bedroom, open at the pages they thought he would find the most offensive.

And he did find them offensive. Offensive enough to read them and then to storm out of his room to lecture them on the true history of colonial nation building. Offensive enough to take the children to Westgrove Public Library and wave a new reading list in front of Mrs Vandermark's face. Her moustache quivered faster than ever before but she took the list and promised she would discuss it with her supervisor. All the titles on Appa's reading list were published overseas, and it would be expensive and time-consuming to source them.

'We pay our taxes too, Mrs Vandermark. The First Fleet and the Anzacs are not the only highlights of Australian history. There's so much more. We're both trying to learn about this country; let's do this together.'

Appa gave Mrs Vandermark his best smile, the one which could persuade Amma to give them all extra milk toffee after dinner.

Mrs Vandermark blushed and acceded. Together, Appa and Mrs Vandermark established a new set of history reference books that no one read except the Ali family and the librarian herself.

It was during these history lessons from Appa that Anji learned that her grandfather was an archaeologist and her father was an expert in temple architecture and restoration, and that they had worked together to write the only book Appa ever published.

One night over dinner, Anji finally asked about the book.

'It was this family's first great creation,' Appa replied, looking at Amma. 'You and Siddharth were our second. You will be stronger and last longer. You are the present and the future. That book was the past.'

'Where is the book now, Appa?' Siddharth asked.

Anji saw Amma's eyes fill with tears.

'Here. We brought it with us.' He nodded at Amma. She went to their room and returned with a parcel wrapped in a stiff silk sari.

She unfolded it gently, each layer releasing a faint odour into the air. It smelled like their Queen's Birthday bonfires in the backyard; smoky and earthy. Inside the sari was a satchel, and inside the satchel was a book.

They all stood around the book on the table. Its cover was darkened, as though ash had seeped into the pores of its skin, embedded deep and beyond extraction.

Amma touched the gold lettering of the book's title.

'*Reclaiming the Past, Claiming the Future*,' Anji read out loud. She opened the cover and continued to read the words slowly,

'This book is dedicated to my wife Maya and our future children. Human beings are storytellers. From the beginning of our existence we have told stories. We have carved, painted and drawn them onto stone and paper. We seek to explain our creation and existence, our death and destruction through stories.

We define ourselves as individuals, communities and as nations through the stories we tell each other. History is the most powerful of all these stories. Ownership of culture, language and land depends on ownership of history.'

She stopped and looked up at her parents.

'It's a little wordy, isn't it?' Appa said softly.

'You were both a little wordy,' Amma replied. 'Couldn't stop talking about it, both of you.'

Appa nodded. He took Amma's hand in his and kissed it. Anji and Siddharth looked away.

Sydney, present day

Old Uncle Gana from Room 5 informed Anji that she was obliged to inform her mother, the legal owner of Cinnamon Gardens, that the nursing home had received a complaint under the Racial Discrimination Act. Anji reluctantly gave the papers to her mother and watched her read it. Maya stopped only to laugh out loud.

'I knew she shouldn't have married him,' Maya said. 'He's an idiot.'

It was true; her mother had known Nikki since childhood and had never thought Gareth was good enough for her.

'What are you going to do?' Maya asked.

'What do you want me to do?' Anji replied. 'You own this place—it's your call.'

'I think you should respectfully defend our decision to take the statue down. It wasn't done on a whim. Your father didn't just wake up one morning and decide that he didn't like Captain Cook.'

'Thank you, Amma,' Anji replied. 'I can take someone with me to the conciliation, a lawyer or a friend, a support person. Preferably not you, if that's okay.'

She wanted to spare her mother the stress of defending their father.

But this was not okay with Maya. She insisted on accompanying Anji, taking Ruben with her.

'He's my translator,' Maya explained. 'According to the Commission website, I'm allowed to have a translator.'

'Only if you need one. You speak English, remember?'

'Yes, but the Commission doesn't know that. I'm also allowed a carer.'

~⌒~

By the time Anji arrived at the office of the Australian Human Rights Commission, she had watched its instructional YouTube video more times than she had watched Chris Hemsworth's impassioned appeal for donations to the Rural Fire Service. Even more times than she had secretly watched his mindless exercise routines on Insta. But while she knew what to expect from the process, she hadn't anticipated how she would feel when she entered the meeting room and saw Gareth sitting at the table by himself.

He stood up, reached forward as if to kiss her hello, but then dropped his hands back to his sides. He looked lost in the clinical meeting room, surrounded by sweeping canvases of Aboriginal art. She stepped forward and shook his hand. She held it in both of hers. They had to be kind to each other. If they could do that, then this would be okay. Then the image of his hands on Nikki's body flashed into her mind, and she let go.

'Anji, Mrs Ali, thank you for coming,' he said. 'Ruben, isn't it?'

If he was surprised to see Ruben, he didn't show it.

Jo Sayidd, the AHRC conciliator—a short, stocky woman in a no-nonsense suit—introduced herself and invited them all to take a seat on either side of the table with herself in the middle. As if reading from the same script used in the YouTube video, Jo talked through the rules of conciliation. Anji vaguely clocked the phrases: mutual respect, non-binding forum, informal but confidential, not a court.

'Do you all understand how this works?' Jo asked when she was done. Her encouraging smile revealed a small piece of salad in her left canine. 'We'll begin with short opening statements from each of you. Mr Barton, as the complainant, I'll invite you to go first.'

Gareth nodded and opened a leather folder. Inside was a set of typed notes stapled together.

'Thank you, Jo. Anji, Mrs Ali, you would have read my complaint form by now. It's all there. Your nursing home performs an important service for our local community. It's well known and well respected. I'm not trying to be difficult and I don't want to hurt you. I just want you to understand that the removal of Captain Cook's statue, even if it was done by Mr Ali years ago, is racist.'

'Like the graffiti on the walls of the nursing home?' Anji demanded.

'Dr Ali,' Jo broke in, 'let's allow Mr Barton to complete his opening statement and then you can talk us through yours. Is that okay?'

'Yes, of course.' She flushed. 'I'm sorry, Gareth.'

'That's all right,' he replied. 'The graffiti on the walls is a reprehensible, hurtful act of racism. It made you angry. So, you know how I feel.'

Anji nodded; she had handed that one to the politician.

'Captain Cook symbolises the foundation of Australia by Europeans,' Gareth continued. 'I absolutely recognise that Australia's settlement resulted in the dispossession and genocide of our First Nations people. But to remove the statue of Cook negates the validity of our presence here, the presence of European people, which is *my* race. It's disrespectful to Cook and disrespectful to Europeans, because of our race.'

He flipped through his notes and found the page he was looking for. Even upside down, Anji recognised the formatting of Section 18 of the Racial Discrimination Act. She had studied its words and read all the cases that Uncle Gana had found for her. Gareth began to read the familiar words of the section: 'It is unlawful for a person to do an act, otherwise than in private, if: (a) the act is reasonably likely, in all the circumstances, to offend, insult—'

'Mr Barton, let's limit our comments to opening remarks, please. Later, during the negotiation phase, we can talk about the law, although as I said at the beginning, the Commission cannot and does not make a determination of discrimination. Have you concluded your opening remarks?' Jo asked.

'Almost.' Gareth looked at his papers again and swallowed hard. 'If the statue had been of Gandhi, you wouldn't have taken it down. I felt "offended, insulted and humiliated" by its remov—'

'Mr Barton, I must ask you again not to bring the words of the Act into this part of our discussion.'

'It's fine,' Anji said. 'Let him finish. You felt offended, insulted and humiliated.'

'Thank you, Anji. I felt all of those things, and I felt like the statue was removed because of Cook's race, which is the same as my race. It's racist. That's it. I've finished my opening remarks.' He exhaled, the final words tumbling out as though he was afraid the conciliator would overrule Anji.

'Thank you, Mr Barton,' Jo said. 'Dr Ali, Mrs Ali, I'll invite one of you to reply.'

'I'll reply on behalf of the nursing home and my family,' Anji said.

Preparing for the conciliation process had been stressful, forcing her to remember her father and prepare a defence of his actions. Since he had left them ten years ago, she had thought about him every day. It was impossible not to. She was surrounded by memories which had been absorbed into the nursing home and could be released with no notice, giving her no time to steel herself for the pain that travelled like lightning from her brain to the furthest reaches of her body. Pain that stalled her breath in her lungs and her blood in her heart. He was as present in their nursing home as he was absent.

Weeks before Sri Lanka's civil war had come to a bloody end on a small strip of beach in 2009, Zakhir Ali had disappeared. He had woken up one Saturday morning, done all of his chores for the nursing home, and met the family for lunch at Anji's house. They made plans for Tamil New Year the following week. That afternoon, he packed a small suitcase and his satchel, taking nothing of importance but his passport and his book. He was seen at Sydney Airport, and the police investigation into his missing persons case revealed he had boarded a plane for Colombo. He left Colombo Airport and was never seen again.

When she looked back on that last meal, Anji asked herself if he had seemed different. Should she have realised? Could she have known? She was a geriatric psychiatrist with training in trauma-informed care. She had chosen this sub-specialty because she knew something about it already.

Did she understand and forgive him for leaving? Didn't he love them enough to stay? Didn't he love *her* enough to stay? Nathan had given her years of free counselling, the kind he gave to any child who felt abandoned by a parent. It had helped some; enough to make her understand that her father's decisions were to do with his personal shit and it didn't mean they had to become her personal shit. His abandonment was not a reflection of his love—or lack thereof—for them.

It's not my fault, Nathan made her repeat over and over again.

I am loved by my parents, she reminded herself.

Gareth's complaint forced her to relive a memory that was strong and happy, one that only reminded her how much she had lost. She could still remember the sound of Appa cheering as Captain James Cook's feet melted towards the earth.

'Dr Ali?' Jo prompted.

Everyone was staring at her, waiting for her to speak.

'Thank you for your comments, Gareth,' Anji said.

Uncle Gana had schooled her on legal etiquette. 'Always thank your opposing counsel; it confuses them. And smile, child: look him in the eyes and smile.'

Anji smiled, not on the advice of counsel, but because Gareth was her friend. At least, he had once been her friend, before he hurt her best friend. They were tied to each other, for better or for worse. And she smiled because the memories of her father had brought her more joy than sadness.

She took her opening statement out of her handbag and placed it on the table in front of her.

'My father was a temple architect. He said that the future belonged to "those who claimed the past as their own". He wrote a book about it and it almost cost him his life, because he came from a country where the right that we take for granted here, freedom of speech, didn't exist. In addition to that, his book offered a version of history that competed with others. If I may, my opening statement is the foreword from my father's book, written in 1978. It's not short . . .' She looked at Gareth and then Jo for permission to read it.

Gareth nodded.

'Thank you, Gareth.'

She flattened the paper on the table and looked at it. She and her brother had re-created it from memory, because the book was gone; it had disappeared with Zakhir, somewhere in Sri Lanka. They remembered it, because as children and even as adults they had read it over and over again, trying to understand their father better. Archaeologists looking for clues about his past.

She began to read:

'This book charts the archaeological discoveries made by Dr KN Sriskandarajah in the Jaffna Province of Sri Lanka between 1943 and 1956. These discoveries—a temple that Dr Sriskandarajah named *Mayanilayam* after his only child, and a surrounding town complex—indicate that a civilisation existed in the north of the island from as early as the seventh century BCE. Comparisons between archaeological findings and operational temples in Tamil Nadu with Mayanilayam, confirm its ethnic and religious provenance. Mayanilayam was almost certainly built by people who had come from Southern India and were of Dravidian origin. The Dravidian civilisation was the precursor to the Tamil civilisation, among others in Southern India.

The discovery of Mayanilayam suggests that an early Hindu civilisation existed in Sri Lanka, predating the arrival of Prince Vijaya in the sixth century BCE and the arrival of Buddhism in the third century BCE.

After its discovery in 1943, Dr Sriskandarajah continued to excavate and explore Mayanilayam for another thirteen years, documenting his findings with the academic rigour expected of a man of his calibre and experience. At his request, the Jaffna Public Library brought teams of archaeologists and historians from the University of Madras to verify his findings.

In 1956, shortly before the passing of the Sinhala Only Act and the Buddha's 2500th Death Anniversary, Mayanilayam was closed by the Sri Lankan government and the site was claimed by the Sri Lankan Army for a military base.

That same year, Dr Sriskandarajah attempted to publish his findings in a treatise entitled *Mayanilayam: The battle between illusion and fact*. He would spend the next five years of his life being censured by the academic community in Colombo and stripped of his previous academic honours. He was later employed by the Jaffna Public Library as its curator of archaeology.

I began working with him in 1977 when I was researching ancient Sri Lankan temple architecture. I attempted to document his findings, drawing on his memory, personal notes from his field trips and archival material at the Jaffna Public Library.

This book builds on the work of Dr Sriskandarajah and extends it by placing Mayanilayam in the wider context of Tamil Hindu architecture in South India and Southern Asia. It openly and defiantly concludes, rather than suggests, that a Tamil Hindu civilisation existed in Sri Lanka before the arrival and existence of the Sinhalese civilisation and Buddhism.'

She paused and swallowed hard against the tightening in her throat. The paper shook in her hands. She concentrated on steadying them, exhaled and opened her mouth, but before she could continue reading, she heard Gareth.

'Anji,' he said softly. 'I know it must be hard for you to read this. I'm not trying to hurt you, but I don't understand the relationship between your father's work and the justification for taking down the statue.'

'Excuse me, Mr Barton,' the conciliator interjected. 'Perhaps we should take a short break before we begin the negotiation phase. We can do this together or you can sit in separate rooms outside and I will move back and forth between you.'

'Thank you, Jo, but I'm fine to continue,' Anji said. 'The connection, Gareth, is this. My father always told me that Mayanilayam demonstrated that the Tamils were first in time. In the battle for historical legitimacy, it mattered who could prove they were here first. If I may?' she asked, holding up the paper. 'My father explained it much better than I could.'

The conciliator looked at Gareth who shrugged and nodded.

'Please, go ahead, Dr Ali.'

Anji continued reading,

'This book directly contradicts the prevailing mythology of Sri Lanka's formation. In the late nineteenth and early twentieth century, Sinhalese politicians, led and supported by bhikkus, Buddhist clergy, created a powerful narrative that Sri Lanka was a Buddhist country that had been designated by the Buddha to protect and preserve Buddhism.

The *Mahavamsa*, a fifth-century CE Buddhist chronicle written by the monk Mahanama, purports to document the history of Buddhism in Sri Lanka from the sixth century BCE to the fourth century CE. The Sinhala Buddhist nationalistic narrative of Sri

Lanka has been built on this rendering of "history". Nationalists have used the *Mahavamsa* as evidence of territorial ownership and supremacy. This narrative claims Sri Lanka for the Sinhalese and frames the Tamils as usurpers from India, who arrived later to steal the country from them.

As I write this foreword, the same mythologised history drives changes to Sri Lanka's constitution that entrench Sinhala supremacy. This history drives policies that have demoted the Tamil language and placed restrictive quotas on Tamils in educational institutions and places of employment. This history drives the state-sponsored movement of Sinhalese communities into land that has been held by Tamils for thousands of years. And this history drives increasing communal violence by Sinhalese people against Tamil people.

This history is wrong. Mayanilayam and the history it evidences make this clear. The Sri Lankan government's response to Dr Sriskandarajah's findings demonstrate their concerns about Mayanilayam and the alternative narrative it offers. Their attempts to stop the book's publication strengthen the validity of our thesis. The foundations of modern-day Sri Lanka are built on ancient myths. Historical fiction can only be fought with historical facts, such as those buried in Mayanilayam.

As Dr Sriskandarajah likes to say, possession of land is nine-tenths of the law; possession of history is nine-tenths of the future.'

Anji put the paper down, her hands still shaking and her voice hoarse. Gareth pushed a glass of water towards her. She nodded her thanks and took it without looking up.

She wasn't ready to see her mother's face. She stared resolutely at the table and saw Ruben's dark hand cover her mother's darker one. She wanted to comfort her mother too, but the pain of her father's words sat so close to the surface of her skin. Any sudden movement and it would surge through the cracks she could feel forming in her body.

Finally, she looked up at Gareth, holding his gaze. Losing her father had been the hardest thing she'd endured, but losing a child was beyond her comprehension. She only understood a fraction of his pain.

'Appa said that in Sri Lanka, the Tamils were colonised by the Sinhalese first, then the Portuguese, then the Dutch, then the British and then the Sinhalese one more time. In Australia, we are taught the mythology of colonisation, that this country was discovered by Captain Cook and settled peacefully because it belonged to no one. Despite evidence and court cases to the contrary, we are indoctrinated and socialised to believe that the British built this country on the foundations of nothing, erasing more than sixty thousand years of history, culture, and people, in one fell and foul swoop.

'Captain Cook represents that mythology, that great lie that all colonisers tell themselves and the colonised. Appa said that Cook had no place in the pantheon of heroes or in our home. That's why he took the statue down, Gareth. And why the statue will stay down.'

Jo closed her notepad with a slap, causing Anji and Gareth to look at her instead of each other.

'This seems like a good point at which to take a break. Mr Barton, let me show you to your room. There's coffee and water there. You can take some time to regroup. Dr Ali, your room is through that door over there.' The conciliator indicated a door at the back of the room.

Gareth followed Jo out.

Anji exhaled and waited for her mother to speak.

'Mahal,' Amma said. Daughter. 'Ende mahal.' My daughter.

Anji missed the sound of her father's voice calling her mahal. She put her face in her hands and cried, a sound, a pain that had been placed in a stone vault, buried deeper than an ancient Hindu temple.

She felt her mother's hands on her hair and then her mother's arms around her.

Maya held one side of her body and Ruben held the other, as Anji released the memories and the anger and the loss which were too immense to be held within her any longer.

GARETH

Sydney

Gareth loosened his tie and paced the small room. He had more evidence of racism at the nursing home, but he no longer felt compelled to present it. As far as he was aware, this was the first time Anji had talked about her father since his disappearance. Seeing the pain in her face and her quiet resolve to honour his memory and his wishes had unsettled him. What was wrong with him? How had he let himself end up here, in this room with cheap prints of Indigenous art and bad coffee?

He felt his phone vibrate in his pocket. It was Davidson.

'Mike,' Gareth answered. 'How are you?'

'I'm ropable. Not surprised at you, not one bit. No, that's not true—I *am* surprised. I didn't think you had the balls, to be honest. But there you go. Finally, after all these years, you did something unexpected. If it wasn't so fucking stupid, I'd be impressed.'

Gareth felt sweat trickle down his back under his shirt.

'What are you talking about?' he asked, pulling even harder at his tie.

'Don't be a dick. I know where you are, and I know what you're doing. I've seen your application to the Commission; you typed

236

it up on a work laptop. It's on our system. You didn't do it in the party's name, but it can be connected to us, if this gets out. This is a fucking nightmare.'

'It's none of your business, Mike.' Gareth's mind was spinning. Bella Davidson, it must have been her. She'd been suspicious ever since he asked for the research.

'That's where you're wrong. You look like a racist, attacking this nursing home. It's one of the most respected businesses in Westgrove. It's run by a Sri Lankan family in a constituency with one of the highest concentrations of Sri Lankans in Sydney. We need these people to win the next election. We need them and you're attacking them.'

'I'm defending our right to—'

'To what, Gareth? To what?'

Gareth said nothing, not sure what he was defending or what he was doing. None of it would bring back what he had lost.

'I thought so. You were on three months' notice, but in the light of your recent misconduct, we have grounds for immediate dismissal. I've asked security to revoke your IT access and they've cleaned out your desk. A formal letter of dismissal will be sent to your home and your settlement pay and super is being calculated.'

'Please, Mike, if you fire me, I'll never work—'

Davidson cut him off. 'I always knew you weren't up to the job. Consider this our last conversation. Everything else can be done by email—or through lawyers, if you prefer.'

The line went dead.

～

'Everyone, thank you for coming back. I thought we had a really productive session and I've had a chance to talk to both of you,' Jo said, looking at Gareth and Anjali. 'I think I have a good idea of what you each want. As you know, the Commission is not empowered to make a decision about whether discrimination has taken place.'

She looked at Gareth meaningfully, clearly expecting him to react as vehemently as he had in the breakout room. He bit down on his lip. It was still unclear to him *what* the Commission was empowered to do. Maybe it really was as toothless as all the free speech advocates claimed.

'The purpose of this conciliation and my role here is to help you reach an agreement with each other rather than a finding of law. If we don't reach an agreement, then the president of the Commission will issue you with a Notice of Rejection and you can decide whether to take this matter to the Federal Court or the Federal Circuit Court.'

Jo continued, 'The offending acts that Mr Barton has brought before the Commission, under the *Racial Discrimination Act*, are the removal of the James Cook statue and Dr Ali's discussion about it.'

She paused to look at Gareth again, giving him a chance to qualify her summary. He remained silent but nodded.

'Mr Barton, these acts—'

'It's more than that,' he said, his heart pounding. Davidson's words echoed in his mind. He could imagine the MP back at party headquarters, telling them he always knew Gareth wasn't up to the job.

'Mr Barton, we've been here for a couple of hours already. If you have substantive acts or words that you consider to be racially offensive, I'm happy to hear them, but please note you have already had ample opportunity to raise them earlier today and before today.'

That wasn't very conciliatory of her. He felt himself losing his nerve. He was such a coward. Davidson was right.

'It's not just the statue,' he said. It was everything about the place, he thought, but knew he shouldn't say.

Maya's hands were locked together, fingers threaded through each other. He saw her hands tighten. On her ring finger, she wore a single gold band, unlike a lot of his Sri Lankan constituents, who carried a small fortune on their bodies. The ring was loose on her thin finger, but trapped in place by her swollen knuckle. He didn't want to hurt her. He wasn't an arse.

'Anji. Maya.' He looked at them both. 'Your nursing home is a warm and beautiful place. You've created a home for elderly people where they live with dignity.' He swallowed hard. They were waiting for the *but*.

'But . . .'

'Just say it, Gareth,' Anji prompted. 'We're all friends and poten-tial litigants here.' She smiled her beautiful smile.

He exhaled. 'It's everything about the place,' he blurted out and then covered his mouth with his hand reflexively. 'That's not what I meant. It's just that, for example . . .'

'Yes?' Jo said.

They all leaned forward a little, even Ruben.

'It's just that everything in the nursing home is orientated around your country, around Sri Lanka and your culture,' he said.

'Such as?' Maya asked. 'When you say, *everything* . . .'

He needed to give them strong examples. He had a list somewhere in his papers. 'For example, I know you celebrate your festivals and religious occasions. But do you still celebrate ours? Do you celebrate Christmas and Mother's Day?'

'Mother's Day?' Anji repeated.

'Yes, I know that might seem trivial to you because it's not one of your celebrations, but it's important in this country and you live in this country.'

'Of course,' Maya answered before Anji could reply. 'We have a calendar of celebrations based on the residents' demographics. This includes Mother's Day. One year, I even gave all the women a Womanizer as a Mother's Day gift.'

'A womaniser?' Gareth asked, confused.

'Yes, it's a small hand-held device that every mother should have,' Maya explained.

Anji put her head in her hands and muttered something to her mother in Tamil. Ruben looked away and the conciliator bit her lip, trying not to smile.

'I can see you're mocking me,' Gareth said, his face hot with anger.

'She's not, Gareth,' Anji replied, a note of apology in her voice. 'Unfortunately, she's serious. In answer to your question, we celebrate Mother's Day, Christmas, Easter, the works. Cinnamon Gardens is a broad cultural, religious and secular church.'

'We orientate our identity around all our stakeholders,' Maya added. 'Unlike Australia.'

'Amma.' Anji shook her head.

Maya shrugged. 'It's the truth.'

He clenched his fist under the table. They were so damn smug.

'What about your food?' he asked. 'It's all Sri Lankan.'

'Actually, residents get a personalised menu based on their health and dietary requirements, and their preferences,' Maya answered. 'Our chef and kitchen staff are versatile, so residents can choose between multiple cuisines. All residents are offered food from their ancestral homeland, whatever that homeland is, because it's comforting.'

'It's more than that,' Gareth said.

'Please explain,' Anji said.

Gareth looked at her sharply, checking to see if she was echoing the words of a famous racist in order to ridicule him.

'I'm serious, Gareth. You seem comfortable eating Sri Lankan food at my house or having a curry after a big night out, but our nursing home menu of seemingly rampant multiculturalism offends you. I'm confused, so please explain.'

'It's the residents themselves,' he said finally. 'They're mostly Sri Lankan.'

Anji opened her folder and leafed through it before extracting a piece of paper which she pushed across the desk. It contained tables and graphs of the demographics of the nursing home.

'Historically, the nursing home comprised anyone who could afford to live there, and it reflected the ethnic and socioeconomic nature of the neighbourhood or the wider catchment area. When my parents took over, that shifted because a significant number of white people moved out. My parents filled those beds with whoever applied.'

She leaned over and tapped a chart at the bottom of the page.

'You'll see from those records that I do the same. I simply allocate beds when beds become available to whoever has applied.

'All of our awards and tender applications to the Department of Health should tell you that we operate the nursing home equitably and fairly.'

'Then what about the staff?' he asked, trying not to look at Ruben.

'What about the staff?'

'They're almost all Sri Lankan,' he replied, eyes firmly on Anji.

Anji pulled another document from her folder. She had been prepared well by someone.

'Here's the breakdown of our staff by citizenship and race. You'll see that when my parents took over the nursing home, many of the white Australian staff left. We recruit in compliance with all Australian fair work legislation. We're looking for people with specific carer experience. In addition to this, we need people with language skills, because as our residents slide into deep old age and dementia, they revert to their mother tongue, to the language of their childhood. We want to communicate with them kindly, and so we need to have a pool of language skills to draw on.'

She made it all sound so sensible. She made him sound so irrational and paranoid. She made him sound so racist.

'It just seems like you're running an affirmative action recruitment policy,' was the best he could come up with.

'This whole country runs an affirmative action policy in favour of white men first, then white women,' Anji replied. 'If you're accusing me of reverse racism, Gareth, please come out and say it so I can explain to you why there's no such thing.'

'I'm not accusing you of anything,' he said, regretting it immediately.

Anji laughed and shook her head. 'Aside from racism and an unofficial affirmative action policy.'

'He's allowed to talk about his concerns, Dr Ali,' the conciliator said. 'That's why we're here.'

Finally, someone helping him.

'Thank you for this report. The records are very helpful for us to understand what's going on at the nursing home and why,' Jo continued. 'It helps us to unpack what Mr Barton has put forward as the racially offensive behaviour.'

Unpack. That was such a psychologist's word. Such a new age meaningless word. To unpack. Nathan used that word a lot. Let's unpack Oscar's feelings. How about we pack up the whole fucking nursing home—and that cottage down the back.

'Yes, thank you for the records, Anji,' he said. 'Really helpful for all the unpacking I'll need to do. You keep surprisingly organised records for a nursing home.' His implication was clear.

'Not really; we're required by the government to keep accurate records and we report quarterly to ensure accreditation,' she replied.

Maya leaned forward to speak. 'Twenty years ago or so, I hired some of the grandchildren of the residents to migrate all of our old paper records to digital. It was a tedious data entry exercise, but my father had an interest in record keeping and the stories that lie behind the data. He called it ethnography. With the right database you can search for citizenship status and race—things that *you're* interested in. And you can search for people's motivations and their feelings—things that *I'm* interested in.'

'I call it Amma's inherent curiosity about people.' Anji smiled at her mother.

'I call it her nosiness,' Ruben said. 'Although, as she said, she's obliged to keep accurate records and does so in accordance with Australian law.'

'You're a lawyer as well as a nurse?' Gareth wondered if Ruben was actually Anji's legal counsel.

'No, I'm a carer not a nurse. But I'm a linguist and interpreter by profession,' Ruben replied. 'I like words.' He shrugged. 'There are a lot of words in these laws.'

'A linguist?' Gareth was confused. 'How many languages do you speak?'

'Ten.'

'Right. Well, it's wonderful that you've come to this country and learned so much,' Gareth responded, with feigned warmth.

Ruben opened his mouth as if to speak, and then stopped himself.

'Yes?' Gareth asked.

'Nothing, Mr Barton. You're quite right.'

'If you have something to say, Ruben—'

'Mr Barton,' the conciliator intervened, 'we're not here to discuss the qualifications of Mrs Ali's carer. Dr Ali has set out the demographic profiles of the residents and staff. Dr Ali has also submitted checklists showing that the nursing home complies with its legal obligations under fair work legislation, other anti-discrimination legislation and aged care regulations.'

'That's why I need to have that report back, too,' Anji said, gesturing at the report in Gareth's hands. 'When you're ready, of course.'

'Sorry?'

'We comply with data protection and privacy laws. I need the reports back.'

'Yes, right. Strictly confidential. Top secret,' he said, trying to smile.

No one smiled back.

'Mr Barton, if we could set aside your concerns about the way in which the nursing home operates for the moment, I want us to focus on the issue that brought us together today.'

The conciliator made it sound as though they were about to get married. He realised what it was about her that annoyed him so much. Her voice didn't modulate in tone or pace. Regardless of what was being said, she maintained the same robotic rhythm and cadence throughout. Sincere but a little patronising.

'If I could now turn your attention to the relevant section of the Racial Discrimination Act.' She placed a copy of an extract in front of both parties. Anji shared her copy with her mother.

The conciliator read it out for them, as though they couldn't read it themselves. Perhaps Ruben would like to translate it into nine other languages for them.

'Mr Barton, even if you could argue that the nursing home's removal of the statue was offensive to you, the act was not done because of *your* race or because of the race of some or all of the people in *your* group.'

He saw Anji nod.

'This second element of the offence is essential. As I understand from Dr Ali, the removal of the statue came from Dr Ali's father's feelings about colonisation and'—the conciliator sifted through her notes to find the words she was looking for—'colonisation and cultural erasure in all its forms. The act was not committed because of white Australians or towards white Australians.'

Gareth felt his head spin and the sounds around him became muffled. He gripped the edges of the table. It was like the last time he took Florence on the inflatable rubber tyre at Wet 'n' Wild. He'd had an ear infection and shouldn't have been in the water, but she was desperate to go. The tyre spiralled down the massive funnel. He could see the children laughing and screaming, but the sound that reached his brain was a paler version of what his eyes were seeing.

Redacted, that was a good legal word for this non-legal, non-binding forum. He felt redacted somehow.

Someone touched his arm. He looked up, startled.

'Gareth,' Anji said. 'Are you okay?'

He shook his head.

'Should we take a break?' Her concern was hard to bear. It was as surprising as it was unwanted. No, that wasn't true. He wanted her to care. He wanted Nikki to care. He remembered his wife's cold indifference the last time he had seen her at the nursing home. The first time he had seen Captain Cook.

He nodded, coughing to clear his throat and summon the words.

'Yes, please.'

In the breakout room, the conciliator talked him through previous cases. The Act clearly wasn't designed to protect white people from racism. The conciliator also cautioned him against appealing to the Federal Court, as this process was expensive, time-consuming and stressful. Unlike the Commission, it wasn't confidential and he would most likely lose the appeal and his reputation with it.

The conciliator called them back to the main room after half an hour. It was time to wrap up and there was only one way this was going to end. Gareth had known that from the moment he pressed send on the AHRC portal, and he was a fool for letting it get this far, but he hadn't known how to stop it.

'Mr Barton, we've been here for a few hours now. You're all tired and hurt. I know you have a long history of friendship, respect and love between you. Your families have been close for decades.' She paused.

'Nikki, Gareth's wife, has been my best friend since primary school,' Anji said to no one in particular. Or maybe just to him. 'Our boys love each other. I want us to be friends, Gareth.'

Our boys. The new boundary of their friendship.

The conciliator nodded and said, 'I've explained to you both how the law operates, even though this is not a court.'

'Yes, thank you. You've been very clear and very kind in your explanations,' Gareth conceded. The conciliator was right, they were all exhausted. He was trapped and tired.

'I hear your grievance, Mr Barton. I'm not saying your claim is vexatious,' she said. There was something about the way she said this that indicated she definitely thought his claim was vexatious.

'But this Act is designed to protect people who are marginalised in Australia because of their race; people who are victimised because of it. The Federal Court will look both to the facts of this case and the public policy reason behind the legislation. The threshold for an affirmative finding under Section 18C is very high, even for people who have historically been the subject of racist attacks.'

'And because I'm white, I have not historically been the subject of racist attacks in Australia,' Gareth said. 'I am from the race that's usually the perpetrator and not the victim, and the Federal Court, like you, finds it impossible to conclude that I have been discriminated against in a racist manner.'

'Mr Barton, as I said at the beginning, I cannot make a finding of discrimination here. I know that's hard for you to accept. So, I'll give you all one last opportunity to speak to each other, with honesty and respect. If we can find common understanding, then you can walk away from this incident and put it behind you.'

There was so much Gareth wanted to put behind him. There was so much behind him that he wished was in front of him, so he could redo it. What he really wanted was a do-over: on his life, his daughter, his marriage, his job, and this stupid complaint. But he would get none of that.

'Mr Barton, as the complainant, perhaps you'd like to go first?'

Gareth shrugged his shoulders. 'Anji, I listened to you read your father's prologue to his book and I read it again this afternoon, a few times. I know you won't put the statue back. I know you don't understand why it matters to me, or what you've taken away from me. I feel like we've said everything that needs to be said.'

He gathered his papers.

'Gareth,' Anji began. The pity in her voice was unbearable. 'It wasn't your fault,' she said. 'It was a terrible accident.'

He shook his head at her. He couldn't do this—not here, not now.

'Guilt is a terrible thing,' she went on. 'It eats away at all of us. We all feel it.'

'Not the way I do. The conciliation is over, Anji. I have to go.'

'Give me another solution, anything. Ask for anything else that will help you to forgive us. Please, forgive me.'

She wasn't talking about the statue now and there was nothing she could do. He couldn't forgive her and he couldn't forgive himself. It was such a fucking mess.

He shook his head and walked out the door.

~ঽ

Gareth stepped into the harsh sunlight, his eyes momentarily blinded. The building next to the Commission was boarded up, thick dust billowing from behind the panes of chipboard, the staccato of cement blocks being thrown from a height, interspersed with the throbbing pain behind his right eye.

'Gareth,' Anji called from behind. 'Wait, please. I don't want it to end like this.'

She pushed through the crowd milling on the Commission steps.

'Don't.' He took a step towards her. He must have spoken more loudly than he intended, because people turned to look at him. Anji put her hands up, as if negotiating with a gunman. 'Don't look at me like you know what I'm feeling. Don't look at me like you feel sorry for me. Don't look at me at all,' he hissed.

Anji took a step back and then Ruben was in front of her, placing his body like a wall between them, as if she needed protection from him. Gareth was asking for the laws of this country to protect *him* from *her*, and they were all acting like *he* was the offender. Like *he* had done something wrong.

'Mr Barton.' Ruben also put his hands up, palms open. A peaceful gesture that was intended to diffuse his angry one.

Ruben the translator who knew how to make Nikki laugh.

Gareth's hands hung by the sides of his body. He felt them clench into fists again. He had found himself doing that a lot since Florence died. He felt cold sweat slide down his burning body.

'Mr Barton,' Ruben said. 'Would you mind stepping back, please?'

Somehow Gareth's body had moved forward again and closed the gap between him and Ruben.

'I've been stepping back all afternoon. I've been stepping back and out of the way for a long time now.'

He took another step forward, close enough to see that Ruben was a handsome man. Tall, dark-skinned and broad. He carried himself quietly, present but discreet in the corridors of the nursing home. Here, in the sunlight, his stance confident and resolute, Gareth could understand his appeal. He could understand why people were drawn to him; his restrained strength. He could understand, and finally he *did* understand.

'I will ask you one more time, Gareth,' Ruben said.

There was something about the familiarity in the way the man said his name. As though Ruben had discussed him with Nikki and, in their conversations, they called him Gareth. What did they say about him? Did they laugh about him? Did Ruben talk about Gareth as he traced kisses down his wife's body and entered her? Did she even think about Gareth or did she simply call out Ruben's name in pleasure?

'You people, you come here and take everything. You act like you own the place. You're not welcome here,' he said, wanting to push Ruben away with his words. 'You're not welcome here,' he repeated. 'You have no idea how hard it is to be me. You've taken everything away from me. *Everything.*'

Gareth lifted his fists and swung wildly at Ruben.

Ruben sighed and stepped quickly to the right.

Gareth's fist missed Ruben but sank into something soft. Something that staggered under the pathetic force of his attempted violence.

Maya cried out, her hand reaching for her shoulder where Gareth had connected with her. Ruben swivelled around and gasped, catching Maya in one arm before she fell. He placed another arm out to block Gareth's advance. Anji was there, behind her mother, and together they steadied the old woman and helped lower her to the ground.

'I'm sorry, Mrs Ali.' Gareth shuddered, realising what he'd done. 'I'm so sorry.'

He stepped forward to help her.

Ruben shook his head, casually raised his fist and hit Gareth once, bringing him to his knees, and once more, dropping him to the cement steps, the screams of people around him echoing above the ringing in his ears.

~⦿

Gareth reached over to turn his alarm off. He touched his face; the right side of it was swollen and tender. He picked up the phone. There were eleven missed calls from numbers he didn't recognise, three calls from Mike Davidson and one text from Nikki. He looked at that first.

> I heard about yesterday. Call me. Just want to check
> you're ok.

Gareth's heart pounded. His phone rang again before he could call her back. No Caller ID.

'Hello?' he asked, hoping it was Nikki.

'Mr Barton,' a man's voice greeted him. Then, when he didn't reply, 'Mr Barton?'

'Yes, yes, it's Gareth,' he answered.

'Gareth, you're a hard man to reach. My name is Brian O'Callaghan. I cover the legal pages for *The Daily Telegraph*, and I was wondering if we could speak. The paper is considering doing a story on you; that clip has turned you into a local hero.'

'What clip?' Gareth's mouth felt dry. Still holding the phone to his ear, he stumbled to the bathroom, horrified by his reflection in the mirror. The bruise was a deep grey and yellow. He touched it again, fascinated by the distortion of shape and hue, intrigued by how much pain he could withstand, prodding himself until his eyes smarted with tears.

'The clip—the one that's gone viral.'

'Viral?' Gareth whispered. 'I don't know what you mean.'

'Look at your phone, Gareth. You're a star. The Twitter wars are already raging and it's barely seven thirty. Morning TV will be calling you. I want to give you a chance to tell your story before—'

Gareth disconnected the call and searched his name on the internet. The first hit should have been his bio on the council website. Instead, it was a clip of him on YouTube, shouting at Ruben on the steps of the Australian Human Rights Commission.

He heard himself say, 'You've taken everything away from me. *Everything.*'

Then he saw himself lash out at Ruben and hit Maya instead. The old lady fell back but somehow Ruben whipped around and caught her. He couldn't see the expression on Ruben's face but he could sense the other man's body coiling in anger. Maybe he was remembering it: the man who seemed emotionless and empty suddenly filled with rage.

The first blow had been such a surprise, he was more shocked than hurt. The second had hurt him so much he didn't remember Ruben raising his fist a third time. He saw Anji restrain him and shake her head. She pulled Ruben's arm and then his body into hers, a gesture that was both calming and controlling. Strangely intimate for an employer and employee. Familiar.

People around them screamed. Several of them rushed forward to help Gareth, not Maya. And then the clip ended as abruptly as it had started.

He sat on the bathroom floor and watched it five more times.

The YouTube counter said it had been viewed 528,734 times. That couldn't be right. And the number was rising.

528,735 . . . 6 . . . 7. Who were these people?

He looked at the comments below the clip, the contents of his stomach churning as he scrolled down.

> Violent black guy hits man while he's down. Typical.
>
> Check out this guy—telling it like it is.
>
> Who is this guy? Want to buy him a beer or ten.
>
> Who does this guy think he is?

Gareth crawled over to the toilet and threw up, the spasm and retching pulling at the muscles on his face, making him cry out.

He sank back against the cool bathroom wall. Stone grey tiles with a purple blossom detail. Nikki had chosen them with Flo. His daughter had loved purple flowers. The tiles were Japanese and cost extra, but he loved to listen to Florence in the bathroom, counting the flowers while she pooed.

He closed his eyes, braced himself and looked at the comments again.

> Someone needs to give this guy a fucking medal.
>
> Finally. Someone calling out the truth.
>
> Angry white guy for PM.
>
> Angry white guy for Australian of the Year, not that other cnt.

Make Australia great again. Go home u black bastard

Gareth closed his eyes and breathed heavily against the panic surging in his chest. He called Nikki, letting the phone ring and ring until it rang out and went to voicemail. He listened to the first few words, longing for that voice to speak to him, to soothe him. He disconnected, called again and did the same, hanging up before the voicemail this time.

The phone rang again. No Caller ID.

'Hello?' he whispered.

'Gareth? It's me, Nikki.' As if he didn't recognise her voice at the first syllable. The first breath of his name.

'Oh, Nikki, thank God.'

'You've seen it then.' It wasn't a question.

'Just now. I didn't know about it. I didn't realise it was being filmed. I had no idea, hon, I just . . . I just woke up and I don't know what to do. I . . .'

He ran out of words.

'You're famous.'

Her voice was completely devoid of emotion. It wasn't a judgement or a criticism, just a fact. An observation about someone she knew.

'You're going to be busy, sorting this out,' she said. 'I think I should keep Oscar with me for a bit. Until we know . . . until we know what's going to happen next.'

'Happen next?'

'Yes. Perhaps you'll get your own reality show.'

'Nikki, please,' he begged. 'I didn't want this. It was an accident. I was angry. I shouldn't have hit him.'

'You hit Maya, actually. An eighty-two-year-old lady. You hit her in the heart and none of the thousands of comments on your thirty seconds of fame seem to have mentioned that.'

'I'm sorry. I'm so sorry. I didn't mean to.'

'It's not me you need to apologise to, Gareth. Anji is my best friend and you've exposed her and her family business to God knows what's next.'

She paused. Gareth tried to hold on to the seconds that passed before she spoke once more, willing a stasis upon them. Wanting to hold on to life while it was terrible, before she opened her mouth again and it became much worse.

'Gareth, after what happened the other night—'

'I'm so sorry, Nikki.'

He balled his fist and hit his forehead, trying to beat the sickness out of him, beat the memories and his actions out of his body.

'Gareth.'

He heard her sigh. He wanted to inhale her breath and hold it in his lungs forever, let it absorb into his bloodstream and run through every cell of his body forever.

'Gareth, I'm getting a lawyer. I'd like to split everything as fairly and as quickly as possible, including custody of Oscar. Please don't . . . please don't cause problems. Let's honour our marriage and our family, the way it used to be, and try to come through this as friends and partners who can co-parent Oscar in the way that's best for him. He's been through enough already. Is that okay?'

He covered the phone with his hands so she couldn't hear him cry out, the sound low and childlike, escaping from his body in waves.

'Gareth?' She waited. 'Gareth, are you okay?'

He took a few deep breaths. 'I'm okay. No, not really. But yes. Yes, I understand. Whatever's best for Oscar, and for you. Tell me what I need to do and I'll do it.'

RUBEN

Sydney

Ruben sat with Nikki while she made the call. He hadn't wanted to. It was her private business. Her marriage and her family. He wasn't the reason she was leaving Gareth. He loved her, but he wasn't the reason their marriage was over.

Did he strike Gareth to punish him for hurting Nikki?

Yes. Absolutely. He would never understand a man who tried to take what wasn't given.

Did he strike Gareth to punish him for touching Maya?

Yes. Even more.

Ruben heard Nikki say, 'Gareth? Gareth, are you okay?' And then he saw her relax when he agreed to her request. Her breathing slowed and her shoulders dropped a little. The human body was fairly simple in its responses to stress, and he knew Nikki's body well now. The clenching of her jaw at night when she was worried about something. The picking of her nails when she was about to give a patient or their family member disappointing news. The lift at the end of her sentence when she was lying.

254

There were also the lines around the corners of her eyes when she was laughing genuinely rather than politely. The spasm of her body and the arch of her back when she came.

She put the phone down on his side table.

'He said he'll do whatever I ask,' she said.

Ruben nodded, not wanting to take hope away from her. There was a long road ahead and plenty of time for Gareth to rethink his approach. Plenty of time for both of them to remember their anger.

'I should go.' Nikki turned back to look at him lying on the bed.

He swung his body around to sit next to her. He pressed his lips to her temple, the place where greying strands pushed through the blonde, the mingling of grey and gold creating a burnished silver. He hadn't asked her for more since Gareth had tried to hurt her.

In Sri Lanka, Ruben had seen torture in all its creative forms. He had seen soldiers use implements—penises, fingers, fists, bottles, broomsticks, barbed wire in pipes, and guns. He had seen these shoved, stuck, and burrowed into the body parts of screaming women, men, and children if they were unlucky enough to be alive when captured. He had seen them shoved, stuck, and burrowed into the body parts of the dead, so deep in the corpse that unseeing eyes bulged from the inside out.

But he had never seen a husband try to force himself on his wife. The only marriages he knew well were his parents' and Maya's. Both were loving, a bond that was respectful in life and transcended death. Nikki and Gareth's marriage was proof that marital bonds were different from the bonds of intimacy. And without the imprimatur of mutual consent, the last bonds had been broken.

He took her hand and kissed it. 'I'm sorry I hit your husband.'

'I'm not.'

'Me neither.'

'The clip has gone viral, Ruben. You might get unwelcome attention. You should talk to Anji about whether she's getting a lawyer and whether you need advice.'

'About what?' he asked. Despite what people on Twitter were saying, Ruben had only been defending himself and Maya.

'I honestly don't think Gareth will get the police involved,' Nikki said. 'He sounded embarrassed by the reaction. Ashamed even.'

'He should be ashamed; he hit an old woman, even if it was an accident.' Ruben looked at his hand. His knuckles were bruised, the skin on his middle finger split where he'd connected with Gareth's cheekbone.

Maya was fine. Shaken and shocked by the blow. Shaken but not shocked by the violence of Ruben's reaction. They had taken an Uber home in silence, Anji holding her mother's hand in the back seat and constantly checking on her. Ruben sat in the front, staring out the window as glass towers and cement ribbons sailed past him. Stuck in traffic, he had time to look at the sunlight dancing on the harbour, millions of diamonds catapulted on the waves, the pink haze of sunset drifting over from the west.

When they arrived at the nursing home, Maya had taken Ruben's bruised hand in hers.

'Mikka nandri, mahan,' she said. Thank you deeply, son. She reached up and kissed him on both cheeks, inhaling him, the way his mother used to do.

'Urimai,' he replied. A small word with a vast meaning. There is no need to thank me, you are entitled to this and more.

Urimai. You are entitled to my love.

Maya's eyes filled with tears. There was no need to say anything. He would have beaten Gareth into the ground if he had to. He would have rendered the dry earth of Sydney wet and red like the earth of his home.

She nodded. 'Urimai.'

～

The voices in the nursing home corridors fell suspiciously quiet as he pushed the laundry trolley along them, collecting piles of sheets from the floor of each room. The Nepali nurses giggled as he passed. He felt his face grow hot.

He emptied his trolley into the giant washing machines and did the same for the other trolleys waiting outside the laundry. He pulled his phone from his back pocket and allowed himself to look at the nonsense.

The YouTube clip had reached 1.1 million views. Who were these people with nothing better to do? And why did so many of them feel the need to comment?

Maya had set up a Twitter account for him with a fake profile linked to a new email address. He found it alarming how easily identity fraud came to her. Her own online presence as Sarah Byrnes was a simple homepage advising readers how to buy her books and telling them why they shouldn't try to find her.

'Your messages, your tweets, can't be longer than two hundred and eighty characters,' she advised him.

'I don't want to post anything. I just want to see what's going on.'

He didn't really want to see what was going on, but the looks from staff and families visiting the residents were becoming too obvious. A few minutes on Twitter and he understood why.

#youvetakeneverything was trending in Australia.

So was #aussiemanlosesit.

And #violentblacks.

And #goback2whereucamefrom.

A few hours later, the following was also trending in Australia: #swampedbyasians.

He looked at a few tweets.

> @SouthernCrossParty
> This is the inevitable consequence of multiculturalism gone mad. Political correctness gone police state.
> #youvetakeneverything

@andrew1974_ford
Wish I was this brave. Truth to power man
#youvetakeneverything

@millie_rob
I'm not racist but its time to think about why this poor
man felt pushed over the edge. I feel for him. He's entitled
to be heard. We're entitled to our frustration too. We're
entitled to have expectations of people who come here.

@lovemyute
It's about time. About bloody good time. We've all been
there. #youvetakeneverything

Been *where*? Ruben wondered. He opened a link to a video of
Senator Graham, from the Southern Cross Party, standing on the
steps of Parliament House. The senator turned his iPad, frozen on
a still shot of Gareth Barton, to face the crowd of journalists and
tourists surrounding him.

'This,' Senator Graham said, 'is what I've been talking about
for decades. This is a simple, quiet Australian, pushed beyond his
limit. This is a mainstream Australian who has been forced into
the margins. He has been silenced for too long. We must listen. We
must set aside our fears of being called "racist". What is that word,
racist? Does it mean an Australian who understands and accepts our
values and culture and expects others to do the same? Does it mean
an Australian who speaks up for the right to keep our culture, our
history, and our language intact instead of allowing it to be diluted
and corrupted and sidelined by others?

'If that's what it means to be a racist, then I am a racist, and you
should be too. This man is a hero. He speaks for all of us. I urge
you to listen. Like he says, migrants are coming here in floods.
They are supported by honest, hardworking, quiet Australians and
their hard-earned tax dollars. *They* are supported, not us. When we
defend ourselves, we are attacked for being racist.

'This is the reverse racism I've been talking about for years. When one minority group receives preferential support and treatment, and we are penalised for being white, that is reverse racism.

'They come here and live off us. They take our benefits and our jobs and jack up our house prices so decent Australians can't afford to buy their own home. The Australian dream is out of our reach because these people grabbed it first; these people stole it from us.

'Mark my words,' he said, pointing to Gareth Barton on his iPad again. *'They've taken everything from us.'*

An article in the *Sydney Morning Herald* noted:

Senator Graham's speech was inspired by recent events outside the Australian Human Rights Commission, where two men had an argument after an unsuccessful conciliation meeting. The argument ended with one man assaulting the other. The incident was captured on the mobile phone of a concerned bystander. Senator Graham quoted the outraged words of the victim, an Australian man who has since been identified as Councillor for Westgrove, Mr Gareth Barton. Mr Barton has not been available for comment and is recovering from his injuries. He has not pressed charges against the Indian assailant, but our sources reveal that NSW Police has now launched an investigation into whether this is an isolated incident, or whether this is part of a series of racist attacks on Mr Barton and he has reason to fear for his life.

Senator Graham's comments were met with criticism and concern from human rights organisations and refugee advocacy organisations. The Southern Cross Party has supported his statements, saying he speaks for all of them. Members of the major political parties have refused to comment.

Senator Graham reiterated his right to voice his patriotism and call out 'unAustralian behaviour by people who are not used to our ways'. He stated: 'Freedom of speech and freedom of protest are a fundamental part of being Australian. I will not be censored by liberals and their accusations of racism. People are afraid to speak out, afraid to speak their minds. What happened to Mr Barton shows us what happens when people are silenced for too long. That man is a victim. There are too many men and women like him, desperate to shout, scream and be heard.'

The exact details of the matter before the Australian Human Rights Commission are not known, but sources close to the councillor suggest he was the complainant and he was bringing a matter under the Racial Discrimination Act. The Commission stated that the incident on its steps does not reflect the Commission's approach to conciliation, which they reiterated is confidential and aims to help both sides come to a better understanding of each other's position and a negotiated settlement.

Senator Graham later noted that the Commission's purpose and value in Australian society was once again brought into question by this incident and he would be raising it with the Productivity Commission later in the year. He questioned the utility of taxpayers funding the 'political correctness police' and giving them open powers to silence everyday Australians. He added, 'As my good old dad used to say, "Lefties are flushing freedom of speech down the loo." He'll be turning in his grave right now, just thinking about what the inner-city elites have done to this country.'

Ruben went back to Twitter where #itsoktoberacist was trending. He found the one account he was interested in.

> @sarahbyrnes_author
> Questionable defence of free speech by @SenGraham
> who tried to ban the hijab #selectiverights

> @sarahbyrnes_author
> Freedom of speech is not a get-out-of-racism-free card.

@sarahbyrnes_author
Freedom of speech: the defence of all racists, sexists,
and homophobes.

@sarahbyrnes_author
Identity politics: harnessed by the right to divide the
country instead of exploring racial inequalities.

@sarahbyrnes_author
@SenGraham, why don't you just come out and say it?
The non-Anglo migrant Australian is never really fully
Australian. They're always on probation.

Sarah Byrnes had been on Twitter for twenty minutes and already
had 93,600 followers. Fewer than Kim Kardashian but more than
the average Australian author on her debut social media appearance.
Of course, Sarah Byrnes was not an average Australian author, or
an average Australian.

Ruben finished up in the laundry, his body still aching from
the last beating he'd taken from a quiet Australian, and went to
Anji's office.

'You okay?' she asked, putting away her papers and bringing
up the ABC website. 'So far, the media's been focused on Gareth.
Thank God for the ABC. They're the only one calling *his* outburst
the incident of racial hatred. Did you read this one?'

'No. I saw snippets in the games room.'

'Yes, I heard they applauded you.'

The uncles and aunties had given him a standing ovation. (Or
tried to; some had fallen over.) Almost every room in the nursing
home was tuned to ABC 24 instead of Sun TV, although there were
a few altercations because in *Idhayam*, the soap opera from Chennai,
Ahalya was just about to tell Gajan that she was carrying his child,
even though she was married to his evil twin brother Vinayak, the
wealthy plastic surgeon who ran a drug cartel on the side.

'You're a hero.' Anji smiled. She looked just like her mother when she smiled, and just like her father when she was thinking deeply about something.

'Not according to Senator Graham,' he replied. 'I'm the man that pushed poor Gareth Barton too far.'

'Yes, apparently you've taken everything. I was there.' Her eyebrows furrowed. She was thinking. 'Ruben, it won't take long before they find out why he was at the Commission. He might tell them himself. Nikki says someone at Westgrove Council ratted him out, so the council might even leak to the papers.'

'Doesn't seem smart. The Sri Lankans make up a big part of the council's support base.'

'They've fired him. He was on notice before this happened. There's a press release on the council website announcing his 'resignation' and their regret over his actions. They've appointed Bella Davidson in his place, and she'll run in the next election. Either way, the story will get out.'

'I'm sorry, Anji. If I hadn't taken the bait, none of this would have happened.'

He realised that since the incident he had slipped into using her first name all the time, instead of by accident. She seemed comfortable with that.

'He wasn't baiting you, Ruben. He was mouthing off and then he tried to hit you. The problem is if he decides to press charges. There will be footage somewhere on Pitt Street that would have captured the rest of the incident, not just the highlights that are making it onto YouTube. So even if he goes to the police, we'll be able to defend you.'

'Because the police are fair and not racist?'

'That's right.' She paused, pushing a thick curl behind her ear. 'Well, in *this* neighbourhood they are compelled by law to be fair and they're not overtly racist.'

'The problem isn't the police in this country,' he said. 'It's the people. The police just reflect the aspirations of the people. And judging by the coverage, a concerning number of people believe that Gareth's outburst was justified; that he was voicing a frustration shared by many Australians.'

Anji shook her head. 'The coverage just reflects what the noisiest, unhappiest Australians are saying, and politicians like Graham use it to amplify their voices and their hateful agenda. Graham's views don't reflect the views of the Australian public, but the clip has given him something with viral power. The more he keeps talking about it, the more he feeds it, the more powerful it becomes.'

Ruben loved Anji's optimism. She got that from Dr Ali. He was optimistic about human nature until the very end.

'You and I are going to have to disagree,' he said to her. 'In polite societies like Australia, you keep your racism in the closet, a set of advantages that are so deeply embedded you can't even see them. In Sri Lanka, we did away with such politeness a long time ago, and we write our racism into laws and state-sanctioned violence. The only difference between our two countries is time. Give Australia more time and you'll end up like us.'

Anji laughed sadly. 'And I'd thought I couldn't feel any worse about this whole thing. Thank you, Ruben.'

'You're welcome.' He smiled at her. 'If it makes you feel any better, I'm going to go sterilise bedpans now.'

'You know you don't need to do that job. You've been here such a long time and I've told you I can give you other work if you need the money.'

'And I've told you I'm happy to do any jobs that need doing.'

'You could get a job teaching languages at a university instead of teaching Tamil at Westgrove Public School on Sundays. Although my children would be devastated if you left Tamil School.'

The boys attended language class with Ruben Mama, as they called him, every week after maths tutoring with Maths Master Parameswaran in Room 13.

'I'll never leave your children,' Ruben said. 'They're natural Tamil speakers.'

'Only because you're a natural teacher. Please don't do the bedpans.'

'Any work done selflessly and offered to the divine is divine work. Including bedpans.'

'You know I can't argue with you when you quote the Bhagavad Gita, even if I know you're taking the piss—no pun intended.'

'No, but it was a pun well made.'

'Ruben, seriously, if the police call, please tell them you need to speak to your lawyer. Call me, and don't resist them in any way.'

He looked at her and nodded. 'Thank you, Anji. I know what to do when the police call.'

Jaffna, 2009

Ruben knew he was on the Sri Lankan government's payroll. He wasn't proud of it, but the job served his purpose. He had earned his family's freedom by working for the soldiers and police in Jaffna. Thanks to his connections, Amma and Nimi were given permission to leave and move to Colombo. Now he was saving to send them to London. His younger brother, Anil, had refused. He wanted to finish his medical studies and stay in the north, helping people, not 'spying for the enemy', as he put it.

For the next year, Ruben stayed in Jaffna, trying to watch over Anil the way Sanjay Anna had told him to. Anil resisted and rejected him, moving out of their small apartment and staying with Periamma, their mother's older sister.

One day, their aunt called him, crying. Anil had disappeared with a small team from Jaffna Hospital. They had heard that the army was moving from the west of the Vanni region, driving a human caravan across the north of the island, towards the east. Men, women and children making their way through the jungle with whatever they could carry. The army shelling them from the west, and the Tigers forcing them to act as human shields as they fired back. The doctors and nurses, some barely qualified, took supplies and joined the last NGO convoy heading into the war zone.

Ruben begged the brigadier to contact the NGO; if he could just speak to Anil, he could convince him to come back. The Tigers would make their last stand. They were outgunned and outnumbered. The people around them were already dead; there was nothing Anil or Ruben or anyone could do for them except encourage them to run.

Brigadier Fernando made the call to the NGO. Anil listened to his brother's tearful plea but didn't reply. Ruben imagined Anil's hands holding the satellite phone. The fingers that had been broken decades before had never reset properly; his left hand looked old and crooked beyond its years. He wanted to reach through the phone and hold his brother's hand one more time, pull him back from the mortar fire, the palmyra trees cracking open, spilling their entrails onto the dark earth, the sweet sap mixing with the sticky blood of children, the sky raining phosphorous and shrapnel, the screams ricocheting inside his head.

Ruben begged him to come home and Anil said nothing. Each of them had struggled with what happened in their childhood and Anil had finally found a way forward, even if the path would end on the eastern edge of the island, trapped between the Sri Lankan Army, the Tigers, and the Indian Ocean.

That was when Ruben started accepting different jobs with the army; jobs that took him into the war zone too. Under the protection of the army and its relentless march east, he scoured every village and examined every dead body in search of his brother.

Brigadier Fernando was assigned a mobile SIU, a Suspect Interrogation Unit, embedded in the Third and Sixth Battalions that were leading the western flank. The Sixth Battalion picked off the suspected Tigers and brought them to the brigadier. His new team had been trained in Colombo by the CID and a special unit of the Chinese People's Liberation Army. They conducted the interrogations and Ruben agreed to help translate the pain-filled screams into military intelligence.

The first time, he threw up for hours afterwards, trying to purge the memories from his mind long after his body had emptied itself. He cried himself to sleep. The next day, he asked the brigadier if he could have a sick day. The brigadier shook his head, his eyes glistening with tears too. Ruben was called back to the same make-shift cell; the same man, not much older than Anil, his naked body covered in cigarette burns that snaked a path from his chest down to his testicles. The soldiers kicked at him where he lay on the floor in his own blood and urine.

Ruben lifted a hand. He stepped forward, the fluids on the floor lapping his sandals and touching his feet. He picked up the man as gently as he could. Every movement caused him pain.

He spoke quickly and softly to him, the words of his father's favourite Thevaram, a prayer to Lord Murugan, the god of Tamils.

With each question the soldiers asked, Ruben added questions of his own, asking the man about his life and family, extracting memories from the recesses of his pain, something to hold on to in the dark. Asking him if he'd seen Anil.

And eventually, as Ruben became better at his job, he started asking the soldiers for water for the prisoners and then food and then short breaks and, one time, for mercy. He travelled deeper into the Vanni jungle with the army as they pushed east. At night, he made notes of all the places where he saw the bodies being buried. He tried not to think about all the places he didn't know. He participated in interrogations from the early hours of the morning to late into the night. He forced himself to be there with his people, taking and translating their testimony, their dying words, their declarations of love for family, their pleas to make it stop, their statements of guilt—some true but many false—and their final prayers.

ANJALI

Cinnamon Gardens

Anji pulled into the nursing home car park and listened to the end of the radio show host's tirade. She'd never listened to 2WMR before and didn't even know how to tune her car radio to find it. Her twin, Siddharth, had messaged her from London to tell her to ignore it.

The WMR in 2WMR stands for White Men Rule, he joked during their recent and increasingly frequent messages. They had a Whatsapp group with Amma and their partners, but this exchange was a private thread, so Anji could tell Sid the truth without upsetting their mother.

It was hard to hide the truth from Amma, though. The news—if she could call it that—was on every TV channel, on social media, the radio, and now on the outer walls of their nursing home.

The conciliation was supposed to be confidential, but extracts of Gareth's complaint had started to be quoted on the radio. Clearly someone had leaked it. She'd presumed it was Gareth, but Nikki said it was Westgrove Council, and she had no reason to defend Gareth.

Anji turned off the car and turned the volume on Mick 'Jonno' Johnson down a notch. As the owner of a diverse portfolio of assets, including part of an AFL team in Victoria, a health spa in Byron and a sheep station in South Australia, Jonno appealed to a broad cross-section of the bigoted.

Anji was sure he hammed up his ocker accent; the twang was too inconsistent, the use of idioms too frequent. No one who'd been educated at Shore Grammar School, holidayed in Courchevel and lived in Woollahra said, 'Struth, mate.' No one born after 1950 or who was not a character in a quirky Australian comedy said, 'Struth, mate.' She doubted anyone had ever really said, 'Struth mate,' except in the imagination of the true-blue mind.

Jonno's rhetoric was building towards its climax. 'Don't get me wrong, I love Indians. I love their curries, and they're damn fine cricketers. Really good at IT too. If I need someone to fix my wi-fi, I'll call an Indian.'

She exhaled deeply.

'But twenty years ago, there were less than a hundred thousand Indian people here. Now, there are almost five hundred thousand Indians. That's *half a million*! They're here, taking our education.'

Subsidising our education actually, Anji thought.

'Taking our jobs.'

Were they really?

'Everyone knows they only employ their own.'

Ah, that old chestnut. Jobs for the boys—who'd have thought that could be so offensive in this country, where most CEOs were the fourth generation educated in the same sandstone neo-Oxbridge colleges and quadrangles as their colleagues?

'And that's what's pushed this poor guy over the edge. He's just saying what we're all thinking; what we're all feeling inside but are too afraid of the political correctness police to say aloud.'

Where were these political correctness police, she wondered, throughout her time at school and university, her early years at hospital? Why weren't they issuing fines to consultants who congratulated her for being so brave and progressive because she got an education, married a white boy and didn't wear a hijab?

And the doctors who kept asking her, 'Where are you from?' and responded to her answer ('I'm from Westgrove') with, 'No, where are you *really* from?'

Once, a junior doctor had asked her if her children played cricket. When she answered no, that Kailash, Hari and Kethes preferred soccer like their father, he said, 'But it must be in their blood?'

'Not so much. Do *your* children have genocidal or criminal tendencies in their blood?' she replied, trying to smile.

In her upward-appraisal, the doctor had provided feedback that she was 'overly sensitive and lacked interpersonal skills and humour.'

Jonno took a deep breath, refilling his lungs with air, getting ready to convert that air into hatred and fear.

'I love this country, and I welcome people to it, people who share our values. For those who come across the seas, we've boundless plains to share.'

Surely he had not just quoted the national anthem.

'But these foreigners, who are escaping their shithole countries, come here and, like I said yesterday, they are a parasite, a cancer on Australia. We're trying to hold back the tide here, mate, with nothing but a boogie board to keep the rest of us afloat.'

A boogie board? She imagined Jonno sitting astride a boogie board in his budgie smugglers wearing an Akubra and sunscreen-based war paint across his face.

They, them and the rest of us.

Immigrants were no more tribal than the locals.

'This nursing home has gone too far,' he said. There it was. The reminder about Cinnamon Gardens. Her heart pounded painfully in her chest, a wild energy urging her to escape the threat. Danger was closing in and her limbic system was in a constant state of fight or flight. She tried to visualise her reptile brain and envelop it in a pink, soothing light, the way Nathan taught children at school.

'Fuck that,' she said out loud. Pink light wasn't going to help her.

'This nursing home, which has benefited from federal grants, which is supposed to look after some of the most vulnerable people in our community—'

God, he was making it sound like they were torturing old people.

'—has taken that money and that trust and, instead of being grateful, they spit on this country. This country which has given its owners refuge and a commercially successful business.'

Australia didn't *give* them more than it gave any other small business owner. And they had given back over the four decades since her parents had moved here and become taxpayers.

'I repeat, when you tear down a founding father of this country, you spit on its foundation. If you spit on this country, you spit on everything the Anzacs fought for.'

The *Anzacs*? Anji shook her head. When had they come into this? She bloody loved the Anzacs. They received a veteran's discount at Cinnamon Gardens.

Jonno continued. 'You spit on all of us. And we will spit back.'

After yesterday's *Jonno in the Morning*, and its 3 pm repeat, #foreignparasites and #foreigncancer began trending. At sunrise, Ruben had started scrubbing the words *parasite* and *cancer* off the outside walls. Her personal favourite was *Cook killer*.

Tomorrow they could look forward to some variation of *spit* on the walls, no doubt.

She had to admire Jonno's approach. Short, simple catchphrases, repeated on a loop. She walked from the car park down the driveway to the outer wall. Ruben was still working. The pressure hose had taken off several layers but she could see the imprint, like a faded tattoo.

'I asked you to stop. In fact, I didn't ask you to start this job. There's worse to come. I think we should just leave it up. Shame these idiots by leaving it there for everyone to see,' she said, turning off the hose at the tap.

'These idiots have no shame,' he replied, standing back to assess his progress. Soap foam flecked his dark skin and hair. 'I didn't want your mother to see it.'

She nodded, her chest tight and painful.

'Jonno in the Morning isn't the worst of them, but he's got the loudest microphone, I suppose.' Ruben dried his hands on a small towel and then wiped the sweat from his body under his t-shirt.

'You've been following him?' Anji asked.

'Following is an overstatement. 2WMR is repulsive, but I feel like I need to know what the people are feeling, if only to know what they'll be spray-painting next. Is it bad that I long for the days of *Fuck off bitch*?'

Anji laughed and felt some of the strain in her shoulders and neck ease. 'You didn't like Gareth applauding you at the Commission for availing yourself of Australia's fine education system?' she teased.

He grimaced. 'There was a lot about Gareth at the Commission I didn't like. To be honest, there's a lot about Gareth anywhere that I don't like. That said, he has reason to dislike me too.'

'Yes, I hear you. But that particular comment?'

He shrugged. 'I was educated largely in Sri Lanka. Jaffna University, before the war, was an excellent institution. My education wasn't driven by Western opportunities. All Tamils study hard. They want an education and, in the past, it's been the only thing that saved us.'

He soaked a steel wool scrubber in the bucket of water. 'That said, I'm washing walls and he's probably recruiting an agent to help publish his future memoir.'

'If he calls it, *You've Taken Everything*, I'm going to scream,' Anji said.

Ruben laughed and returned to work.

~♪

The next day, the nursing home's outer wall was covered in the words *we spit on you* and *ungr8ful bitch*. The word *bitch* always scared her. It seemed more personal than all the others she'd read on her wall.

She stood on the footpath, looking at the fuzzy spray-painted lines and letters in erratic sizes and angles but consistent in their accusation. Ruben had finally agreed to leave the graffiti there, at least until she emailed today's photos to the police, so they could ignore them like they had yesterday's photos and the photos from the day before that.

Ungrateful.

She *was* grateful to Australia for the refuge it had offered her family. She had never been ungrateful for that.

She. Was. Gr8ful.

But she had started to hate that word over the years.

You should be grateful, Anji; grateful that you've been able to build a life here in Australia. Grateful for all the opportunities this country has given you. Grateful that you've been able to do so well.

So grateful to Australia that you were not allowed to criticise it.

She'd heard that so many times from so many people; well-meaning, casually racist people who would never feel such vertiginous levels of gratitude from themselves for having the same opportunities because they were somehow entitled to them, while she wasn't.

Opportunity and refuge: the privilege of the migrant Australian. Our lifelong responsibility and debt to be repaid.

Opportunity and refuge: the entitlement of the white Australian. Your lifelong expectation.

Absorbed in tracking the words across the wall, she didn't notice the woman pushing a pram towards her until the woman drew close. Anji turned and smiled. The baby was leaning forward, one hand on the safety bar, the other pointing at the sky. There was a little dog tied to the pram, one of those caramel-coloured curly ones that looked like a toy bear. The baby clapped and Anji clapped back.

She glanced at the mother in time to see the woman moving her closed mouth in an elliptical manner, as though something was stuck and spinning inside it. As she passed Anji, the woman opened her mouth and coughed. Anji felt a cold, wet mass hit her cheek and spray across her face. She screamed and raised her hands, too shocked to do or say anything.

The woman ran, pushing her pram, its cross-country wheels rattling in front and the little dog stumbling behind her. She picked up the animal, threw it into the pram and sprinted away down the street.

Anji wiped the saliva and tears from her face on her sleeve and ran inside to the safety and refuge of her nursing home.

Anji insisted that the police officers attend the scene of the crime. They arrived in a pair, one male and one female, both young and unsure of how to help her. She showed them the vandalised wall and the broken CCTV cameras.

'It's not really a crime scene,' Officer Arkell said, flipping his notebook to a blank page.

'It is actually,' Uncle Gana answered. He had eschewed his plaid sarong and fake Lacoste polo shirt, and dressed up for law enforcement in a starched business shirt, grey slacks and Bata slippers. His hair was immaculately Brylcreemed as always and shone in the mid-morning sun. He stood behind the officer, watching him take notes.

'The graffiti on the nursing home wall is malicious damage,' he explained. 'The spitting is a public order offence. Malicious damage attracts a custodial sentence if the damage is severe. Spitting attracts a fine.'

'You're a criminal lawyer?' Officer Newton asked the old man, while she took photos of the words shouting at Anji across her wall.

'Mostly civil law, but I dabble in criminal when the need arises,' Uncle Gana said smartly. He smiled at Anji, prompting her.

She nodded nervously and said, 'This is the third time the graffiti has happened this week, the first time for the spitting, and it won't be the last for either of them. I'd like you to open an investigation.'

'An investigation?' Officer Newton stopped taking photos and looked at her. 'Dr Ali, we log your complaints, but unless we catch someone at it, or have suspects, or you identify the kids who are doing this—'

'*Perpetrators* is the word,' Uncle Gana corrected her.

'Right—perpetrators,' Officer Newton said. 'Unless we know who's doing this, there's nothing we can do about it.'

'That's the purpose of an investigation,' Uncle Gana replied.

'I'm sorry, sir, are you Dr Ali's lawyer?' Officer Arkell looked from him to Anji with irritation.

'He is my lawyer, thank you, Officer,' Anji replied. 'And he's right: it's not my job to hand you the perpetrators. It's your job to investigate what's happening here and find them. Walk the streets, knock on doors and ask questions. Tell people, tell the whole neighbourhood, that you're watching them. Tell them that vandalism and spitting aren't acceptable, that they're crimes.'

Do your fucking job, she thought.

Officer Arkell shut his notebook and took a deep breath. 'Look, Dr Ali, I know it's hard. This seems like a really nice place and you seem like a really nice lady—I mean doctor. It's just that, I don't think you want us stirring up the neighbourhood.'

'I'm not asking you to stir them up; I'm asking you to investigate them, or look at the CCTV footage at the train station and see who's coming into Westgrove at night. If we're lucky, they'll be openly and brazenly carrying cans of spray paint because they know they can vandalise with impunity, if they hit the right homes.'

'Look, it's not like that.'

'I think it's exactly like that, Officer,' she replied, her voice trembling. She hated that tremble. It made her sound weak.

Don't apologise, Uncle Gana had coached her. Do not plead when asking for your rights as a citizen. If they refuse, then you can take it up the line if you want, but don't give them a way out. Don't be deferential and quiet. Don't accept it, he coached her. She could see him looking at her now, waiting.

She exhaled. 'I think if this were the local fish-and-chip shop, run by Mr and Mrs Desmond who make killer calamari rings, you'd be canvassing the neighbourhood like you were Gary Sweet in *Blue Heelers*. I think you'd care enough to do your job. Even if you didn't care about the Desmonds, you'd do your job. But this is different, I'm different, so your approach is different.'

Officer Arkell opened his mouth and was about to speak but Officer Newton touched his arm lightly and shook her head.

'You are different, Dr Ali. But my colleague Rob is right and he means you no disrespect. What he's trying to say is, if we start knocking on doors, we'll draw more attention to you. We'll make you more of a target instead of less of one. We'll take a look at the station CCTV and see if there's anything suspicious happening at night. But if we ask too many questions, too loudly, we'll stir up trouble. You'll become the problem.'

'I'm pointing out the problem. You're asking me to just shut up?'

'I'm asking you to be patient.'

'Why do we always have to be patient?' she asked, her voice splitting and betraying her again. She swallowed hard, trying to imagine her throat relaxing and opening up, releasing the words into the world whole and strong.

The woman shook her head. Her kindness and confusion hurt more than if she'd been a racist dick about it.

'You're telling me *don't cause trouble*?' Anji said. By defending my rights. Don't cause trouble by asking for what's mine, she thought. Don't cause trouble by telling the truth. She felt the rebel tears well up in her eyes, angry and uncaring of the shame they caused her as they cascaded down her face.

'For now, Dr Ali, just for now,' the officer replied, handing her a packet of tissues from her pocket.

Anji's phone rang. She looked at it, grateful for the excuse to look away. It was the kids' school. Her heart hammered as it always did when the school rang.

By the time Anji arrived at the school, the other parents had already squeezed into the head teacher's office, facing Mrs Lang, who sat safely behind her large desk. From the far side of the small room, Mel and Dave smiled at her apologetically, Jacob sitting between them, tears and mucus running down his face. They all looked as though they were on detention.

Gareth and Nikki sat in the middle, with Oscar positioned like a guard rail between them, each of them holding on to one of his arms tightly in case he ran away and left them with each other. Gareth looked straight ahead, but Nikki smiled at her when she entered the room and mouthed the words, 'I'm so sorry,' to her.

Sorry for what? Anji thought, looking to Nathan for reassurance. Kailash sat on the last seat, his jaw set stubbornly forward, the muscle in his cheek jerking erratically from the effort of striking that pugilistic pose. He looked so much like her father when he was angry that her heart filled with sadness at the memory and then relaxed with relief. The school receptionist had reassured her that everything was fine, all three boys were safe. But she'd burst out crying again in front of the police, which resulted in a ride in a police car to Westgrove Public School.

'Sorry I'm late,' Anji said, gently nudging Kailash from the seat and taking it. She pulled him awkwardly onto her lap—just what every ten-year-old boy wanted in front of his peers and head teacher.

'No problem at all, Dr Ali. I was just about to explain what happened and why we're here. There's been a little misunderstanding, but I think if we all talk about it together, we can clear things up quickly.'

Mrs Lang smiled at everyone encouragingly and Anji had a terrible sense of deja vu. This was her second conciliation with Gareth for the week. She prayed it would go better than the first one.

'I know that all of your families are friends and things are a little strained at the moment.' She looked meaningfully at Gareth and then Anji.

Anji felt her face flush. Nathan placed his arm along the back of her chair, not touching her but just there, lightly. She shifted back in the chair and his hand touched the top of her shoulder. She breathed in for three seconds and out for four, quietly and slowly. She placed one arm around Kailash's waist, her hand at the base of his rib cage. She could feel the tension coiled in his small body, poised for flight.

'It seems that Kailash called Oscar a bad word in the playground today and that some of the other children—Jacob in particular— followed suit.'

Jacob's whimper escalated into uncontrolled sobs at the sound of his name. Mel and Dave covered his mouth with tissues and hissed frenetic *shhh*s, hitting his back as though they were trying to save him from choking rather than soothe him.

'Careful,' Mrs Lang admonished them. 'Let him breathe, Mrs Richardson.'

'What happened, Mrs Lang?' Gareth asked.

Anji saw Nikki's body tighten at the sound of Gareth's voice. She leaned away from him towards Nathan, on her other side.

Mrs Lang coughed nervously. 'Well, today at lunchtime, Kailash called Oscar'—she cleared her throat again—'a racist.'

Anji felt the air rush out of the room.

'I wonder where he could have learned that from,' Gareth said to no one in particular and yet directly to her. She felt Nathan's hand on her shoulder tighten a little.

'Why don't we hear what happened from the children, Mrs Lang?' Nathan asked. 'This is a safe space for them to practise telling us how they feel and why they've done what they've done. Then, together we can help them understand the consequences of their actions and help them take responsibility for those consequences. We love them and support them. And, to be honest, as adults we're still learning how to do those things too.'

Anji smiled and relaxed further into Nathan's embrace. Complex children, broken families, and toxic playgrounds: that was her husband's domain, the place where he wasn't a unicorn but a fucking magician.

'Right, yes. Of course,' replied Mrs Lang, not used to losing control of her own meeting. 'Ah . . .'

'Kailash, how about you talk us through what happened first. Sometimes people have a different interpretation of an event, so after you, we'll ask Oscar to tell us his side. Does that sound okay, mate?'

Oscar nodded at Nathan and Nikki smiled at him, grateful to him for chairing the meeting instead of Mrs Lang or Gareth.

Nathan touched the top of his son's hair to prompt him. 'Go ahead, Kailash.'

'We were playing handball when Tom, Hugo's little brother, said that Oscar's dad, Uncle Gareth, was on the news talking about immigrants. He said that Uncle Gareth was angry at all of us for taking everything away.'

Kailash paused, looking at Anji with those hurt, confused eyes. She kissed his head and breathed in the reassuring smell of her child's sweat and sunblock.

'Keep going,' she whispered.

He nodded. 'Oscar said people said the immigrants were taking over. There were too many of us . . .' He paused again.

Mrs Lang leaned forward across her desk. 'Yes, Kailash?'

'Then Oscar organised everyone,' Kailash said, as if that explained everything.

'Organised everyone, darling?' Nikki said.

'Yes, Aunty Nikki. He sorted us into groups—all the kids on the handball court.'

'How did he sort you, mate?' Nathan asked, even though they could all guess the answer.

'He put the white kids on one side of the handball court and the rest of us on the other side. There were four white kids, including him and Jacob, and nine other kids: me, Gopi Ravi, Muraly Krishnan, Eric Tse, Kiran Mongia, Ray Sim, and a couple of others. There were more of us, and Oscar said, "See? Dad was right: they're taking over." Then I said, "That's racist," and then he said, "You can't call me that, I'm telling."'

'And now you're here?' Nathan said.

Kailash nodded and buried his face in Anji's body.

'Okay,' Mrs Lang said. 'Okay.'

Anji could see Nathan raise his eyebrows at his boss's eloquence.

'Oscar,' he said softly. 'You heard what Kailash said. If you disagree with any of it, even the tiniest bit, I want you to tell us, mate. Tell us what happened, from the beginning, in your own words.'

Oscar bit his lip and receded into the space between his parents.

Nikki turned her body towards Oscar and Gareth, even though it cost her. She took her son's face in her hands. 'I know it's hard, but you can do this. I know you can. You're not in any trouble, darling. Mummy loves you.' She stopped. 'Mummy and Daddy love you. We just want to help you all. Okay?' She smiled at him reassuringly.

He nodded back at her. 'That was it,' he whispered.

'What was?' Gareth asked, his face pale. 'Speak up, Oscar.'

'That was it,' Oscar repeated. 'What Kailash said. I put them in teams so I could show them what you said was true, Dad.'

Gareth shook his head. 'And then he called you a racist?'

'Yes. Then the others started calling me racist too, even Jacob and Kiran. I called Miss Taylor, because it's a bad word.'

'It is a bad word, you're right, Oscar, and I'm sorry you had to go through that,' Gareth said. 'Perhaps you and Kailash can apologise to each other and we can move on.'

Anji had to catch herself from laughing as the head of every adult in the room whipped around to stare at Gareth in disbelief.

'Mr Barton, the situation that Kailash and Oscar have described for us is more complicated than mere name calling. Your son, he, well, he . . .'

'Gareth . . .' Anji leaned forward. She heard Nathan whisper, 'Kavanam,' asking her to be careful. Nathan had an excellent grasp of the right five Tamil words at the right time.

Mrs Lang raised her hand. 'Maybe we can send the boys out to get some fresh air, so we can talk?' She shepherded the three boys into the arms of Miss Taylor, who was waiting outside, and shut the door behind them.

'Gareth . . .' Anji repeated his name, but he wouldn't look at her.

'Mrs Lang, I see exactly what's happened here. Kailash is a great kid but he's very sensitive; a little—how should I put it?—fragile. They're just kids playing a game; kids can't be racist.'

Mrs Lang looked at him over the tops of her glasses. 'I've been an educator for forty years, Mr Barton,' she said, pushing her glasses back up the bridge of her nose, 'and in my experience, unintended racism is just as hurtful as intended racism. Sarah Byrnes, my favourite author, has just tweeted about this very thing. She says we can't hide behind wilful ignorance.'

'Sarah Byrnes?' Anji said. Her mother had a Twitter account? 'But that's—'

'Absolutely, Mrs Lang,' Nathan interrupted her before she could out Amma. 'People who criticise others for being overly sensitive, who claim they didn't mean to be racist, usually feel entitled to their racism, whether they're prepared to call it racism or not,' Nathan said.

'That's *exactly* what Sarah Byrnes said,' Mrs Lang replied.

'I know,' said Nathan. 'She's my favourite author too.'

'I had no idea, Nathan.' Mrs Lang blushed.

'Mrs Lang, if I may?' Gareth interrupted. He turned to Nathan. 'Your son *is* overly sensitive. As I said before, it was just a game. A stupid game but, still, just a game.'

'Your son segregated his handball friends on the basis of race. In another country that was once called apartheid,' Anji replied.

She saw Nikki cringe and nod at her. Gareth saw it too but ignored his wife.

'Oh, come on, Anji. Don't be so dramatic. You and your family have certain personal heightened sensitivities around colour and oppression, which I can understand, but that doesn't mean the rest of us have to pander to it.'

Anji took a deep breath and ignored Nathan's warning look this time. 'Gareth, your *lack* of sensitivity around colour segregation cannot be assumed to be the universal norm on this. But once again, as a white cis-gendered male, you've assumed that your perspective is the neutral perspective and people who differ from you are wrong.'

'What the hell are you talking about, Anji? Don't forget you married a white cis-gendered male too.'

'I'm right here, Gareth,' Nathan said. 'And I know I'm the king of the jungle, whereas you behave as though you're an endangered, persecuted species. By the way, these *sensitivities* of Anji's that you dismiss as personal? They're not personal sensitivities. They are concerns about your son's behaviour that we all have. You have them too, but you're in a deep hole of your own making and you don't know how to get out.'

'I'm concerned,' Nikki whispered. She strained her body even further away from Gareth, holding her hands together tightly. 'I'm concerned about his behaviour. What he did was wrong. I can see where it came from; we all can.' She took a deep breath and spoke again, her voice clearer. 'But he was still wrong. I'm as shocked and upset as you—much more, actually. I'll talk to him, Mrs Lang. I know I need to. And I'm sorry, Anji and Nathan. I'm just so sorry. I don't know what else to say.'

'Don't do that, Nikki,' Gareth said. 'Don't apologise to them, after everything that's happened.' He reached for her and then pulled his hand back.

'Don't tell me what to do,' she said, the words gathering a force of their own. 'You're not in a position to offer parenting advice to me or anyone.'

Gareth flinched as though Nikki had hit him. Anji had heard those words from Nikki before, but only in the privacy of their friendship, in the throes of unbridled grief and obliterating rage. But she'd never said them to Gareth's face, and never in public.

'I . . . I . . .' Gareth couldn't speak; he just stared at Nikki as if seeing her for the first time.

'Mr Barton,' Mrs Lang said. 'I think more than one apology is required and we may need some time together to talk about that.'

'No. Nathan's making something out of nothing.' Gareth shook his head, exhaling loudly, his face flushed a deep red. Anji knew it was shame, not anger, but he was attacking her husband and her son, and in that moment she hated him for it.

'He's a school counsellor,' Gareth continued, 'and that's his job: to see problems where there are none. Nikki *and I* will speak to Oscar about the game.'

'Game?' Anji repeated. Only Gareth would keep spinning in this situation.

'Yes, a *game*. Jesus, Anji, you've heard a few podcasts, shared other people's Facebook posts, read a *New York Times* bestseller, and now you think you're so woke.'

'Not woke, and not racist.'

'Neither am I, and I resent your suggestion that we are. I resent your suggestion that this is a racist country. I don't know what's happened to you, Anji, but you've changed.'

'*I've* changed?' She exhaled and waited. She gave Gareth one more chance to be less of a dick and more of the man she had met at university.

Instead, Gareth nodded and said, 'I will handle my child. But you need to handle yours. Kailash can't call people names like that without consequences. He hurt Oscar's feelings and he needs to apologise for that.'

Nathan leaned over to her and whispered, 'Inside Voice. And don't swear; Lang will card you.'

Anji felt the rage rising up from her feet—or maybe it was from the earth beneath her feet. Molten rage from the centre of the earth rising through her blood and bone, a volcano of words she had swallowed her whole life and more words swallowed in the last week since the meeting at the Human Rights Commission. Words that sat in the bottom of her gut and had become swollen and bloated, choking her from within.

She remembered her Inside Voice and spoke slowly, so the fuckwit didn't miss anything.

'He needs to apologise? *He* needs to apologise? For telling the truth? Your son is copying your behaviour, repeating your words and finding ways to justify them, finding ways to reconcile the ugliness of what he's hearing at home with the love he feels for you. Kailash is not the problem; he pointed out the problem.'

Gareth swallowed hard, his hands clenched into fists. She saw Nikki look at his hands, but this time her friend didn't shrink back. Nikki exhaled and straightened her back, her body strong and resistant. She moved her chair away from Gareth, towards Nathan and Anji, towards the side—the family—she had chosen.

Gareth saw it too, tears in his eyes.

'You think you're so much better than us, Anji,' he said. 'So much better than me. I'm not stupid. I see the way you all look at me; the way you still judge me.'

He stopped, breathless.

Anji smiled sadly and shook her head. 'Gareth, I suspect we all see you more clearly than you see yourself right now.'

She felt Nathan's hand on hers.

Gareth had said enough. He had revealed enough.

'Mr Barton,' Mrs Lang interjected quietly, 'as I said, I need to have a much longer conversation with your family about this. Not with the others, for now.' She looked at Anji and the rest of the adults with a practised neutrality. 'I'll contact you all by email this afternoon. May I suggest that you find your children and take them home? Let's allow them to settle down and reflect on what's happened today.'

'Thank you, Mrs Lang,' Nathan said, standing up. He grabbed Anji's hand and led her out into the playground, where Kailash, Oscar, and Jacob were playing handball together.

As they approached the boys, Anji heard a rush of footsteps behind her. Worried it was Gareth, she quickened her pace. But it was more than a single pair of footsteps, she realised; it sounded more like a stampede.

Nathan tugged her hand, swearing loudly. 'Keep going, avoid eye contact. Jesus, these bastards move fast.'

Anji looked around to see a swarm of journalists converging on her.

'Dr Ali, Dr Ali! Is it true your son called Councillor Barton's son a racist? Do you really think the playground is the right place to air your personal grievances?'

Turning, she pushed Kailash behind her body, away from the camera lenses that were aimed at her.

'Call Jane Butler,' she shouted to Nathan. 'Tell her to get the twins.'

Another voice, more aggressive than the first. 'How do you respond to accusations that you and your son have no respect for freedom of speech, one of the pillars of Australian democracy?'

A long boom mic extended from the group and dropped in front of her face like an alien limb. It had a 2WMR badge on it.

'Surely children should be allowed to be children and say what they feel on the playground. If not on the playground, then where are we free to speak, Dr Ali? Aren't you taking us one step closer to censorship disguised as political correctness?'

Anji stepped forward to exercise her freedom of speech and argue with the defender of Australia's shaky democratic pillars, when the crowd of journalists veered left and circled back towards the school building as another, more interesting target came into view.

'Mr Barton! Mr Barton! Have you seen Senator Graham's Twitter feed this afternoon?' one called.

Another broke in: 'He says this is a terrible day for freedom of speech in this country. He says your son's a hero, like you. He agrees with little Oscar that this school is a perfect example of immigration gone too far; immigration that has become a kind of colonisation of its own. He says migrants and the radical left-wing are driving race divisions by giving preferences and handouts to foreigners. He says that's racism towards white people.'

'Mr Barton, Mitch Hillard here from Radio 2WMR. We'd love for you and Oscar to come in and talk to Jonno in the Morning and speak directly to the Australian people. They've been waiting for someone like you to tell it how it is.'

Anji saw Nikki sprint past the journalists who had formed a tightening circle around Gareth. She grabbed Oscar from the handball court, whispered, 'I'll call you later, I'm so sorry,' to Anji, kissed her quickly and kept moving towards the car park.

'You've got Jacob?' Anji said to Miss Taylor. 'Mel and Dave should be right behind us.'

Miss Taylor nodded; she couldn't take her eyes from the drama.

Anji heard her phone ping. It was a text message from Mel.

> So sorry abt this mess. I feel terrible. Am ashamed. Will
> talk to Jacob asap. He's so sorry too. Pls call me lets
> talk soon. xx

There was an emoji of a heart.

Anji felt the tears starting to fall again. She grabbed Kailash and followed Nathan to the car park.

That night, after the six o'clock news on every channel reported the Playground Politics, as the incident was now known, #whitelivesmatter and #itsoktobewhite started trending on Twitter.

According to *Media Watch*, the words 'free speech crisis' were used over 963 times in the next twenty-four-hour news cycle.

The fiasco in the playground was all over the media, and people were spitting on other people they assumed to be South Asian immigrants. Spitting and running. A spate of spit-and-runs. In the western suburbs, the spit-and-runs quickly became spit-shove-and-runs committed by young men in hoodies. At Westgrove station, the spitting and shoving resulted in three schoolchildren and two women falling off the platform onto the train line. They were rescued by onlookers, but it was only a matter of time before a sari pallu became trapped under the tracks and bodily harm became homicide.

The ABC and SBS reported the racially motivated attacks. The race commissioner of the AHRC condemned them. *The Daily Telegraph* didn't notice them.

Terrified South Asian parents started driving their children to school. East Asian parents started doing the same, just in case all Asians looked the same to angry white people. Anji started carpooling with her neighbours, Jane and Paul Butler. The children usually walked to school, but she wasn't taking any chances.

Westgrove Police Station installed cameras in reinforced cages at the station and Officer Newton called to tell Anji that they would now have an officer stationed on the train platform from 6 am to 9 pm; two officers during peak times.

Anji disconnected her barely used landline after she started receiving abusive phone calls at home. The receptionist at Cinnamon Gardens was instructed to write down the number of every phone call that appeared on Caller ID before she answered it. The previously disengaged receptionist was now alive to the media storm she was part of, and after the eleventh abusive call, she returned fire. Her part of the call appeared as a soundbite on 2WMR and was cited by Jonno in the Morning as an example of 'the disgusting way immigrants talk in this country'.

Jonno quoted Senator Graham's endless Twitter feed, saying, 'There was no racism in Australia until multiculturalism became fashionable. Immigrants brought racism with them from their home countries. That's where racism and multiculturalism should stay. It should go back to where it came from.'

The next day, *COOK KILLERS go back 2 where u came from BITCH* appeared on the nursing home wall.

Nathan, Ruben, Nikki, nursing home staff, and families of the residents helped her to scrub the graffiti from the wall every day, but every night some variation of it returned. Cars slowed down to watch them on the street. One car, a dirty white van, crawled past often, its passengers hidden behind dark windows. She tried not to look at the driver, but she knew he was looking at her. Once, the van followed her home from the nursing home. She called Officer Newton, her voice shaking as she gave the policewoman the fragments of the number plate she could remember.

The Westgrove Chronicle ran an interview with the new councillor, Bella Davidson, who drew on her years as a human rights advocate for an unknown human rights organisation to urge racial harmony.

'Australians are kind people who give everyone a fair go,' she said, speaking from her penthouse apartment in one of the latest high-rises to be built next to Dartmouth Station, the suburb on the easternmost boundary of their western suburb electorate.

'This kind of behaviour is unAustralian and uncalled for. I love the different cultures of our great country and our beautiful suburb,' she said, from thirty-two floors above the densely populated, spit-covered streets of Westgrove. 'It's what makes this modern-day masala so rich and nourishing. Just like the butter chicken I make from scratch.'

The article was followed up by Instagram posts from Councillor Davidson, attending local Deepavali celebrations in a sari, her plastic bangles and sequined bindi sparkling in the light of so many well-placed cameras. Her hashtag #moderndaymasala did not begin to trend.

The piece in *The Westgrove Chronicle* was posted on the Democratic Alliance Party website, and then a screenshot of it appeared on the Southern Cross Party Instagram account, with the caption, *Today a sari, tomorrow a burqa.*

The Daily Telegraph ran a page-two article about Gareth Barton, investigating the timing of his 'resignation' and revealing that he had been fired by the council, possibly unfairly, at the time of the concili-ation conference at the Australian Human Rights Commission. The piece noted that the Barton family were recovering from the sudden and tragic death of their three-year-old daughter, Florence, ten months earlier.

The article suggested that Gareth had been fired because he was courageous enough to call out the nursing home's systemic racism and the Westgrove Council, fearing it would lose the support of the significant Sri Lankan Tamil population in the electorate, jettisoned the concerned local councillor. The article noted that Gareth's wife, Dr Nikki Barton, who worked for the nursing home, had moved out of the Barton residence, probably fearing reprisals from her employer, who hired migrants and fired Australians with impunity.

The morning after the article was published, the nursing home walls were no longer covered in graffiti. The nursing home bus, parked inside the nursing home grounds, was covered in faeces and the contents from many sanitary napkin bins. Anji's car, parked in the driveway of her home three streets away from Cinnamon Gardens, was painted with the words, *Racist Cunt* and, *Die Black Bitch*. Its windscreen was smashed in and Anji watched as people in hoodies emptied another sanitary napkin bin on top of it and ran away.

She called the police and stood silently while Officers Arkell and Newton took photographs. They were accompanied by a third man in plainclothes who introduced himself as Peter Woodbury. She assumed he was their boss because the younger officers were deferential and edgy around him as he instructed them on how to record the crime scene.

She sent the children to the Butlers' next door, Nathan hoisting Kailash, Hari and Kethes over from their side of the fence, Paul Butler waiting on the other side to receive them. Jane Butler put the kids in the car in her garage and sped them out, narrowly avoiding the growing crowd of journalists and strangers who were congregating outside Anji's house to take photos.

'I think it's time to upgrade the old Volvo,' Anji said to Nathan, trying hard not to cry. She loved this car. It had carried her babies safely for ten years. It was a gift from her parents five years before that, when she had taken on more formal responsibilities at the nursing home. Appa had made her take the car to the Murugan temple for the priest to bless it. The priest stood in the car park wearing his white sarong and nothing else, the morning sun shining on his ample man boobs. For twenty dollars, he anointed the car with holy ash, holy sandalwood, and holy water. Anji broke a coconut on the ground near the car and a shard bounced up in slow motion, narrowly missing the windshield and cursing the car with bad luck.

'But it's the safest seven-seater on the market,' Nathan said, handing her his cup of coffee.

'We should lean into our immigrant coloniser new money status. If we're going to get hated on, we may as well deserve it,' Anji said, taking a big sip.

'Really? Does this mean we also get to knock down our tasteful Federation-style cottage and build a perimeter to perimeter McMansion in greige? If so, there's a showroom in Harwood I've been desperate to check out. I hear they have the best neo-Corinthian columns and multi-layered water features in Western Sydney.'

'I'm in, but first we need a new car.' She returned his cup to him. The hot coffee had helped diffuse the constricting pain in her throat a little; not a lot. Her whole body hurt with anger and fear.

'Please can I get a fuchsia-coloured Lexus convertible? The Tses have one and it looks hot. Vanity plates and all. It's the Asian banker's vehicle of choice.'

'You're not an Asian banker,' Anji said, laughing finally.

'No, but if we play our cards right, one of our children will become one and we can retire early.'

'Okay, but only if I get to choose the number plate,' Anji replied. She tried to imagine showing up at the temple in a fuchsia-coloured convertible for the priest's blessing. The temple car park was full of grey Mercedes, BMWs and Volvos, all bearing vanity plates with auspicious words and numbers, such as SAI108, VSNU108, KRSNA108 and AUM108.

'Anything for you, kunju,' Nathan said, his Tamil endearment pronounced badly but lovingly. 'How about FKUYTS?' he suggested. 'Too aggressive?'

She nodded and sighed. 'I know I sound angry all the time. I hear myself giving everyone the same lectures my father gave us, correcting people and pushing back. I wasn't always like this,

Nath. It's just, since having the children, I worry more about the world they're living in.'

'You're allowed to worry. Have you seen our car?' he said. 'No hurry on the plates, we can work it out later.'

'I was thinking about something simpler.' She walked towards the police officers who had completed their photo shoot and were getting ready to leave. They smiled at her apologetically, handing her paperwork to sign.

She thought about her father, who had held Kailash as a baby and named him at the temple. Appa had never met Hari or Kethes, the twins named Haridhwar and Ketheeswaram. All three of their sons were named after the most beautiful temples in India, in honour of their religion but also in honour of the grandfather they would never know.

'Anbu,' she answered. 'Maybe ANBU108.'

Anbu. Her favourite Tamil word. Her mother's favourite too. The first word in Tamil Amma had taught her, after she taught her to say Amma.

It meant *love*.

NIKKI

Cinnamon Gardens

Nikki flicked through the channels on her father's television while eating his leftovers for dinner. Although Aunty Vidya had died, the legacy of her kale curry lived on. She had invented it decades before kale became a superfood, using the local species but also adding vallaarai, the sharp Sri Lankan salad leaf Ruben grew in the nursing home garden. Ray flatly refused to eat his greens. Even when he wasn't lucid, he was consistently resistant to it, but she loved it.

She stopped flicking when she arrived at her desired TV destination. Anji had been approached for a comment before the interview aired on *30 Minutes*, but declined. Bradley Preston's square jaw filled the screen, his casual stubble and craggy face giving him the aura of a foreign correspondent speaking to his audience from a bomb shelter in Aleppo, instead of the shiny studio in Ultimo that was residence to a team of make-up artists who helped him achieve the look. Bradley—or Presto, as he was known to his fans—cocked his head to the side and leaned forward, this trademark arrangement of features and body language intended to convey concern for public wellbeing and deep journalistic integrity.

'Senator Graham,' he said to the older man in front of him, 'you're a polarising figure in Australian politics.'

'Thank you, Presto,' the senator replied.

'It wasn't a compliment, idiot!' Ray shouted at the TV, waving his fork.

The corner of Bradley's mouth lifted a little. 'You're loved and hated in equal measure—'

'I don't mean to interrupt you there, Presto, but I'd venture to suggest that I'm loved more than I'm hated. It's just that some people are so afraid of the political correctness police, they don't want to publicly support me. Thankfully the ballot box is confidential—a safe space, shall we say, for people to air their legitimate concerns and to have their voices heard through their vote.'

'Rightio, Senator, this is not a free political advert—let's stick to your most recent revelations on Twitter. You say you've been conducting an in-depth investigation into the Cinnamon Gardens Nursing Home, its owners and its staff, is that right?' Presto asked. 'Since when did the Southern Cross Party dabble in investigative journalism?'

'Exactly!' Ray interrupted again. 'You tell him, Presto.'

'Dad!' Nikki shook her head.

Graham laughed as though Presto was sharing a joke with him. 'Since we hired a dark arts media operative last year to help us stay on top of these hipster liberals who are corrupting our country. Hipster liberals, left-wing radicals and immigrants. They're changing the face of Australia and infiltrating all our institutions, from our universities to our corporations, making it harder for small businesses and workers, the quiet Australians, to say their piece without getting shot down as racists.'

Nikki had to laugh as she watched Presto shift uncomfortably in his chair, seemingly sensing he had finally met an interviewee who controlled the mic better than he did.

'There's a lot there to unpack,' Presto said. 'Let's start with your investigation and perhaps circle back to your dark arts media operative; I definitely want to know more about him or her. So, your investigation: you tweeted about this today, linking to an article you wrote for your website. The article has been considered inflammatory by some, and has been referred to the Australian Human Rights Commission—'

'By the hipster liberals. The Commission is run by the left-wing radicals to listen to the complaints of hipster liberals and immigrants, while being paid for by the taxes of quiet Australians.'

The senator threw his hands up, mirroring the emoji Oscar often used when messaging her about his forgotten cricket kit.

Nikki wasn't worried about left-wing radicals; it was the right that terrified her. And angered her. Everything made her angry at the moment.

'Let's stick to your investigation and article, Senator. The Commission is investigating it, and Twitter has removed your post in anticipation of it triggering anti-vilification laws.'

'Gag laws.'

'Anti-vilification laws. But why don't you talk us through your article. Just the facts, Senator, as you see them.'

As Senator Graham saw them? What does that mean when talking to an inveterate racist? The facts according to white supremacists were a little different from the facts according to everyone else.

'Thank you, Presto, I'm glad you asked. Our investigation has revealed that not only are the owners of Cinnamon Gardens racist against white Australians, not only are they opposed to Captain Cook and the founding of this great country, not only are they ungrateful for the privileges that this country has given them, that they would not enjoy in the country they came from, the country they should go back to, but—'

The senator paused for effect, and the camera switched to Preston's piercing blue eyes, clipboard balanced on his bent knee, pen in one hand, the other hand sweeping back his thick brown hair with strategically placed flecks of mature-but-not-old grey. He cocked his head and leaned into the camera. Australia leaned into their TV screens and Nikki with them, her spoonful of kale and vallaarai curry poised in mid-flight.

'Yes?' Presto prompted.

'They're also Muslim.'

'Fuck me,' Ray said.

'Too right, Dad.'

That night, the internet went mad.

> @lovemyute
> It all makes complete sense now. Its always the Muslims. Always.

> @AustraliansforAustralia
> I knew it. Be like 9/11 all over again. Its just a matter of time. The stuff at the commission is just the start. Mark my words. Just the start. Shit just got reel.

> @millie_rob
> I don't see colour. I honestly don't think of people as black and white. I think only people of colour see colour and that's a big part of the problem. We should talk about that respectfully too. I think they'd feel better if they knew how we really saw them.

> @George_JacksonQC
> What's happened around the world to Muslims is terrible. Iraq was a deep injustice and Syria a humanitarian disaster. But they have to realise that they need to be careful. They need to think about what they say and do because they're easy targets during these testing times.

@FirstFleetTheOnlyFleet

No wonder they hate Captain Cook. We have allowed
immigrants to overrun the country. We have allowed
Muslims to overrun the world. We need to protect
Australian values and Australian culture. The Quiet
Australians have had enough of the Murderous Muslims.
We were here first and we will be here last.

@AustraliaforAustralians

We will all be beheaded under sharia law. Need to strike
first. Spread the word. Be ready.

The next morning, a dead pig was left on Anjali's front doorstep. Kailash opened the door to get the paper and started screaming. Nathan moved the children and their dog into the Butlers' house next door. Ruben offered to move in with them and sleep in the front room, but Anji wanted him at the nursing home, just in case.

Gareth called Nikki and left a hesitant voicemail when she didn't pick up. He sent her a more coherent email an hour later. It involved a full-bodied apology for what he'd started, and a plea for her to come home.

'What did you think was going to happen, Gareth?' she said when she finally called him back.

'I didn't mean for it to go so far. I'm so sorry about everything. I had no idea this would happen,' he said, the words hurtling from his mouth as if he was afraid she would hang up.

'You had no idea? No idea,' she said softly. 'A dead pig on the doorstep. That child will have nightmares about this; they all will. They are terrified. Children scared to go out. Oscar's best friend. My best friend. Good people.' The tears rose up and choked her. 'My people, Gareth.'

What was there left to say?

'I'm sorry,' he repeated.

'I know you are,' she said, exhaling. It surprised her that it still hurt to see him in pain. 'I know you are.'

Nikki turned off her phone and opened up her laptop. She checked the only 'news' that gave her comfort, a surprising new Twitter feed. Sarah Byrnes was her mother's favourite author, but Bek South had died never knowing the secret Anji had eventually told her.

> @sarahbyrnes_author
> Muslims? Took you long enough to work it out. Thank god the security of this country isn't in the hands of Southern Cross #notASIO I am confident no nursing home residents have been beheaded, circumcised, fitted with vest bombs or denied pork against their will. Reject Islamophobia #multiculturalAustralia

> @Minister_Multiculturalism
> Australia is a multicultural society, a peaceful, safe, and beautiful place to live, study, and visit. @sarahbyrnes_author come talk to us about it we love your books #multiculturalAustralia #clementinekellyrules

> @sarahbyrnes_author
> @Minister_ Multiculturalism backs #multiculturalAustralia as long as it exists in a fundamentally white Australia, on the terms of white Australians, and facilitates tourism and the inter-national student market. #whatthebloodyhellareyouthinking?

> @sarahbyrnes_author
> Hosting Bollywood-themed birthday parties does not make you culturally competent. Also, chai means tea. There's no such thing as tea tea.

Maya's loyal fanbase responded to @sarahbyrnes_author's tweets with hundreds of thousands of retweets and posts, urging the author to speak out more, to show her face and lead her readership away from the storm brewing over their sunburnt country. *Women's Weekly* ran another 'Who is Sarah Byrnes?' feature, the eighth one in the four decades since she'd started writing. Sarah had insisted on being interviewed for this piece by Tanuza Rahman, an up-and-coming Australian Bangladeshi Muslim social commentator and author. *Women's Weekly* also ran a feature profiling famously eloquent and photogenic Muslims, including Tanuza Rahman and, of course, Waleed Aly.

@ANZACs_4_SarahByrnes got a Twitter account and started retweeting Maya's messages. So did @TheRealHughJackman and @NicoleKidman.

RUBEN

Cinnamon Gardens

The siren ricocheted off the crumbling walls of the church. Carried by the wind, the mechanical scream followed him down the narrow lanes of their village, telling him the army was coming. Ruben heard himself whimper, the short bursts of fear that came out of his mouth in a language he hadn't learned to control yet. A wordless sound that bubbled out of his lungs and collided with the same sound coming from the people around him. Fear flying through the air, crashing into more fear, like mercury droplets coalescing and growing in size and sound. Its crescendo pierced his sleep, the staccato sound and the adrenaline waking him.

He sat up and looked around, confused. He was in bed, in his home in Westgrove, and his phone was ringing, casting sound and light into his dark room.

'Hello?' He coughed to clear his throat. 'Hello?'

'Ruben, I'm so sorry to disturb you.' It was Anji.

'It's no trouble. What's wrong?'

'Malathi just called me; Uncle Saha has gone missing again. I don't know how he does it. The doors are all locked and alarmed, there's no way out. I'm heading over to the nursing home now, but I thought since you're there . . .'

'I'm on my way.' Ruben was already half dressed. A call from Anji or one of the managers in the middle of the night could only mean one of two things: a resident was having a health incident or the midnight headcount had revealed that Uncle Saha was missing. If a resident died during the night, it was usually silently and only noticed in the morning on pre-breakfast ward rounds.

Ruben slipped on his shoes and checked in with Malathi, the night manager, to make sure the old man hadn't been found in a bathroom or raiding the kitchen. He hadn't. In that case, Ruben knew where Uncle Saha would be.

He ran the three blocks to the public oval attached to Westgrove High School. The moon was bright overhead, shedding a milky light over the dark pool of grass in front of him. He stopped to catch his breath and scan the field. On the far-left side of the grounds, the Westgrove Cricket Club's weatherboard clubhouse stood tall over the bleachers.

On Saturdays and Sundays, the Jaffna Old Boys Cricket Union organised Twenty20 games before the concept had become a BBL smash hit. The union comprised cricket clubs drawn from villages and schools across the Jaffna Peninsula, alumni and their descendants. It had more than 900 members and was divided into ancestral and academic teams as well as age divisions.

From time to time, Ruben played in the St Johns College (Jaffna not Cambridge) under-forty-fives. The union had progressively capped its one-day games at 20/20 to ensure that Tamil children could attend Tamil class in the morning, play a quick but competitive game of cricket, and then leave on time to attend four hours of tutoring to help them beat the Chinese and Korean kids and secure their place at Sydney's finest selective schools.

Ruben walked across the oval towards the clubhouse, but as he neared it, he saw movement—three ghosts moving in the dark, swirling around and above another dark form writhing on the ground. They were masked by the shadows of the clubhouse eaves but, although he couldn't see their faces, he recognised the movements of pain, even from that distance. Pain being delivered, pain being received. It followed a familiar rhythm; dance steps he had seen before.

He ran as he called 000 and told the operator there was a girl being raped at the Westgrove Cricket Club. He repeated the address and broke into a sprint. As he neared the bleachers he heard the sound of fists and feet being pummelled into a body.

'Hey!' he shouted as he ran up the aisle between the rows of wooden benches. 'Hey! Get the hell away from him.'

Ruben picked up speed as he ran, his lungs burning, taking the steps three at a time, his hands balling into tight fists. He charged into the first shadow, using his momentum and whole body to throw him off the old man on the ground. The shadow tumbled into the second shadow, both of them falling into the river of moonlight.

Ruben recognised their faces: it was Lynx—Ned—and one of the brothers. The shadow behind him tackled him at the waist, but Ruben was expecting him. He absorbed the tackle and fell forward, crashing into Ned and the brother, who were still lying in a tangle on the ground. Ruben punched and kicked, his arms and legs landing on different body parts. He didn't wait for the men to recover or to realise there was only one of him. His hand brushed against a familiar instrument. He picked up the cricket bat and swung wildly. He sliced through air on the forward sweep and then heard a grunt when the wood connected with a body on the return sweep. There was a satisfying dull thud as a body hit the ground, heaving and desperately trying to draw air into its body.

One of the shadows pulled away, dragging another with him. Ruben heard the sirens for the second time that night, only this time they were real, not the remembered sirens that haunted his sleep. A police car, its blue lights strobing, came screaming down the street and slammed on its brakes in the car park, its urgency radiating towards the three men who picked each other up. They swore, stumbled, and ran down the steps of the bleachers, onto the oval and into the night.

Ruben rushed to Uncle Saha and rolled him over. The old man groaned and then fell silent; his bloodied face was starting to swell. Ruben held him close with one arm, and with his free hand checked the old man's neck for a pulse. He bent his face to Uncle Saha's mouth and listened for his breath, but he couldn't trust the rapid heaving of his own lungs, the erratic pounding of his own terrified heart. Feeling moisture on his arm, he reached behind the old man's head. His hand came away wet and sticky with blood. He placed his hand at the back of Uncle Saha's head again, holding the pieces in place. A futile gesture; one he would wonder about later when the nightmares of Jaffna were supplanted by the nightmares of Westgrove Cricket Club.

A torchlight flashed in his eyes. He looked up, through the tears blurring his vision, and saw the forms of two people; police officers, he assumed. They shone their torch beam on Uncle Saha in his arms, then kneeled beside him. One of the officers, a young woman, called an ambulance. He heard words, fragments of sentences: *Officer Newton . . . elderly male victim . . . GBH . . . get here as fast as you can.* And then the words: *Not good, mate; not good. Call Woodbury.*

The other officer flashed his torch around them, looking for the assailants, perhaps looking for the rape.

'Did you call us in?' he asked.

Ruben nodded.

'Not a rape,' the officer said rather than asked. He looked up at the sound of an ambulance rushing towards them.

Ruben shook his head. 'No, I thought you wouldn't come. There were three men; someone called Ned and two others, brothers. The same men who attacked me before.'

He looked down at Uncle Saha. The old man was completely still. In the moonlight he looked grey and lifeless. Ruben knew he would look the same in the sunlight.

ANJALI

Sydney

Anji agreed to accompany her friend Tanuza Rahman to the studio, and not just because her mother wanted her to meet Waleed Aly. When they arrived at the show's green room, they were told Tanuza had been bumped down from *The Project* to *The Panel*. Sally Bentham-Jones, *The Panel*'s anchor and proud endorser of Swisse's gut-health formula, was already mic'ed up and ready to speak to her past-prime-time audience.

Anji watched as Tanuza adjusted her long black hair, moving some of her blonde balayaged tips to the front. As an advocate of Muslim rights and racial harmony, she provided evidence-based eloquence coupled with stereotype-defying style. Her make-up was perfect: beauty-enhancing but not intellect-undermining. The whole look said 'Earnest and Sophisticated Muslim' not 'Angry and Dangerous Muslim'.

The mic guy shook his head and motioned to the small mic pinned to her lapel. Tanuza nodded and pushed her hair back again. The mic guy put his thumb up and she gave him a thumbs-up in return. She smiled at Anji, pointing to the small TV screen to her left and the teleprompter, beyond the circle of light that haloed *The Panel*'s U-shaped table.

The mic guy handed Anji a set of headphones. 'You can hear the conversation without the ambient sound,' he said, flicking a switch on one side.

After the profile in *Women's Weekly*, inspired by author Sarah Byrnes's Twitter defence of the nursing home, Tanuza had received numerous media requests to speak about 'being Muslim in Australia'. She had invited Anji to be a part of the coverage but Anji refused.

'Eventually, you'll want to speak out and defend the nursing home. Violence should not be met with the silence of the oppressed. Come to a few interviews with me, see what they're like. That way it'll be easier when it's your turn.'

Anji never wanted it to be her turn. But this interview was different and she had agreed to support Tanuza, although well away from the camera. She exhaled deeply, pushing the image of Uncle Saha, intubated in a hospital bed, from her mind.

Sally Bentham-Jones leaned over and patted Tanuza on the arm.

'You're doing great,' Anji heard. 'Just say what's on your mind and in your heart.'

Anji could actually hear her friend's eyes rolling through the headphones.

Christ, she thought. Were all television types so cheesy?

The camera guy adjusted his headphones and made a helicopter sign with his hands.

'Quiet, everybody—stations!' someone shouted. The red light above the cannon-like-camera started flashing faster than her heartbeat, and then suddenly switched to green.

Sally Bentham-Jones's sombre face reflected yesterday's tragedy.

'I'm joined here today by Tanuza Rahman, author of the bestselling book, *The M-Word: Staying sane and staying alive in White Australia*. Her satirical blog, *Islamophobics Anonymous*, has just been

305

bought by Netflix and will be developed into a TV series starring Mindy Kaling and Hasan Minhaj.'

Ah, Hasan: Anji's back-up husband.

Tanuza nodded her appreciation of Sally's plug.

Sally smiled back at her encouragingly. 'Thank you for joining us, Tanuza. I can't imagine how the Muslim community must be feeling today, after the tragic bashing of Mr Sahadevan, a resident of the Cinnamon Gardens Nursing Home. Mr Sahadevan—or Uncle Saha, as he is known at Cinnamon Gardens—is in a medically induced coma. Councillor Bella Davidson, who visited the hospital today, says he's in a critical but stable condition and would have died if not for the timely intervention of local police.'

Local police? Anji tried to keep her head from shaking.

Sally smiled again, prompting Tanuza to speak.

'Yes, thank you, Sally. There are many Muslim communities in this country and we are united in our grief and respect for Mr Sahadevan, a Hindu Australian of Tamil ancestry. He was brutally bashed. An elderly man who wasn't doing anything or hurting anyone became the victim of a savage racist attack.'

Tanuza exhaled. She looked straight into the camera, with the look she'd been practising since Anji had first met her at high school debating, thirty years ago. Bradley Preston had nothing on Tanuza Rahman.

'This attack was a direct result of Senator Graham's call to arms on his website and on the recent episode of *30 Minutes*. Since his maiden speech twenty-five years ago, he has been sowing the seeds of racial division. This is the harvest he wanted all along. This violence against an unarmed, elderly man, in the shadows of a children's cricket oval. Violence committed because of his colour, because he looked like an immigrant, because he looked like a Muslim. This is the inevitable murderous harvest.'

Tanuza wanted this gig because it was the first panel about the recent violence and people of colour that actually included a person of colour. Other than Waleed, of course. She was being called on more and more by 'concerned' white people to speak for all Muslims and now it seemed all Hindus too.

Sally nodded, her eyes distant, as if listening to a voice in her mind. Anji realised it was a voice in her earpiece giving her instructions.

'Thank you, Tanuza. I can feel your rage and I appreciate the restraint and the respect that you're displaying here today.'

'Respect and restraint are the mark of a civilised society,' Tanuza interrupted.

'Yes, absolutely. Tanuza, tell me, Westgrove was once a quiet suburb, now it's a hotbed of racial hatred. What went wrong? When people from one ethnic group live together and mix together, in these kinds of ethnic ghettos, isn't *this* violence an *inevitable* consequence?'

Respect, Sally Double-Barrelled, Anji thought. You totally had me with your 'say what's on your mind and in your heart' routine.

'Sally.' Tanuza smiled beautifully. 'I hope you're not suggesting this violence is our fault. White people live in ethnic ghettos too; you just don't think of yourselves as ethnic or your suburbs as ghettos. You also don't notice you're doing it, or maybe you do, but you feel entitled to do it because you're the ones doing it.'

Sally paled under her matte pancake, her eyes darting and then distant as she took more instructions from what Anji assumed was a room full of white men reading a live ratings monitor.

The journalist focused again, looked down at her notes and then at Tanuza. 'Senator Graham, as you know, was invited to join us on today's show but he declined. In a statement published on his website, he said that the people who did this—'

'Who committed this crime,' Tanuza clarified.

Yes, the *criminals*, Anji thought.

'Yes, the people who committed this crime,' Sally corrected herself. 'Senator Graham described them as well-intentioned. He said that they, and I quote, these are his words, not mine, "got carried away". He said he can understand their rage after the clip of the bashing of former Councillor Barton went viral, and the revelation that the nursing home is run by Muslims.'

There it was again. Nursing home and Muslims. The adrenaline in Anji's body spiked erratically. She tried to focus on Sally's voice, quoting the Senator's usual vitriol. At least it wasn't prime time.

'He said people love this country,' Sally continued, 'and they want it to be great again; they want to protect the heritage, identity, and future of Australians. The immigrants brought the violence on themselves. We are a tolerant society but even a tolerant society has limits.'

Tanuza laughed bitterly. 'Yes, we're a tolerant society, as long as the model minority knows their place. We're tolerant until the minority speaks out and criticises. Then *they*—which is to say *we*—are the ones creating divisions and undermining Australian culture. We are always auditioning; we are always proving our patriotism and our loyalty. We are always called on to be reasonable with bigots and now with murderers. No more. No more.'

'Are you suggesting that minorities should meet violence with violence?'

Tanuza shook her head. She looked past the cameras and directly at Anji. 'I'm suggesting that violence should not be met with the silence of the oppressed. Even if it is being met with the silence of our government and our Prime Minister. Senator Graham has been making racist statements for years. The bigger story here is that the Prime Minister, the Minister for Home Affairs and the Minister for Immigration and Multiculturalism are saying nothing at all. Well, nothing meaningful.'

She turned back to Sally Bentham-Jones.

'A man is fighting for his life in hospital and there has been no condemnation of the violence from our leaders. Instead of dissecting Senator Graham's "policy statement", which is really nothing more than a series of populist slogans appealing to an increasingly large and now brazenly violent segment of Australian society, the government remains silent. And the press—you included—simply repeat the slogans, giving him a free and enormous platform. You just repeated his words on *The Panel*; you didn't interrogate them.'

A red flush snaked up Sally's neck and into her cheeks. She opened her mouth to say something and then closed it. Anji found herself feeling sorry for the woman, God knew why. Tanuza looked at Anji again, and Anji shrugged. It had been a long week. They were all exhausted.

'Sally,' Tanuza said, more gently, 'you mentioned to me earlier that Sarah Byrnes, Australia's whitest author of contemporary romance, has come out for the first time in her career, making statements criticising Senator Graham?' Tanuza raised her eyebrows, indicating that the lifeline was Sally's for the taking.

'Yes, that's right, Tanuza.' Sally smiled gratefully. 'Sarah Byrnes, author of eleven books in the Clementine Kelly series about the gutsy frontierswoman, is condemning the Southern Cross Party and this senseless attack by white supremacist thugs.'

Sally read from a teleprompter where extracts of Sarah Byrnes's recent social media posts appeared.

'The reclusive author writes: *When the nursing home owners took down the statue of Captain Cook, they were exercising the rights we expect and demand for ourselves. The problem here is that the nursing home owners exercised these rights in a way that offends our narrow and exclusive definition of what it means to be Australian. They offended our notion not of how Australians should behave, but how* migrants *should behave.'*

Sally paused for dramatic effect, certain that her viewers were as intrigued by Sarah Byrnes as she was.

'In a searing criticism of Australia, the four-time winner of the People's Choice Torn Bodice Award for Historical Romantic Fiction, goes on to say: *We feel these migrants displayed a lack of gratitude for this country that has given them no more than it has given us. In some cases, this country has given them less. They challenged our triumphant, erroneous, and white supremacist notion of the founding of this country. On a conscious level that offends us. On an unconscious level, it delegitimises our right to be here. It reminds us that we have no more right to claim this land than immigrants do. It reminds us that we are all immigrants on stolen land, and that everyone needs to buy into the lie for the lie to work; for the lie to hold true. If we don't, we feel threatened and afraid. When we feel threatened and afraid, we attack them.'*

'Pretty bold for a white lady,' Tanuza said, aware that white people would listen to a white lady rather than her. Also aware that this white lady wasn't so white after all.

Pretty bold indeed, thought Anji. The Torn Bodice Awards were all hidden under her bed.

Sally smiled. 'She is. I've read all her books. She's such an inspirational Australian. And she sounds just like Clementine Kelly.'

RUBEN

Cinnamon Gardens

Fire had a distinctive voice, a language of its own. Its structural characteristics would place it in the typological classification of an isolating language. Each word in the language of fire was composed of an individual, original and unanalysable morph. Fire's genealogical classification was equally unknown to him. Ruben had only ever heard fire speak to him in Sri Lanka and in his dreams, so while he assumed that fire was Afro-Asiatic, he had never interrogated its diachronic relation to any of the other families of languages in the rest of the world. Until he heard fire speak to him in Australia.

In Australia, fire whispered first. A slow hum that hypnotised him into a dangerously deep sleep. A warmth that was so beguiling, so comforting in its embrace, so gradual in its heightening, he could only sense the danger at precisely the same moment he lost his ability to escape it.

He heard the fire whisper. His breath synchronised with its steady heartbeat. His lungs opened to the smoke and welcomed its heavy sedation. He would have let it fill his body and carry him away, but his mind threw him one last memory, a call back to life; a promise he had made to another old man at another old time in another old country.

Ruben woke up and looked across the garden towards the nursing home. Spirals of smoke billowed white in the moonlight against the dark night sky. Yellow tongues of fire ruptured the windows of the ground floor and stretched themselves towards the floor above, where Maya slept.

He realised fire spoke its own language, universal and transcendent. He understood it immediately. He was an intuitive interpreter; sounds and syllables always revealed their meaning to him. He didn't hesitate. Ruben ran into the fire.

ANJALI

Sydney

The phone rang, its siren cutting a pathway through Anji's sleep. Nathan stirred next to her, reaching over her body to answer it. She found it on her side table first.

'He-llo?' the syllables were fragmented, her mouth sticky with sleep. 'Hello?' she tried again.

'Dr Ali?'

'Yes?' Her heart pounded. Calls in the middle of the night terrified her. She prayed it wasn't her mother.

'Dr Ali,' the man repeated.

Her body went cold. She didn't recognise the voice. It wasn't Ruben or any of the night staff.

'Dr Ali, you need to come down to the nursing home. I'm afraid there's a problem.'

'What kind of problem?' She tried to remember Nathan's self-calming advice, but her body had begun to shake. She gripped the phone with two hands to her ear to steady it.

'My name is Charlie Blythe,' the man said, 'and I'm with the Westgrove Municipal Fire Department. The nursing home is on fire.

313

Luckily your alarm system is wired back-to-base, so it automatically alerted us at the first sign of trouble. We're evacuating the residents. How soon can you get here?'

'Which nursing home?' she asked.

'Sorry?'

'Which nursing home?' she repeated. 'There's the big one at the back where most of the residents are, and the old house at the front.' The old house, made of wood on the inside and brick on the outside. The one her parents had lovingly restored first.

'The old house at the front.'

The one where her mother lived.

MAYA

Cinnamon Gardens

Maya heard the fire before she felt it. She heard its triumph as it cracked and gobbled the floorboards in the games room, as it inhaled the paper in the office, and shattered the equipment in the kitchen. She heard the stairway leading from her floor to the ground floor collapse as its wooden girders were reduced to cinder and ash. She heard all of this but didn't understand what it was until a familiar voice shook her fully awake.

'Aunty! Aunty, wake up!'

Ruben was dragging her to her feet. They touched the floor and she recoiled in pain at the heat. He kneeled down and helped her into her shoes and then ran into her bathroom. He came out with Zakhir's cardigan, soaked in water. He placed it over her shoulders. The air around her was hot; every breath in hurt a little more than the last.

'Come, Aunty, we have to go,' he said, pulling her to the door.

Her glass window was starting to warp, its prism refracting the outside world she sought. There were red flashing lights, like stars spinning, on the street. A siren screamed at her, demanding that she follow Ruben.

'The others?' she asked. There were six residents remaining on this floor. No one in Mrs Vandermark's room or Saha Anna's. No one on the ground floor. Another fifty residents in the brick building behind them. Sivam, she had renamed it; the auspicious one, the Lord of Destruction.

'They're being evacuated; they'll be okay. This house won't make it, though. *We* won't make it if we don't hurry.' He had his arms around her and held her close to his body, whispering into her ear so she could hear him. Around her the fire bellowed and howled, demanding to be fed.

'The others?' she repeated. Her eyes smarting and then watering from the smoke and heat. She looked at the man—the frightened boy—whose arms were holding her up, his face, hair, and hands burned, new wounds to add to the record of suffering that was already written across his body.

'I've woken as many as I can. Most are moving. I'll get the rest, I promise. But you first.' He wrapped a wet cloth around her mouth and secured it at the back. 'Trust me.'

She nodded as he pulled her into the corridor, the wooden floor glowing and bubbling, pustules of heat breaking through its skin; heat and fire erupting from the ground beneath her feet.

RUBEN

Cinnamon Gardens

Ruben had been chased by fire before. He had felt fire falling from the sky, mortar bombs that exploded on impact, sending molten shards of metal into the bodies of men, women and children. Phosphorous weapons whose white clouds streamed and spiralled through the air until they touched skin, and then ignited into pellets of fire burrowing deep into flesh. All fire stripped the skin from the bone, the bone from the body, the body from the earth.

Ruben knew how to run from fire. He dragged and half carried Maya's light body down the corridor, feeling the heat at his back, singeing his shirt, the sweat from his body barely sitting on his skin before it vaporised into floating mist behind him. He felt the soles of his feet burn through his rubber shoes. He didn't stop moving. If you stopped, you died.

From the corner of his eye he saw Uncle Gana from Room 5 stumble towards him. The old man's back was on fire, and there was a halo of light around him as his body thrashed and convulsed in pain. Pieces of him ignited into sparks and then fireballs that left his body. Freed from his gravity the flames took flight, seeking other sparks around them. Maya stopped, reaching towards him.

317

'No!' Ruben shouted. 'No. Leave him.' He would come back, he promised in his mind. He would come back. He would come back. He just needed to get Maya out. He kept moving towards the room that would save them.

He pushed the door open and almost threw Maya into the shrine room where Aunty Ragupathy and Aunty Devaki were already waiting, huddled by the front window. There was a man on a ladder outside, prying the window away from the swollen frame with a crowbar. Another man on the ladder crouched underneath him, doing the same to the lower half of the window. They had smashed in one pane and were speaking to the residents through it.

Ruben did a quick count. Maya plus two residents here in the shrine room, one on fire, two missing. Aunty Shanthi and Uncle Ray must still be in their rooms.

'Stand at the window, Amma,' he said to Maya. 'Go with the firemen. Don't think about the others, don't think about me. Just go. Get out of here.'

'Where are you going?' she cried, her brittle hands holding him hard.

'To get the others. I'll be right back, but don't wait for me. Do what you are told and don't look back.' He pulled away before she could stop him and pushed her gently towards the window.

He ran down the corridor towards Room 5. The heat in the floor stabbed at his feet. The scorched air warped around him, shapes shifting like a terrifying mirage. He forced one foot in front of the other, in the direction he had walked a million times before.

'Thambi,' he heard a voice call. Little brother. He ran into the heat.

Uncle Ray and Aunty Shanthi were beating down the flames on Uncle Gana's lifeless body. They were both crying, their skin blistered and peeling.

He took the blanket from Aunty Shanthi and shook it, wrapped it around her with one arm. With the other, he grabbed the old man firmly and pulled his face towards his.

'He's gone. Think of Nikki, Uncle. Think of Nikki and follow me.'
Ray nodded.

Ruben heard Aunty Shanthi whispering, 'Om Namah Shivaya,
Om Namah Shivaya,' over and over again. She took a step and
cried out, stumbling against him. He looked at her feet. They were
blackened and bloody.

Ray followed his gaze to her feet and then back up to Ruben's eyes.
He bent down and started to take his shoes off. Ruben stopped him.

'Aunty,' he said to Aunty Shanthi. 'Endu muthuhile erango.
Endu muthuhile erango.'

'I'll help you, love,' Ray said to her. Together, they put the old lady
on Ruben's back. Ruben stumbled down the corridor with Aunty
Shanthi whimpering her prayers in his ear, Ray close behind him.

Ruben pushed against the shrine room door; his hands recoiled
from the heat. The old lady slid down into Ray's arms. Ruben used
his back to shove the door open. To his horror, Maya and the others
were still there, crowded around the window, crying.

He ran to the circle of old women and pushed through to the
closed but cracked window. Cracked but still closed.

'Mate, they're stuck,' the fireman told him. 'The windows—we
can't move them.' He was wet, sweat running down his face like
tears. He looked past Ruben to the old women, now holding each
other and crying.

'Is there another way out?' Ruben asked, knowing the answer
to that question already.

The fireman shook his head. 'We're bringing up the rotation
saw,' he said, pointing to the truck beneath him. The ladder he was
perched on swayed in the torrents of burning air exhaled by the
blazing nursing home.

'I can try to set small explosives. Or use liquid nitrogen. I'll have
to go back to the truck. Everything's there. You'll need to help me;
the metal joints of the window are on the inside.'

The man's eyes told Ruben what he was thinking: they were running out of time and options.

'We can do it,' the man lied. Such kindness in that face. A man trained to run into fire. A man who needed them to stay hopeful because once hope was gone, life followed it quickly.

'What's the problem?' Ruben asked, looking at the window. It had expanded in the heat and pushed hard against the frame of the building, fusing with it, refusing to yield to the firemen's crowbars and tools.

'Ancient wood. We don't use it anymore; not code. They couldn't have known. The outer frame has expanded to cover the inner frame, locking the window in.'

Ancient wood.

'Let me try something,' Ruben said. 'Move away from the window.' He ran to the altar. Ray was at his side again, with a wheelchair. Ruben nodded his thanks and together they toppled the bronze statue of the meditating Lord Shiva and others into the wheelchair. Aunty Ragupathy grabbed the lingam, her arthritic hands wrapped around the smooth river stone she worshipped every morning. Ruben pushed the wheelchair to the window.

He ran back to the altar and swept aside Maya's wedding sari, which had served as the altar's dressing for the decade since Zakhir had died. Underneath the altar table was a box of Uncle Saha's tools which Ruben also pulled across the room to the window.

He took out the cannister of compressed liquid nitrogen. 'Stand back,' Ruben shouted. He released the safety on the can and lifted the rusted chisel he had seen Uncle Saha use to make stone into god. To release the form of god that exists within all of creation, as the old man used to say.

The fireman's eyes widened. He nodded and spoke into the radio strapped to his collar. The fire truck inched back, taking the man on the ladder away from the window, putting a safe distance between them.

Ruben sprayed the joints of the window with the liquid nitrogen, once, then twice, then a third time. He counted to thirty and then made himself count to thirty again and then, because some of Maya's superstition had worn off on him, he counted to forty-eight. One hundred and eight in total: a sacred number.

Maya was at his side holding the iron Brahma idol that had so deeply offended Aunty Shanthi. The god's four faces blurred and then focused, one of them staring directly at the window. Aunty Ragupathy used the meditating Lord Shiva as a stepping stool and she was ready, with the lingam poised at the upper joints. Ruben took the iron Vishnu, the god of protection, and held it over the base of the chisel which he had set to the hardened nitrogen. He nodded at Maya and Aunty Ragupathy, his throat raw from the heat. Together they hit the joints with as much strength as they could send through the Hindu trinity of Creator, Protector and Destroyer.

Over and over again, Ruben smashed the chisel, tipped with diamonds that were thousands of years old. He swapped positions with the others, giving each hinge the full force of Uncle Saha's priceless tool. The joints loosened and then cracked. Ruben motioned for the others to step back.

In the wheelchair, one last god remained. He looked at the bronze Lord Nataraja, his face calm and peaceful, lost in deep meditation. His four arms and two legs were outstretched in the motion of the god's cosmic dance, which created the universe and destroyed it, so that it could be created anew. Around him was a ring of bronze fire, signifying the divine energy that pervaded them all. They were born from this energy, and when they died they might, if they had lived dharmic lives, merge with it. He wondered if his life had been good enough.

He remembered the words of the prayer his mother taught him.
Hara Hara Mahadeva.
Hara Hara Mahadeva.

He repeated them in his mind. He hadn't prayed since Zakhir had died. But he prayed now.

Hara Hara Mahadeva.

I bow to the Great Destroyer.

Ruben hefted the enormous statue up. He felt his back shudder under the strain as he braced his hips and legs to balance the god. He inhaled and exhaled rapidly, like he had seen weightlifters on the television do. Every breath hurt his scorched lungs. He inhaled deeply once more, and as he exhaled he pushed his body and the statue at the loosened window.

Wood and glass relented and shattered outwards. Air roared inwards, and in the bowels of the building the mighty god of fire, Agni, felt the breach Ruben had created and sensed that some might escape his hunger. Ruben heard the fire race towards the fresh air from beneath him. He felt himself topple forward, his body half outside the window, still clutching the cosmic dancer.

As the weight of the god pulled him out into the hot air, towards the incinerating light and darkness of fire, he felt hands on his back pulling at his shirt: the withered hands of men and women who'd lived long, hard, good lives; whose strength was leaving them but had returned for one last act of love. The crushing weight of bronze and gravity, drawing the god back to the earth's core and him with it. The strength of his elders anchoring him to their home that was itself burning to the ground.

The fireman on the ladder sailed slowly through the air again towards the now-open window. He climbed through the frame and placed a blanket over the windowsill to cover the remaining shards of glass and splintered wood. Another man appeared at the window, and the two firemen worked together without speaking. This was a new language for Ruben; the language of men who had done this before and didn't need to speak. They worked quickly, one guiding the residents to the window and lifting them out one by one; the other receiving them like a mother receives her newborn, wet and sticky and breathing and safe. He then handed each resident into the arms of another man further down the ladder, and so it continued, an umbilicus formed between the men and the trembling residents.

Ruben pushed Maya towards the fireman. 'Go, Amma,' he said. 'I'll be right behind you.'

She always knew when he was lying although she had never worked out what truth his lies were hiding.

'Leave it,' she said, holding on to his burned arm. He flinched but he didn't pull away; her touch was cool on his feverish skin. 'Ippa vahngo,' she said. Come now. 'Ennodu vahngo, mahan.' Come with me, son.

'I just need to get it.'

'It's gone.'

'No.' He refused to believe that. Ten years of hard work; of meaningful work. 'I'll be right behind you,' he repeated.

'Leave it, mahan—it's not important,' she said, black tears running down her face.

He shook his head. He understood Zakhir, finally, after all these years.

'When we leave this earth, the stones we carve, the stories we tell, the records we keep—these are all that remain. *These* are the temples we build, to remind others that we were here, we mattered, we were loved. These are the temples that honour our existence and our efforts. They must not be erased.'

'Leave it, I beg you.'

He smiled and kissed her head, holding her as a child holds its mother. He pushed her towards the fireman, who took her from him and lifted her out the window, screaming his name.

He ran back towards Maya's room, towards a book he had hidden there so her husband's words would be close to her heart without her ever knowing. Towards the small hard drive containing the work they had been doing together. He ran back into the fire.

GARETH

Cinnamon Gardens

Gareth sat in his car, parked on the other side of the road from the nursing home. He steeled himself to get out and find Nikki. His phone told him she was here, among the blackened remains of the old building.

Lights swirled around him, charged particles thrown off kilter by an unseen solar wind. An aurora of blue and red, accompanied by the keen of sirens. Police cars lined the usually quiet street. Ambulances filled the driveway of the nursing home. They were no stranger to death, but they were gathered in unprecedented numbers.

Channel Seven was the first on the scene, their early morning crew called away from the pre-dawn sausage sizzle being prepared for the consecration of a new Captain Cook statue at Cook's Reserve. It was James 3.0, the younger years, rendered in recycled blackbutt.

Gareth recognised Claire Burgess standing on the footpath, the sign reading *Cinnamon Gardens* behind her, the words emerging in the tentative sunlight. He watched her massage and loosen the muscles of her face. She applied a well-practised expression of mournful concern, like make-up. Then she took it off.

The camera-man swivelled the tripod and brought Claire within its crosshairs. He raised three fingers above his head and counted them down.

On three, Claire smoothed the line of her tailored green jacket over her shift dress.

Nikki looked lovely in that colour. It contrasted beautifully with her long blonde hair.

On two, Claire ran her tongue over her teeth one last time, perhaps making sure they were shiny and ketchup-free.

Gareth got out of the car and walked quickly towards the nursing home, finding refuge in the shadow of a towering eucalypt.

On one, Claire put her concerned face back on.

'I am standing here outside the Cinnamon Gardens Nursing Home. Once a safe haven for the elderly of these western suburbs, now a scene of devastation. There have been reports of injuries and several deaths. Somebody's grandmother, somebody's grandfather . . .'

Her voice picked up tempo, the measured cadence of mourning giving way to the pulse of a sniffed but not yet seen scandal.

'Yesterday, their frail bodies held on to life with the tenacity of battlers who had one more battle left; explorers who were undaunted by the final frontier of . . . age.'

Gareth could tell she was riffing quite convincingly. She might not be Walkley material, but there was probably room on her dressing-room shelf for another Gold Logie.

'Yesterday, they played bingo and waited for their grandchildren to visit. Today, they will wait for their families to identify and claim them.'

Claire pressed her earpiece, receiving her question from the two anchors of the breakfast show back at the studio.

'That's right, Deb,' she replied. 'In recent months, the nursing home had received some unwelcome attention. It was at the heart of an investigation by the'—she coughed, swapped the microphone in her hands and pushed the earpiece into her other ear to better hear the instructions from the staff researcher—'the Australian Human Rights Commission, as the subject of a complaint by former local councillor Gareth Barton.'

Gareth flinched at the sound of his name. He watched as Claire paused again, allowing the anchors to fill in the blanks using their studio teleprompters.

'Yes, Stevo, his allegations of racism under the Racial Discrimination Act were being investigated. The case is still pending.' She nodded sagely.

Pending was a good legal word. She clearly had no idea where that investigation was at. *Pending* would do.

'The residents of Cinnamon Gardens came from many different parts of the world, but as you can see behind me, they are all covered in black ash and white sheets. They are all the same. They are all . . . Australian.'

The cameraman panned to the right to follow a stretcher being carried from the home to the waiting ambulance. To his left, there was a rush of activity, the clatter of cameras hitting each other as two more crews arrived on the scene and headed straight for him.

'Mr Barton! Mr Barton!' a journalist shouted. They formed a tight sphincter around him. 'Do we know what's happened here, Councill— Gareth?'

Gareth ran a hand through his hair. Ash was falling on all of them.

'I know as much as you do,' he said. 'Very little.'

'Is it true this was a racist attack on the nursing home, Gareth? Three men have been detained at Westgrove Station. Police haven't commented, but it seems likely they're the perpetrators.'

Gareth didn't say anything.

The journalist continued. 'Since your case at the Human Rights Commission, both Cinnamon Gardens and the home of its owner, Dr Ali, have been vandalised. Residents and workers have been attacked, one resident is still in intensive care and unlikely to survive. And now this. Do you feel responsible, Gareth?'

Gareth watched the teams of firemen direct their high-powered hoses at the last of the fires. 'All we know for now,' he said, 'is that the community of Westgrove has been rocked to its core.'

No one could have expected this. No one wanted this. *He* didn't want this.

'Will there be an inquiry?' the journalist asked.

'I'm sure there will be many inquiries,' Gareth replied. Maybe even a Royal Commission, he thought. A Royal Commission with a panel of credentialled elderly white men convened to explain what systemic racism looks like in Australia.

The journalist wasn't letting it go. 'Gareth, you've been criticised for your action against the nursing home. It's been suggested that *you* are the racist, not the nursing home, and that you're trying to resurrect your failing political career and further your own personal agenda rather than further the public interest on this issue.'

'Further my own personal agenda? Who said that? The ABC? SBS? Mate, my career is over. I cleared out my desk last week. Today is not about my career. It's about these people.' He gestured to the nursing home behind him. 'They are us and we are them, and as a private citizen rather than a local councillor, I will find out what happened to them.'

Nikki hated this kind of rhetoric, but right now she also hated him. Maybe he hated himself too. And right now, he didn't have much choice. Every news camera and hundreds of mobile phones were on him and he had to keep his shit together. Stay on message, no matter how empty that message was. He'd never work for the Democratic Alliance Party again, but he needed to find work. An articulate suspected racist was better than an inarticulate one. Plus, he wasn't a racist; he had never been one. He wasn't like Senator Graham or the bastards who had done this.

He turned and pushed his way out of the circle, towards the police cordon. He saw Anji in her pyjamas, held by Nathan, nodding her head and crying as the police briefed her, her hand clamped over her mouth as if to trap the screams inside her body.

Nikki was standing next to a stretcher. She pulled the sheet back, nodded her head and said something to the police officer with her.

The second stretcher was brought to her. He saw her sway and then steady herself. She pulled back the sheet gently and her body collapsed, like a building detonated from within, like a nursing home set on fire, each floor collapsing on the next one down until she was just a pile of rubble on the driveway, crying at the wheels of the stretcher. The police officer crouched down next to her. Nikki spoke a name and nodded, letting the officer hold her as she sobbed. He had forgotten what it meant to love and be loved like that.

He remembered taking Florence to see Grandpa Ray at the nursing home. He remembered taking his jacket off and hanging it on the back of Ray's chair. Flo was showing them her new dance routine, something she'd learned from the internet. His phone rang, a work call. Mike Davidson, wanting notes urgently for a speech he was giving at some gala on the weekend.

'You okay with her, Ray?' Gareth asked his father-in-law.

'Sure,' said Ray, smiling at the three-year-old who was in her own world of high kicks and mildly inappropriate hip gyrations.

Gareth stepped out into the corridor of Cinnamon Gardens to take the call. Standing next to a medication trolley, he fed Davidson the lines his boss would use but not credit Gareth for. Flo came out of the room and tried to talk to him, shaking a small container. One of her Shopkins toys, he thought.

'Go and play with Grandpa, darling,' he whispered, his hand over the phone. He returned to Davidson and the speech.

He was gone no more than twenty minutes. When he came back, Flo had been eating something—blue lollies she said, from Grandpa.

By the time he drove her home, not ten blocks away, not six minutes away, she was asleep and couldn't be roused. He knew something was wrong. Nikki was there, screaming at him to call the ambulance. He called 000 but could barely speak. Suddenly all the empty words that had come so easily to him in his job were gone; the meaningful ones too.

Nikki pulled Florence out of the car and set her down on the grass, checking her mouth and her pulse. She turned the remains of a blue tablet over in her fingers.

He watched his wife then, amazed at how she stopped screaming and started working. Her beautiful mouth over Florence's sweet one. Air from her living body given to the still one on the grass. Gareth would have ripped his beating heart from his body and given it to his child if he could have.

Florence's only movements were from Nikki's pounding on her chest. She didn't stop until the ambulance arrived and the paramedics guided her away.

'She's taken something,' she said. 'Maybe ten minutes ago. Not sure what. Maybe Valium.'

She emptied Gareth's briefcase onto the ground and checked it for medicine, her hands shaking.

The men who worked on Florence were kind and capable. They tried so hard, all the way to the hospital, in the ER and then in the ICU, but there was nothing anyone could do.

Through the black smoke of the nursing home, Gareth watched Nikki grieve once more; her body shaking in the arms of a policeman, her cries of pain so familiar to him, and so clear above the wail of the sirens.

MAYA

Sydney

The fireman—Toby—visited her in the hospital. He was taller than she remembered, although she didn't remember everything from that night. He was younger, too; so young to be so brave. He stood politely as he told her what had happened. Ruben had run out of the shrine room into the burning corridor. Toby waited for him on the ladder, longer than he should have. The hot winds buffeted him on his perch and Toby could hear his sarge shouting instructions to pull out: the ladder was unstable, the walls of Cinnamon Gardens would fall at any moment and topple onto him and the fire truck whose engine was revving, the driver ready to floor it on Toby's command. Toby begged them for a few more moments. It felt like hours but it had only been minutes. Every minute counts in a fire, he said.

Maya nodded. She knew that now.

Ruben had run back into the shrine room with the satchel Toby was holding now. Maya recognised it, although its presence in her hospital room confused and then scared her. Like she was seeing a ghost, although she didn't believe in ghosts.

The bag was singed black from the fire. It was stained brown with old blood that she later learned was Zakhir's, and red with fresh blood that could only have been Ruben's. Inside it was her husband's book and her hard drive. Two objects she loved but had never seen together before. The book she had not seen for a decade; Zakhir had taken it with him the day he disappeared and returned to Sri Lanka.

Ruben had leaned out of the window and given Toby the satchel. Toby slung it around his body and turned back, arms outstretched, to help Ruben. Ruben stepped forward and then he was gone. The walls and floors of Cinnamon Gardens crumbled and collapsed in on itself, taking him with them. The building had wept fire.

Later, with Anji's help, Maya opened the hard drive on her daughter's laptop. It contained all the stories she had recorded in Tamil and English over the four decades of interviewing every resident who had lived and died in Cinnamon Gardens. It contained stories in languages she didn't speak but Ruben did. He had continued her work and expanded it. He transcribed her notes and her tape recordings. He invited people to speak to him in the language of their ancestors, the language of their mothers, and he translated every one of them so they could be understood by others; so they could be loved by others. The stories we tell are the temples we leave behind. They should not be erased.

He recorded the stories of everyone at Cinnamon Gardens, including his own.

RUBEN

Vanni jungle, May 2009

This was the sixth village Ruben had been to with the army and he knew the drill. Smoke billowed into the sky from the tops of the palm trees, their crowns still smouldering. Ash drifted to the earth, the soft fog settling on the buildings. Bodies littered the streets, segments of people covered in the hot dirt thrown up by the impact of shells. Segments missing, obliterated by bombs and flying shrapnel. Blood running into the drains meant for monsoon rains.

After the attack, the Sri Lankan Army swept through. The school had been converted into a makeshift hospital. It had taken fire, shells crashing through the red cross that was painted on its roof. The doctors and nurses who stayed behind had pulled as many patients as possible to safety. They sat, too exhausted to cry, in the schoolyard, huddled in groups.

The soldiers lined up the dead outside the temple. They inspected the bodies for the dog tags worn by Tiger cadres and signs that they had been in battle.

Then they began to search the living. The soldiers walked slowly through the playground, separating the groups into lines for closer inspection. People cried as the children were prised from their arms. Some still held their dead and they began to scream as the bodies were wrested from them and dragged to the temple.

This village was large, more of a town, and the army had received intelligence that the hospital was sheltering wounded Tigers. A soldier used the tip of his rifle to draw lines in the dirt. He spoke to Ruben, who translated into Tamil.

'They want you to sit on the lines, leave proper spaces between you. Please let go of your children; it will be easier for you. If you hold on to them, they will suspect your children. Just relax. Breathe deeply and look straight ahead. If you avoid eye contact, they will suspect you. If you make eye contact, you may provoke them. If they take someone, please let them do it. Don't try to stop them and don't touch them. They will hurt you.'

The crowd settled and did as he instructed. He exhaled with relief. Sometimes people were so traumatised they couldn't understand basic instructions. The soldiers took this for rebellion.

The violence had been growing over the months he'd been with the army. The soldiers were killing faster, asking fewer questions, sparing fewer lives. Maybe they had been fighting too long and lost too many of their own friends to the war. Maybe they enjoyed it. He didn't know and he wasn't sure he cared; the outcome was the same.

He had nightly briefings which drifted into conversations with Brigadier Fernando. Despite the carnage of the other leaders and soldiers in the Sri Lankan Army, he had come to believe that the brigadier was sincere when he had said at their first encounter that he wanted to build a bridge.

The soldier nodded at Ruben and a group of them walked along the lines, this time looking more closely at each person. Their choices were predictable. They pulled out the young boys and girls. The parents cried and called out despite his instructions. Some started to stand up and pull their children back.

The soldiers swivelled their rifles around and hit the parents; a hard and fast blow to the head usually made them release their children. The soldiers kept pacing along the lines, sometimes lifting people's faces and looking into their eyes. An old man stood up, his white coat covered in blood and dirt, a satchel slung around his body.

'Doctor,' Ruben said in Tamil, 'please sit down. There's nothing you can do for anyone. You'll only make it worse for yourself and they need you.'

The man raised his hands and kept walking towards Ruben, the words tumbling out.

'These people are civilians. Only the injured and the old. There are no Tigers here. They left days ago, as soon as we heard you were coming.'

'What's happening?' a soldier asked, chambering his rifle and lifting it into position.

Ruben spoke rapidly to the soldier and he dropped his weapon.

'You need to sit down,' he repeated to the old man. 'Your patients need you.'

'I'm not a doctor,' the old man replied in English. 'Not a medical one. I'm from Sydney, in Australia. My name is Zakhir Ali. I came here because I need to go to the Jaffna Public Library. I need to return something.' He reached into the satchel.

Soldiers started shouting and four of them raised their guns.

'Aiyya,' Ruben said respectfully, raising his hands and walking towards the old man. He placed his body between Mr Ali and the nearest soldier. 'Keep your hands up, where they can see them.' He motioned to the soldiers who were circling closer. 'Please. If you make any movements that frighten them, they will shoot you.'

One of the soldiers stepped forward and pulled the bag from the man, causing him to stumble forward. The soldier opened the bag and emptied it onto the ground; a book spilled out along with a collection of papers. The man cried out, reaching for them.

The soldiers shouted again, one of them hitting Zakhir on the back of the head. Another picked up the papers and examined them.

'Get the brigadier,' he called to his comrade. Then, pointing to the man on the ground, he shouted at the others, 'Get him up.' He shook a fistful of the papers at Ruben. 'Maps. Maps of this area. He's a Tiger. Take him with the others.'

~◌

Ruben signalled to the young soldier to stop. The soldier looked at his commanding officer for approval and then stepped back, allowing Ruben to help the old man. Zakhir had been questioned for two days. At each interrogation session, he gave the same answers, despite the intensity of the pain and his deepening exhaustion. At Ruben's request, the soldier stopped beating him with a rifle after the first day. Ruben explained that the man was more than seventy years old and it wouldn't be hard to break every bone in his body. This would kill him fast and yield no answers to their questions.

'Why do you have so many old maps?' the officer asked again. 'Where are they leading you?' The officer spoke in Sinhalese, and Zakhir, a Colombo Tamil, understood him perfectly. There was no need for Ruben to be there as translator, but he felt compelled to stay to support the older man.

'I told you,' Zakhir whispered, his words whistling through his broken teeth. 'They belonged to my father-in-law. They were prepared by cartographers in 700 AD. My father-in-law copied them by hand. They show the kingdoms of Sri Lanka. I was taking the maps and the book back to the Jaffna Public Library.'

The book lay on the floor, where the officer had thrown it. Zakhir's blood and urine trickled towards it, as if seeking the comfort of its pages.

'The book—again the book.' The officer nodded at the soldier who wound his belt around his hand and then flexed his wrist, stretching the tendons, before he flicked the leather strap against

Zakhir's chest. The buckle hooked into his body and created another fissure in his skin. His chest was covered in a lattice of deep cuts and bruises, the colour of crushed jacaranda flowers. Ruben could tell by Zakhir's breathing that at least one rib was broken and pressed on his lungs. Each breath was ragged and shallow.

'You've told us that this is the book you and your father-in-law wrote together. The book that he died for. The book that you're trying to return to Jaffna. My children have books they need to return to their local library, but they wouldn't leave the safety of their home and travel thousands of kilometres into a war zone to do it. We're not fools, old man. Why are you really here? Who are you meeting? We know you're in the Tiger leadership. It's only a matter of time before you tell us everything.'

Ruben had seen countless interrogations. He could tell within the first ten minutes how long a person would last under torture. He could tell who was telling the truth and who was lying, telling the soldiers whatever they wanted to hear in order to make the pain stop.

Zakhir was different. He was not as young or strong as the others. He was telling the truth about why he was there, despite the insanity of his story. And despite Ruben's secret prayers, Zakhir refused to lie. When the blows from the belt rained down on him, he closed his eyes and bit his lip to a pulp. He screamed and cried, begging them to make it stop. But he would not change his story.

Ruben placed the bowl of warm water on the floor and kneeled beside the old man. He touched him, rolling him gently onto his back so he could see his face better. Zakhir whimpered. His face was covered in dried blood, his grey hair matted dark brown with it. Ruben dipped the cloth in the water and began to wipe Zakhir's face clean. The pressure made him cry out. Ruben instead let the cloth sit on Zakhir's skin to absorb the blood. Ruben imagined he was absorbing Zakhir's pain into the cloth and then rinsing it out in the bowl. As if pain was something he could remove and then discard.

Zakhir reached out and held Ruben's hand, bringing it to his chest.

'You. The translator.'

'Yes. Ruben.'

'I know: *Ruben*. It means world. You are the world. Every child is their parents' world.' Zakhir coughed and groaned. 'Do you have children?'

Ruben shook his head. 'No. I'm not married. My mother and sister are in London now, and my brother, Anil, is a doctor with the refugees. I'm looking for him.'

'Thank you for staying with me in there. In the room.' Zakhir opened his eyes as much as he could and tried to lift himself upright. Ruben helped steady him into a sitting position, his back against the wall.

'I brought you some things. Water, food . . .'

Zakhir nodded.

Ruben held the water bottle to his lips so the man could sip from it. Each mouthful touched the open nerves in Zakhir's gums, causing more tears to stream down his face. He pushed the bottle away but Ruben was insistent. People died from dehydration almost as fast as the torture in these rooms.

'You work for the army?'

'I used to be a teacher and a translator. I speak a few languages. Now, I do this.'

'It's a great service.'

'I'm not sure everyone sees it that way.' Ruben shrugged his shoulders.

'You speak Yalpanathamil,' Zakhir said.

'Yes, my father taught me. He was a language teacher too. In Jaffna, we speak something closer to the classical form.'

'Not like us in Colombo, with our Thanglish,' Zakhir joked. Colombo Tamil included as many words in English as Tamil.

Ruben laughed, and began opening out the compartments of the tiffin carrier. He tore a small piece of dosai, dipped it in the warm sambar and fed the man. Zakhir chewed slowly, closing his eyes and leaning back against the wall again.

'Almost as good as my wife's,' he said.

'Tell me about your wife, Zakhir,' Ruben probed gently. 'Tell me who you are.' He didn't doubt Zakhir's story. The man had come back home to return a book that was important to him to the library. He had become trapped in the current of refugees, Tamils forced to leave their homes by the oncoming army. He could have fled but he decided to stay, to help if he could. Zakhir had already told him and the soldiers this during the interrogation sessions. But translation was more than just taking the author's words and converting them into another language. Anyone could do that. Computers could do it now. Translation was about understanding the motivations of the author.

'Tell me who you are,' Ruben repeated. 'Tell me why you're here.'

Zakhir began a story that would continue for the last three days and nights of his life. With a historian's precision, he spoke about his life in Australia. The architecture of his world that gave it meaning and value.

'My name is Zakhir Ali, and I am married to a beautiful woman called Maya,' he began.

With Brigadier Fernando's permission, Ruben brought the doctor to Zakhir's cell. His body was covered in bruises and cuts, but Ruben was worried about the dark purple bloom that appeared after his last interrogation session. It was slowly unfurling under his skin, a dark stain that threatened to consume his entire torso. His abdomen was swollen and stretching.

The doctor was a young man, not much older than Anil. His skin was dark and blistered, his arms and legs covered in mosquito bites that he scratched at anxiously as he passed the soldiers at the door. They checked his medical bag and then pushed it back into his arms.

'It's fine, you're safe, thambi,' Ruben said, addressing the younger man as his brother. 'You're with me.' He led the doctor into the room and saw him flinch.

'I've been trying to keep him clean,' Ruben said apologetically.

The man shook his head. 'I'm used to that. He's just so . . . broken.'

The doctor kneeled down in the muck and stroked Zakhir's head, pushing the old man's sweaty, matted hair back from his face.

He opened his medical bag and began examining his patient, flashing the torch in Zakhir's eyes, and putting the stethoscope to his chest and back.

'His stomach, look at his stomach,' Ruben urged.

'I know, I'm getting to that,' the doctor said, taking the scope gently down Zakhir's body. When he reached the stomach, Zakhir cried out.

'This is going to hurt a little, but I need to feel what's going on, Aiyya. I'm going to touch you here. I'll be as gentle and as fast as possible.'

Zakhir nodded and cried while the doctor finished his examination.

'Enough,' Zakhir whispered.

'Yes, enough.' The doctor pulled down Zakhir's torn shirt and stood up, motioning for Ruben to follow him to the other side of the room.

'He's bleeding internally. It's significant. He's losing blood to organs which will be dying inside his body. The blood is pooling in his abdominal cavity; that's the swelling and discoloration you see. It must be so painful for him. There's nothing we can do here; I just don't have the equipment or even the supplies. I'm out of antibiotics and down to my last painkillers. You have to get him to a hospital.'

'I've asked. I've begged. Even the brigadier has called. They're not interested in one old man who could be a terrorist.'

'He's not a terrorist,' the doctor said. 'You know that.'

'Of course he's not, but they just keep asking him the same questions over and over, and he keeps giving them the same answers over and over, so they hurt him over and over.' Ruben's voice faltered as he tried to hold back the tears. He'd seen so many interrogations and wondered when one would break him. This was it. Zakhir was it.

'Make him give in,' the doctor whispered. 'This is madness. It could take him days to die. Terrible pain; more than he's endured already.' He paused and looked at Ruben. 'If you stop giving him water, it might happen faster. And there are other ways.' He touched Ruben's arm.

Ruben had thought of nothing else for days. He put his hand in his pocket and felt the small cylinder he had taken from the doctor's bag without him realising.

'Let me speak to him. I'll persuade him.' He pulled away, tears streaming down his face.

~

Zakhir was sitting up, waiting for him, when Ruben returned from seeing the doctor out. He was slumped against the wall; the effort of raising himself had drained him.

'It's not good, is it,' he said. It wasn't a question.

'If you don't get to a hospital, you're going to die.'

'I don't think they're going to let me go to a hospital. Best to bury the evidence deep underground, with the rest of the temple.'

'What?'

'I said—' Zakhir started coughing.

'Rest, Aiyya. Let me do the talking. Tomorrow they'll interrogate you again. Mayanilayam, the temple in your book, it's now part of an army base. They think you're going to use the maps to bomb the army base, or show the Tigers an ancient escape route.' Ruben shook his head.

Zakhir smiled at that, revealing his cracked teeth and a blackened mass where the infected root of one had started to rot.

'If you admit to this, they'll stop torturing you. Just admit it. Just say you're here to help the Tigers. There's no shame in that. We all want to help them. We would if we were brave enough.'

'You want me to lie,' Zakhir said. 'To save my life.'

'Yes, to save your life. There's no honour in death. Think of your family; think of Maya and Anji and Siddharth. Think of all your friends at Cinnamon Gardens who are waiting for you, worried, imagining what's happening to you.' Ruben realised the human imagination did not extend as far as its cruelty. 'Please, lie to save your life,' he repeated.

The old man shook his head slowly, although the movement cost him. He stopped, breathless from the pain. 'I can't.'

'Why?' Ruben cried.

'Because I already did that once before, and I promised myself I would never do it again.'

~ↄ

That night, Zakhir told Ruben one last story. He told him how, when he had been taken by the police with his father-in-law, a man he loved like a father and who had loved him like a son in return, they were both tortured for hours. Zakhir knew almost immediately that he was not a brave man or a strong man. He knew he would not last. He begged the policemen to stop. He pleaded with them to tell him what to do, tell him what to say so that it would stop.

'They asked me to sign a piece of paper. A confession—no, an accusation. I was to say that my father-in-law had lied. That he had falsified his findings at the archaeological site at Mayanilayam in order to seek fame and glory for himself. That he had done so at the behest of the Tamil nationalist movement that was seeking to prove that the Tamils had an ancestral claim to lands in the north.

341

They asked me to say that he was a fraud and that Mayanilayam was all a lie.'

Zakhir's tears, sweat, and blood sat heavy on his face.

'I did everything they wanted. My father-in-law's reputation was destroyed. His previous publications were all withdrawn from universities across Sri Lanka. Only the Jaffna Public Library continued to hold the entire collection. All but one of his books were burned when the library was torched.'

'All but one,' Ruben murmured. He thought of the book that was sitting on the brigadier's desk, under a pile of papers. He could take the book one night, with or without the man's permission.

'The only mercy was that my father-in-law died in prison. He didn't live to see the shame I brought on his name and on his life's work. I think he knew, though; I think he knew what I did to him.'

'If he knew,' Ruben said, 'he would have understood and forgiven you. I can tell from everything you've told me about him. Parents always do.'

Zakhir nodded. 'Siblings do too, son. Remember that.' He looked at Ruben closely then said, 'I'm tired now. I can't take any more.'

Ruben nodded.

'Help me.'

Ruben looked down. The old man reached for his hands and held them tightly.

'I'm grateful for everything you've done for me already. Everything. You've done as much as a son would do for his father. More than I ever did for mine. Now, please, do one more thing.' He squeezed Ruben's hands with all the strength he had.

'Kill me, I beg you,' the old man said quietly.

Ruben reached into his pocket for the syringe, wrapping his fingers around it. He checked the door. Then he exhaled quietly and nodded.

NIKKI

Cinnamon Gardens

Nikki read Ruben's story. Finally, she understood the scars and the nightmares, but also the loyalty. And the love. She understood that family was not just the one you were born with or married or buried, but the one you rebuilt. Ruben whispered to her from the pages of his story, locked in a hard drive, unlocked by a fire. He explained that although he was surrounded by death, he chose to keep living. It was possible to keep living.

She closed the front door of the cottage against the wind. The southerly lifted the ashes of Cinnamon Gardens from the bones of what was left. She imagined fragments of him flying above her, diving towards the earth and then rising again, towards the sun. Fragments dancing and finding other fragments, pieces of Florence still whispering to her from the sky.

The moment of imagining and pretending always ended. The time of loving and missing never ended. The time of living continued, if she chose it.

Together, Nikki and Anji helped Maya with her interviews, transcribing tapes, typing up notes, and eventually teaching her

343

to use a digital recorder with voice translation. On Mondays and Wednesdays, Nikki attended Aunty Yagnik's yoga class with Mel. On Fridays, Mel took Aunty Yagnik to Bondi, where Aunty taught at the Energetic Mindfulness Centre. On Saturdays, Nikki took her father to Aunty Shanthi Segaram's poosai in the makeshift shrine room that had been set up in the remaining nursing home until a new one could be built. The battle of the deities continued, but with more affection than acrimony between Aunty Shanthi and Maya.

When Nikki stood at the kitchen window of the cottage, she could watch the slow rebirth of an old home. The bulldozers were outside, razing the remains of Cinnamon Gardens, pounding it into the earth, creating a foundation for the new nursing home Anji would build. All of the residents had chosen to stay in the larger building behind it, which had been spared. No one wanted to leave their family.

They renamed the nursing home's library the Ganapathipillai and Vandermark Library. It was a bit wordy, but Maya thought that was appropriate. And last week, at the front of the cottage, they planted a tulasi tree, the holiest of trees, in honour of Ruben.

Nikki heard Oscar in Anji's old room, unpacking his boxes with Kailash. They were already planning sleepovers and bagsing the top bunk. She straightened Florence's Shopkins toys on the bookshelf next to the set of Clementine Kelly novels in Spanish. She dragged her last box to Ruben's room, once Maya and Zakhir's room, now her room, and began to unpack it.

MAYA

Cinnamon Gardens, 2010

When Zakhir left her to return to Sri Lanka, Maya waited alone in their home. She wanted to be punished with death, and when death didn't come, she realised that Yama, the god of death, would punish her with life instead.

One year later, old Mrs Venkatraman in Room 1 died, and Maya made a decision. She began packing and called Ruben from the nursing home to help her. He had come to Australia as a refugee after the war ended and had worked at the nursing home ever since. It was only years later that she would reflect on how his industrious presence had helped to fill the void left by Zakhir's quiet one.

Together, they had created an ambitious vegetable garden. Under her instruction they planted manioc, neem trees and rosella bushes. He also suggested banana chillies, turmeric and five more curry leaf trees, revealing the small details about himself that hid bigger tragedies. He had a sister who was allergic to raw vengayam and a mother who brewed turmeric into an anti-inflammatory tea for an older brother whose name, Sanjay, it hurt him to speak. None of these family members were with him in Sydney and she didn't have the courage yet to ask him where they were.

Ruben stood in front of her, quiet but not diffident like some of the other employees at the nursing home.

'You're still living in Pendle Hill?' she asked. It wasn't really a question. She knew the answer.

'Yes, I've been living there for a year, ever since I came here.'

'You're here as a student?'

He blushed at the question. She hadn't meant anything by it; she was just leading into her request. She already knew his background. Her daughter interviewed their employees rigorously and always requested proper documentation. They would lose their government accreditation if they did anything wrong.

'I am. I'm studying linguistics at the University of Western Sydney.'

'Linguistics?'

'Yes. I'm getting a diploma that will be recognised in Australia. Mathematical linguistics.'

'Mathematical linguistics? Do those subjects go together naturally?'

'Mathematics and language are the building blocks of our universe and our civilisation. One depends on the stability of the other to exist. I think they go together quite well.'

'Indeed.' Good answer, she thought. 'I need your help. I need you to move boxes for me.'

'Where to?' He surveyed the cottage. It looked like it had been ransacked.

'Those three boxes must go to my daughter's house.'

They were the things she wanted her children and grandchildren to have. The things that recorded a lifetime of blessings and burdens. Photographs, letters from her father and husband, a small jewellery box shaped like a temple that her father gave her when she married.

The book Zakhir had written with her father was missing. He had taken it with him the day he disappeared. It was the only possession that mattered to her and it was gone, just like him.

'This suitcase must go to Mrs Venkatraman's room. The deluxe one.'

Local families, some with their elderly already living in Cinnamon Gardens, others with their elderly on the nursing home's lengthy waiting list, were campaigning hard to get Room 1. It was on the top floor of the restored Federation home and it was the largest, with a private bathroom, a kitchenette and the best mobile phone reception in the building. It was close to the two most important amenities: the shrine room, which was on the same floor, and the TV room downstairs, where Tamil TV (on a cinematically wide screen) was played around the clock.

When Mrs Venkatraman died, Anjali received more proposals for her room than shaadhi.com.

Maya's name was still on the title deed to the nursing home, however, so Mrs Venkatraman's room was now hers.

'Would you please also move the writing desk to the nursing home? Everything else must go.' Maya looked around the cottage one last time.

Ruben lifted her one suitcase. 'Where do you want everything else to go, Aunty?' He looked around again, confused. There was a lifetime of furniture and clothes strewn around the room.

'Pack it all up. Box it all. Label it. Old Men's Clothing, Old Women's Saris, Old Women's Oversized Underwear,' she tried to joke. She was already wearing Zakhir's brown cardigan with the leather elbow patches. According to one of her grandchildren, it was retro cool. It still smelled like Zakhir.

Ruben didn't laugh. He waited.

'My husband left me,' she said simply.

'Your husband *left*,' Ruben said. 'But perhaps he didn't leave *you*.'

Maya's eyes filled with tears. 'Zakhir told me he wanted to go back home; he told me for years that he needed to. I wonder what would have happened if I'd listened to him. I've spent my life listening to the stories of others, but not his.'

Ruben shook his head. 'Maybe he wasn't ready to tell you.'

'Maybe,' she said, her voice breaking under the strain of her torment. 'Or maybe I wasn't ready to listen. When he left, I was almost relieved. I *was* relieved. I was tired. Is that terrible?' she asked the young man in front of her, as though he would know the answer.

'It's human, Aunty,' he said. 'It is so very human,' he repeated in Tamil. 'And we are only human.'

She nodded. It felt a little lighter, the guilt, now that she had placed it outside her body, in the air between her and Ruben. In her cottage.

'Please take whatever you want for yourself. And then talk to the Tamil Rehabilitation Organisation. The number is on the kitchen bench.' She was sure he would know it already. 'Give it to refugee families here and then ask Kuhan at TRO to post the rest of it to Sri Lanka. I'll pay for the postage. Is that okay?'

She kept her eyes on him. She couldn't look around again.

'Of course, Aunty.' He paused, seeming to understand the weight of the decision she had made. 'Your daughter will be back on Monday.'

In two days, her daughter and family would return from a holiday to London. They were visiting Siddharth, Anji's twin.

'Yes, I'd like to move in today,' she said. Before Anji could talk her out of it. 'You work long hours at the nursing home, Ruben. Would you like to stay here, instead of Pendle Hill?'

She would never know why she offered the cottage to him. Something about his resolve, the way he approached all tasks. Did it remind her of Zakhir? Maybe. Perhaps it reminded her of her father. She didn't know. She just liked the idea of him being close to the nursing home, as though its walls would keep him safe, as though he could keep her safe.

'I don't know if I ever told you,' she said, an unusual opening because she was quite sure she had never told anyone except Zakhir, her children and the original residents of Cinnamon Gardens, all of them now long dead, 'but in Ceylon, when I was young, I used to write. It helped me. It calmed me.' It did more than that. It connected her to herself in a way that prayer did not.

'What did you write?' Ruben asked. 'Books?'

'Yes. Well, no. Initially stories that I published locally. My professors at Jaffna University said I had talent, that I should develop it.'

She didn't know why she said that. He would hardly be impressed. Why was she trying to impress him?

'And did you? Did you develop your talent?'

Ruben listened and asked questions. She liked that about him.

'In a way. When we moved to Australia, I wrote stories about our life back home. I even wrote about the residents of Cinnamon Gardens; their stories of migration and navigating life. I couldn't get anything published, so I wrote something else. Other books, which *were* published.'

She looked at the bookcase with its shelves of Clementine Kelly novels, which had been published all around the world in dozens of languages. Every sequel, every translation had helped look after Cinnamon Gardens.

'I've worked alongside my husband, raising our children and running this nursing home for decades,' Maya said to Ruben. 'I want to rest. I want to retire. Apparently all retirees need a hobby. I'm going to write again. Bingo and balloon animal-making is not for me.'

Ruben laughed, still obviously confused by his role in her plan.

'I want to hire you to be my personal . . . person.'

'Your personal person?' He raised an eyebrow. 'Will I be asked to do anything illegal or inappropriate for you, Aunty?'

She looked up, startled, and then saw the grin on his face and knew she had read him correctly.

'No, nothing illegal or inappropriate. I'm not that kind of pensioner.'

~ᓚ

Maya bought herself a lightweight laptop. This was such an ingenious invention, she bought ten more for the nursing home.

Ruben converted the old billiards room in the Federation home into a computer lab, and the daughter of one of the residents ran training sessions. By the end of them, the residents were proficient in online solitaire, online share trading, and online astrology, and they were able to skype their relatives in London, Toronto, Colombo, and even Jaffna.

In her new room, Maya put Zakhir's cardigan on, sat down at the desk with her laptop in front of her, and began to write.

She gave Ruben the keys to the nursing home's Golf, a tax-deductible purchase by Zakhir before his disappearance, and paid him to take her places she needed to study for her new book.

Sydney, 2018

Ruben had brought her to a cafe in Avalon. He sat with her and typed up the notes from her interviews while she worked on her final project. Clementine Kelly's last adventure would be published in time for Mother's Day. Her agent, Clara Rose, was excited. Something called data analytics had suggested that Clementine Kelly sales would exceed expectations, and expectations were high.

The waitress asked her what she'd like and Maya politely ordered a piccolo.

'Not chai tea?' Ruben asked.

She laughed. Tamils didn't say chai or drink *tea* tea but this joke had become a feature of their outings. She enjoyed these excursions to extremely-white Australia with him, a chance to study her subjects and work in situ.

The most commercially successful Australian novels, she explained to Ruben, began with a dead body. The protagonist must (a) be white and (b) return to their home town in rural Australia to uncover closely guarded secrets from the past and present, which (c) converge neatly at the end of the novel.

Maya reviewed her work. It was not her best writing, but it began with a dead body. An attractive older man killed by a Thermomix blade to the neck. Only on Sydney's North Shore. She needed more scenery. Australian readers loved a mythologised landscape and, in this novel, her most complex yet, Clementine's great-granddaughter had (a) fled the North Shore for the refuge of her ancestral home in rural Australia, where she would (b) solve a contemporary murder and one from Clementine's past, both of which would (c) converge neatly at the end of the future bestseller.

Maya tried again:

Kate slid the window of her Land Rover down and allowed the heat in. It had wrapped itself like a blanket around her hybrid car, its fingers tapping gently at first and then, with each passing kilometre, more insistently, more urgently. She could feel the dust settle on her sweaty skin, a layer of fine grit that heralded her return home. She stopped at the rusted iron gate and read the sign: Go Back to Where You Came From. *She was tempted. It wasn't too late to turn around. But both Kate and Clementine had come from here. This was once her home. A place she had outrun, erased from her memory and identity just as the hot winds would now be erasing the tracks of her expensive tyres. She had indeed gone back to where she came from, although she was not sure this place still wanted her.*

She lifted the catch of the gate, the grating of metal against hot metal as one swelled and expanded in the heat against the other, warped by the elements. She rolled her car forward onto her father's property, got out and locked the gate. An old habit. The first and last time she had forgotten to lock the gate her father had taken his belt to her. There were no animals left to escape, though. Her brother told her the last of the cattle had been sold for what little meat there was on them. The crops had failed for six years in a row.

Maya really wanted to insert a rice paddy field, but that would have to be saved for a sequel set in Far North Queensland, which she'd heard was tropical like Sri Lanka. For now, she needed to ride the heatwave across this sunburnt country, a land of sweeping plains, although not really boundless plains to share.

> ~~Clementine~~ *Kate drove up the dirt track to her father's home. Her home. She was careful to go slow so as not to startle the stones on the track or the dogs in the kennels.*

Ruben leaned over and read her words on the screen.
'That's a great story,' he said. 'But it's not your story.'

Cinnamon Gardens, present day

Maya reconnected the hard drive to Anjali's laptop. Its plastic and metal body still smelled like the fire, even months later. She read the contents of the hard drive again; she'd lost count of how many times she had done this. Each reading hurt a little less and revealed a little more. She still cried but often she laughed, too.

Saha Anna, recovering in Westmead Hospital, seeking the cricket matches that reminded him of his sons. His tools, which saved their lives. Shanthi Segaram and the Tamil Christian boy she loved but wasn't allowed to marry. Uncle Gana and his unfinished textbook on the decline of the rule of law in Sri Lanka. Cedric, the self-proclaimed dilettante, who restored the nursing home because it helped restore Zakhir. Mr Petsas and his love for Soula, the northerner with the sunflower hair, and his ten tips for removing a statue of Captain Cook. Mrs Borkowska, her family's escape from Krakow, and the pierogi she used to make for her children. Ray South and the Valium bottle he opened for his granddaughter Florence, without realising it was Valium. Vidya and the nursing home menu she designed to make people feel that at the end of their lives they were loved just as much as they were at the beginning.

Zakhir and his need to return home, to seek forgiveness from his birthplace for the lies he told out of fear.

The forgiveness he finally gave himself.

The forgiveness Maya could now give herself.

The forgiveness Ruben should have given himself years ago.

Decades of stories from hundreds of residents who had lived and died at Cinnamon Gardens. The stories we tell each other and the stories we tell ourselves. The stories we reveal and those we hide. The stories we tell our children.

'These are the temples we build,' she whispered. They must not be erased.

Maya put Zakhir's cardigan on and began to write.

AUTHOR'S NOTE

Chai Time at Cinnamon Gardens was written with respect on the lands of the Darug people.

A lot of great academic and creative literature sits behind this book, but I'd like to note and thank, in particular: *Decolonising Criminology* (Blagg and Anthony, 2019), *The Good Immigrant* (Shukla, 2016), and the commentary of Riz Ahmed, Waleed Aly, Ghassan Hage and Stan Grant.

People have asked me if Dr Sriskandarajah, Maya's father, is based on a real archaeologist and if Mayanilayam is a real temple. Both are fictitious. The events of the civil war portrayed in this book are real.

The Jaffna Library was burned by security forces in 1981. It contained 97,000 books and historical and cultural records about the Tamil civilisation and its presence in Sri Lanka. Some texts, such as the *Yalpanam Vaipava Malai* (a history of Jaffna), were the only copies in existence and have been lost forever. In 2009, the civil war ended on a small strip of beach at the far east of the island. During the last months of the war, it is believed that 40,000–70,000 Tamil people died. A 2021 United Nations Human Rights Council resolution has called for the collection of evidence of crimes, violations of human rights and violations of international humanitarian law.

Sri Lanka's nationhood and the historical narrative of its formation has always been contested. The island was once three kingdoms, forcibly unified under British rule for the purposes of colonial administration. The north and the east were historically a Tamil kingdom that sometimes lived peacefully and sometimes conflicted with the two Sinhalese kingdoms of the south. The city of Jaffna, which features often in my novels, is the capital of this ancestral Tamil kingdom. It was also the capital of Tamil Eelam, the proposed separate Tamil state that the Liberation Tigers of Tamil Eelam fought for from 1983 to 2009. This is a simplistic, one-line explanation of a brutal and complex war. If you want to know more about it, my first novel, *Song of the Sun God*, covers seventy years of colonisation, dispossession, erasure, and the struggle for self-determination. It's a long story, but you might like it.

In *Chai Time at Cinnamon Gardens*, Dr Sriskandarajah and his son-in-law Zakhir define a people's right to be where they are, their right to exist on that land, as territorial legitimacy. In Sri Lanka, the battle for territorial legitimacy is fought on many grounds. It begins with the battle of contested histories and competing mythologies; with ancient tales of who arrived first.

As Tamils, we have learned about the existence of the Dravidian or proto-Tamil civilisation on the island, the evidence of religious places and practices that worshipped an early form of Lord Shiva, the Hindu god of destruction and renewal, and the naming of people and places in Tamil and the Brahmi script that preceded it. We have been taught that evidence of our existence in the north and the east was destroyed, and that Sinhalese Buddhist temples were built over Tamil Hindu ones. Tamil historians and archaeologists have faced extraordinary pressure from the government and bhikkus (Buddhist clergy) to hide certain findings and emphasise or even contrive others. Sinhalese people are taught a completely different history, one in which Tamil people are the late arrivals, the usurpers, and the threat to Buddhism. I don't assert the truth of one history over the other, only that, as Dr Sriskandarajah says, possession of land is nine-tenths of the law, but possession of history is nine-tenths of the future.

On my last trip to Sri Lanka, in January 2019, I returned with three generations of my family. We went to our ancestral villages and saw the continuing effects of the war. My parents showed our children all the places they had loved and left behind. We also saw how much of our history was being erased by the government and army's 'rebuilding' of the north. Sometimes the rebuilding hid the mass graves and the evidence of war crimes. Sometimes, the rebuilding hid the evidence of the Tamil civilisation's early existence in Sri Lanka. Conquest and colonisation often involve this 'architectural approach'.

There are many forms of cultural erasure, none of them exclusive to Sri Lanka, and many of them used in Australia and other countries. These include (but are not limited to): the destruction of temples, the burning of books and libraries, the prohibition of languages, and the stealing of children and their forced assimilation. And, of course, there is genocide.

A lot of my work looks at the narratives in Sri Lanka that created one particular national identity (i.e. a Buddhist Sinhalese one), which excluded and othered the Tamils in their own country. This harnessing of history, its appropriation and control, was the first step towards civil war. It happened in Sri Lanka but—of more relevance to Australians—it happened and still happens in Australia. Worryingly for us all, the appropriation of history and the rewriting of narratives happens all over the world. So while this novel is located in a Sri Lankan Tamil community, I think its themes are relevant to modern Australia and to the world.

First Nations people tell us about the erasure that commenced upon colonisation, its continuation and its consequences. They tell us about the defensiveness of non-Indigenous Australia when it comes to understanding those consequences or acknowledging our responsibility to address them. This story of erasure is integral to the formation and continuation of the modern nation state of Australia. This story is our collective shame, but if we acknowledge it, and if we listen to First Nations people, then it is also our opportunity to do much better for all Australians.

Dr Sriskandarajah is named after my uncle, who is a doctor of medicine, like all good Tamils of his generation, and a Tamil political historian. He taught me a great deal about Tamil history, and he introduced me to key political figures. Along with his wife, Aunty Nalaini, Uncle Rajan has reviewed, challenged, and improved my work. The character Dr Sriskandarajah is a composite of and my tribute to all the historians and archaeologists who have been silenced. Mayanilayam is not a real site but a representation of all the sacred places in the world that have been destroyed and erased. Both Dr Sriskandarajah and Mayanilayam exist only in my imagination and now, hopefully, in yours. As Ruben says to Maya, the stories we tell are the temples we build. They must not be erased. *Chai Time at Cinnamon Gardens* is a story I told; it is a temple I built.

Thank you for reading it.
Anbudan,
Shankari Chandran

ACKNOWLEDGEMENTS

Nandri and thank you—these are such small words for a long and important list. Such small words for the emotion I feel and the debt owed to the following:

Wendy Beckett, the Blake-Beckett Trust Scholarship and Create NSW, this book could not have been written without your support. Government and philanthropic funding is essential for the creation of diverse stories that reflect who we are and remind us who we could be.

Robert Watkins, for valuing and believing in this story; I am honoured to be included in your slate, and so very grateful for your support and your gentle reminders to exhale.

The team at Ultimo, for bringing *Chai Time* into the world: James Kellow and Brigid Mullane, my patient editor; Jessica Cruikshank, that cover is The Story; Emily Cook and Kat Rajwar, for selling an introvert; Simon Paterson, that font is The Boss. Ali Lavau, a very special thank you, you are an exquisite wordsmith. Alex Craig, for reading my first book in 2013 and inviting me to call you.

Tara Wynne at Curtis Brown Australia, for your constant, optimistic and ferocious advocacy of my work.

My artist friends: Karen Radzyner, Emily Maguire, Indu Balachandran, Jay Woods, Christine Shamista, Marie-Claire Collyer and Arjunan Puveendran for taking the lonely journey with me.

Emily Maguire and Maxine Beneba Clarke, your reviews over-whelmed me. Your work has supported me to claim my rage and trust my voice.

My Book Club: Narelle, Sandra, Tina, Carmela, Su Lin, Alex and Ange for fearless critique and endless friendship. Here's to our books and our babies (in that order).

My First Readers: Rachy, Reema, Indu, Keda, Bekster, Anjali, Eagle-Eye Franksy, Kate and Slaney for suffering through poor drafts and making them better.

My Subject Matter Experts: Tanu, Subha Akka and Brami for keeping it real; and Luckshmi for understanding my intention.

Aunty Shamani for generously scouring the streets of Colombo for me.

The organisations that fight for the writers: Writing NSW (Jane McCredie, long may you serve the storytellers of this great state), the ASA and Sweatshop.

Cinnamon Gardens is based on a nursing home where generations of families go to see their Ammammas and Appappas. Thank you Periappa, Periamma and Logie for that place to call home.

My lifelong reading/writing partner: Kate Kelly for all the things we've found in books and friendship together.

Everyone who let me borrow their name for this book: thank you, I hope you enjoy the Easter Eggs as much as I did. In particular, L&T, please accept my offering.

Finally:

Amma and Appa—the love and sacrifice of parents in my books is always based on you. Thank you for everything; nothing would be possible without you.

Narendran, Brother—my first best friend.

Haran, Husband—my Kunj and my last best friend.

Ellora, Kailash, Hari, and Sid—these stories are for you. Thank you for sharing yours with me every day.